BLOOD

Alexi Sokolsky: Hound of Eden

Book 1

James Osiris Baldwin
A Gift Horse Productions Book

Copyright © 2016 James Osiris Baldwin

All rights reserved. This book or any portion thereof
may not be reproduced or used in any manner whatsoever
without the express written permission of the author or publisher
except for the use of brief quotations in a book review.
For permission requests, please contact James Osiris Baldwin:
author@jamesosiris.com

Layout and design by James Osiris Baldwin.
ISBN: 0994407017
ISBN-13: 978-0-9944070-1-6

Gift Horses and the Dermal Highway setting are Copyright ©
2017 Canth Decided-Baldwin

All illustrations are by James and Canth Decided-Baldwin

Books in the Hound of Eden Series

Prequel: Burn Artist

http://jamesosiris.com/alexi-sokolsky-starter-library/

Book 1: Blood Hound

http://hyperurl.co/bloodhoundnovel

Book 2: Stained Glass

http://hyperurl.co/stainedglassnovel

Book 3: Zero Sum

http://hyperurl.co/zerosumnovel

Other Titles

Fix Your Damn Book! A Self-Editing Guide for Authors

Find all my books, bonus chapters and more at
http://www.jamesosiris.com

WHEN SHIT GETS TOO WEIRD FOR THE MOB TO HANDLE, HITMAGE ALEXI SOKOLSKY IS THE GUY THEY CALL TO FIX IT.

Set 5 years before Blood Hound, Burn Artist is a prequel to the series which reveals more about Alexi's past. What were the events that shaped him? Why did he murder his own father? And what are his true feelings for his best friend?

Get your free copy of Burn Artist when you sign up for my author newsletter. You can unsubscribe at any time.

Visit: HTTP://JAMESOSIRIS.COM/ALEXI-SOKOLSKY-STARTER-LIBRARY/

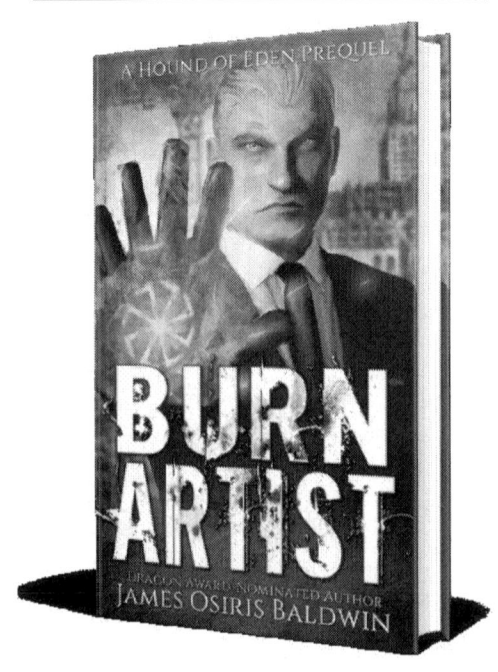

CONTENTS

Chapter 1	11
Chapter 2	32
Chapter 3	44
Chapter 4	63
Chapter 5	74
Chapter 6	79
Chapter 7	87
Chapter 8	99
Chapter 9	111
Chapter 10	120
Chapter 11	127
Chapter 12	138
Chapter 13	147
Chapter 14	165
Chapter 15	177
Chapter 16	190
Chapter 17	210
Chapter 18	231
Chapter 19	238
Chapter 20	254
Chapter 21	264
Chapter 22	279
Chapter 23	296
Chapter 24	313
Chapter 25	325

Chapter 26	342
Epilogue	349
Stained Glass: Chapter 1	353
Get your Free Copy of Burn artist	366
More Books by James Osiris Baldwin	367
Other Titles	367
Structure of the Yaroshenko Organizatsiya	368
Afterword & Acknowledgments	369
About the Author	371

DEDICATION

For canth?, the loveliest of all Gift Horses.

"Every step closer to my soul excites the scornful laughter of my devils, those cowardly ear-whisperers and poison-mixers."

— C.G. Jung, *The Red Book: Liber Novus*

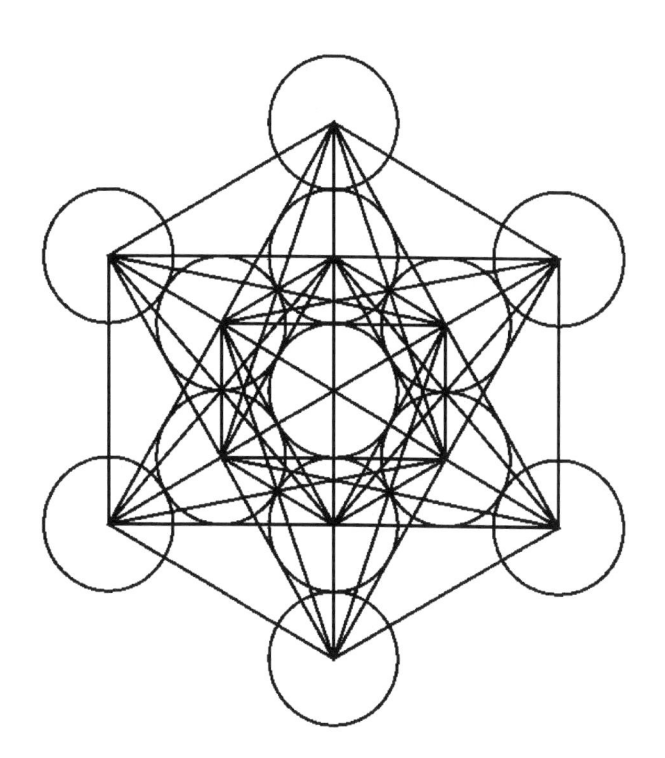

CHAPTER 1

It was a hot summer night in New York, and I was on my way to kill a man. The target was my boss's oldest friend, Semyon Vochin, currently hiding out at his safe house on East 49th Street. It was a solemn affair. Semyon was one of us; we thought we'd known him well.

My driver, Nicolai, was as grim as a pallbearer at the wheel. He was Old Crew, one of the first *muzhiki* to come from Ukraine via Afghanistan and make a name for himself in New York, just like Semyon. There was none of the usual shit-talk and banter that usually went on before a job. Semyon was a friend to nearly all the old guys in the Yaroshenko *Organizatsiya*... as much as anyone in the Russian Mafiya could be counted as a friend.

My partner for the evening was nervous. He wasn't a rookie by any stretch, but I was the first mage he'd ever met and he was clearly uncomfortable. Every anxious shift of his ass on the seat prickled my ears with the sound of wool on leather, squeaking like insect legs. His name was Mari, Manny, something like that... a Bulgarian, fresh off the boat, older than me by around five years. His face was pug-like and flat, like someone had one smashed it in with a skillet. I'd been sure to look him in the eye when we were introduced. We wizards can tell a lot from a man's stare, and all I'd seen inside of him was a flat, dull nothingness, a void of old anger and self-entitled spite. The whites of his eyes were yellowed from too much cheap vodka and *krokodil*; he walked with a cock-swinging swagger and had tried to crush my hand when we shook. Unfortunately for him, he reminded me strongly of my father.

"You cool, spook?" As if feeling the weight of my thoughts on him, Manny-Mari grunted the question aloud for perhaps the fifth time that night.

I ignored him and continued gazing out the window. My stomach swooped giddily as I watched the orange streetlights caress the pavement past my dim reflection in the glass. I realized, with a nervous little lurch behind my ribs, that we were nearly at 49th Street.

Naturally, he took my silence as a challenge. "Hey, Sokolsky. Shortass. I was talking to you."

"And I was very carefully not listening." I didn't give him the benefit of a glance. All proper mages must know how to perfect an aura of impenetrable sourness, the better to discourage people from bothering us. Otherwise, they start on with the inane questions, like "Where does magic come from?" "Can you make my cock bigger?" "Why don't you set this cat on fire and prove it?"

"*Iaz mi huia*[1]." My partner cursed me in Bulgarian. "Fuckin' freak."

I blinked, once, and resumed my meditation. I'd been called worse things by better men.

With these kinds of jobs, repulsiveness was the most important quality I needed in a good partner - the other requirements being religious fervor and an IQ less than a

---

[1] 'EAT MY DICK'.

hundred. To my great relief, Manny-Mari ceased trying to get me to turn my head and settled for grumbling and cuddling into his new jacket. His suit was a better cut than anything he could have gotten in Sofia, and he was already superbly ungrateful to us. America did that to people.

I've imagined getting off the plane or a ship from the old country the way my parents did, taking that first yellow cab through the mythic brownstone buildings and Art Deco monoliths of New York. As far as immigrant *brigadi*[2] like this guy or Nicolai were concerned, America was a soft carcass with all the organs they eat, a place ripe for the picking. But Nic had told me once that as hard as life in the USSR could be, the USA had its own kind of poison. The country corroded something inside you, and I'd bet anything that when the cabbie took off, spraying snow from the curb all up your nice new coat, and you realized he stiffed you because you didn't know how much twenty bucks is worth here... well, suddenly New York wasn't so romantic anymore.

We turned the corner onto the silent road and came to a gentle stop in front of the apartments sheltering our target. Nic cut the engine and sat back, fingering a cigarette. Manny-Mari dropped the seatbelt clip he hadn't fastened and fussed with his hair, his belt, and his gun.

"Hold your whiskers, tiger." Nic's terse, staccato Russian punctured the air of the cabin. "Briefing."

"Oh." The other man dropped back into his seat.

I hadn't moved, save to look sidelong so I could watch Nic's face in the rearview mirror. Nic was my *Kommandant*, the Commander who oversaw all the street teams working in Brighton Beach, Red Hook, and Queens. He was a dry, thin

---

[2] BRIGADI – ONE OF THE SLANG TERMS FOR RUSSIAN MAFIOSO

man with sun-weathered skin, heavily tattooed, and missing the tip of his left ring finger. His blue eyes were slightly cloudy with premature age, but even in his fifties, he was still as lean and sharp as a razor.

"Okay. Vochin hired his own spook to do him up with some heavy magic. If you know what's good for you, Moni, you'll shut the fuck up and do what Alexi says. Anything he says. Whatever Sem's got up there ashed the last two guys who tried to pay him a call. Hit Vochin and anything else alive you find. Make a scene, but not too much of a scene. Got it?"

Moni—that was his name—looked sidelong at me and furtively licked his teeth. By the shift in his manner and the look in his eye, I knew what he was thinking before he said it: "And if the wife's up there?"

"Don't leave a mess." Nic's flat voice turned a little stiff with distaste.

Pig. I finally stirred from my seat and left the car, masking my own opinions behind a pleasant nothing-face. I put the wave of disgust aside with my first breath of fresh air. Fresh, at least, by New York standards. I could taste pennies on my tongue. The wind was metal-tinged, heavy and humid after the last summer rain, and ripe with magic.

After you pierce the Veil for the first time and make the switch from 'dabbler in the Occult' to 'mage', something in you changes forever. You develop a sense of presence, of something else thinking behind your own thoughts. Many of the greatest mages describe it almost like another person, and it has many names: The Holy Guardian Angel, the Genius, Anima, Neshamah. I had never had the compelling relationship with this presence that other mages had described to me, but I could tell that it was less like an angel and more like a large, patient snake gazing upon a world of mice. As I tuned into the street, I could feel it looking out through me. Magic crept and crawled and waited in a thousand places. Some of it was old and ghostly, arcane architecture coded straight into the design of the city itself. Some of it was newer, still shining like spiderwebs. Burglar alarms, house-blessings, benedictions, curses, wards of all kinds. Wards are the most common form of magic found in cities: static enchantments written onto the energetic matrix of a structure, place, or object. Of those wards, most are really just simple alarms: they alert someone when the ward is breached. Evocation wards—complex, dynamic spells that can do all manner of wonderful things—are in the minority. They are used, for instance, to blow people up.

Only about two hours ago, my *Avtoritet*[3], Lev, sent two men to kill Semyon Vochin in his car. Surzi and Boris pulled up alongside him at a red light, where Surzi stuck his pistol through the driver's-side window and promptly exploded. Boris hadn't been any luckier. Semyon's protective wards turned them both into cat food and caused a six-car pileup on Water Street. Then, like a frightened rodent, he'd scampered back to his burrow.

I know if someone had tried to pull a hit on me the way Lev had done with Semyon, I'd have split town while I was still in the car. Clothes, money, they could all be replaced. But life? Not unless you knew a good necromancer. Heavy magic and big guns had a way of making men overconfident, though. The apartment lights were on, shielded by heavy drapes.

---

[3] 'Authority', the Russian mafia equivalent of a Don.

Moni trailed behind as we headed for the foyer, hats pulled down. Even with the heat, this was an occasion for Russian Mafiya formal—hats to hide our faces, overcoats to conceal our weapons, and gloves to hide our fingerprints. We had ski hats on under the brims so we didn't lose any hair for the cops to find later on. With forelocks, we could have passed for a couple of rabbis.

"So, uh, what'cha gonna do up there?" Moni spoke as we passed the desk. "Sacrifice a goat or somethin'?"

"If there just so happens to be a goat handy in this New York penthouse suite, why not?" My voice stayed deep and dry, a little flat.

He scowled. "Are all Americans assholes, or is it just you?"

"I have on good authority that I occupy the extreme end of the bell curve." God, he was nervous. I could smell him, the sour red tang of spent adrenaline. The Bulgarian was half a foot taller than me, big and brawny, but he was sweating like a new side of lamb. "But in all seriousness, I will look over the wards, examine them for flaws, and either use those flaws to destroy them or find another workaround."

"The hell does that mean?"

And here was why I discouraged questions about magic. Very few people really want to know what they think they want to know, and even if they do, the information rarely sticks. I sighed.

"Heap big magic," I said in English. "Wizard do things good."

Moni's brow furrowed. He didn't understand a word. "What?"

I half-opened the door and turned back to glare at him. "Blood magic. Now, please. I need to concentrate."

The foyer was stripped clean of spells, but like so many of these old buildings, it had been made to handle them. The Freemasons and Rosicrucians once had and still do have a significant hand in the building of America, and sure enough, we passed across a checkered floor and between two columns, one black, one white. Beneath the dome overhead lay the compass within a circle, a very powerful magical construct in its own right. A chandelier hung down from the center of the dome over the compass rose, like a knife poised over a beating heart. The core of these old buildings channeled magical energy like a lightning rod. If I concentrated, I could sense its unimpeded flow.

"We take the stairs," I said, already heading for them. The security desk was unmanned. Lev had called and arranged the bribe in advance. "The elevator will be trapped."

Moni made a stupid, thick sound in his throat, but he followed. Thank goodness I only had to work with him for one night. I clamped my teeth together and locked them just to feel them click.

The stair climb was a good way to relieve some tension, and by the time we hit the fifth floor, I felt better. Sweating, laboring, thighs trembling a little—but not too much—my heart thumping with every step, I felt properly alive. My intuition was playing my body like a violin, and my fingers vibrated more the higher we went. I don't know how I knew Vochin and his wife were still in their rooms when common sense told me they should have already fled. I am not very powerful as mages go—with the right tools and a lot of my own blood, I can break wards and move paper clips around on a table without resorting to magnets—but this sense of fatedness has been my guide ever since I was a child, and it has yet to fail me.

The first ward was on the sixth-floor landing. I pulled up hard as the hum washed over me, holding up a hand to wave Moni back. The hissing ozone smell of magic filled the echoing stairwell, but we hadn't pushed past the threshold. "Wait. It's here."

"What?" Moni drew his pistol from his coat, as if it would do him any good. "Where?"

"Put your pistol away. And don't move." I breathed in deeply, scanning the greasy walls, and focused my will into a sharp point of intent. The faint dizziness from the climb helped my vision split between the two closely knit layers of reality on Earth: *Malkuth*, the material plane, and *Yesod*, the subtle aetheric layer. On one level, I saw nothing but stained concrete and peeling metal railings. On the other, my vision swam with fine blue lines that danced and glimmered like strands of hair in sunlight. The threads led back to the landing door in a fine web and were bound to a square foot of wall beside the exit. A freshly enchanted sigil, crawling with energy. The mage had drawn it in lemon juice and salt water, that old invisible ink recipe we all learn as kids.

"Go back down, and watch the stairwell. Try and head anyone off," I said. "Magic draws attention. People might come out to gawk."

Moni holstered his pistol and glared at me reproachfully, but to his credit, he obeyed. He excelled at following orders. That was good.

I reached into my coat for one of my oldest tools: a knapped obsidian knife with a small, leaf-shaped blade. Calmly, I rolled back my sleeve with two precise turns of the cuff, exposing my forearm. The humming of the magic rose an octave and spilled out, reacting to the stirring energy that built in my blood and hands. Wards fed off ambient energy, and this one sent out little tentacles towards any focused source of power, like a plasma globe. Moni couldn't see it, but he could feel the creeping weirdness. He looked back. That was not good—he was too jumpy, and it made the energy wobble and shift slippery around us.

"*Bi-en bol baltoh.*" The words bubbled up as I faced the sigil, eyes closed. I brought the knife up and around, drawing it through the soapy film of energy to find its flow and pattern. The words themselves were fragments of Enochian, a language which had to be spoken slowly, each letter intoned at a specific pitch. "*Comselha cilna nor-molor.*"

Enochian was invented by John Dee, the court wizard of Queen Elizabeth I. He believed he'd discovered the language of the angels. I suspected he'd actually taken a lot of drugs and made it up, but it was the ideal magical language for someone who saw sounds in color. Every sound had a unique color and texture, and I could taste both with every well-shaped word. They tripped sweet and syrupy from my tongue, rolling, weaving into the ward, and my senses began to expand. I could feel Moni twitching and flinching from ten feet away through my fingertips. This was not even the high weirdness, but magical disturbance was unnerving for Blanks with no ability to understand what was happening. They feel dread, I am told: a twisting in the belly that screams "wrong!" like a siren going off in the animal part of the brain.

I carefully pricked the skin of my wrist and watched the red well up, only to be sucked away. The first drop twisted upwards and vanished, then the next. A giddy rush of energy flooded me then, pushing and clamoring. I tipped my head back and let it connect, feeling out along the ward as it fed from my body. It did not take long to find what I was looking for: the chink. The delicate error where the mage's drying finger had not quite connected the circle. I felt it out with the prying fingers of my mind, braced myself, and shoved.

My arm bled. The ward swelled, then snapped. My grasp on it turned from caress to assault as I shunted hot power through the fine filaments of magic. The air of the stairwell blackened and buzzed like television snow around us; the lights flickered, one of them bursting with the pop and fizzle of spent Freon.

"Jesus have mercy!" Moni's voice echoed up and down the stairs.

The magical net snapped one last time, flickering with pearly light, then burnt itself out and fell dormant. The ripples slowed. The lights returned to normal. The ward was inert, while the big Bulgarian, a veteran of hundreds of smuggling runs and God-knew-how-many murders, was white and bunched with fear. He watched me warily in the swelling silence.

"That was what we colloquially refer to as a 'snatcher.'" Scanning the wall for anything I might have missed, I tugged my gloves up and adjusted the cuffs of my jacket. "A spell designed to extract intention and memory. If we'd passed the door, we'd have forgotten what we were here for. If Nicolai asked about the job, we'd have said it was finished, and as far as we'd know, it would be."

Moni's eyes bugged. Slowly, he clambered up towards me from the bottom of the stairs. "So you're saying that maybe some of the things I remember, I don't really remember? Like, maybe I didn't even do 'em?"

"Perhaps, but spells this powerful are not especially common these days. They're very expensive to hire for. Now, we move on. Come."

I led the way into the hallway, and for a time, we heard nothing but the rhythm of our shoes tapping against marble. I counted the doors out of habit, but I knew which one we needed. The penthouse floor was like a wind tunnel, the pressure of arcana drawing me towards its core.

The ward scribed into Vochin's door was a delight, thrumming the Yesodic substrate with a deep bass hum. The hairs on my neck thrilled as we approached, and I paused for a moment of appreciation for such a beautifully wrought piece of work. The one in the landing had been quick and dirty, a first-stop defense. This ward throbbed with power and malevolent, bated heat. It was written to connect with the energy of Mars, which meant it would respond—and act—with some kind of physical force. Explosion, implosion, kinetic burst. No wonder Semyon had run home.

Moni couldn't see the lines, but I could see him sense the force in them as the ward rippled warily in my presence. Gooseflesh crept up the big man's neck and arms, and his fingers tightened on the trigger. "Fuck this place. Feels like them air pockets, huh? You know, like when you're on a plane."

"I've never flown." I held a hand up towards the door, and the ward thrummed sensuously in response. Who on earth had this kind of ability? I could only dream of creating something like this. It was impossible to suppress a twinge of envy, but given what had happened to Surzi and Boris, I'd expected Semyon's inner layers of defense to be greater than what I myself could cast or dispel. "This is the same kind of ward that killed the men earlier today. Masterful, and the product of a great talent. Very dangerous."

"What did it do to them?"

"It turned them into two buckets of red paint and ground beef," I replied. It was hard to keep the right tone of voice at this point in the game. "This is a very powerful piece of magic—and I need your help."

"Me?" Moni turned to face me, a gleam of avarice finally lighting the spark in his wolfish eyes. No doubt he enjoyed my loss of *blat'*[4], respect, and the boost to his own authority. His mind was already stoked on whatever he planned to do to Vochin's wife, and the money he expected to get after the job: twenty thousand, minus Nic's cut. Even after he greased the Kommandant's palm for his excellent driving, Moni would have more money than he'd held in his entire life. "What the hell do you think I can do about this shit, shortass?"

"You believe in God, don't you?"

"Yeah." His eyes narrowed warily.

"I need you to stand right in front of the door and pray while I speak the incantation. Belief in the divine is more powerful than normal magic. I need your help and your faith." I pitched my voice low, gentle and authoritative. "Make sure you don't touch it, but get as close as you can."

Moni nodded, licked his chapped lips, and moved slowly towards the door. The ward geared itself expectantly, poised like a weaving cobra, but Moni did what he was told. He lifted his hands and prayed earnestly. He was scum, but he could definitely follow orders. None of us joined the Organizatsiya because we were nice, pleasant people, but I made sure Nic gave me the worst of the worst for these jobs. Rapists, bullies, pedophiles... My last partner had a thing for

---

[4] *BLAT'* IS LIKE THE CONCEPT OF 'FACE' IN ASIAN CULTURES, BUT MORE RELIANT ON ASSERTIVE BEHAVIOR THAN SOCIAL HARMONY.

teenage girls, fourteen or fifteen years old. My stomach curled at the memory of his banter in the car.

While Moni mumbled earnestly at the sigil, I drew my most powerful tool from my coat, a tool I have worked on enchanting for most of my professional life: The Wardbreaker, a silver Colt Commander engraved with symbols down the length of its barrel. I checked the silencer was properly aligned, then leveled it at the back of Moni's head.

"*LAL!*" The word of power burst from my lips like the bullet from the gun.

There was almost no sound: just a small 'click', like a Hollywood silenced pistol. The Wardbreaker sounded like a toy, but it didn't affect the power of the round. Moni's face exploded in a wet spray against the ward, body jerking in surprise, and the air buckled and warped with a sub-audible screech. The sacrifice flooded the ward with energy, so fiercely and so suddenly that the magic spent itself before the man's soul snapped its link and closed the Gate. I helped it along with another bullet, shoving as much of my own return force into the spell's weave as I could. Moni didn't even hit the floor: the ward sucked the remaining life out of him and compressed his flesh into something the size of a baseball, which landed with the full weight of a two-hundred–pound man and shattered into chunks of super-dense charcoal. A frightened cry came from inside. The job could begin.

I kicked the door in and stepped in over the mess, into a white-walled hallway decorated with gilt mirrors, marble tables, and bad art. A cat ran from me, silent as it scuttled under the furniture of the sitting room.

A door slammed from back in the house. I followed the banging and swearing, hugging a wall and circling in.

Semyon's clatter turned deadly quiet, and the air of the apartment trembled with his silent terror as I drew closer. I heard suppressed, panicked cursing from inside the master bedroom. Carefully, I reached for the door and tried to focus, to sense for wards. Before I pushed down on the handle and threw the door open, a cloud of bullets sprayed through the flimsy wood and blew white paint chips across my coat and into the hallway with the 'spat-spat-spat' rattle of a machine pistol.

I returned a single shot through the gaping splintered hole, whirled around from my cover, and put a booted foot through the remains of the door. It took most of the next hit. I rolled across and had a brief vision of Semyon cowering by his bedside table, a gun wobbling in his damp, shaking hand.

"Stop! Stop! I'll k-kill you, you crazy white-eyed fuck!" he called out. He sounded high.

"You know why I'm here, Semyon," I called back and measured the familiar weight of the Wardbreaker in my hand. *Five bullets gone, four left.* "Your protection is useless. You can't stop me."

I dove around the corner of the open door. His reply was an auto burst that tore the bedsheets off his bed and sprayed me with shreds of fabric and foam, but Semyon couldn't aim the barrel straight. The strength was draining out of him. He'd never been a strongman. He wasn't a street soldier. He was a gemcutter and appraiser, a fussy white-collar who relied on men like Moni and me to do his dirty work and protect him, and I only had to wait until the final bullet and the guilty click of an empty cartridge to roll out from around the bed and aim my gun at his beaky, milk-white face.

"A-Alexi. God, Molotchik, look look look... you know me, you know me," he stuttered, still holding the useless gun. "There's coke, lots of coke. And money. Money under t-the bed. Take it and I'll g-go. Away. Moscow, Israel. I'll go and you can t-tell Lev—"

"That I let a snitch escape to Tel Aviv?" And coke? I frowned. I knew him, but he apparently didn't know me very well at all. "You betrayed the Organization to the Manelli Family, and they went straight to the FBI. Or did they? What do you know about this, Semyon Milosivich Vochin?"

"B-business. It was just b-business," he whispered, shaking his head. "Look, you have to talk to Nic about this, he—"

"No, Semyon. No, this isn't about business. Men like us have no business selling out." I got to my feet, keeping him centered down the sight. "Lev paid for you to come to America and help our people. Not rat us out to the Manellis, and certainly not the police."

Semyon said nothing, staring at me with cringing, red-rimmed eyes.

"He shared his home with you. He found you a job. You prospered, and you owed him your life here. You turned on him for drugs. Not for justice. Not because you thought you were doing the right thing. You turned for drugs and money."

Tears leaked down Semyon's face. "Alexi, I swear they made me take the deal, I didn't have a choice! Nic—"

"We always have a choice." Five years ago, New York had no 'Russian Mafia.' No one knew about us, our *Organizatsiya*. We were a nebulous, seemingly unconnected collection of businessmen, racketeers, gambling bosses, spooks, bookies, bouncers, and attorneys.

We kept an easy peace among ourselves and our community, and the police never connected the dots—until Semyon Vochin. The Manelli family had passed on his information because, like all the old Italian crime families, they had a strict code of honor they broke when it suited them and a policy of never working with the law unless it achieved their ends. "You chose to steal. You chose to stick product straight up your nose. The Manellis can't order you to turn in your friends, Semyon."

"You don't understand! They—"

"I understand that five men are dead because of your choices." A tic rippled across my face. I advanced a little more, carefully. Whatever magic he'd had, it must have been on the car, not on his person, but it paid to be cautious. "So now I am here, the logical conclusion of the bad decisions you have made. You only have one last choice to make. Die well, or die poorly."

"Fuck you," he hissed.

"Come now. It's a yes or no question, Semyon." My aim did not waver.

Semyon's fingers twitched on the trigger, and before he could throw the pistol at me, I fired. Fully charged with blood, the gun was truly silenced.

Blip blip. One took him in the chest, the other in the thigh, and with a hoarse shout, he pitched to the carpet.

Blip. His wordless scream cut into nothingness.

I found the cases of money under the bed: fifty thousand in cash, mixed hundred- and fifty-dollar bills. It smelled like new Government money. I left the case arranged neatly on the end of the ruined mattress, the rows of bills facing Semyon's open bedroom door. Let the Feds find it, and wonder.

As I nosed back through the house, I heard a sound from the den. Neck prickling, I slid along the wall and around the corner, gun leveled.

The cat who'd run from me was nosing around the lines of coke laid out on the table, sniffing at them with her tail held high. She was a Siamese with pale gray points, lithe and bold. When the cat lost interest, she trotted across to me with a friendly chirp. Before I could think to move away, she pressed herself against my pants leg, purring and meowing.

"Huh." I looked down at her, chagrined, and holstered the Wardbreaker. I shouldn't have let her touch me. The fibers of my trousers would be on her fur now.

I tried to step back, but she rushed under my feet, making for one of the doorways, where she turned and yowled. Against my better judgment, I stepped around the blood and followed. She led me into a large, clean kitchen and paced around an empty dish of kibble crumbs. I felt a pang of something that might have been guilt.

"I see." I found the box and poured until the bowl was full. "I suppose you'll be going to the pound when the Feds come by, won't you?"

The cat looked up at me, and for a moment, I was transfixed. Her eyes were a gray so pale they were white. Just like mine.

"Mrrrr-raow. Mrrr," she replied.

Some hitmen were in the practice of killing animals to 'warm up' before moving on to taking contracts. The notion had always disgusted me. Animals can only be victims; marks are targets because of the choices they made. Moni's choices had led him to die here; Semyon acted similarly, making decision after decision that led him to the moment of his death. His decisions shaped the fate of this cat, a creature with the misfortune to have been under the guardianship of a snitch. She was as stuck with him as I was with the Organizatsiya. This wasn't her fault.

I turned to leave but then paused, looking back. The cat had an expression of fatuous contentment, crunching on her kibble. It would take the police days to find the corpse. Would she have enough food and water? What if she ate Semyon's coke-addled body and got sick?

No, no, don't start on this. Damn it, brain. Her welfare was not my responsibility—but I am the son of an alcoholic and a Jew besides that, and the impulse to take responsibility runs deep and true.

I jerked my shoulders and forced myself to walk away. This time, I made it as far as the doorway before turning. The cat had stopped eating. She was watching me, her white eyes wise and wide, imbued with subtle intelligence. If she was afraid or regretful at the loss of her human companion, she showed no sign.

"Don't try and pull a fast one on me." I folded my arms, wavering in place. "I'm wise to you, cat."

The Siamese responded by flopping onto the floor and rolling to her back. When I hesitated, she squinted and began purring, kneading her paws in the air, a sound that intensified when I crossed to her, crouched down, and petted her belly.

"You're a manipulative bitch, you know that?" I said. But we both knew I'd lost. Her reply was to grab my hand and groom it, purring all the while. Her slender neck could produce a surprisingly deep sound, and it felt nice: a pleasant rumbling mouthfeel, a sound my brain translated to a delicate sky blue.

Five minutes later, I was back outside. Nic grunted with satisfaction when I threw open the car door and climbed into the backseat, then again in surprise when he noticed the bundle in my arms.

"The fuck is that?" he said, turning the engine.

"Mraaaow," the cat replied.

"Her name is Binah." I rested a gloved hand on her head, flattening her ears. She relaxed under my palm. "Don't ask."

"Uhn." Nic pulled away with his headlights dark, only turning them on at the end of the street. "You did the job?"

"Of course."

"And Moni?"

"A non-issue."

"Good," Nic replied. "Piece of shit."

We settled into a comfortable silence, broken only by the sound of Binah's purr and the rustle of fabric as I shucked my outerwear. Nicolai was not known for being chatty. He was an old soldier, an Afghan veteran and a hardened killer. I couldn't say I liked or trusted him, but I respected him. He was my teacher, my superior... and less fortunately, my creditor.

"So, about my fee," I said after a time. "I'm waiving it towards Vassily's prison bribe."

"Okay. But it's not gonna cover it," Nic replied. "Ten grand to go."

The pleasant afterglow faded, and fast. "Ridiculous. I already paid five. How much did it really take to get him out early?"

"Thirty, plus interest. Five years of interest. That was the deal, kid."

The Vochin job was worth twenty. I'd already paid off five. The rest of my money had gone to my father's old debts,

Chernobog[5] take him. My jaw worked, muscles tightening and bunching. "You get one more round of work from me. That's it."

"I got one lined up already. You two can come talk to me about it when he's back," Nic said. He didn't look over at me, steering laconically with one hand. It was the closest he got to sympathy. "Vassily's out of the can tomorrow, isn't he?"

"Today." My voice sounded tight in my own ears. I petted Binah, who restlessly explored the seat beside me. "Nine thirty."

Nic grunted. "Come to Sirens tomorrow. I'll tell you more there and—fuck."

I perked up as the tinny sound of Nic's pager cut through the cabin and tensed as the car listed to one side of the road when he pulled it off his belt and read it.

"Fuck," he said again. "Motherfucking piece of shit."

"Pardon?"

Nic threw the pager back to me and stomped the accelerator, pitching me and the cat against the door as he strove to make the exit. I somehow caught it as the car righted and held it to the light. The code was a string of symbols: *T1RH#4C*.

T was for *trup*, the Russian word for corpse, and the number showed how many bodies. The location, *RH#4*, stood for Site #4 in Red Hook: the AEROMOR shipping yard. The last letter in the paging code showed the nature of

---

[5] CHERNOBOG ('BLACK GOD') IS THE SLAVIC GOD OF DARKNESS, MISERY, AND POISONING. CHEERFUL GUY. 'GIVING SOMETHING TO THE BLACK GOD' IS A WAY OF 'CASTING OUT' BAD LUCK.

the problem. 'C' stood for *cherny*, 'black'—but to me, raised bilingual in Brooklyn, the C was for Crisis.

CHAPTER 2

The greasy violet taint of decay carried on the wind and coated the back of my throat before we'd stopped the car. AEROMOR was our biggest cover business, and Dockyard Number 4 was normally like every other unremarkable shipping yard in Red Hook. Tonight, the old docks were absolutely lifeless. It smelled like a charnel ground.

I left Binah to nap in the car. Lev and his posse were already waiting for us next to the guardhouse. The *Avtoritet* of Brighton Beach was nearly the spitting image of Bill Gates: a deceptively soft-looking man with an earnest pudding face and a receding hairline. He had weird, calm eyes, level and lightless, the gray-tinted green of the sea at dawn, and waited to receive us like a dignified heron in long sleeves and light slacks, unbothered by the heat. He was flanked by Vanya, a corpulent pufferfish of a man, and his favorite bodyguard, Mikhail. Most of the Yaroshenko men were Ukrainian and proud of the fact. Mikhail was *katsap*, Russian, a sleek and dangerous Doberman in human skin. He glared at me as we approached, but like most men in the Organizatsiya, he did not ever meet my eyes.

"Alexi, Nic. Good of you to join us." Lev was terser than usual, his reedy voice stiff and halting. "Vanya's man is bringing a truck to clear up the mess, but I wanted both of you to have a look before he arrives."

"Uhn," Nic grunted. He kept his chin down, scanning the docks. "What happened? I can smell it from here."

"I am hoping we can work that out." Lev glanced at me, and he did meet and hold my gaze. Thieves are a superstitious lot, and even though I can't actually read minds, nearly everyone in the Organizatsiya thought I could—except Lev. "Someone was left here for us to find. We don't know why, or who he is. He's not from the Organization."

"Has anyone disturbed the body?" Too much interference didn't only destroy physical evidence, it also disturbed any spectral evidence I might be able to sense.

"Minimally." Lev frowned, lips pursing. "And if you can tell us who or... what did it, that would be even better."

"That bad, is it?" I had probably seen worse and, in all honesty, had probably done worse. Deal with enough dead bodies, and the shock wears off.

"You'll have to see for yourself." Lev motioned with a hand as he swept off towards the waterfront.

My self-assured cynicism began to fade as we came up on the corpse. It was a decidedly long way from where we started, and the stench slowly thickened to a skin-prickling, sinus-clogging cloud of unnatural filth. I felt sick by the time Lev stopped and turned back to look at us.

The body had been left in a ring of shipping crates in the stacking yard, under the container cranes near the threshold of land and sea. Our Ivan Ivanovich was crucified, nailed spread-eagled to the planking with thick iron spikes longer than my hands. The skin of his face was torn away to expose the meat and bone beneath. One eye was sewn shut over the eyeball, while the other socket was empty, gaping up at the gunmetal sky. He was shirtless, barefoot, his fly torn open. The front of his jeans was crusted with blood.

But the mutilation was not the focus of the ritualized pose. A large symbol was carved into the corpse's chest. It was one of the demonic seals found in the Key of Solomon, a common grimoire often abused by novice Occultists with the hankering to dabble in "black" magic. Whoever this man was, he wasn't a random guy somebody had thrown out the back of a van. His killers had turned him into a display. A sacrifice.

Nicolai went around the other side of the body, hands jammed in the pockets of his cargoes. A cigarette hung listlessly from one chapped lip. "Jesus."

"No. Aamon," I said. The smell was curdling the air in my lungs. It was not natural. The heavy, leaden sensation of rotten magic is difficult to describe. It is as if the air itself was cut up, as if this patch of reality was molding, full of holes. It sucked the light out of the immediate area. The associated color of the scent was an intense, vibrant violet, the sickly color of a fresh bruise.

"What?"

"The sigil is the seal of Aamon." I took a penlight from my pocket and set it between my teeth, trying not to breathe through my nose as I crouched beside the body. I searched under his dead weight for the telltale outline of a wallet, mildly surprised when I actually found one. The money was missing, but there were half a dozen cards with different names. I flipped the penlight over to use the blacklight end, scanning them for government seals. Even the best fakes always get the seals wrong. "Here we are. Frank Nacari?"

I waited for a response. When none was forthcoming, I looked back to see that Nic had joined Lev, and they were standing shoulder to shoulder in grim silence. They were both pale. As the pregnant pause stretched on, Nic tapped a new cigarette from his case, lit up, and drew a quarter inch off the end.

"Well. We're fucked," he said on the exhale. He blew a plume of smoke down into the metallic sea wind. "Not as fucked as Nacari here, but still pretty fucked."

"Nacari is John Manelli's *Consigliere* [6]." Lev sighed, reaching up to rub the bridge of his nose. "My god. I didn't even recognize him."

Now that I thought about it, the name was vaguely familiar. My stomach flinched. That he was dead hardly bothered me, but the stench was painful, and my head was beginning to throb. "Well... that's no good."

Nic's lip had curled from the smell. He was fighting not to bring his hand to his face. "You know anybody who could do this? Any spooks who could pull something like this off?"

I did not because, unfortunately, that class of mage did not include me. My sorcerous ability had hit a hard wall in my teens and never advanced any further. I was moderately good at a very few things, and there was no way I could know which mage had done it. All I knew was that I didn't like the way the air around this body felt. It was toxic, unnatural. Frank didn't smell like rotten meat. He smelled oily, like kerosene or turpentine. "I'm sure there are, but I don't know them. If they needed a human sacrifice like this, they are either a powerful mage trying to do a very bad thing with a common ritual or a weak mage who needs the intense energy generated by a death to properly summon at all. All I know

---

[6] A CONSIGLIERE IS THE ADVISOR TO THE DON IN THE ITALIAN MAFIA, AND USUALLY ONE OF THE MOST TRUSTED MEMBERS OF A MOB BOSS'S INNER CIRCLE.

is that his death was probably used to fuel the summoning of Aamon, who is a moderately powerful demon from the Goetia. But that doesn't make much sense to me, either."

"What the fuck is an Aamon?" Nic crossed his arms over his chest.

"Marquis of Hell, the ruler of the creation and resolution of feuds. He is summoned for questions pertaining to finding people or causing and resolving arguments. What confuses me is that the rite to summon Aamon doesn't require a human sacrifice, and Aamon, by and large, is not a violent demon."

"There's violent demons and nonviolent demons?" Nic squinted, the lines around his eyes deepening, and moved around to stand by Nacari's feet. Lev did not say a word, but he was listening intently.

"Yes. The demons of the Goetia are teachers and tricksters, and they reflect parts of human nature. They're not... corrupt like this." Nic's ignorance was irritating me. The Goetia was easy to find, and even Blanks—non-magical people—could pick up a book and read it. We needed to change the subject before I said something inappropriate. "Was there security footage? Anyone working late who might have seen anything?"

Lev finally spoke up. "Someone took out the camera. The nightshift shipwrights were all at Number Two. This dock was cleared for the night."

My frown deepened, and I touched a gloved finger to the head of the huge nail that had been driven through Nacari's hand. Pushed it. It didn't budge. "These are dog spikes. Railroad spikes. They either brought a borer and pre-bored the holes, or they found a spike driver. It would have made a lot of noise. In any case, whoever did this must have a connection with the construction industry, probably rail."

Nic said nothing for several seconds, lighting his next cigarette from the tip of the old one. "You know Georgie, right? The new Laguetta Don?"

"Of course." The Manelli and Laguetta family war—with the accompanying body count—had been the start of our troubles with the Manellis in the first place. "Not personally."

"Laguetta has a hand in the Concrete Club. Man of his is in charge of Pinnacle. Skyscraper developer."

"No, no, I can't believe he'd contract this and leave the body here. They've been with us for years." Lev shook his head, but he sounded uncertain.

The Laguettas were the second largest of the four big Italian Families, the Manellis being the largest. Affording a ritual like this one was out of reach for most people on the street. At the highest levels of power, spooks on the payroll battled a cold war in gridlock, ensuring their own Don or Avtoritet or King was untouchable while others tried to pick away at their defenses—but this was something else.

I crouched down and leaned in. In the center of the seal of Aamon was a deep, festering puncture. The flesh around it was fragile and pallid, laced with branching trees of black veins. Carefully, I lifted the edge of Nacari's fly. What little flesh remained was torn, blackened at the edges. He was completely emasculated, and the amputation looked to be older than the stab wound that killed him. Awful, but in that train wreck-kind of way.

Nic grunted and shifted uncomfortably. "Yeah. If this is Laguetta's dirty laundry, it don't make no sense. No reason for any of his crews to take a dump on our turf."

While they debated, I turned my attention to the dead man's face, leaning in with my hand clasped over my nose. His one remaining eyelid was distended and dark, the nearly transparent skin bulging over something underneath. I took a knife from my pocket and popped it open with a small click. Balanced on the balls of my feet, I stretched out and flicked the tip of the blade up under the stitches.

Frank Nacari's eye had been replaced with a large lead caster. The dawn light reflected dully off its surface, and with a soft sound under my breath, I reached forward to push it out. The caster was roughened on the underside and rasped against my gloves when I rubbed the blood away. It was only slightly smaller than an eyeball, roughly polished, and etched with a symbol:

On the ground and facing away from Nicolai, I could conceal the moment of shock and vague recognition. It was an Occult sigil, and I should have known it. I *knew* I had seen it before. I stared at it, fighting with half-memories of planetary tables and pages from very old books on ceremonial summoning. At a loss to remember which books held what, I held out the caster to Lev. He took it, puzzled, and his nose wrinkled.

"The hell is that?" Nic said.

"I have no idea. But it is deeply idiosyncratic." I shrugged.

Nicolai stared at it. "Idio-what?"

"Unique. Singular," Lev replied.

"And honestly confusing," I added.

"Huh." Nic glanced past me, looking over at the entry gate. "Looks like... whatddya call 'em? The swinging tick-tock things. Not clocks."

"Pendula." Lev turned it around and held it back out to me. Absently, I accepted its hot weight as I looked down at the gaping sockets, now empty, and frowned. The other socket was a blank, but now that I was up close, I could see where the skin had been stitched together, just like the one with the caster. The stitches were torn, with a foamy residue crusting the socket.

From behind us came the roar of a large truck. The cleanup crew. While Nic, Vanya, and Mikhail turned in distraction, I bent down and sniffed, then snorted. Even blunted by the scent of decay, Nacari's face smelled like wet dog.

Lev watched me curiously. "Anything else?"

"Nothing definite, Avtoritet. This symbol is possibly a calling card." I picked up the caster with careful fingers, wrapped it in a tissue, and pocketed it with a certain reverence. "I'll research this symbol and find out. Ask around, as well—it might be turning up with other hits around the city."

"Could be the Zetas. They've been getting real up themselves lately." Nicolai shook his head. "Don't know who else'd cut a man's dick off. You can't tell us what did it?"

I shook my head. "There's literally nothing here. Nothing at all."

Lev exhaled thinly and pushed his glasses up along his nose. "If Manelli finds out what happened to Nacari, he's going to be very, very angry. It must be kept under wraps. No discussion. Am I understood?"

I nodded. Six years ago, the Manellis hadn't been a large Mafia. Back before the crack boom, they'd been scraping by under their old protectorate, the Scappetis. The Manelli-Scappeti coalition spent their time scrapping with the other three big Families, mostly the Laguettas. The Laguettas were an old, old Family who ran all of Brooklyn and a good part of Manhattan out of Queens. After John Manelli arranged for Don Scappeti to have a premature heart attack, he took over his op and played the hand he'd been building for years. John Manelli was young and willing to bend the 'code of honor' he theoretically embodied to deal in drugs directly. While the old Mafioso clung to their ways, John was running the crack boom in the Eastern United States, taking over gay bars and discos and cutting into our much older and well-established party drug business. That wasn't enough for him, either. Young Dons like John were inevitably aggressive, ambitious, eager to fight. He wanted us bought under heel. For all we knew, he'd ground up his own *Consigliere* and thrown him over the wall, so to speak, just so he could point in our direction and get his men fired up to wage open war on us.

"I say this must've been a pro-team job. Three or four guys." Nicolai watched me, his hands restless. He patted down his khakis as if looking for something. He was nervous. I'd never seen him nervous before.

"Can I let Vassily in on this?" I had to get up and back away, as the first waves of real, unstoppable nausea swept up and rolled me. I felt dizzy. Everything smelled like rotting peaches and meat. "I'll be picking him up in five hours or so. He will want to know."

"I will tell him, at my discretion." Lev drew his coat around his arms. Even though it was still in the low seventies, he looked as cold as I felt. "Nicolai, could you leave us for a moment? Alexi and I need to take a walk."

"Sure. We'll get him loaded up." Nic jerked his face to one side and sloped back off across the yard, disappearing into the shadows beyond the beam of the truck lights. I jammed my hands in my pockets, suddenly stranded in the presence of authority.

"Come, Alexi. I need to talk to you about something which no one else needs to hear." Lev motioned with his head. He looked greenish, as ill as I felt.

"As you say, Avtoritet." Was it the question of involving Vassily? I followed warily. Being alone with your Avtoritet was never particularly safe. "Is this about the money I owe Nicolai?"

Lev waited until we were some distance away before speaking. "No. I want to know how Semyon died. Did he admit that he wronged me?"

I looked down. "I regret to say it, Avtoritet, but no. I asked him, as you ordered. He died a coward."

Lev heaved a deep sigh. "Did he confess anything? Anything about his magical activities or about the FBI?"

"No." I shook my head. "Though regarding the latter, he implied they'd forced him into a deal."

"I don't doubt it. But he shouldn't have accepted." Lev was very, very unhappy. The tendons of his shoulders and wrists were taut under his skin. Even so, his face was as placid as Lake Baikal in the summer, and just as deep. "You will not tell Vassily what happened between Semyon and yourself. I don't want anyone knowing what happened up there. I trust you'll obey; Vassily is a good man, but he is as gossipy as a gypsy grandmother."

I let the insult slide. "Of course."

"I'll take your word." Lev stopped, and I halted mid-step so I didn't pass him by. "There aren't many men in this organization like you left. Loyal, quiet, sensible."

"Thank you, Avtoritet," I said, cautiously.

"You're wasted on this grunt work, Alexi. Once you clear Vassily's debt, you should finish your degree. Come and work for the firm." Lev's mouth lifted at the corners, but it never reached his eyes. "And speaking of Vassily, please do pass along my regards when you pick him up. He is welcome to take one of the Sirens lounges for a private session with the women of his choice. As are you, of course."

The very notion turned my stomach. Lev's voice was as pleasant as ever, but it raised the hackles on the back of my neck. Some instinct nagged at me, telling me to tread carefully. The Organizatsiya had given Vassily and me everything, but our benefactors—Lev, Nic, Sergei—kept a fistful of strings tied to every offered gift.

I forced a brief smile. "Of course, Avtoritet. I am sure he will take up your offer at the earliest opportunity."

"I hope he does. No matter how well we handle the events of the night, I fear we are all soon going to have to turn our energies to war." Lev dipped his head slightly, turned, and left me to stand there in the middle of the yard, watching him disappear into the humid night.

The lead caster was cold through the leather of my glove, colder than the overripe air. My fingers clenched in the moment before I started after him, boots ringing out against the hard ground. The only certain thing about the mess had been left largely unsaid. Someone had summoned a demon: Aamon, the lord of feuds, and was driving my small Organizatsiya from skirmishing with the largest Mafia family in New York to outright war. Nacari's murder transcended brutality and moved well into the realm of horror, and Lev was right. If John Manelli ever found out what had happened to his favorite Captain, he was going to give us Hell.

CHAPTER 3

By the time I arrived at my apartment block, my head was a little clearer. It was a temporary reprieve: it was close to five in the morning, and I was exhausted, weary, blood-spattered, and looking forward to a cold shower before the grueling three-hour drive to Fishkill.

Binah hung placidly along the length of my forearm on the way up the stairwell, which smelled of old urine and cigarettes. My door was on the third floor, near the exit to the roof. There's a stereotype of wizards locked in ivory towers, but my apartment was a meat locker with balconies, Spartan and uncluttered save for the Tetris-like mass of bookshelves lining the walls: Row after row of books, neatly filed in floor-to-ceiling shelves by color, height, and subject. The shelves spanned most of the rooms and over some of the doorways. There was even a small one in the bathroom.

Enfolded in the papery silence of the hall, I shucked my shoes, unbuttoned my cuffs, and rolled them up to the elbow. Binah leaped from my arms and wandered off into the house to explore. I lost track of her on my way to the kitchen. The lead caster with the sigil was burning a hole in my pocket, but when I extended my senses towards it, feeling for any imprinted magical residue, it came up blank.

Still, Alexi Grigoriovich Sokolsky is not known for being an incautious man, so before anything else, I got a clean tin chalice and filled it with coarse rock salt and water, burying the caster in the center. Tin is the metal of Jupiter, the Greater Benefic who oversees abstracts such as justice, purification, and good fortune. Salt and water are to magical effects what containment pools are to spent nuclear fuel rods. They don't fix the problem, but they keep it confined and—temporarily—safe.

I found Sir Purrs-A-Lot's old litter box and food bowls and set them up for Binah in the bathroom, then shed my gloves and threw them and my keys into the tub to wash up. Exposed, my hands rang like a tuning fork: I pressed my teeth together and forced myself to touch the tap and turn it. The chilly metal sent a shock of bright sensation through my fingers. The sound of the screeching faucet and rushing water obliterated my vision with white haze while I washed the keys, my gloves, and then myself under the shower—twice with soap, once with lanolin cream. Too much heavy magic and not enough sleep turned up the dial on my nerves, overstimulating my senses to the point of disability. The sound of the water had color and shape I felt in my mouth.

The whole time, I was haunted by a strange, nebulous discontent. I couldn't say if I was disturbed by the course of the night or not. Death has never particularly disturbed me. It is nicely certain, one of two events—the other being birth—which are guaranteed and irrevocable. The only variable is how you go about it, when the time comes. Do you die well, or do you die badly?

For different reasons, two men had died badly tonight, and bad deaths bothered me in a way I could not even articulate to myself.

Once I was clean, I felt around over the sink and opened the mirrored cupboard with the point of my wrist. Inside was a glass tumbler and a new pair of gloves. Even after all that, I still felt dirty, as if I were covered in a faint sheen of blood and filth. It had been a very long night, and it was going to be an equally long, hot, difficult day. I had to pick up Vassily, and then maybe—if I was lucky—I'd get six hours sleep before we drove in to report to Lev.

God, Vassily. The thought of having him back made my mouth turn dry. I still had surfaces to clean, books to sort. The place needed to breathe: it needed to be everything that prison wasn't for those precious first minutes when Vassily stepped in and found everything the way it should be. He'd been gone for five years. I guess it wasn't that long, not really. Not on the scale of, say, the time between the present—1991—and the day I'd run away from my parents' house, but five years is a long time to be missing your right hand. We'd practically lived together from the day I'd been adopted into his family to the day he'd been convicted, and for five years, I'd come home to this heavy silence after every job, hanging my coat and setting down my gun in the buzzing nothingness of an empty apartment.

Before I left, I spent some time in front of the mirror practicing. Nic told me soon after Vassily had gone in that sometimes, the prison wouldn't admit you if you looked wrong. I'd never been refused a visit, but this was a release, and I wasn't completely certain it was the same sort of occasion. I tried to appear more pleasant and less severe for several minutes, but no mirror in the world could bring a warm light to my eyes or soften the thinness of my mouth. No matter what I did, I looked like a short, sharky man-eater. It was Vassily who taught me how to socialize outside the confines of a hit. Thanks to his patience, certain kinds of interactions were manageable. Hellos, goodbyes. Business. Intimidation. Dealing with people like Moni is easy: I have those men down to a science. But being likeable, attractive, relaxed? They were Vassily's skills.

I fiddled with my face and clothes until my cheeks ached. Frustrated, restless, I stood back, gut tight, and breathed deeply of the clean vacuum smell of the house. Overriding it was the faint perfume of frankincense and myrrh. My altar took up one wall of my bedroom, a plain table laid out with a well-organized, eclectic clutter of Judaica and Occult paraphernalia from no particular country or point in history: a knife and chalice, a statuette of Santa Muerte, the Mexican cartel saint who protected those who worked by night, and an effigy of Veles, ancient god of magic, in honor of my Slavic heritage. A tarot deck wrapped in a scarf sat in front, the card for the week propped up against the rest, and a hundred other items of curiosity, awe, and personal significance were arranged in concentric rings from the central point. The Wardbreaker lived there, resting next to a gold ankh I'd given to Vassily on his twentieth birthday. He'd pressed it into my hand just before he was led out of the courtroom after his sentence was handed down, his fingers shaking and hot against my palm.

I took up the ankh, folded my fingers around it, and squeezed. It was time to go and see what remained of my best friend.

* * *

Fishkill Correctional was located just off Route 84, an old New York State Psychiatric Center converted into a prison. My gut was sour with tension by the time I cleared security.

Dry-mouthed, I waited in reception with my hands twisted on my lap, staring down at them in stony silence while I tried to think of things other than the dangers and vices of cellblock life. Jaundice. Drugs. Alcohol. Especially alcohol.

A buzz preceded the opening of the inmate release doors, and each time, the sound jerked me from my reverie. Three ex-convicts went by, one after the other. One of them, a black man with the hollow eyes of a serial jailbird, was picked up by a stoic woman with big hair and big teeth. Next out was a bald, fit hardcase with an underbite and piercing blue eyes. He marched out the door alone without a backward glance. The third was a bewildered little rabbit who lingered around the reception desk. I watched him with slow eyes. He had the wire-strung build of a junkie and the quick, jerky manner of prey.

The buzzer blared a fourth time, and my gaze shifted from Rabbit to the door. My eyes lit on a familiar pair of hands—long, fine-boned philosopher's hands, lettered and tattooed over the knuckles: the tattoos of a *Vor v Zakone*. Vassily and I were both too young to actually be considered Vor v Zakone, the oath-taking sworn thieves of Nic and Lev's generation. Vassily's tattoos were well deserved in many other ways, but they were a memorial to the father he'd never known.

I stood up in alarm as my sworn brother—thinner, harder, and more wolfish than I remembered—let his mouth stretch in a chagrined smile as he was led to the desk for processing. His black hair was shorter, and his old suit strained visibly across his shoulders and hung loose around his waist, but he was just as lean and tall and handsome as I remembered. I stared at his back in shock as he signed the release, pulse hammering under my tongue. Finally, I heard the final stab of the pen from across the room, and Vassily threw it down as he broke apart from his escort in a rush. We collided as I stepped into his long-limbed embrace, wrapping my arms around his chest as he swore and laughed and squeezed his whole upper body around my head. Under the weird clinical smell of institutional air, without cologne or aftershave, he still smelled the way he always had. He smelled right, like fur and blue and spice on my palate. For a long moment, I found my mouth full and cottony, unable to speak from a place of perfect stillness.

"Jesus," Vassily said hoarsely. "Alexi. Jesus."

"You're back where you belong," I replied in Ukrainian, clapping Vassily's back. "Here."

Vassily did not let go. I felt his fingers clench the skin of my shoulders through my shirt. When he spoke again, it was quiet, lips beside my ear. "Get me the fuck out of this place. Food. Sun. Coffee. Please."

I peeled back enough to look up at him, gripping his arms. Intensity hummed like a weight in the back of my throat, and white heat burned behind my eyes as I leaned forward, my gaze locked with Vassily's. "We will go to Gletchik's. I'm certain they'll be glad to see you again."

Hesitantly, he nodded. Behind him, the guards were waiting impatiently by the door, their lips drawn into disapproving lines. I fought the urge to stare back and pulled him away, and neither of us said another word on our way outside. I was light-headed. The fears tumbling around in my imagination during the drive were lost to the wind.

We listened to the radio on and off, but after a while, our need for music petered out and we spent the rest of the drive in comfortable silence. I watched Vassily out of the corner of my eye and sometimes caught the glance of the hot summer sun over his cheekbones or the shadows of his throat. Vassily let his elbow rest outside the threshold of the car window, drinking in the sight of the sky. He couldn't keep his eyes from it, and as the clouds rolled in, a massive front from over the mountains, he grinned broadly with delight. It made me smile, too.

"Space, man," Vassily finally said. "Nothing but wide open space."

I relished the pleasant mouthfeel of his voice for a moment, then spoke. "These years must have been hard."

"Meh. No different to how it was out of prison really. You eat your peas, you roll some jackass every other day, you shave and shit. Nothing to it." Vassily snorted, rolled his eyes, and tipped his head back against the seat. "The only thing... man. No girls. THAT sucked."

Being a virgin, I had no idea what to say by way of reply. We drove in silence for nearly five minutes, and this time, it was slightly awkward.

"So, uh... tell me what's happening. I heard what I could from you or Nic, but he said a lot of shit's changed."

"It has." Goodness, where to begin? "Sergei still has not returned from the continent, and as you know, Lev is now *Avtoritet*."

"Feh," Vassily chuffed.

"Nicolai is now *Kommandant* of Brighton Beach. He absorbed Rodion's old team when Rod was gunned down last year. No one knows if it was Lev who had him killed, but my theory is that he did. We also lost Mo, and my father, of course." I recited the changes and deaths perfunctorily. They were little more than statistics: movements on the grand chessboard where Vassily and I had been making moves since we were teens. I mulled my next words, considering what Lev had said. We weren't to talk about Nacari, and I wasn't to divulge the intimate details of Semyon's death... but everything else was kosher. "I dealt with Sem Vochin last night."

"Sem? Sem the Jeweler?" Vassily's surprise was audible. "Lev's—"

"He went to the Manelli family and sold out all of the details of Lev's new cocaine operation. Naturally, the Manellis took his information and fed it to one of their pet cops." My lips thinned. "As you can imagine, Lev was not pleased."

"*I'm* not pleased. The little rat was probably the one that landed me out here." Vassily scowled, drumming his fingers on the dash. "But that was Lev's mistake. He should have kept his cards close and his mouth shut. This is the problem with the old guys, Lexi. They can't keep their metaphorical dicks in their metaphorical pants. Sergei was the only one with any real wit, you know?"

Sergei Yaroshenko, that grand old patriarch, was our *Pakhun*.[7] the man who'd established the Yaroshenko Organizatsiya in the 1950s. He ruled Brighton Beach for thirty years and put Vassily and me through school, priming Vassily for the leadership and me to be his *Advokat*, his advisor. That goal was why I'd done the Organizatsiya's dirty work for most of my life. But it was a goal that was looking more remote with every passing year.

---

[7] THE PAKHUN (LITERALLY 'PRINCE') IS THE FOUNDER AND ABSOLUTE AUTHORITY OF ANY GIVEN RUSSIAN MAFIYA OUTFIT. UNLIKE THE AVTORITET, A PAKHUN IS RARELY 'HANDS ON' AND MAY EVEN BE A LEGITIMATE BUSINESSMAN, POLITICIAN, OR AUTHORITY FIGURE. THIS IS ONE OF THE MAJOR ORGANIZATIONAL DIFFERENCES BETWEEN SLAVIC AND ITALIAN ORGANIZED CRIME.

When we'd turned twenty, Sergei left America to take care of business in Ukraine, vanishing into whatever bureaucratic spiderweb he'd spun in Kiev. The leadership had passed to Rodion Brukov, an old-school captain with a pompadour, a vodka and gin habit, and the uncanny ability to make good decisions while drunk. He'd been about to make Vassily Kommandant just before he went to jail on trumped up credit card fraud charges, which we now knew was Semyon's fault, as was Rod's death. Rodion's passing left a power vacuum, and Lev was the man who conveniently stepped in to fill the void. He was an attorney and trust fund guy, a real white-collar intellectual, and even though he'd averted an internal war and built the Organizatsiya into an immensely profitable force, he was not popular with the rough-and-tumble men who had willingly worked for Sergei and Rodion.

I made a noncommittal motion of head and shoulders. "Sergei is apparently securing our place in the new system, now that the USSR is collapsing around our ears. The continent is in chaos."

"*Perestroika*.[8]" Vassily made a face.

"Indeed. The system is crumbling, jobs are disappearing, and every louse with more muscles than brains is looking to get rich. Mikhail has been hiring rogue players from Bulgaria, Georgia... Nic's been feeding them to the dragon, so to speak, to keep the numbers in check. I dealt with another one just last night."

---

[8] PERESTROIKA WAS THE RESTRUCTURING OF THE SOVIET POLITICAL & ECONOMIC SYSTEM, AND A MAJOR CAUSE IN THE DISSOLUTION OF THE SOVIET UNION AND THE SUBSEQUENT COLLAPSE OF COMMUNISM IN SEPTEMBER 1991.

"I heard it was getting rainy out there. Lots of guys dying." Vassily sat back, hands restless in his lap. "I just hope I can hit the ground running."

"You will." The USSR might have been changing, but things in Brighton Beach rarely did. We worked the same trades our fathers had done before us: fake fuel and guns, contraband, and policing the *krysha*, the protection racket. Before cocaine, the krysha had been a big part of my life. I collected the rent, pressured the guys who didn't pay, and protected the ones who did. "Lev, to his credit, has been a good leader, but he is not well loved. They think he is changing too much too fast."

"Well, yeah. Because Rodion was a great Avtoritet. Lev's nothing but a bureaucratic jerk-off."

"You shouldn't challenge him yet, Vassily. Lev is still Sergei's Advokat. You shouldn't even look at him askance until Sergei has returned and confirms you."

"If he ever does. It's been nearly ten years. He's just about forfeited his claim to the Beach, and I don't care how many million fucktons of money he has. This is where you and I grew up. It's our turf, Lexi, and Lev and Sergei treat us like serfs on their land. We're the ones who collect the cash and do all the work. My brothers all died for this place, and for him. And for what?"

His words had some truth. I ran my tongue over my teeth as we turned off the highway, barely slowing for the exit. Most traffic was moving in the other direction, away from New York. Cars full of families and fishermen, heading for the Hudson and its promise of slow days and cleanish air.

As suddenly as it had come over us, the grim mood began to ebb in the lull of conversation. Vassily made a thoughtful sound and drummed his long fingers on his thigh. "Anyway... I was wondering if—"

"Your room is as you left it." I cut him off, anticipating what he was about to ask, and merged onto the busier lane that would take us into the city. "I sorted your washing and vacuum-sealed it. It's as good as new."

"Of course you did." Vassily rested his head against the back of the seat and snorted. "That wasn't what I was gonna ask, though. You still into the woo-woo?"

Magic was the one part of my life he had never understood and I never shared. "Of course. Why?"

"Maybe you can explain something for me, Mister Wizard. I thought about the sea a lot while I was in." Vassily's brow furrowed. "Dreamed about it. What do you make of that?"

"Emotion. The sea is symbolic of ocean and the mystery."

"The mystery, huh? What mystery?"

"*The* Mystery. Ocean is a powerful symbol for the subconscious mind, for the things we don't know and can never know about ourselves," I replied, gesturing to the road ahead. "We know it is the origin of life, but we cannot survive in it. It is full of oxygen we cannot breathe, animals we have never seen, forests we cannot walk through. It's the mystery which represents the greater mystery of our existence."

"I don't really know what you're talking about, but I'll think about it. 'Mystery' wasn't ever much of a big deal for me, except for like... you know, 'what's in the fridge that I can still eat for breakfast?' But I had a lot of time to learn how to think."

"That is probably the most profound thing I have ever heard emerge from the sphincter you pass off as your mouth," I said.

"Fuck you. I was the token Russkie in prison. I got along by keeping my mouth shut." Vassily jerked his shoulders back, rolling them, but there was laughter in his eyes. "So, did you ever get around to the *Tao Te Ching*?"

"I did." Books had kept our friendship alive while he was in prison, a point of connection when everything else had been taken away, and I smiled. "*He who knows how to live can walk abroad without fear of rhinoceros or tiger. He will not be wounded in battle. Why is this so? Because he has no place for death to enter.*"

"Yeah, I knew you'd love it. Verse forty-four's my fave. It helped a lot with these weird nightmares I had. I was always dreaming about falling up into a black hole. Black holes, or the sea, but it was always up. I felt like I was coming apart sometimes, you know?"

Yes, I did know. You couldn't work in my profession and not encounter it, that void of no-future. My father had fallen into it, and had tried to drag everyone around down with him. "Indeed. Though bear in mind that black holes are often associated with feelings of guilt."

"Guilt? Yeah, right. Anyway, off topic. I held off asking for as long as I could, but are you still single? Do I have to keep worrying about you never getting laid?"

He switched topics so quickly I almost lost track of his voice. Fortunately, I had been preparing for this question for years. What I needed to say was technically a lie, albeit one with a kernel of truth. "Not entirely."

"I mean, I know you're basically a monk, but I... wait." Vassily paused mid-thought, hand raised. His mouth worked as he struggled to process what I'd just said. "Hold on. 'Not entirely'? As in, 'No, Vassily, I'm no longer a sad and lonely virgin'?"

"I know a woman." Not knowing how to elaborate, I shrugged a second time.

"Is she... uh... is she real?" Vassily's brow furrowed in concern. "Like, alive, and not a magazine cutout with a hole for your dick?"

I tch'd and rolled my eyes. "Don't be a putz. Her name is Crina Juranovic. You met her once, at Sirens."

"I don't remember her. And Juranovic? She Serbian? Croatian?"

"Possibly. She speaks Ukrainian, but she grew up in Germany."

"Well, I... huh. Right." Vassily trailed off and began to twitch, drumming his fingers on his thighs. He hesitated for a moment before speaking again, voice catching. "That's good, because guys like you end up in the Weird Obituaries section of the papers, Lexi. I worry I'll come in and find you've choked yourself out from the doorknob with a pair of dirty stockings someday, and—"

"Vassily." If I rolled my eyes any harder, they were going to burst out the back of my skull. "Please, give me some credit. The stockings would be clean."

He busted up laughing. "Okay, fine, fine. Girl or no girl though, I'm glad you haven't really changed much."

"What do you mean by that?" I gripped the steering wheel and fixed my eyes ahead. I was surprised at myself, how immediately defensive I sounded. "I've worked my way to independence. Nic trusts me, Lev trusts me... I have a lot of work from them. The money is excellent."

"I'm not talking about what you do, Lexi. I'm just talking about... you. Like the heart of you. It's still the same." Vassily looked back out towards the rush of gray and brown as we entered the gaping oven of New York City. "I'm not saying that's a bad thing. I mean, it's good to get out and have at least one thing still be how it was, 'specially after all the hard news. You're lucky you weren't wasted when Lev took over."

"I'm more worried about the Manellis," I replied. "Lev does a good enough job. His maneuvering has the best interests of the collective at heart. I'd rather have him as Avtoritet than, say, Vanya."

"Well, yeah. I'd rather see a dog turd as Avtoritet before Vanya."

"Indeed. The biggest test will be how we hold against one of the Five Families," I said. "This new Colombian cartel arrangement has been incredibly successful. Every yuppie from Miami to Boston is buying at the moment. Now that John Manelli knows who's in charge, I have no idea what we'll do. Lev hasn't really talked about it. Nic has only fears. Unfortunately, I am no seer."

I trailed off when I noticed Vassily had fallen uncomfortably silent, staring down at his hands. Unspoken was the same anxiety I had also nursed, off and on, for the past half a decade. His incarceration had driven us both to think about our friendship for the first time, how tenuous our freedom together really was. His release was already overshadowed by fresh violence, and both of us would have to be there when the shit hit the fan, parole officer or no parole officer.

After a few minutes of silence, he smiled, and I watched his light flicker back to life. "So, we're going straight to Gletchik's, right?"

"Of course." I desperately needed food. My stomach had given up trying to tell me how hungry I was, and I imagined it shrunk down to the size of a bean, the walls of my gut gnawing at itself for sustenance.

"Thank God. I'm gonna hit that menu so hard."

The idea was utterly perplexing. I frowned. "Why would you hit the menu?"

"For fuck's sake." Vassily rolled his eyes. "Alexi... I'm not actually going to hit the menu."

"You order from menus." I shook my head stubbornly.

"Fine. Okay. I will order from the menu. Everything from the menu." He sighed. "Fucking hell. I forgot how literal you get when you're tired."

Ordering everything on the menu didn't seem a whole lot more practical than hitting it, but I kept my mouth shut and focused on my driving. In any case, if buying everything was what he wanted to do, well... I guess we could make space in the refrigerator for it all, if we tried hard enough.

Gletchik's was as good as usual. We ate as much as we could, but there was no time for rest. Vassily needed ID, a new bank account, new clothing, and all the other minutiae of mundane life after being released from prison. We returned to my apartment with far too much food for the old one-person refrigerator and wet food for Binah. My new cat greeted us enthusiastically at the door, and when Vassily stooped and picked her up, she stuck her head out, purring, and began to wash the bridge of his nose.

"Who's this pretty little guy?" Vassily paused for a moment to check under her tail. "Girl."

"Binah. She's..." I almost said "Semyon's cat," but Semyon was dead. "New. I thought you'd like her. To replace Sir Purrs-a-Lot."

"R.I.P Purrs-A-Lot." Vassily said mournfully. "I still owe your dad a punch to the face for murdering my cat."

I glanced away. "My father's dead."

That froze Vassily for a second. "Oh... shit. No one told me. Grisha's really dead?"

"Yes. I didn't think it was a good idea to tell you at Fishkill."

"Sure." Vassily cleared his throat, suddenly nervous. "Was it-?"

"I don't want to talk about him." I jerked my shoulders. "Not today. We're supposed to be celebrating your release."

Vassily smiled awkwardly, but then brightened again. He flipped Binah onto her back in his arms like a baby. Most cats would have lost their shit, but Binah simply lay there, purring. "Well, okay. This cat's great, anyway. I love Siamese. They're like the best parts of dogs and cats rolled into the one furry package."

Once everything was put away, I left Vassily to play with Binah in the den and stumbled gratefully to my bedroom. I was delirious, dizzy by the time I was finally able to turn off the light, undress, and get into bed.

Sleep came easily, but it was not peaceful.

As I often did, I dreamed of my childhood home, the white house on Brighton 6th Street. Like an automaton, I walked up the foggy sidewalk and opened the gate. The peeling bungalow door was usually locked, as inaccessible to me as the memories of my teens. Tonight, the front door was open as wide as my hand, large enough for a cat to squeeze in. The cool air coming from underneath the entry smelled rotten and sweet. I knew I was dreaming but couldn't stop myself from reaching out and pushing the door in. Couldn't stop myself from walking inside.

The living room was cluttered to waist height with the stacks of old paper my mother hoarded and trash bags full of the bottles my father discarded. The carpet was thin and dull, and the only light was from two sickly green lampshades in the corners of the room. The wide arch that would have led to the kitchen was bricked over, painted with a strange symbol. It looked like an eye with a cross where the iris was supposed to be. It was drawn in blood, pressed into plaster the texture of dead flesh. Crumpled face-first against the wall was a tall, white-haired, dark-skinned, sexless figure. Its fingers were bloodied stumps.

"You believe in G.O.D., don't you?" The figure did not speak, but its voice echoed around the room, breathless and fluted. It spelled out each letter slowly, shaping them like soap bubbles that burst in my ears.

I froze. The shadow of a man much larger than I loomed around me, cutting the light from the door behind. I heard a click, like a finger on a trigger.

"I need your help and your faith."

My vision began to crawl with black spots, dancing specks creeping in from the sides of my eyes, but I could not move as I heard the trigger pull home.

In the split second before impact, the head of white hair snapped around like an owl's, eyes wide with surprise. I saw Blue. Twin points of blazing white-blue that ate into me, drowned me, and filled me as my head shattered.

"... *Bat'ko?*"

My body hit the bed and bounced, pitching me to the side and then upright as I scrambled for purchase on sweaty sheets. My hand flew to my face: it was numb. Disoriented and heaving for air, I stumbled up, searching for a light. The room was pitch dark and freezing, the air thick, silent except for the rattle and spit of the air conditioner. I found a lamp and pulled the chain, leaning back against the wall beside it. It was the lamp on the bookshelf beside my altar.

I looked around and down, and my eyes were drawn to the tarot card I had set out for contemplation earlier in the week. The Devil, the card of material entrapment, confusion, false self-image. It sat next to the tin dish of salt and water which held the caster I'd retrieved from Nacari, and as I stared at it, trying to figure out what was gnawing at me, I realized: The water had boiled off, and the salt was brownish, dull and stained. I could see the top of the caster protruding from the remains, like a half-buried skull.

When I could move, I pushed away from the wall and got the chalice on the way out. The rest of the apartment was gloomy, the air hanging still. I nosed through the darkness until I reached the kitchen, ran gloved hands over the edge of cold metal and the small gap between the fridge and the overhead shelf. I found the door and cracked it open: Light spilled over the brown linoleum tiling. Squinting against the glare, I got a jug of cold water and refilled the chalice to drown the sigil in fresh salt water. I put the whole thing in the icebox, tucking it securely between bags of frozen *pilmeni*. It wouldn't evaporate again.

"Mrr. Mrraw." Binah's was still getting used to the place, flighty and shadow-shy, but she arched against my bare legs like she'd always known me. Her fur was warm, a little damp. Sleeping on Vassily, probably. In the lapse of sound just as I bent down to pet her, I caught a flash of bright green noise: the telltale beep of the answering machine from farther back in the house. I'd slept so hard I hadn't heard the phone.

I grimaced and stalked out at a quick walk. My stomach was twitchy as I strode into the den in the dark and then stopped, sniffing. It was humid in here, and smelled like male scent. Vassily was sleeping on the sofa instead of in his bed. I crept past him, snoring away in his duvet, and unlocked my office door with Binah on my heels.

My office was the size of a large closet, barely big enough for a desk, shelves, and the case that held my father's old sledgehammer. My work library was in here – references of old criminal cases, journals on forensic technology, a record of murders solved and unsolved, and local police bulletins on organized crime. My desk was surrounded by pinboards covered in news clippings and notes. You had to stay on top of what the other side was doing to be good at your job.

A long glass case next to the desk held the sledgehammer on its bed of purple velvet. It was a plain prison camp tool, unremarkable in every way except for the memories of mingled horror and victory it aroused in me. My father had used it for his executions, and I had used it to execute him. The haft was worn smooth, but the oiled iron head was dark and pitted with old blood. As always, I glanced at it as I shuffled into the chair and pressed the play button, switching on the desk lamp with the other hand. The machine whirred and clicked, winding the tape. While I waited, I rubbed at my itching jaw. My mouth was very dry. *Bat'ko*. I had heard that word very clearly, but it made no sense to me. 'Bat'ko' meant 'father'.

Nicolai's grating, dull voice spoke from the speakers, rough and flat from the electronic distortion. "Lexi, it's Nic. and Lev needs to see you at Sirens as soon as you get this message. Shit's going down."

CHAPTER 4

Sirens was my own special hell. Between the clashing smells, the pounding music, flashing lights, and hordes of sweating, hooting twenty-something men, it was a purgatory of sensory agony. The colors flooded my mouth as soon as I stepped out onto the warm asphalt. The syrupy amber of bass, the high and wavering papery texture of treble, and the kaleidoscopic flow of muffled vocals from inside and around the club bubbled somewhere between the back of my tongue and my sinuses like a mixture of popping sherbet and razor blades.

"Whoo-whee." Vassily was making the best out of a five-year-old Hawaiian shirt, new slacks, and Brylcreem. "It's still baking out here. They got air-con in the club yet?"

"Uhn." I didn't want to have to talk, not until I had no other choice. I fumbled for a packet of peppermint candy while walking, put one in my mouth, and started chewing. The chill took the edge off.

The guard at staff entry, Ovar, could have modeled for a harem romance novel. At six and a half feet, Ovar was half a foot taller than Vassily, a full foot taller than me, and broader through the shoulders than both of us put together. The Georgian towered over every stripper, most of the other bouncers, and nearly all of the patrons like a mountain of muscles, black glittering eyes, and mustache.

"Ho, if it isn't our star dancers!" he boomed in Russian over the lot as we trudged our way across. "My Zmechik and Charivchik, look at you! Back together at last!"

"Ho-lee shit. Look who it is!" Vassily advanced, beaming. He clapped hands with Ovar, who pulled Vassily into a brief hug. "How you goin', big guy?"

I chewed my candy and tried to look pleasant. The white-blueness of peppermint overrode the mashed odors of perfume, bleach, sweat, and sex I could smell from the door. One could only hope I'd brought enough to carry me through the night without a migraine.

"Good, good. Healthy and fat. But you, out of prison already and looking meaner than you ever did." Ovar flashed a mouth of wet gold teeth. "Makes you a man, doesn't it?"

"Sure does." Something was missing in Vassily's smile.

"Ha! Mind you, it's soft here, in this country. Karaganda, now *that* was a prison." Ovar was one of those relentlessly cheerful men whose voice, unfortunately, grated on my nerves. Words tumbled out of his mouth like black gravel, and I couldn't shake the sensation or image as I shifted my weight uneasily on my feet. "But America? It'll end up the same way, you watch. Land of the free, hah!" The huge Georgian hawked a gob of spittle onto the concrete. "Free to rot in jail."

"Sorry to interrupt, but Lev is waiting for us." I spoke up before Vassily could open his mouth and keep chattering. "We were called in with some urgency."

Ovar's eyes lit up, and the mustache bristled in excitement. "Oh-ho, fresh business. Well, he will wait. Go see Nicolai first. He has to be on the floor in twenty minutes.

Lev can wait around in his fancy office, acting like he's important. We have to make sure we remind him who really owns this city, eh?"

"Hey, he had big boots to fill. From everything I've heard, Lev's doing a decent job of keeping the place clean," Vassily said.

"Ha! He is half a man, at best. You'll see. Sergei will come back someday and set this place right again. Go and deal with him, kids. I'll stay here and hold the fortress against the horde of idiots." Ovar aimed a clumsy, friendly slap towards my shoulder as I swept past, and I adroitly sidestepped his hand and pushed ahead into the corridor. The gauntlet cleared, I drew a deep, steadying breath.

"See what I mean, Lexi?" Vassily spoke when we were out of earshot, eyebrow arched. "Why'd you shrug him off like that? You hate people."

I grimaced and fixed my eyes ahead. "I respect Ovar, but his voice sounds like a truck laying out bitumen on a new road. Also, he's a little bit... grabby."

My friend's laughter rang out sharply against the concrete walls as we turned the corner. A pair of girls talking and laughing about the other dancers teetered down the hallway towards us. Vassily tipped an invisible hat to one of them as she pushed out her bubblegum-pink lips and winked. I gave them a wide berth. Their voices were yellow and jagged, and I could barely relate to the men here, let alone most of the women. Morosely, I sucked on my mint. I could feel the club's music in my teeth.

We found the security office and muster room nearly empty, with four of the nine radios already checked out for the night. Only two of the bouncers were in. Petro and Maxy were playing dominoes with their handsets turned off. Typical.

If Ovar was a refugee from a harem romance, Petro was an escapee from an Armani fashion show: tall, strikingly handsome, always well-tanned and well dressed. Maxy was a small guy with a pinched face and a mullet, a mustache considerably less impressive than Ovar's, and hard black eyes. On the way past, I glanced curiously at their tiles and rapidly calculated the odds. Petro was going to win.

"Oh my god. Look who just walked in like he owns the fucking place!" Petro rose up from his seat, his face alight. "Vassily! You look like a million bucks, man!"

"I feel like something a bear shat out. How's it going?" Vassily went in for handshakes and shoulder-pounding, while I hung back and glanced at the corkboard, looking for the security roster. Unconsciously, my mind pieced together shapes made by the pieces of paper: they were arranged in a hexagonal pattern, alternating colors. I like patterns. Patterns don't move, unlike people, and don't nauseate me in the way that human faces did.

Vassily's dark blue voice and the pink-and-gray nattering of the other men ground on behind me as I stepped in to look over the roster. Six men were on shift, including Nic, but only four radios were missing. Idly, I left the table and went to the register, flicking back through the logbook to check the sign-ins. Mikhail, Petro, Nic, Maxy, Ovar, and Yuri were on shift, but Yuri's sign-in was missing.

"Hey, shorty. Was it your body they found today?"

"Body? What body?" I replied absently and glanced over at the trio. They called me a few different names here. Men like Ovar stuck with the names I'd earned as titles of respect—*Charivchik*, Magician, or *Molotchik*, 'Little Hammer.' Not all of my nicknames are so flattering.

"I heard that one of Manelli's boys turned up weird and dead on our turf this morning." Petro crushed his cigarette into the tray.

"We was betting it was Vanya that called the hit. He's been all kinds of happy the last couple of days since that last shipment of snow came in," Maxy added.

I stiffened in place. Rather than lift my chin to look up at Petro's face, I glared at him from under my brows. It was never good to look up at taller men, because that allowed them to look down on you. "No, it wasn't, and that's business that doesn't have any place in the staff room."

"Nic told us, jeez. Calm your tits." Maxy grunted unhappily around his own cig as he swept the dominoes together and mixed them around. "Why don't you try pulling the stick outta your ass for once, Alexi?"

My stomach twisted angrily, dropping like I was on a roller coaster: a roller coaster that would end with Maxy's nose being smashed against the edge of the table if he didn't shut up. I took in a slow breath, threw another mint in my mouth, and crunched down on it to feel it splinter under my jaws. "My ass, and the contents thereof, are none of your business."

"That stick's shoved up so far it ain't ever coming out." Petro wiggled his fingers at me as he dropped back into his seat. "But you gotta keep that hole nice and warmed up for your boyfriend, right?"

"Lexi's right. Shut your cockholster, Petro." Vassily stepped up to my side before I could retort. His shoulders were slightly hunched, defensive—but I didn't need a guard dog. I needed respect.

"Come on, Vasya. Alexi can take a little shit." Petro smirked around his next cigarette, cupping a hand around the end as he lit it. "We're all grown-ups now, even if he ain't exactly the man his daddy was."

"I'm twice the man that *suka*[9] ever was." I ground the words out bulldozer-flat, and stared at him until he met my eyes. "And putting him out of my misery was the best thing I ever did."

A toxic silence descended over the room. Vassily's head turned sharply, eyes wide with genuine surprise. "Wait, what? *You* killed him?"

I stared at Petro. "Yes."

Petro's bravado flickered like a candle, briefly flaring before he turned back. Maxy's silent scorn faded, and he began to toy nervously with the dominoes in front of his fingers.

I'd screwed the pooch. There was one guiding social force within the Organizatsiya: respect. To be respected, you built a dual reputation as being both useful and dangerous. If you maintained a suitable ratio of competence and intimidation, people didn't have to like you, so long as they respected you. Being useful without being intimidating got you trampled; being a bully without being useful led to people getting a lethal grudge. Waver in either quality, and someone was always waiting to shove a pistol in through the chink in your armor. As usual, I was off the mark. My retorts were always either too slow or too sharp.

---

[9] SUKA LITERALLY MEANS 'BITCH', BUT THE CONNOTATION IS DIFFERENT IN RUSSIAN THAN IN ENGLISH. THE WORD IS MOSTLY USED FOR SNITCHES, TRAITORS, PEOPLE WHO COOPERATE WITH THE AUTHORITIES, ETC... AND IF YOU CALL SOMEONE 'SUKA', YOU BETTER BE ABLE TO BACK IT UP.

Vassily looked back and forth, mouth twitched to one side. "So uh... is Nic in his office?"

"Yeah. Fuckin' slackass." Petro did not look at me. "Boozing it up before he goes on the floor."

I didn't look away from him; instead, I made a point of staring at the side of Petro's face, counting the pulse that jerked rapidly in his throat.

"Well, I better go in and pay a visit before shit hits the fan here." Uncertainly, Vassily glanced back to me. "Meet up afterwards?"

"Yes." I pulled my gloves up higher on my wrists, tight enough that they creaked around my fingers. I bowed from the neck. "Excuse me."

Maxy looked like he was about to say something smart, but seemed to think better of it. I swept out of the room, and once I was alone, ground my teeth until they groaned. Dammit, Vassily. He hadn't meant to, but he had just cost me a lot of face. And what the hell did Nic think he was playing at, defying Lev's orders? Gossiping with Maxy and Petro, of all people.

Resignedly, I ate another peppermint. To get to the offices, I had to walk out past the dressing rooms, cut behind the main stage, and go up the stairwell. I headed backstage around the end of the stripper's catwalk and was greeted by the sound of pandemonium from beyond the heavy velvet drapes. The lights beyond were flashing, lighting up the star dancers who rested their feet while they waited on their sets. Quite suddenly, I felt my mood lift. Perched on one of the stage boxes in her corset and feather-tufted heels was the Woman. Crina Juranovic was smoking a black clove cigarette in a long holder, wrist cocked back, her eyes closed. She was tiny and curvaceous, with a hard-planed, boxy little face on a long slender neck. Her hair was very dark, her skin only a few shades deeper than cream. Had she been blonde, we could have passed as brother and sister.

"You look tired." Speaking from down below the back of the stage, I had to raise my voice so it was loud enough for her to hear me over the music.

Crina opened her eyes to look down, her expression softening with relief. Like me, she spoke Ukrainian, but her accent was interesting: part Balkans, part Germany. "Alexi, thank God. Please tell me you're bouncing tonight."

"Unfortunately not. I'm only here for a quick meeting." I looked towards the exit door and ran my tongue over my teeth. Lev wouldn't miss me for five more minutes.

Crina smiled tiredly as I pushed myself up to sit on the edge of the stage, resting by her ankle. I stayed a modest distance from her bare leg.

"*Drecksnest.*" She chuffed, leaning back on her hands. "It's a bad crowd. End of exams, so all the frat boys are out, dicks in hand. My ass is going to look like a glazed donut by the end of tonight."

Solemnly, I lay my hand over my heart and bowed my head. "I pray their wallets are well stocked and their seminal aim is poor."

She laughed, rocking back on her rump. Crina was a magnificent person, everything I knew I should be attracted to in a woman: clever, bookish, well-educated. Because no attraction existed beyond a meeting of minds, we had become friends, and we played beard for one another. Crina was near the end of a degree in English language and comparative linguistics, and she appreciated being able to tell people like Petro that she was not available. I had only tried to date seriously once in my life and had no desire to make a second attempt. It had been a humiliating disaster.

Crina leaned forward towards me, her eyes glittering with conspiracy. "So. Have you heard that Jung's family is finally releasing *Das Rote Buch*? Not that I'm hinting or anything, but the library at my college might have pre-ordered a first print copy..?"

My breath caught. The Red Book: C.G. Jung's handwritten masterpiece, rumored to be a dialog between the psychologist and his own soul, and supposedly one of the greatest Occult tomes ever written. I straightened, and my mood lifted a little more. "Have they, now? And how much is this book worth, exactly?"

"Twenty *thousand* dollars." Crina's hand flew up in excitement, hovering near her face. "Can you believe it?"

"I certainly can," I replied. Twenty thousand or twenty million: it didn't matter. The Red Book was a priceless Occult text written by one of the most insightful psychonauts in modern history.

Crina bit her lip, swinging her ankles out over the edge of the stage box. "Well, I could, in theory, sneak it out when it comes in... and could, in theory, share it with a certain gentleman, if he's interested?"

I nodded slowly, feigning consideration, and rolled the mint around my mouth. It took the edge off the nausea brewing in the pit of my gut. "I think that would be quite acceptable. And if the lady wished to bring it to the gentleman's home…?"

Crina blossomed like a magnolia before my eyes, her face suffused with pleasure. "Let's make it a date. How about Tuesday?"

I snorted. Her choice of words made something deep inside my chest tense warily, but I was mostly grateful. "Me? Date? Come now."

"You know what I mean. We both know the date's with *Das Rote Buch*." She flashed me a little crooked smile. "Dirty bibliophile."

"No date," I replied. "And you have a deal."

She reached down to me, fingers poised like a dancer's. I clasped Crina's small hand and shook it carefully. She giggled, and I wasn't certain if she was making sport of me, if I'd done something inappropriate, or if she was just pleased.

"By the way, my friend Vassily was released from prison today," I said. "He is sleeping over and will still be in the house by next Monday, I assume. So, perhaps you could…"

"I will be a perfect stuntwoman." Crina laid a delicate hand across her heart. "Cooing and makeup and everything. Pat my thigh a couple of times and give me a glass of wine in front of him. Don't worry about a thing."

We shook on that, too. She had literally been a lifesaver. A man without a woman on each arm is greatly suspect in our world, and if there was one thing that would seal my outcast status with the rank and file, it was my distinct lack of activity with the opposite sex. There were some things about me none of the men needed to know.

My skin vibrated in the relative silence of the elevator on the way upstairs, humming against my clothes. Yes, the dream bothered me. Nacari bothered me. Lev's growing reliance on my services bothered me. He was competent, but not popular. I was similarly competent and unpopular, and he was reeling me in, perhaps trying to win me over to his inner circle. The problem, however, was that unpopularity in the underworld is often terminal for more than one's career.

CHAPTER 5

The Sirens VIP Lounge was a whole other world compared to the pigpen below. The entry hall had grayish-purple carpet so deep it scrunched under my shoes. They kept the music low and rhythmic, the perfume expensive, and the decorations tasteful. I heard the raucous laughter of a small party of drunk men from one parlor, and dimly, the moans and cries of people screwing from behind another closed door. The double doors at the end of the hall guarded the manager's office, which had been Sergei's lair, then Rodion's, and which was now sparingly used by Lev. Our Avtoritet was not a strip club sort of person: he spent most of his time in Manhattan overseeing his legal firm, another important subsidiary which kept the money flowing, our men out of prison, and the words 'Russian Mafia' out of the press.

Before I had a chance to touch the intercom box outside Lev's office, the lock clicked. I let myself in, and a hush fell around my ears. Always cool, the room was decorated entirely in muted tones of aquamarine, turquoise, and pearl. A copy of Botticelli's *Birth of Venus* took up most of the opposite wall. Lev's desk was glass-topped, like most of the furnishings. Lev was already standing, the fingers of one hand elegantly splayed over his desktop. He looked up from them, smiling. He really looked like the kind of guy you'd find doing your taxes, not managing the second-largest gun- and drug-running operation in New York. "Good evening, Alexi. Did Nicolai brief you for the meeting?"

"He did not, Avtoritet. I didn't have a chance to speak with him." I waited until he offered his hand before we shook. Lev had a firm grip for such a small man. Like Nicolai, his hands were covered in old smoky-blue tattoos. "His message implied there was a problem."

"A very inconvenient problem indeed." Lev considered me with piercing scrutiny. For all his physical softness, he had the intensity of a hunting tiger. I realized, almost as an afterthought, that he was coldly furious over something, the anger tamped down under a shivering veneer of calm control.

Maybe he knew Nic had been gossiping. "Have the Manellis learned about Nacari?" I asked.

"Not to my knowledge. Possibly. This is a related but separate matter." Lev folded his hands behind his belt. The arch of his lower back was stiff with anger. "It's a lot more important."

I crossed my hands in front of me, and waited.

"Our primary lead into the cocaine market was meant to be here by six," he said, the words a little too crisp. "The man who cracked Colombia for the Northeast Coast. He's been absolutely reliable for the entire three years we've worked with him, but he didn't show up tonight. I am... concerned. No response to phone calls. I sent someone to his house. Nothing. I need you to find him."

My gut began to crawl with an uncomfortable sensation that had nothing to do with my sensory overstimulation. This was something new, and I didn't like it. I had never, ever been asked to bring someone in like this. "Well, Avtoritet, I will, of course, but..."

"But?" His gaze sharpened a little.

"Generally speaking, I don't bring men back to you alive, and if he's run... well, sir, I'm not a private investigator."

"But you will," he said.

There wasn't a lot I could say to that. "Yes, sir."

"Then I will tell you what I know of him." The charge between us ebbed slightly. "The man you will be searching for is named Vincent Manelli."

My eyebrows arched. It was not unheard of for people to move from one organization to another, but it was much rarer for blood family members to do so. "Manelli? A relation?"

"Yes. John's youngest son. Vincent humbly defected from his family in eighty-eight and became a critical ally of George Laguetta. He is a personal friend of the Santos Twins, the brothers who run the cartel in Cali that supplies our operation." Lev rose again, pacing aimlessly. "The likelihood of Vincent's return to his father is very low. George is the sole confidant of whatever sensitive matter drove Vincent out from his family in the first place, and he assures me that his return is impossible."

"I see. When did you last speak to him?"

Lev paused, and briefly, his expression fell. "I only talked to him recently, yesterday. He was concerned about his safety, so I had my contact put him up with protection."

My eyes flicked over Lev's face, then down. While I was thinking about these things, I couldn't watch people's faces. "When you sent someone to his house to find out what was going on, was his bodyman absent?"

Lev's whole face sharpened. "Yes."

"Out of interest, was it Yuri? Yuri Beretzniy?"

Lev's gaze bored into me with renewed focus. I could feel it, even if I wasn't looking directly at him. "I know we call you Charivchik for a reason, Alexi, but didn't know your ability extended to fortune-telling."

"It doesn't. If he disappeared from his home, it's natural that his bodyguard would either have been killed or taken with him. Otherwise, he'd have informed you straight away." Staring at the painting, I chased the breadcrumb trail of events with a sense of faint exhilaration. "Yuri was your bodyguard before Mikhail, a trusted resource. He is supposed to be on shift. The only reason he would accept a work assignment was if his charge was coming with him. Vincent was scheduled to meet with you while Yuri was on the floor, and they would have gone home together."

"When you put it like that, it seems obvious, doesn't it?" Lev's voice held a hint of genuine regard. He folded his arms across his stomach. "Yes, you are correct. Yuri was guarding him, and neither of them were at Vincent's house when the driver went to pick them up. He was to be assigned a safe house tomorrow. Do you think you could find him?"

It wasn't really a request, and my reply wasn't entirely truthful. I hate lying, and the honest answer was really 'maybe', but Lev was fishing for one answer, and one answer only. "Yes, sir."

"Yes." Lev smiled a tense smile. "You'll be well paid for it. And incidentally, I should mention... Sergei will be back later this month."

Lucky us. Even so, I was surprised to hear it. Lev seemed... glad. If I were Avtoritet in place of a ten-year-absent landlord, "glad" is not the response I would see myself having. "I see."

"I intend to put in a good word for you to him." Lev dipped his chin. "There will be something of a reorganization when I return the leadership."

My heart lurched. That was as much a threat as a promise. Regard from Sergei was worth a great deal, and if anyone could wrangle it, it was Lev. By the same token, if I failed... well. I'd failed Sergei once, and only once, and that had been enough for me to never want to do so again. "How much is Mr. Manelli worth?"

"Three hundred thousand to find Vincent. Another ten for Yuri."

I blinked, once, and managed to control my expression. It was difficult. I didn't care much for money—not, say, compared to something like *Das Rote Buch*. I've driven the same old Mercedes since Sergei gifted it to me on my eighteenth birthday. But three hundred grand was nearly ten times my normal fee. It was enough to pay off my father's debs and end his influence on my life, forever.

"Well..." I cleared my throat in the pregnant silence that followed. "That is generous of you, Avtoritet. I will begin with the contact who helped arrange the money and safe house, if you will give me his details."

"Her name is Jana Volotsya," Lev said, as he went around the desk and took his seat. "Of Moskalysk, Volotsya and Goldstein."

CHAPTER 6

The waiting room of Moskalysk, Volotsya and Goldstein enfolded my senses with cool, perfumed solace. I'd gone home after the meeting, tried and failed to sleep, and ended up throwing back three antacid pills with a cup of coffee and calling it a night. Mentioning Lev's name got me a nine a.m. appointment, which left plenty of time to talk to Jana and hopefully get a proper day's sleep.

The lawyers at Lev's firm were rarely available to the public. He and the other two partners were constantly booked, with waiting lists that accepted no new clients. Their client list—Sergei, our bankers, and high-level American trustees—filled up their time with more than just court appearances.

Jana had a private consulting suite, and the door had a brass plate bearing her name and a shortened list of her degrees. *Tetyana Volotsya, J.D.* I read her full name over as I knocked, leather-covered knuckles thumping on wood. Six syllables that tripped nicely over the tongue.

"Let yourself in." Her voice was faint through the walls.

Jana's office was immediately, overwhelmingly white—white and cream and light beech wood. Poised, pale, and elegant, the attorney stood by a small beech-and-glass flower stand, dressing and arranging a bunch of fresh lilies, their waxen buds and petals still untouched by the heat of the day.

"Good morning, Mr. Sokolsky, a pleasure." She turned her head and paused in what she was doing, smiling gracefully. Jana had a strangely proportioned, but not unattractive face, heart-shaped and strong-jawed, with green eyes a shade brighter than Lev's. Her Russian was thick, a prominent American accent coloring her words. "Come in and take a seat. I won't be long."

I inclined my head stiffly and took the edge of a chair in front of her desk, cataloging the details of the room. It had the sterile feeling of a doctor's office, with high shelves laden with books on criminal law. Everything was built of light-colored wood; her desk was topped with a cream leather desk pad, and it was immaculate, no ink stains or pencil smears. Jana herself wore a pantsuit of the same eggshell color, with sharp shoulders and solid, low-heeled shoes. I found myself watching the back of her head while I waited for her to finish. Her flossy blonde hair was braided up in a coil like a girl's, a tight halo around the back of her skull held firm with a tortoiseshell pin.

"There we go. Sorry... you caught me just as I had them out of the paper." Jana took her seat in the other guest chair across from me like a counsellor, rather than behind her desk. The scent of the flower arrangement followed her passage, spreading the thick smell of lilies throughout the room. With her knees pressed together, her hands folded in her lap, she mirrored my pose. This piqued my interest immediately. I was dealing with someone who had trained in the art of manipulation for many, many years.

My gaze flickered down momentarily. A single ring—platinum—on the wrong ring finger. She had very clean nails, polished like the inside nacre of a seashell. "It is hardly a problem, Ms. Volotsya."

"Lev called me early this morning." Jana leaned forward a little and pressed her lips together, wetting them just a bit. Not too much—she wore her lipstick expertly, testimony of long practice. "He's an old friend of mine, you must understand. I'm very concerned."

If news of Semyon's demise had filtered into the firm offices, no doubt she was concerned about the fate of 'old friends'. Letting a guy she'd arranged protection for slip through her fingers wasn't good for her reputation, even if it wasn't actually her fault. I pressed my tongue to the roof of my mouth to banish the odd sensation the scent of the flowers caused. It was associated with a fairly neutral shade of reddish pink, but my nose translated it into a sandy, slippery thing on the palate. The whole experience, taste and sensation, blended with the sound of Jana's unfamiliar voice. "As are we. Tell me what happened in the days leading up to this."

"Well, I'll give you a little background. Vincent came across from his family a few years ago, seeking asylum with the Laguetta family over some private business." The attorney sat back in her seat, her face a mask of concern. The chair was a starker white than her suit. "Something drove him out of the family very suddenly. Of course, he knows a lot about their business. I don't know the details of what he does for us, of course, but given that he knows the Twins personally, you can imagine how valuable he's been. Both for the Laguettas and for your people."

Your people. She nursed the fantasy of clean hands. Discreetly, I let my vision slip, reaching out to sense for any kind of arcana out of idle curiosity. "I see. He's worth his weight in gold, from what I hear."

"Not quite gold." Jana's mouth curled at the corners. "But close. Since then, he's been the boy wonder of the family. I can't lie—part of the reason he's been so consistently reliable is because George and Lev keep him in a very fancy cage. However, Vincent has made an incredible amount of money for himself, so I doubt he minds."

"It is always best to bind allies with the cords of gifts that cannot possibly be repaid." I bowed my head.

Jana's eyes danced. She reached up to her collar and pulled a chain free from her jacket. It was plain, with a large silver teardrop pendant that she rubbed between her fingers as she thought. "I see why they put you on this. You're a real detective."

I dropped my gaze to glance at it. The pendant trapped dancing pinpoints of light, shimmering flecks which seemed to twist and bend under Jana's fingers as they slipped across its surface. Despite that, it had no magical weight to it that I could sense, other than the way it drew attention to her hands. She really did have good hands, dexterous and finely boned. "What does Vincent look like?"

"He's a tiny little guy. Five foot five or so, thin build. He's nervous and has big eyes, like a deer. Short beard, a lot of stubble." Jana watched me watching her and dropped the pendant back to her chest. "Black hair, dark complexion. He always wore a Hornets baseball cap, whenever I saw him."

"Did he or Yuri report to you?"

"None of the men report to me. I only arrange the legal side of the contracts. Identification, number plates, addresses, that sort of thing." Jana pressed her lips together again. "Vincent came here and told the management he'd seen strange men hanging around his house, and he was concerned he was being scoped out. He asked for protection, so Lev delegated it to me. Yuri was assigned to stay with him three days ago at his house in Douglaston."

I repressed a grimace. Douglaston. That meant a big house with lots of security that would make getting in and out difficult. Not impossible, but difficult.

"I know, right? Typical Gold Coast Mafia." Jana seemed to read my thoughts. She looked down, smiling uncomfortably. "I have to say, I'm a good judge of character, Mr. Sokolsky, and Vincent is a silly, nervous man. He's got that tough guy front they all have, but his facade is very superficial. I think he's gone and done something stupid."

"I have no doubt." What I did wonder, though, was what Frank Nacari had to do with it. If he had anything to do with it. "Was there anything else he was wrapped up in that I should know about?"

Jana sighed and looked at the wall past my head for a moment, then back to my face. "That's about all I know. I'm sorry. But feel free to ask me any questions as they come up, and if you'd ever like to go with me and get a cup of coffee some time, you should definitely ask about that."

I was suddenly awkward in my seat, struck by a nameless gnawing sensation in my stomach. Maybe it was her voice, sighing like a flute. It had a strange champagne quality when she spoke, smooth and sweet and bubbly. Not that I ever drank champagne. I found it difficult to look away from her wrists. Maybe it was that. Her wrists. They were long and graceful, the skin flexing over the sharp point of bone each time she moved her hands.

"Well, there's nothing I can think of to ask, and I have places to be... Vincent's residence, notably." I gave the woman a quick, forced smile and rose on wooden feet. "Thank you for your time, ma'am. It was greatly appreciated."

"Not a problem." Jana stood without any of the same haste, her voice light and playful. "I'm glad I was able to fill you in, Mr. Sokolsky. I just wish I knew where the little rat has gotten to."

"Alexi... is fine." I nearly stuttered. "Just Alexi. And yes."

Unlike the men of the Organizatsiya, Jana didn't hesitate to meet my eyes. Hers were very green, and for a moment, I flashed back to the figure in my dream: the chalk-like skin, the fall of white hair as it—she?—turned to look at me in shock in the second before I blew apart.

Jana smiled, and her face came back into focus. "Well, Alexi, good hunting. And if you need anything, anything at all... you just let me know."

My face only started to burn when I emerged from the office and hit the wall of heat outside. The odd heaviness that had clogged my throat vanished as soon as I was clear of the building and could draw a lungful of air that didn't smell like lilies. Outside, I leaned against the doorway and rubbed my face. I was a magus, I reminded myself. A spook. A killer. Predator of man. But the dead generally don't have attractive hands and clean nails or flirt with you, and they unsettled me far less than that woman had.

A throaty caw broke through the fugue of shame, then another, long and languid. Across the lot, a glossy black raven drifted down to the ground and strutted across the concrete. It flashed me a brazen look, then fluttered and hopped up onto the hood of my car. I frowned, then scowled as the bird turned its head back and forth, before reaching down to pluck at the windshield wiper.

I stepped out from the doorway. "Hey!"

The wiper blade slipped from the raven's beak and

slapped back against the windshield, and the bird cawed at me. It was a huge animal, larger than a cat, with a vicious horny beak and white-gray eyes. They were so bright and so startling that, for a moment, its presence slapped me like a glass of cold water to the face. I felt like I was looking in a mirror: it was the exact same sensation I had felt when Binah had looked up at me from her mistress's dead hand, but even more powerful.

My gut lurched. Without thinking, I pulled my wallet from my pocket, heavy with change, and threw it hard. It struck the hood and bounced. The bird cawed in alarm, but instead of flying away, it launched towards me with its talons outstretched. Throwing my hands up, I barely got out of its way as it shot past, ruffling the air near my face. I spun around to track it, only to see it caw and strike at a wiry stray dog cringing by the dumpster. The dog shrieked, a high yelping cry as the raven's talons scored an ear. The cawing, hissing bird drove the mutt along the wall, and it backed into the gutter with a shrill, strangled sound before it fled from the alley and out onto the street. Victorious, the raven landed on one of the dustbin lids, flicking its wings across its back with arrogant finality.

I jerked my chin up, arms crossed. "Someone's a prize fighter, aren't they?"

The raven quorked low in its throat, then launched itself up again with powerful wings. It landed on the eaves of the building next door, fluffed its head feathers, and rattled a laugh that sounded so human it made my skin crawl.

My eyes narrowed. "Who are you?"

The bird did not reply or even acknowledge my attention, preening under one wing. It stopped, fluffed itself, and launched off into the heat of the day.

Feeling somewhat foolish, I pulled my gloves up along my wrists and shivered. The perch the bird had occupied was vacant darkness, a yawning space of shadow that endured under the hot summer sun. Slowly, I went across and reached down to pick up my wallet from the ground. It had gone under the edge of my car, so I got down on my knees to reach for it. And there, on my knees and looking under the chassis, I glanced up and stopped. My ears started ringing.

A plain steel box, maybe five by ten inches, was bolted to the underside of my fuel tank.

A bomb. Well, fancy that. Someone just tried to kill me.

CHAPTER 7

There're two kinds of car bombs commonly used by most professional wetworkers in this city. The first is an explosive device—putty, usually—attached to the engine. They rig a block of plastic explosive near the sump and run wires back into the dash. When you insert the key and turn the engine, the ignition triggers the explosion. The second kind has the explosive device mounted in a casing under the fuel tank. That type of bomb can be set off in a similar way—when you start the car—or from a remote control.

Then there's the third kind used by spooks: a bomb set up with a triggering sigil, which is activated in any way the creator pleases. Body pressure on the seat, engine ignition, opening the car door. Generally speaking, a professional is going to style it so the car explodes while the intended victim is inside, not outside, and the sigil ward is triggered automatically. The mage triggering the device doesn't have to hang around, if they're smart enough to account for all the variables.

I was fairly sure, from the brief look I got before I backpedaled rapidly on foot out of the parking lot, that it was the cheaper and nastier gas tank setup, but I couldn't rule out the sigil. Given the magical firepower I'd seen around

Semyon and now Nacari, it was entirely possible that it was the latter.

The first thing I felt was anger, anger at having my property violated. Then came the confusion, then the fear. My heart continued to try to dig its way from behind my ribs as I feigned calm and kept myself at a quick walk. Not knowing what else to do, I found a payphone and called Lev's office number. He didn't pick up, so I phoned home in the hope that Vassily was still there.

"Mister Sokolsky's House of Hedonism, how can I help you?"

"Someone rigged my car." I ran my fingers back through my hair, massaging my scalp. "I'm stuck at Lev's firm. Can you go get my tools and bring them here?"

There was a long pause. "Wait. Rigged? What do you mean 'rigged'?"

"A bomb, Vassily. A bomb." I rolled my eyes.

"Jesus Haploid Christ," Vassily said. "No, Alexi. No, I'm not bringing you your fucking tools so you can tinker with the *bomb* in your fucking car."

"It's *my* car." And it had been my car since I was eighteen. It had my things in it. "I'm not letting them destroy my car."

"Fuck the car, Lexi. Leave it there and get a cab to Mari's." Vassily sounded manic, on edge. "I'll call Nic or Vanya and get them to send in the pros, man. We have guys who are paid to deal with that shit."

I'd set up enough rigs in my time that I was righteously convinced I could defuse this one, but he was right—Nic's ex-military men had dealt with so many IEDs in Afghanistan that they had affectionate nicknames for the different colored wires. Either I did it or they did; there was no calling the cops. "Get a hold of Nic, if you can. It'll cost me either way, but I'd rather owe Nicolai an extra couple grand."

"I've got money coming in if you need it. Meet me at Mari's, okay? Don't you dare go near that fucking thing."

I hung up and let myself lean against the side of the phone booth for a few minutes before I dialed the taxi. One did not need precognition to know it was going to be a very, very long day.

Mari's was a glass-fronted deli owned and operated by my elder adopted sister. The white-and-blue awning brooded a dense cluster of chipped metal lattice tables outside, set up beside a simple sign in cheap gold paint and chalk with three words on it: *Torty ta Chay*, 'Cakes and Tea.' The deli had no written menu. It'd been the cover business for the Lovenko family for two generations, started by Vassily's adventuring parents before they took their final flight over the Gulf of Mexico. Their will passed it on to Vassily's grandmother, Lenina, and then when she died, to Mariya.

I pressed a hand to the glass door and let myself in, the cool sanctity of the place settling over me like a waterfall. The bell tinkled over my head, as it always had. Mari's smelled of sugar, fried butter, old aftershave, and cigarettes. The Ukrainian community news was always playing under the soft music that looped on the overhead speakers, blasting out of an old radio on the menu and cutlery table. The customers, perched around tables with their cake and chessboards, simply picked up their voices to talk over them.

"Alexi!" Mariya's rich voice punctuated the burbling chatter. She appeared out of the storeroom and came around the counter, her face alight. "Handsome as ever. How are you? You look exhausted!"

Handsome? Me? I smiled, briefly, as she touched my shoulders very lightly and kissed me hardly at all. I returned the gesture on her other cheek, taut with discomfort. "Maritka, I am well enough. Work has run late the last couple of nights."

Mariya clicked her tongue, examining my shirt. She fussed with my tie, even though it was already straight. "Alexi, I know you gotta do what you gotta do, but you'll work yourself to death someday."

"Vassily said men like me kill themselves a lot." I regarded Mariya levelly in return, looking for signs of ill health. She was in her early fifties, a good twenty years older than her youngest brother. The eldest living Lovenko had the same dark blue eyes and coarse wavy black hair as Vassily, her face strong and weathered from hard work. Mariya was almost six foot in flat shoes but less wiry than Vassily, with carefully curled and teased hair. She still did not speak much English. "You are well?"

"Me?" She smiled widely with a sly, thin mouth. Both siblings were vaguely serpentine in their build and expression, and Mariya's eyes were only slightly less hard. "Of course I'm well. But you need tea and something to eat."

"Is Semych here already?" Only in family company did I call Vassily by that name.

"Out back with his deck of cards. I'll bring you the usual something. Go catch up. Gossip is heavy today." She waved me off with a little shooing motion.

That reminded me. I moved only a step or two before looking at her over my shoulder. "Before you go, Mari... I was wondering. How do you think he is, now? Really?"

The woman's expression shifted into something I found nearly unreadable. Sad? Resigned? "He's thin. Changed, somehow. I don't know if you were with him before, but he went out last night and got really drunk. Bad drunk."

That was to be expected. If he'd taken Lev up on his offer and partied with the kind of women he liked to sleep with, he probably had five different kinds of herpes on top of his failing liver. "I wasn't there. I left early."

Someone else entered the store, raising a hand and moving to the sandwich counter. With a last reproachful look, Mariya broke from me to serve up. I made my way through the shop, past the display of cakes I had never tried, and through a curtained doorway to the back-of-house. The halls were cramped, stacked with old boxes and sacks of stock used in the restaurant. A door near the rear entry was ajar, and the familiar smooth smell of Chesterfields wafted out from behind it.

Inside, Vassily was engrossed in a hand of Solitaire, his cigarette hanging absentmindedly from his fingers. He jerked his head up as I came in, then sighed, setting down his spares and pushing his hair back from his face. "Jesus Christ, Alexi."

"They only call me Alexi, these days." I bowed and spread my hands to the sides, but I don't think he got the joke.

"Okay, so, I'd just like you to know that I'm really happy you didn't explode," he said. "And also, I thought telling Mari that your car is sitting downtown loaded up with C-4 might not be a great idea. So I didn't."

"I think that was a very sensible conclusion," I replied as I took my seat. "Neither did I."

"Well, you know how it is. Great minds think alike." Vassily drew hard on his smoke and exhaled with a sound of pleasure and relief. "Come on, sit down. We can get lunch and go home. I called Lev, and he said he'll send Ivanko and some other guy to fix your car."

Ivanko was one of Nicolai's old comrades in the Spetznaz GRU, and he probably knew more about car bombs than I ever would... assuming it was not magically triggered. "Thank you."

"No problem. You look like fifty kinds of shit." Vassily stubbed out his cigarette in the tray. He didn't light another. "Am I gonna have to start going places with you? Make sure you don't get into trouble?"

That reminded me acutely of the night before, his stepping up to Petro. I scrutinized him as I had Mariya. She was right: he looked dreadful. Thin, eyes sunken, brow sheened with sweat. He smelled of smoke and expired brandy. "We're not in school anymore, Vasya. Petro was right. I can take shit and solve my own problems."

"I ain't questioning that." He looked away and turned a few cards over, shuffling through the deck. "Not at all. But do you really think that bomb was set up by some other crew?"

I made a tutting sound. "I have no reason to think Lev would send me on a job and then try to kill me the morning after, if that's what you're implying."

Vassily sighed. "Not necessarily Lev, but I wouldn't be surprised, you know? You *did* just kill Sem Vochin, and that dead Italian guy turned up yesterday. And I mean... he looked like he was killed with magic, didn't he?"

I grunted. Now that I was in cool, familiar surroundings, I was really feeling that tiredness. The burn in my muscles, an ache deep in my joints. "I was told not to discuss it with anyone. So was Nic. I don't know why he didn't keep his mouth shut."

"Because Nic doesn't trust Lev as far as he could kick him, and he wants people to know what's going on." Vassily's voice took on a familiar stubborn tone, one I hadn't heard in many years. Insistent, distracted. He was a very intelligent man. Cavalier as he was, we both had earned our scholarships, and he'd always been my better at mathematics and chess. "Nic says a lot of guys have been dying since Lev took the throne."

"Nic was also the one who told me to tell you not to try and take him down."

"Well, sure. I'd be fucking crazy to. One bad word to my parole officer, and I'm back in the slammer." Vassily scowled and toyed with the crushed cigarette. His usually restless hands were shaking, trembling as they roamed. "But I'm going to collect the information, and I'm going to hold onto it because damned if I let some white-collar desk monkey destroy this place. I've got an MBA, Lexi. I know what guys like this do. They come in and clean an organization out, strip it bare, and fuck off to Miami with all the money. The only reasons he's in the big man's chair is because he's got Sergei, Vanya and all of AEROMOR's union guys backing him, *and* because of this cocaine gig. He's got the boats and the goods."

I exhaled thinly and rubbed my mouth with the palm of my glove. "For now. He... has me on another job already."

Vassily pursed his lips, cocked an eyebrow enquiringly, and mimed shooting someone with thumb and forefinger. "Another friend of his?"

"No. A contact. He wants him alive."

"Huh." Vassily began to layer and sort the spares. His fingers were still shaky, but he played three-card Solitaire with the kind of skill that spoke of long practice. "Well, speaking of business, Nic already set me up with something. I can't fucking believe it. Same day I get out, and he's hanging the millstone around my neck. Oy. I have to see my parole officer on Monday."

"He asked you to work already?" I rested my forehead on my hand, leaning on the tabletop. "That's... unnecessary."

"Tell me 'bout it. But it's good money, and good *blat'*. Lev has a million or that needs cleaning at Atlantic City, so we set up a date with George Laguetta. Says that he and Lev need my silver tongue to butter up the Family. We'll cycle the cash, wine and dine them. I'll get enough money to set me up for the year once it's all said and done."

Putting Vassily under all those cameras alongside a known Don and in light of Vincent's disappearance? "No. Vasya, I have a dreadful feeling about this."

"Why?" He frowned.

"Because the man Lev has asked me to find and return is the man who arranged this whole cocaine business for Laguetta and Lev in the first place," I said. "He was supposed to be at a meeting last night and never showed. The whole thing—"

"Smells like shit, yeah." Vassily cut me off, shaking his head. "But I already gave my word. I won't lose face to Nic by backing out. And honestly, man, I need the money. The government took all my stocks. I have to get a hold of my old broker and hope he's willing to work my fake ID and build up my portfolio from scratch."

I ground my teeth until they creaked and crossed my arms. "Well, if you have to go, I go with you. I'm your bodyman for this event. Let the Laguettas wonder how you're able to field a spook as personal protection."

"Even if you weren't a spook, you're the hardest man in this crew. Of course I want you there." Vassily smacked another card down. "And you know what? I told Nic I want Yuri on my other side. You know, Yuri Beretzniy? His old war buddy. He's like a million years old, but I'm pretty sure that guy eats lead and broken glass for breakfast. Figured that'd remind Nic who calls the shots around here."

"He's missing." I rubbed my face again. The fatigue was eating into my ability to focus. "Yuri, that is."

Vassily looked up sharply. "What?"

"Missing." I glanced down at the rows of cards. "He didn't show for work last night."

"Yuri? Missing? But I mean... how?"

"Probably the way most men go," I replied. "By surprise."

"No way. That guy's a seriously tough motherfucker."

I looked up at him pensively. "Sometimes it doesn't matter how tough you are. He's gone missing with the man I've been tasked to find, Vincent."

"Huh. Maybe Yuri cut some money and ran off with him, then. That happens, even with the old guys."

Yes, it was possible Vincent was worth enough to the various underworld high rollers that Yuri stood to gain more by handing him over to someone than by protecting him for Lev. But in that case, who? Vincent's blood family?

"Who is this guy, then? Vincent?"

"One of Manelli's boys, oddly enough." I made the decision to talk it out, no matter what Lev thought. If I could trust one person in the Organization, it was the man sitting across from me. "Vincent Manelli."

"Blood family? Never heard of him. There's Lou Manelli, Celso Manelli, and his little brother, Joe. They all work out of a big chicken factory over in Jersey. Elite Meats, something like that."

"Perhaps because he's the youngest of the sons? He defected to George's team."

"No shit? And he went missing on our watch? Well, bad as it sounds, at least Yuri went missing with him. If he fucked up, it'd be more than just his head in line for the guillotine. How much are you getting out of it?"

"Three hundred thousand."

Vassily's eyebrows nearly hit his hairline. "Lexi, that's a lot of cash for one guy. Too much cash."

The observation sat with me uncomfortably because it was true. It was a lot of money, though I'd managed to rationalize it somewhat. Vincent made the Organization millions of dollars in trade. The Twins hadn't run shipments to anyone except Mama Perez in Miami until Vincent talked to them.

Vassily seemed to notice my struggle and shook his head. "Seriously. That's too much. I don't mean that in the 'you suck and you shouldn't be paid that much' way. I mean in the 'that's a lot of fucking money that's being used to hide something from you' way."

"Not compared to what he's worth."

"After your car got rigged this morning? I don't have to be a wizard to work it out, my friend." Vassily looked away, his jaw working. He was down to only a few spares now. "There's something we're not seeing."

"You're right," I said, after a minute or two. "But I have to do it. Not just that I'm obliged, but I'll be able to clear the money Grigori owed."

Vassily leaned in toward me. "Lexi, if you're hurting for money, just leave it to me. You broke me out of prison, for fuck's sake. I'll rake it in on Monday and we can pay it off."

I shook my head. "I appreciate it, I really do, but I want to do this. Lev will put in a word for me to Sergei."

"He shouldn't have to. We're *blatnoi*[10], we were made for this. Sergei should be back here and paying attention to his own men."

"He will be. Lev thinks he'll be here by the end of the month."

"And that just makes me twitch harder over the whole damn thing." Vassily tch'd and opened his mouth to speak again just as Mariya arrived with tea and plates of food.

"Here we go," she said cheerfully. She'd brought crepes for Vassily, salad and chicken cutlets for me. "You eat everything, now. The pair of you look like you haven't slept in a week."

Vassily changed tack, cheerfully masking his fatigue with a grin and a wave. "Sure thing, Mom."

Mariya slapped him without force, and he sputtered in protest. "Vassily Simeovich, I spent five damn years worrying about your skinny ass. Don't you give me cheek. What would your grandmother say?"

"She would have said I needed to lay on the bullshit better."

I made a motion with my hands, silent agreement. Lenina Lovenko had been a fearsome, pipe-smoking *Ruska Roma* hellcat with more tattoos than her son and grandsons.

---

[10] *BLATNOI, AS THE NAME IMPLIES, ARE PEOPLE WITH A LOT OF BLAT, OR SOCIAL STATUS. THEY TRADE IN FAVORS.*

Mariya rolled her eyes. "Impossible. Are you two going to gym this evening?"

"I will be going to bed," I said, as I took up my knife and fork.

Vassily swatted his sister away from his chair. Mariya shoved her brother's head forward, and he made a rude gesture back at her. She motioned at him with two fingers. *Come get it.*

"I will. I feel pretty good, actually. It'll be good to work out without someone trying to shank me." Vassily chuckled and started furtively on his early dinner, glancing aside at her. "Sisters, man, I'm telling you. Can't live with them, can't shoot them."

Mariya scowled. "I'll take that plate back, Vivy."

"The hell you will. These are amazing. Don't call me Vivy."

I watched them both contemplatively, folding salad onto my knife and fork. I often envied Mariya her simplicity and strength. She had lost parents, grandparents, and three brothers over the span of a decade. She took charge of her household when no one else could or would, a self-made and self-taught matriarch. As the years had gone by and more Lovenkos had died, she became increasingly fussy over us. Now that I had the time to look at her under yellow light, I thought her deep-set eyes were a little shadowed.

It was good Vassily hadn't told her about the explosives. And it was good she and Vassily both didn't know that tonight, I would not be going to bed. Instead, I would be jacking a car, finding a way into Vincent's house, and looking for clues to his whereabouts.

It was time to begin the hunt.

CHAPTER 8

Vincent Manelli's mansion on Turner Drive was faced with high fences that protected lawns so large and lush they looked like golf courses. The pavement here was new and uncracked, the cars clean, and my overall impression was that the whole street was strangely sterile and vacant. Vincent's house was a huge Colonial villa that loomed over a winding gravel driveway lined with solar lamps. They cast muted light over the empty driveway and the clean-raked paths leading up to the front porch.

B&E is the one time you will ever find me in anything other than slacks and collared shirts. Some men do all black, but it's a color that stands out under the muggy New York summer sky. Charcoal and brown work better. I like sportsgear for this: riding breeches, a light tracksuit jacket, and shoes with restaurant tread for extra grip. In this wealthy part of town, the outfit doesn't stand out too much, either. I could always claim to be 'the help'.

I have a toolkit especially for this kind of work, and none of it is particularly supernatural in nature. The problem with B&E is that thresholds of all kind—walls, doorways, and especially circles—have strange power of their own. They are built with the intent to keep outside things out and inside things in. Intent is the basis of magic, and the focus which underlies the construction of any barrier acts as a weak enchantment of sorts. On the physical level, walls and locks don't mean a whole lot. Without wards, the worst you get is the skin-prickling, uncomfortable sensation which accompanies trespass, the ghostly understanding that you are somewhere you do not belong. However, walls and doors that don't belong to you make even easy magic harder than it ought to be. Lockpicking, for example: I can pick a practice deadbolt with magic, but not a deadbolt mounted on someone else's door. For this kind of work, I have effective, but mundane tools.

After the drive-by, I parked down the road and covered the distance on foot. The front gate was unlocked, so I let myself in and had a look over the barriers to entry. They were formidable: The front facade was separated from the rear yard by a high brick-and-steel spiked fence. The front door was locked, the windows closed and locked with roller shutters. There was going to be an electronic security system, maybe even cameras.

The gate into the backyard was locked with a classic cylinder deadbolt. I set my messenger bag down there and crouched, removing a ring of bump keys. Bump keys are evenly notched along their lengths, like a comb. Three of the keys had small rubber O-rings fitted near the head. To use bump keys, you match a key to the size of the lock and insert it, slowly, while tapping it with a heavy object. I took my knife from my pocket, fixed my eyes ahead on nothing, and used the key to feel for the tumblers and bump them open. One, two, three, four. It clicked, and I was in. Sticking to the shadows, alert for the sounds and smell of dogs, I made my way down the white pebbled path that led into the rear yard.

Vincent's backyard was a gaudy concrete courtyard full of statues, pots, and cheap-looking—though undoubtedly expensive—Faux-Classical ornaments. A swimming pool lapped and gurgled in the darkness, storm-gray under the heavy, smoggy sky. The night wind had a bitter edge that stirred the hairs on the back of my neck, and I held the knife low, the blade turned away, as I advanced around towards the back door.

The garden bed just next to the attached sunroom was planted with rows of mature angel's trumpets, and my nose was full of the dizzying vanilla smell of them as I unlocked the door with my bump keys. It was a strange plant to grown in a heavily trafficked place like this. Angel's Trumpets, Datura, are very poisonous and are used to make one of the more terrifying drugs to come out of Colombia, scopolamine. I knew of it because it was an ingredient used to create zombies: the living slave sort, not the walking dead.

I turned on a small flashlight to scrutinize the second lock on the inside door. It was of better make than the last one, with a heavy bump-proof cylinder. Frowning, I put the keys away and, with the flashlight clutched between my teeth, got out a small tension wrench and picks. After five minutes and two broken picks, I was finally able to press in the trick tumbler and carefully, delicately turn the lock. Done.

I pulled a cap down over my ears, shouldered my tool bag, and padded inside with the knife up and ready, warily navigating the sunroom in the dark. Light spilled across the floor from a door further down. I let my eyes adjust, my breathing harsh in my own ears. The sunroom was pretty enough, like the rest of the house, though the plants that lined the glass sill along the far wall were brown-lipped and dying. Something about the stillness of the air was acutely uncomfortable, an eerie disturbance of the ear like a badly tuned violin being sawed at its highest key. Nothing was visibly wrong, but the place felt... hollow. Wounded and bleeding, like Nacari's dump site.

The kitchen was expensively furnished, the air of the interior house cool and temperate, but I did not step inside. Every room had a motion sensor, but judging by the sensor lights, only the rooms beyond the kitchen were armed. The control panel was just outside the kitchen door in the sunroom, a ten-digit number pad with newish numbers.

The unsubtle way to deal with any electronic device is to draw a sigil on it and blow it with a push of blunt force power. A more skilled mage could probably do it without setting the wall on fire, but they'd still probably draw the cops. The problem a lot of spooks have is that as a true magus, capable of the Art, they tend to over-rely on their eldritch might. Being caught out by a problem that can't be solved with magic has been the downfall of many spooks better than me. They have a prison just for us, somewhere out in Wisconsin, and you can bet there are mages in the police force: The Adepts of the Vigiles Magicarum. They track and profile spooks. Legends say that magi are a subtle breed, and it is always good to prove them right.

I took my flashlight and a small mirror and used the intense, reflected light to scan the surface of the keypad. The thing about ten-digit number locks like this one is that the owners very rarely change the numbers. If there are no break-ins, they forget to change the code, or they do it infrequently—perhaps twice a year, if that. The codes are always four digits. People also often use their birth day and month or the year of their birth. I knew Vincent's, but it was important to look and check first.

The light caught the delicate prints and smears of grease on the buttons. I leaned in and exhaled hoarsely against the metal a few times until they could be seen more clearly. To my surprise, only three digits were highlighted: Vincent had better sense than most. Three buttons, four numbers. One of them was a repeat. Zero had the heaviest prints and the most smearing, followed by one and four. I tried it: 0104. When I hit the key button, the sensor lights shut off.

Yes. Good password, but he had greasy hands.

Something clicked overhead. I froze, gut tightening, and only eased down when a puff of cold, crisp air blew against my face from an overhead vent. Air conditioning. There was mail on the kitchen counter, but it was all bills and junk. I rubbed my gloves on a soft cloth, then started my investigation from the counter outwards. The pantry was stocked with snacks, and the refrigerator shelves were packed full of food of all kinds: amongst them was a box of reasonably fresh pizza with a half-empty bottle of beer beside it. The lit lights, the air-con, the alarms, the lack of mess... everything told me the same story. Vincent's home had not been invaded and its occupant removed. It had been abandoned.

I trod quietly through the rest of the house, which was unlit, and the lights behind me gleamed off the knife blade. I passed through spills of cold, stale-smelling scent. The air of the den was heavy, humming with faint electrical discharge from the abandoned appliances. Signs of Vincent and Yuri's habitation remained: impressions of their buttocks on the plastic sheets that covered the Romanesque furniture, an empty bottle of beer on the table, the small flask of cheap Polish vodka beside it. Two half-filled glasses and a stack of video cassettes sat beside the VCR.

Something nagged at me. There was no planning, but also no signs of a hasty, panicked exit. It was like they'd gotten up to go to the store and never returned. I glanced over the shelf of videotapes: half of them were pornography, the rest racing and action movies. The bottom shelf was devoted to videotaped TV shows Vincent had wanted to catch later on, recorded while sleeping or working. I ran a gloved finger over the stickers. The last date was the second day of the month. Vincent recorded the late-night wrestling for the morning.

I eyed the VCR, sitting on its shelf underneath the television. It was still turned on, and a red light blinked fitfully next to its shuttered mouth.

Tape slithered, and the cassette clicked and clacked its way to my hand when I hit the button. The sticker had no date or topic, but the tape had rewound. I pushed it back into the machine and turned the television on, cycling through the channels until I found the one which showed the video. After a flicker came the characteristic fanfare of the WWF theme music blaring while a wrestler stalked the studio hallways with a scowl. Satisfied, I reached out to turn it off but then paused, hand extended, as the video began to bleed to gray. The image and voices flickered, wavered, then dissolved into black-and-white snow with an ear-splitting, hair-raising whine. The sound rose and fell, and as I watched, the fizzing snow began to separate and congeal into shapes like crawling insects. Like a carpet of bees. My skin crawled on my flesh, mouth full of the blinding white the sound created in my mouth and behind my eyes. Hastily, I turned it off and backed away. Well away.

The next thing was to see when the wrestling had been on. I took the TV guide to the lit kitchen to flip through it.

WWF was on Friday nights, starting at nine p.m. The distortion had begun not five minutes afterward, and the four-hour tape had recorded all the way through to the end of its feed and rewound. My imagination filled in the blanks. Vincent and Yuri, nervously trying to develop some rapport over junk food and alcohol, had settled down to watch the wrestling after a trip out to the store, and then... something happened. Something which removed them from the living room as if they'd vanished.

I pulled my gloves up along my wrists before pressing on deeper into the silence of the house, up the spiral stairs that led to the bedrooms. I was accompanied by an eerie sense of displacement as I trod down the carpeted hallway, opening doors to peer inside. There was a personal gym, a studio, and a monstrously large bathroom. Nothing was upset. Nothing was broken or rushed. There should have been something other than the confirmation that Vincent, and probably Yuri as well, had both gone missing between eight and eleven the night before, but there was nothing. No scattered clothes. No missing toiletries. No sign of violence.

Vincent's bedroom was easily the messiest room in the house, a tragedy of Baroque lacquered furniture and leopard-print velvet. Dirty laundry was strewn on the floor next to the bed—a silk robe, boxers, and a T-shirt with pizza stains down the front. I dropped it as soon as I picked it up, disgusted. My eyes flicked from the wallet bulging with money that had been left on the dresser, to the picture of a captured unicorn that dominated one wall of the bedroom, to the line of photos mounted on the wall beside it. The beam of the flashlight lit on one of them, an ornate silver frame holding a faded photo of a woman with the dark skin and proud aquiline face of a Sicilian. Even in sepia, her black eyes glittered, full of quiet power. One hand was resting palm-down on an arrangement of large cards on a tabletop, the other held out of sight. Her hair was covered, but what drew my attention were the details of her shawl. It was decorated in planetary symbols. I took the picture off the wall and carefully pried the back off the frame. As I suspected, the photo had writing on it, in Italian. I could discern a name, though, and the date. *Drina Mercurio, 1942.*

Inside the dresser, I found a vial of testosterone and needles sitting next to a deck of cards carefully wrapped in pink fabric. I knew what they were before I unwrapped them. The tarot deck was very old, the edges worn and waxy. The topmost card was La Torre, The Tower. Frowning, I turned it over. The back face of the deck was the same unicorn image Vincent had on his wall. It was the last panel of seven famous tapestries, *The Hunt of the Unicorn.* I'd seen this image many times in the course of my Occult study, as it was often featured in books on the Rosicrucian tradition. The tapestry was titled 'The unicorn is in captivity and no longer dead', and it showed the chained unicorn resting in a small corral. In the six previous panels, people had hunted it with dogs and spears, until it was caught by a virgin woman, killed, and eaten. In this seventh panel, it was alive again, but enslaved; a tree grew behind it, strung with yellow fruit. The unicorn wore a collar. Its expression was one of stoic grief.

From the dresser, I wandered to the bed. Amongst the cast-off socks and candy wrappers was a quarto notebook. The cover had handwriting on it in Sharpie. *Sogno Diario.* I wasn't sure what the first word meant, but I cracked it open to the last used pages to see what I could make from it.

"La scorsa notte, ho sognato la bianco donna di nuovo. She was running away from the ~~dog~~ again. She says they killed her Hound. Why does she think I can do it?"

I froze, careful not to bend the spine as I read the first line over and over again. I spoke minimal Italian but knew enough to get the gist of the sentence. *Last night... something, the white woman.*

"L'ho inseguito nella foresta di cristallo... and when we came to a stop, lei mi ha detto: Scegliere!" Vincent's dream diary read. *"Per favore, scegliere!"*

"Choose... please, choose," I muttered, frowning. I could only make out pieces here and there. Something about running after her, "like a dog." I flipped the page, and on the back was a crudely drawn series of figures. One of them was a spiked ball, scribbled over with filaments and labeled "the fruit." There was a tree—or at least, I thought it was a tree. It looked like a coral polyp with drooping willow branches and diamond-shaped leaves. Its branches were thrown around itself, as if it were recoiling in pain or terror.

Something banged downstairs. I dropped the book with a clatter and brought the knife up. My heart leaped; my body flushed hot, and I sniffed, snorting out the stale air as I cross-stepped to the doorway and looked around the jamb. I could see nothing, but as the moments passed, a rushing, deep-rooted sense of wrongness built in my chest. My pulse hammered in my throat as I strained to hear any and all sound in the house. As time crept and nothing happened, I eased down, breathing quickly, and turned back to look at the book I'd dropped on the floor.

And then, I heard it. Downstairs, the unmistakable sounds of yipping and snarling and claws clicking against tiles. Dogs. Someone was here, and they'd brought dogs. Large, quick dogs, which were already on my scent.

My next breath flared through tight nostrils. I pushed myself away from the doorway, temples throbbing, and toed the door closed. This was definitely time for a gun, so I drew the Wardbreaker as I backed away into the room, twisting the silencer onto it and holding it up in a teacup grip. Ghostly baying rang out from the downstairs kitchen, followed by the thunder of feet up the spiral stairs that cut off abruptly when the dogs hit the carpet.

I licked my teeth, steadying my breathing, and the tip of the barrel stopped trembling. Dogs. They were just dogs. Why was Vincent dreaming about dogs?

Something huge and heavy hit the door, scrambling at it. I dropped to a crouch, breathing deeply, and barely got my second hand on the grip to hold it steady when the door burst open and a flaming pinscher the size of a pony lunged for me with a mouth of huge, glowing basalt fangs.

I emptied half the clip on reflex as the massive weight surged towards my face. The dog's momentum carried it screaming, bleeding, then crashing into the end of the bed, riddled with gunshot. A second dog was hot on the heels of the first, moving with unnatural alacrity as I fired once, twice. I caught a glimpse of cracking black skin rippling over glowing molten rock before the wind tore from my chest and my world narrowed to a square foot of snapping jaws, blasted heat, and ear-shattering noise. Pain lanced through my forearm and filled my mouth with sulfur. Heat washed over me in a dizzying wave. I smashed the butt of the pistol into the animal's ear, desperately trying to get away from the wall and throw it off. The heat grew—it was overwhelmingly, scaldingly hot. The dog's eyes were blazing, filled with inhuman intelligence. They were the hot red-orange of a caldera.

The other dog was getting up, the bullet wounds sealing with small gouts of flame. My eyes widened in the skipped heartbeat before jaws clamped shut on my hand. I roared, jamming the gun in against its ribs, but as my finger depressed the trigger, the weapon was ripped away by invisible hands. Shock built on shock, and the dog, foaming with animal rage, threw me away from the wall with a twist of its neck. I careened and landed heavily, rolling and smashing into the foot of the dresser to roll, choking, onto my side.

The gun. Where was the Wardbreaker? I saw it near the corner of the bed.

Ears full of the sound of claws, I scrambled to my hands and feet, but before I could throw myself forward, my wrist was grasped, yanked, and twisted. I fell on my chest, only to be wrenched up to my knees like a puppet. I couldn't see anyone. The same force contorted my fingers into knots, and my shout of anger turned to a choking cry of agony as white fire flashed through my mouth.

"Attaboy." A thick Jersey accent penetrated the room from the doorway.

I heaved, staggering forward, and tried to turn around to look at whoever was behind me. No such luck. The invisible vice on my body tightened. Through watering eyes, I watched the huge dog limp past me, back to the doorway. The other one was struggling, but it was healing. The bullet wounds smoked and sputtered as they filled in... with magma.

The other man's footfall was soft as he approached. Each step increased the pressure on my hand. I gagged, retching with pain. Caught in a tightening vice of nothingness, I could only jerk fractionally as a bag was pulled down over my head.

"Well, you ain't no Rasputin." The voice that filtered through the back of the bag was snide. "Guess they don't always make wizards like the old days, huh?"

My mouth was full of knives. I managed to choke out a sound of pain and confusion just before something solid hit me across the back of my skull and pitched me down into darkness.

CHAPTER 9

"Wakey wakey, princess." A cold voice rang out from overhead.

I was naked. That was the first thing I realized, as my bare skin stuck and squeaked against a cold, rounded metal surface. I was in agony, and I couldn't feel my hands. My arms were pulled back strangely, and every motion brought a lance of bright pain from elbows, wrists, and shoulders. Every sound was too loud: the rustle of cloth, the sharp jangle of change in a pocket. *Fuck. Fuck fuck fuck. Get yourself together.*

I had to focus. Had to. My pulse beat a bright tattoo against the backs of my eyes. Past the dancing lights and stabbing pain, I made out a shrewd, hawkish face with a mouth full of big white teeth. Early thirties, with short dark hair and three days of stubble. He reached over my head, and seconds later, my head and shoulders were hit with a spray of cold water that struck my nerves with a slap.

"We can do this the nice way or the way that gets you fucked up the ass with a baton." My tormentor caught my hair in his fist and pulled, and I realized my hands were cuffed to a sturdy assistance rail behind my back. "What the fuck did you guys do to Frank? Why?"

I wheezed with pain, unable to speak. The man held his other hand up threateningly when I couldn't find the words to reply. He wore a thick gold ring embossed with an eye within a pentacle, and I fixed on it in confusion. That earned me a hard slap across the face, and then a much more solid backhand in the other direction.

Black lightning crackled around the edges of my vision. *Oh look*, I thought blurrily. *He has no idea what the fuck he's doing.*

He leaned in, fixing me with wolfish intensity. "You think I'm joking, you son of a bitch?"

"No," I slurred, my voice thick with blood. "Didn't do it."

"The fuck's that supposed to mean?" His eyes narrowed. They were amber, more orange than brown, like the dog's eyes. The dogs. Hell, what the... where the fuck were those dogs?

The water was turned on again, and I jerked back to cold reality, gasping shower spray and harsh, clinical air. "Didn't do it! I didn't do the hit on your guy."

"Bullshit," my interrogator said. "Fucking bullshit."

"Didn't."

Do something, or he's going to kill you. He cocked his fist. I swallowed a mouthful of water and blood and mucus and pressed my tongue behind my teeth to protect them in the split second before he punched me again.

"Like fuck you didn't. I know what happened to him, you piece of shit. Someone set a fetch on him. Your side, punk, not ours! None of us did it. Who? Laguetta?"

It took a moment for the word he'd used to sink in. Fetch. The pause earned me another slap across the face and another dose of water. The spray left me shivering. It hurt. Pain was all I had to center on. "Fetch... fetch what?"

The man snarled in my face. "Come on! You fuckin' stink of magic! What was it? Demon? Elemental?"

I struggled against the inertia, tried to gather my wits. Carmine was acting like a Hollywood action movie villain. You can't beat the shit out of people you want information from, because baby can't talk with a broken jaw—but even if he was a shitty interrogator, Jersey-Shore here was as powerful a mage as any of the old masters. Merlin. Dee. Crowley.

"Wait," I gasped out. "Wait. Can't speak."

He trembled in rage but held off for a moment, chest heaving. It was enough to give me space to see just how hyped up and unsure he really was.

I rolled my eyes up to look at him, flinching at the light. It stabbed all the way to the back of my skull. "You're so much... more powerful. Than him."

He clearly hadn't expected me to say that. Jersey-Shore obviously didn't play poker, either. "More powerful? More powerful than who?"

"Guy that... did the job." I forced myself to think past the teeth-drilling agony of my hands. "Gave me a... I don't know. Ball... caster. He engraved it... with some symbols, weird symbols. Said it would keep me safe. He wanted..." What? I groped for something, anything. "The diary. Diary in V-Vincent's bedroom."

"Why the fuck would he want..." Jersey trailed off, scowling, and then some kind of realization seemed to dawn and he bounced back in agitation. Somehow, I'd nailed it. He hadn't even looked at the diary, he'd been so worked up over finding me. "Shit. That lying *sorca, cazzo*! Piece of shit!"

Get him talking, Alexi. "You..." I tried to speak and ended up mumbling as a tooth wobbled. It shifted around every time my tongue moved. "How'd you... do that? Your dogs?"

"None of your fucking business. You don't get to ask questions. What's in the diary?"

"Don't know." I leaned towards him, as far as the handcuffs allowed, and licked at the blood running over my lips. "Italian. Couldn't read it."

"Was it a grimoire? Big book of magic?"

I stared at him blankly.

The man jerked his face to one side, looking down at me imperiously, and jogged a little on his feet. He was evaluating me with a touch of uncertainty, and I realized something. He'd been expecting the Russian spook, sure, but he'd been expecting a mage like himself. Someone powerful, someone brassy. He maybe had a secondhand description of what I looked like, but it must have been tentative. He didn't recognize me. Was he from out of town?

Finally, he scowled. "Fuck. You don't have any idea what I'm talking about, do ya?"

"Pick-up job," I mumbled, sinking down. "That's it. Pick-up job. Collection."

"Jesus Christ. Okay, fine." He ran his fingers back through his hair. Hyperaware, I read a hundred tiny signs of stress. He thought he'd picked up the errand boy, and that suited me just fine. "What's the spook's name? The one you talkin' 'bout?"

This time, I looked away and said nothing. My interrogator's mouth turned down as the seconds ticked on, then he struck again. And again. A fist connected with my ribs, with my stomach, my neck. My vision blacked. When the light reappeared, it was hazy, fizzing at the edges with a black halo.

"Give me his fucking name!"

"Dunno," I managed to say. "They call him... call him Molotchik."

"Molotchik. Jesus, was that so fucking hard?" He stalked back, pacing an anxious circle.

I watched him blearily. If he bent down that close to my face again, I was going to go for his throat.

"Fine. So you don't know anything about the spook. Well, this is your last chance to be useful, Russkie. If you don't know who did Frankie in, who's this Vincent? You know, Vincent 'Manelli'?"

Hang on... what?

My reward for my real confusion was another punch to the gut.

"Don't... know." I spat and tasted blood, lots of blood. "A-aren't you..."

"Carmine." He pronounced it the proper Italian way, *Carr-mi-nay*, and sneered. "I work for John, shithead, and I want to know who is going around using his Family name on the street without his knowing."

I remembered what Vassily had said in the car. John Manelli only had three sons? It was getting harder to focus through the pain. "Isn't he... isn't he a M-Manelli?"

Something invisible wrapped around my throat and squeezed. I could smell ozone. My skin crawled as the air bent, gathering around me, and lifted me back up to my knees on the hard, wet metal. It was the same force that had torn my gun from my hand. This guy was incredible. He was also out of control. He threw his magic around like a toddler with his toys.

"Let me make this as clear as possible. Uncle Jo hears some punk off the street has been throwin' his family name around like fuckin' confetti, so he calls in me. Mr. Fixit. Now I've got my means and ways of finding out who's who, where they are, then dealing with them." As Carmine spoke, he gestured with his fingers, and the choke intensified. My face was turning numb. "So a little bird calls me up, tells me that the Russkies are working with Vincent Manelli, who doesn't fuckin' exist, and that they axed Frankie. Frank Nacari. So I go to 'Vincent's' house, thinking I'll go ask him some questions, and find you. And now you're sayin' you don't know who he is?"

Someone was playing us. Someone had summoned the demon of feuds, Aamon, and they were playing us off against each other. "No... no, you don't—"

He let me loose as suddenly as he'd seized me. I fell heavily, coughing. The relentless pain, the fading adrenaline were dulling my thoughts.

"You're sayin' that you don't know who he is?"

The quaver in Carmine's voice spoke of underlying desperation. I was bubbling at the corners of my mouth, but I could hear it. He was mining for something. It was a weakness and exploitable. All I had to do was make it up.

"Frankie... was a part of a deal." The strain in my voice was genuine and cracked with every other word. "With Vincent. He's... faking. Not really a Manelli."

"Yeah, that's more like it. Go on."

"Frankie... he came over... to deal with us. Sell John out to us."

Carmine's wolfish eyes were gleaming. "Keep going."

"We knew... we knew Vincent wasn't real Manelli." The words boiled together, rising blithely of their own accord. I was lying, and for once, I didn't care. "But we never told anyone."

"What was Frankie trying to sell you guys?" Carmine crouched down now, leaning in excitedly. "What deal did he set up?"

I wanted to spit on him. Five inches closer, and I'd tear his stupid larynx from his stupid chicken neck. Instead, I swayed, feigning a lapse of consciousness. Sure enough, the splash of cold water followed, and under the searing, sense-clearing spray, I put two and two together. This was where I had to guess. It felt insane. Sounded insane.

"Some kind of... relic." I managed to keep the simultaneous question and disbelief out of my voice. "A book or something. That's... what I heard. He was dealing with Molotchik. I don't know his real name, I swear."

"Is that so?" Carmine was very intent. "What's he look like?"

I was reaching out on a limb. "Dark. Big. Kind of fat. Weird eyes. Bulgarian, maybe."

Carmine's eyebrow arched. He held up the Wardbreaker. "So you don't know his name, but you let him juice you up with this? Cause I swear, you have the taint on you. The mark."

"Y-yes." I fought the urge to lick at my split lip, staring at the gun. "Pakhun ordered it."

"Huh." He looked down on me. "So you got something else you want to tell me? Because that's not enough to save your ass."

I shivered, rattling from the base of my spine to the back of my neck. The next words came to me unbidden, almost as if I hadn't even spoken them. They were from the images and the snatches of English in the dream diary, still lying on Vincent's bedroom floor. "What is... The Fruit?"

Carmine rubbed the ring on his finger with his other thumb, staring down in silence for several long, thick seconds. His hand dropped away, slowly. Watching him watching me, I hung from the rail and waited.

"That ain't any of your business." Carmine stepped back and turned, his shoes tacking gummily against the tiles. "Too bad you don't know anything useful. Go kiss God's eternal ass for me in heaven."

I watched Carmine's back as he walked to the door. It opened into a fathomless black rectangle; he disappeared, and I heard him quip something in Italian to someone outside. I couldn't understand him, but made out the tone well enough. Words to the effect of "All yours."

This was not how I'd planned to die, but I was slipping and couldn't stop it. This was not going to be a quick death, or an easy death, or a good death. I'd beaten enough men in basement interrogation rooms to know what happened from this point on. If I was lucky, they'd just shoot me. And if I wasn't? Nothing is more depraved than a man hopped up on a cocktail of testosterone and righteousness. I felt for something, anything I could do, but I didn't have my gun. There was blood, but no energy. The only sacrifice available was me. This wasn't a ward I could break or a threat I could contain.

My nose was full of the smell of water. It smelled like glass. I licked my lips and settled into place, grounding in the pain, in the cold, in the wet. I'm not religious, but I've seen and done enough to know that magic comes from somewhere. The best hymn to the Higher Self was written by old Aleister Crowley, and it was that long-memorized verse I started to mumble. "You who art I... beyond... all I am. Who has no nature... and no... name..."

Staccato bursts of tense laughter from outside the bathroom punctuated the words. That didn't bode well. Professional executioners didn't chitchat and laugh just before the dirty work started. Bullies did. Old jailbirds, the type of guys who liked to rough up and torture.

"Who art, when all but thou are gone... the s-secret and center of... the Sun."

The invocation continued to pull itself from my lips. It seemed to catch fire and fuel itself. "You hidden spring, of all things known and... unknown, thou aloof alone..."

Thou the true fire within the reed, brooding and breeding, source and seed... Of life, love, liberty and light? You are no Thelemite, my Ruach.

I heard a flutter and the tic-tac of claws as a raven with white eyes landed on the edge of the bathtub. His irises steamed into the humid air, spitting like burning magnesium. "*Why quote Crowley's daemon when you can talk to your own?*"

CHAPTER 10

Over the bird's head, I saw the executioners enter, moving like shadows behind plate glass: two men, a combined four hundred pounds of hurt. Left was bald and Right was bearded and wore a baseball cap, but they both had the same shark-eyed, dog-jawed look I saw every morning in the mirror. These were hardened men, killers.

"Keeps me calm." I don't think I managed to speak aloud.

"These men are about to bleed you like a calf in this bathtub," the raven said. The feathers of its plumage boiled in the air like a black liquid. *"You will undergo Shevirah here, or you will die."*

Shevirah. Now there was a magical term I hadn't heard in a long time. That was straight-up Kabbalah: Shevirah, the breaking of the vessels. Supposedly, YHWH created everything through a series of emanations. Shevirah referred to the point when the divine light of self-awareness within God grew so intense that it burst outwards into nothingness like a harpoon. As it grew farther away from God, it became more solid, more tangible, cooling and creating the myriad layers of reality.

I felt a rough hand haul my face up by the hair and refocused on the arm stretching down towards me. It was the bearded guy. He laughed, lewd and derisive, but the sound seemed to come from far away. The raven was still there, and I fixated on it. It looked back at me, through me, with eyes the color of blazed winter skies. My gaze was drawn into a swirling vortex of pure white that took my breath away, a spiral galaxy contained within a single point.

The tub vibrated under and around me as one of the men climbed in, standing over me. He hauled me up until my jaw was level with his fly. I could smell diesel oil, male musk, the faint odor of unwashed skin through his jeans. For a moment, I was reminded of Moni, the way he'd talked about Semyon Vochin's wife. With distant disgust, I realized the man was hard, but he didn't unzip; instead, he pulled a gun and pressed it between my lips as he jeered back at his friend.

"What do I have to do?" I knew I was speaking in my mind now, as the oily point of the gun waggled in past my teeth. *"I don't want to die like this."*

"I can't lie, Alexi." The bird had sidestepped around so I could still see it on the rim of the tub, flicking its glossy blue-black wings. *"The road to understanding is long and bitter. You will bleed. Your dead flesh will come back to life. You must take holes to be whole. Are you ready to say YES?"*

My mouth was full of metal. I felt the shuffling boot soles through the tub, but my whole body, my whole mind, felt like a gas. A floating web, hovering between the black sky overhead and the green sea beneath. The nothing overhead, the no-sky, sucked at me hungrily. The sea was deep and fathomless, patient, and full. I felt like something tiny looking into a well of impossible size.

"Yes," I replied. The word felt like an incantation, as if it had power all of its own.

"Hang on a sec, Robbie. Don't shoot him," said a voice from far away. "I want some target practice. Haul him up."

"I ain't taking the cuffs off," Beard said, laughing.

"You don't have to, man. Just get him up so I can get his knees."

The barrel slid out, and my head snapped to the side as I was struck. The light was creeping into my vision. Through filmy eyes, I watched the blond thug heft a baseball bat and start across to the bathtub.

"Yes. I accept." The raven opened its beak, revealing a blue forked tongue. *"You will know me as Kutkha. I am the eye of your I... the one you only half-opened in the time before."*

My vision seared white as Kutkha threw itself forward in a heavy downbeat. It funneled into light so blue it was almost black, and pierced me through the front of my chest. I felt the impact, shaking as coils and loops of it braided itself through my mind, through my spine, through my heart and tongue and fingers. The freezing indigo of its substance meshed through me in a tenth of a second, and suddenly, I understood something I had never known. Some part of me had been caged, all this time. But now, the vessel had broken.

I was lifted higher as the other guy came up on me. I saw his face, a mask of rictus pleasure, and a pair of black, lightless eyes. He swung around, hefting the baseball bat, and then brought it down and around at my left knee.

The contact was like a detonator. As dead wood caved through bone, it tore apart the shredding virgin film over my mind. My will consolidated with an involuntary scream of naked agony, a force that pushed up from under my sternum and out of my mouth—a return thrust that wracked the air of the room in waves. Baldy's face blanked into a mask of shock. Then, he exploded.

Escape.

The backlash of life force returned to me like iron filings to a magnet, sucked in and transmuted. My veins were hot, thrumming, every part of my body drawn in sharp relief. The handcuffs turned to liquid around my wrists as the air twisted and weirded, distending. Energy boiled white-hot in my mouth, in every bone and muscle, but I wasn't in control as my hands reached down, grabbed my knee, and wrenched. The bones shifted together with a wet crunch I barely felt. One word hammered through the delirium. *Escape.*

I got one step forward before the world came back into awful focus and my knee collapsed underneath me. I tumbled over the slippery porcelain, striking the edge of the tub with a heavy crash as silenced gunshots burst over my head and sprayed the wall where I'd been chained. Whatever heavy magic I'd just done, that was it. It was all I had. My knee seared, and I screamed rawly a second time as I lunged for the bat, the only weapon within reach, and managed to grasp the handle.

Beard was stumbling up, terrified, covered in minced meat and sprayed blood. The muzzle of the gun was a black hole, a point in space trying to track my head as we slipped uselessly on the wet floor. I got up first and charged him, limping. He got an arm up; I knocked the gun free, and we went to ground, grunting and struggling. His mouth was in my face, gaping; I headbutted him, sending him sprawling to one side, and my oversensitive hand clapped down on the fallen pistol. I pulled the trigger and it clicked, empty. Before he could recover, I rolled over on top of him and hit him in the face with the butt of it. Eyes, temples, skull, until his arms dropped and he stopped moving.

Fuck. Fucking hell. I threw the gun away from me, retching with pain, and fought to breathe. I tried to stand up and limp away, but the fragile healing job the burst of power had given me didn't hold up. I fell back on my ass. The room was suddenly very quiet, very still, save for the etheric hum of the light overhead.

Jesus Christ. My goddamned knee. My hands hovered over it, not touching. I was terrified of what I'd find. Before I could look down, a filamentary shadow reappeared in my vision, translucent and fluid through the tears.

"There's no time. Get up."

"I can't." Every movement felt like too much effort. My eyes ran; I heaved, even though there was nothing in my stomach. I was still naked, covered in drying dead flesh.

"You have no choice. Get up, or die."

Die? No. I didn't want to die here. I wasn't meant to die here. He was right. I needed to break each one of Carmine's stubby manicured fingers and feed them to him. I fixed on this, on the fuel of revenge, while I grasped the bloody baseball bat and used it to lever myself up to my feet so I could shuffle-hop out into the hallway.

Outside, I found my things crammed into a calico shopping bag. With shaking hands, I fumbled with boxers and slacks, then dropped the bat to get my gloves on. The gloves gave instant relief, shutting down the worst of the pain in my torn fingers. The Wardbreaker was underneath my clothes, but the clip was gone. My knife was at the bottom of the bag. I opened the blade, and a strange, immediate sense of impending safety washed over me. No matter how disgusting I felt, I knew how to do this. The dance of violence and survival, the feel of a knife in my hand and the power of the Art in my blood, however tenuous.

Carmine had taken me to a warehouse. The hall had concrete floors, and the ceiling was cobwebbed and unkempt. The bathroom was part of an open corridor, one of several doors set into the wall to my right, and faceless wood paneling to the left. A bolted door was at the end of the hall behind me. Ahead was the warehouse proper. I could try to unlock the back door and get out that way, but I had no idea where it led. The storage part of the warehouse was a crapshoot. Maybe there was enough cover to make a run for it, maybe there wasn't. It depended on how many people were outside.

I heard the snap and rattle of a large roller door, and the lights came on ahead. Decision made. Male laughter followed me as I limped quickly for the back door, the sound growing stronger as I pulled the bolt out and flung the door open into the surprised face of a jowly, dark-eyed thug. His hand was cupped around the end of a cigarette, and he reared back like a deer in the headlights as I threw the bat at him as hard as I could. It hit and bounced; there was an expletive and a short gargling scream as I leaped on him, blade first and drove the knife through his neck. We spun in a lazy circle and tumbled to the ground, me on top. He was a goner, even if he was still flopping around. I dragged him off, shut the door, and rustled his pockets for keys, money, and weapons. No weapons, no money, but he had keys. The bundle was heavy, and amongst them, I found a white numbered tag and a blue-and-gold burnished keyring with a long, thick key, the squared-off kind that fits a truck or bus. The keyring had a logo on it, a crown with seven points and seven dots. *Elite Meats.*

The Manelli family front? I snorted blood, looking up ahead. Across the lot was a row of trucks. They were refrigerated cargo trucks, not quite big enough to be semis. I grabbed my crutch and stumbled sideways into a wall. God help me, I was tired.

"*No.*" Kutkha's voice hissed through my mind. "*Get to the truck.*"

Pushing away from the wall cost me energy. Hopping towards the trucks cost more. "I've never driven a truck."

"*There's always a first time.*"

I had no idea where Carmine was, no idea if there were other men. But that wasn't exactly correct. As I thought about it, sluggishly, I had a dim sense of their presence on the other side of the warehouse. Carmine's aura was the largest, a red-and-orange haze in my mouth and nose that lingered like a bad day. They were hanging around in the storage area, waiting for their buddies to finish with me. They probably had a truck of their own in there, waiting to receive my body so they could dump me out in the bay.

Which raised a good point. Where the hell was I?

CHAPTER 11

We reached the first truck and had a brief battle with gravity and inertia to try and unlock it. Not that one. The next truck in the row was the one: the key fit. At first, I wasn't sure I could use the step to pull my weight up to the door, but I felt another wave of subtle pressure from within. My Neshamah, burning the energy of blood sacrifice to save our goddamned lives. Every muscle screamed as I grappled my way up, hauling with my arms and pushing with the good leg until we collapsed across the worn driver's seat.

"Lev," I muttered. "We need to get to Lev."

I didn't know why I needed Lev. Common sense told me that Lev could have put me here in the first place. He was the one who'd known where I was. In the moment, though, I had genuine, immediate, fully rational problems. The truck had a manual transmission, and I had only one functioning leg.

"Use the bat."

"You fucking use the goddamn bat!" I growled aloud, finally losing my temper. My body was wracked with pain, nothing but pain, as I pushed and pulled and found my way upright in the seat. I jarred the ruined knee. "Mother of fuck!"

Kutkha fell silent, but I could feel him, it, hovering in the fringes of my awareness. Out of the corner of my eye, I watched a shadow cluster on the passenger's seat, swirling anxiously as I heaved for air. As the pain settled back to berating my nerves instead of screaming at them, I reached up to stab at the key slot with the key. Once, twice, and then it slid home.

Across the lot, three men burst out of the door, shouting at me, at the dead body, and at each other. One of them was Carmine. They were briefly transfixed by the dead man on the ground, pausing to stare.

Panic surged through my gut like a shock of cold water. *Use the bat. Right.*

I braced the bat against my leg and down onto the clutch, holding it as I somehow used all limbs to turn the engine and put the stick shift in gear all at the same time. The truck roared to life, stuttering as I fumbled with the controls. Thanks to Nicolai, I'm an excellent driver. Thanks to genetics or memetics or whatever it is that causes me to be so neophobic, I am not excellent at dealing with unfamiliar arrays of buttons and dials. I got the headlights on as the first of the men ran out towards me, gun raised.

"That's right, rabbit. Come on!" I shoved my foot down on the pedal and accelerated at full speed towards him. The Italians scattered in terror; I hauled the steering wheel one-handed as I let off the clutch. Stalling meant death, but now that the machine was working, I knew what I was doing. The truck was more responsive than I expected, and as I spun it, it nearly tipped on its side. My skin flinched as bullets sprang off the hood and struck the windshield, but we had speed and, most importantly, momentum. The vehicle roared straight through a chain-link fence that we mowed down and flung aside, charging across some slippery dead grass and out onto the road.

"Magic," I gasped. "Carmine. Can we—"

"He has to be low on Phi," Kutkha replied, coiling around the cabin like an agitated mist. *"He can't risk much now."*

Phi? I had no idea what that was. I gritted my teeth so hard they felt like they were going to crack as we turned out from the warehouse street onto a main road. In the distance, I could see the George Washington Bridge, and my heart sped. We were across the water and over the state line, in Jersey. This was nuts. Talking to my imaginary raven friend was nuts. I was buzzing and fought to not be conscious of anything but the dance of clutch, shift, and the wheel in my hands while I floored the truck with the help of the baseball bat. My knee felt three times its usual size, too large and swollen to be real. I hadn't looked at it and wouldn't. Not until we stopped.

An engine roared behind me, revving hard. I swerved to one side on raw instinct as bullets whizzed and pinged off the side of the cab. They were chasing, and they were faster than the truck. One bullet struck the mirror, and it shattered just as I swung back and rammed broadside into the pursuing car. It spun away, screeching, and smashed into a telephone pole behind us.

"I can't believe this!" I fought to right the truck before we followed it over onto the side of the road. It was finally dawning on me, through the fog of adrenaline, that I was talking aloud to... what? My soul? A hallucination? "I just... can't fucking believe this. And if you're my Neshamah, you better explain how the hell I did that and how the hell I do it again!"

"Then listen, and learn. Five parts has the human soul, like a small cell within the greatness of the Cauldron. Your being is a tree. Under and around the roots is GOD itself, and then come the roots, called Chiah. From those grow branches, your Neshamah. Then there is you, the Alexi of this world, who is Ruach. You are the mind, the breath which animates the fifth part, your Nephesh, which is your body."

That was pure Kabbalah, for the most part. "What do you mean by God?" I replied. We took the next left and merged the bullet-riddled truck into the traffic of Interstate 95. "And Phi?"

"The Greater Optimistic Direction. The Giant Organism of Dimension," Kutkha replied. *"The YESbeast. It is the Great I."*

"It?" This sounded mad. "That doesn't make any sense. I don't believe in God."

"You don't have to." Kutkha chortled. *"The YESbeast doesn't care. You are one atom in a single cell of its body. You could destroy everyone on this world but yourself, and it would not notice."*

I scowled but had no answer. The whole exchange was so fluid and strange—semi-telepathic, hyper-real—that I couldn't piece the information together. "Great. My Neshamah is some kind of Mormon."

Kutkha guffawed. *"Was I not being mystical enough? Pardon me, your humble soul. Ahem: I am the gate and the key. I am the watcher, your guardian."*

"And a smartass." Fantastic. The road ahead was swimming in front of my eyes, wobbling like a black ribbon. I checked the rearview mirror, but couldn't see any especially suspicious cars. I certainly didn't see Carmine's flaming black dogs. "Guardian? If you're my guardian, why weren't you there when my dad was thrashing the shit out of me and my mother?"

"I was waiting," Kutkha replied, wistfully. *"Waiting for you to see me. But you were afraid... you only saw me briefly, Alexi."*

"Well I—shit!" As I spoke, the engine stuttered, and I worked the clutch, hissing through my teeth. "Don't you fucking fuck up now, you no good piece of shit!"

The traffic slowed as we rolled up to the toll gates, and it took every shred of concentration to keep the truck moving. We rolled up to the window, and I set my jaw, resolving to breeze on through. When no one asked for my toll, I looked out and down. The woman in the booth stared back mutely, her eyes bulging slightly in the bright lights. That's when I remembered I was covered in shredded meat and dried blood, gunpowder, and sweat. And I was half-naked. In a bullet-hole riddled truck.

"Same old New Jersey, huh?" I peered at her dark face, trying to open both my eyes. One of them was swollen shut tightly enough that it was going to need a crowbar to get it open. "How much?"

"Four dollars. And, uh, sir... do you—"

"No." I glared at her with all the dignity I could muster and fumbled for my wallet—or maybe the dead guy's—one-handed as the truck shuddered and lurched a little. I fought to keep the balance on the accelerator and clutch and ended up pulling out a twenty. "Just... you just take that, ma'am. Tip."

Her eyes tracked me as we rumbled off, the engine coughing. The cabin was warm now and brighter than I remembered. The pain was getting worse, not better. The magical outburst had probably saved me from permanent brain damage from Carmine's beating, but I wasn't sure if it was the lights of the bridge blurring into one another or the aura preceding the worst headache I'd ever have.

"We are deplete," Kutkha said, picking up on my silent query. *"The sacrifice was our fuel."*

"You mean every time I want to cast big magic, I need to kill somebody?" I hoped not. I had done a good job of staying out of the hands of the law, but that was only because I killed infrequently and well. And, of course, I guessed that killing people just to cast spells probably raised some ethical concerns.

"No," Kutkha replied. *"But you're so blocked up that you have next to no Flow. The magic worked because you were close to death."*

Oh, right. So I had to die, or nearly die, to be a proper wizard. *Do zla boga.*[11]

We got the truck most of the way to Central Park before I passed out at the wheel. One moment, I was intent on the lines and whirring tarmac, and the next, I was hanging from my seatbelt and the hood of the truck was folded around a lamp post. I was pleasantly, distantly surprised to find that my legs weren't crushed as I hauled myself out of the smoking cab and tumbled bonelessly to the pavement, the bat still in my hands.

My heart shlupped in my chest. It sounded as squishy as I felt, and I was glad that it, at least, was able to move. The rest of my body refused to respond. My brain was a haze of white noise. Carmine and friends could drive up beside us right now, step out and put a bullet in my head, and there was nothing I would be able to do. Whoever killed Frank Nacari could take me off the street. At least I had made it back to New York.

"Get up," Kutkha hissed in my mind.

---

[11] 'GIVE IT TO THE BLACK GOD.'

"I can't." Its urgings were like prickling claws. I struggled to rise, but my wrists buckled from my weight.

"Get up or shut up. You're almost there."

My vision swam, but I still didn't want to die. Sleep, yes; die, no. I tried again and managed to clumsily roll up to my ass and get a look around the crash site. It was a clean, broad boulevard, full of high-rises. It smelled green. Cast-off newspapers rustled down the nearly empty road. Someone was running away towards the park, away from the scene of the accident, and some apartment lights had turned on overhead. Of course, I'd crashed the truck in one of the few neighborhoods in this city where the people cared what was going on outside. The cops would be there soon, and if they found me, I was worse than dead.

I choked a curse, set the butt of the bat on the ground, and used it to push myself up to the better knee. They were both screwed up by this point. With some shuffling and a lot of growling, I got to my feet. Took a step forward. Then another. I lost awareness of my surroundings as I fixed my eyes on the pavement and walked towards the payphone at the end of the street.

I careened into the door before getting inside, dropped my change when I tried to feed it in the slot, and settled on digging the wallet out to find another quarter instead of contorting myself to find the first one on the ground. I tried the house first, but no one picked up. Vassily was out, of course. Next I tried the other number that came first to mind: Lev's office number. I had to think about it, stabbing each button with clumsy fingers, trying to moisten my lips as I summoned the words.

"Sirens Office." Lev's fluted voice crackled over the line.

"Lev. 'S Lexi." My tongue felt too big for my mouth. I slumped against the side of the booth. "Ambushed. Manellis."

"Alexi? The Manellis?" Lev's shock was mild, almost affected, but that was Lev for you. "Where are you? I'll send someone right away."

"No idea." I heard the slur in my voice and swallowed, glancing around. Park. Green. It had started to rain, heavy pattering drops that formed a mist around the tall buildings. I looked up at the skyline, orienting myself. "No... wait. Central Park. South."

"Tell me the number on the payphone."

I peered at it, but it took a while to make it out. My eyes were refusing to focus. "Two... four, five... nine, seven...nine... zero."

"Okay, I'll look it up. Stay down, stay safe."

Was that it? I held onto the phone for several seconds after it clicked, not certain I'd heard my Avtoritet correctly. Then I dropped the receiver, staring at it numbly until the wail of sirens pierced the night air, getting closer. Shit. My fuzzy-headedness was abruptly cleansed by fear. Fear of arrest tapped reserves of energy I never knew I had, and I hobbled desperately out of the booth, across the street, and into the park, like a wounded cat. I huddled down in a cluster of bushes, burning and freezing under the metallic summer rain, peering out through the green wire netting at the road as it began to flash red and blue. My gut clenched to something the size of a walnut as the siren hooted and then went silent. Voices called out, cops getting out of the car. God help me.

"Kutkha?" My mental voice was very small. *"Please tell me that I didn't just go through all that to get pulled up."*

The response was a subtle fluttering of pressure around my shoulders, like someone's consoling touch, the kind of touch I had never been able to stand. Kutkha felt weak and distant now, but even the smallest sense of his presence somehow balmed my mind and took my attention, however briefly, off the relentless and otherwise all-consuming pain. I thought back to Vassily in the car, the long stretch of his throat and the words of the *Tao Te Ching*. The man who walks without fear. I wasn't dead. Not by rhinoceros or tiger, or Guido hellhound, or NYPD.

It was an age until the street outside my green sanctuary descended into silence. The doors slammed, the sirens withdrew. The cops had likely called a tower in to get the truck, but with no one around, there was no reason for them to linger. My heart beat rapidly and shallowly in my chest, and lurched when a car door slammed outside the park fence not too far from the ruined truck. I heard a pair of old army boots hit the pavement. The sound roused me from my damp fugue.

"Marco." Nic lifted his voice to be heard. He sounded tired.

"P-polo." I choked on the word. It wasn't loud enough. "Polo!"

The boot step swaggered over in my direction. A few minutes later, the foliage over my head rustled, and Nic's dry, wiry fingers snapped around my forearms. I was too exhausted to protest as he hauled me out, except to snarl and chomp my teeth as I put weight down on the wrong foot and felt an invisible knife wrench up through my leg.

He clicked his tongue. "They fucked you up."

"Lev." I turned my head to the side and spat blood. "Need Lev. I have to... have information... the operation. Vincent."

Nic paused for a moment, looking at me with narrowed eyes, then hmmph'd and shrugged, offering his arm. I accepted, and he helped me hobble to the car. I let him load me face-first onto the backseat and lay there watching the world spin in an elegant loop ahead of my nose.

"Lev," I croaked.

"You're real beat." Sympathy never really touched Nic's voice, but his tone held a certain urgency I'd never heard before. Maybe he cared. "Keep talking. What happened?"

I couldn't talk. Instead, I rolled over, struggled up to my elbows, and finally looked down at my leg. I immediately regretted it. It was stuck out to the side, the kneecap pushed up strangely from underneath my pants. Legs weren't meant to look like that, so I lay back and stared at the lines of leather on the ceiling overhead. "Had to kill a couple of guys. Lev."

"We're on the way to Lev. Don't sweat it. You're tough." Nic revved the engine and backed out of his space too fast for anyone's comfort, least of all mine. "We got your car fixed."

You're tough. He'd given that same piece of encouragement since he started teaching me how to box and shoot and boost cars. "Okay."

Dizzy, dry-mouthed, I covered my eyes and tried to relax on the backseat, bumped forward and back by Nic's flippant one-handed steering. We turned a corner, and I had to bury my teeth in my own arm as my leg jerked, bracing the other hand against the seat in front. The longer I lay there, the greater the shock. It flushed through me like a wave of hot anger but without the accompanying energy. I had been naked. My mouth was still oily and sour from the gun. It wasn't anger. It was disgust. My body was full of holes, my flesh weak and bloodied, invaded. And yet... past the slow and continual shattering of my remaining dignity, past the stench of blood on my wet clothes, I could feel the crooning, cold presence of Kutkha. He enfolded my consciousness with wings as breathtaking as the clouds passing over a wild steppe. Every touch, every brief synaptic moment, carried a litany that slowly overwhelmed my thoughts.

...LoveYouLoveYouLoveYouLoveYouLoveYouLoveYouLoveYouLoveYouLoveYou...

I could smell night-blooming flowers. Jasmine, maybe, or honeysuckle. Was I dying? Drifting, distant, I was surprised to find my vision fading to green.

With no other recourse, I surrendered. Maybe death wasn't so black after all.

CHAPTER 12

One moment, I was watching the orange lights of the highway marching through the back windshield of Nicolai's car; in the next, I was hanging off his elbow in a white-lit elevator. The unlit buttons were numbered into the thirties. Foggily, I stared at them, unsure where I'd been taken. I could distantly smell Nic beside me, a brown and green and muddy blue scent, and was mulling over the weird mouthfeel of his cologne when I fainted again.

The next sensation was one of lapping water against my cheeks. When I opened my eyes, I found myself floating on the surface of an endless expanse of water, looking up through a passing gallery of luminous white aquatic creatures extending far up into the green sky above like a field of stars. Or... not quite endless. Somewhere very high overhead, the green turned abruptly to black, a blackness so deep it looked less like a form and more like the absence of form. It was vacuuming up the eerie, peaceful fauna that swam innocently back and forth, hoovering them in like a screaming mouth. The Void hurt to look at for long.

I closed my eyes against the darkness. When I opened them a second time, there was light. My face was running with streams of water. My gaze met one overhead, as placid and calm as the green sea at dawn.

"Ah..." Lev said. He wiped my face with a hand towel. "There we go. Back with the living."

My knee wasn't hurting nearly as much as it should have. I lurched up to try to look at it, and it was Lev's clammy, firm hands that pushed me back down. I was lying on a black leather sofa as big as a single bed.

"Nothing's wrong." Lev's prim voice was firm. "It wasn't as bad as you thought it was. I reset it... it will be fine. It doesn't even hurt."

And for a moment, it was true. Lev's words washed away the pain and doubt like seafoam, but like seafoam, the wave vanished as my memory swept clear and my own thoughts, my own knowledge, flooded back into place.

"You..." I rasped. "I don't... believe you."

Lev's face froze into neutral lines, but he slapped the mask over his expression of shock just a split second too late.

"My knee." My chest ached as I drew another ragged breath and struggled up to my elbows. Dizzy, yes, and sore. My lips were parched and I was uncomfortable, exhausted, but I was not in agony. I looked down at my leg. My trousers had been cut up and taken off around mid-thigh, baring my legs. The knee still didn't look right: it was puffy and swollen, purpled up, but it was mostly straight underneath the swelling and bruising. I tried to flex it and immediately let out a harsh bark of pain as it reminded me that, yes, it was still royally screwed.

"Stop that." Lev swatted my hand away. "The bones are still setting. Whatever you did to it, it will take time."

Whatever 'I' did to it? I lay back, nostrils flaring. Lev stood up, carrying a bowl of water and a green cloth away with him.

"You tried to control my mind." I glared up at the ceiling. The paint was smooth and new. I had no idea where I was.

The room smelled clean and air-conditioned, vaguely oceanic, and mild. What furnishings I could see were expensive and new-looking. Brown leather, cream carpet, mahogany cabinetry. Was I at Lev's house? "Why? How?"

Lev sighed from across the room. "The how and why is not really your business, I'm afraid. In general terms, though, I tried to suggest that perhaps your pain isn't as bad as you suppose. Apparently, it was ineffective."

The blank canvas of the ceiling danced with spots and flecks of light that stung my aching, itching eyes. "You're a spook," I said, flatly.

"Not as such." Lev's footfall was soft on approach. A straw was touched to my lips. Water. I tongued the straw into my mouth and drew greedily. The cool liquid chased some of the scratchy tightness from my throat. "Do you remember anything?"

"Yes, but I have no idea what happened. By the time I roused, I..." The taste of the gun barrel flooded my palate, my body reliving the humiliation and pain. The muscles of my face tightened. I clamped my jaws together until the enamel squeaked, flexing them until the taste and smell of Carmine and his buddies passed over and through me. "What day is it?"

"The morning of the twelfth." Lev tugged the straw from my gritted teeth and set tdshe glass aside. "Monday."

Monday. So, I'd been out at least a good six hours. I knew there was something I was supposed to be doing on Monday, but the faint shadow of memory flitted just out of arm's reach. Whatever it was, it couldn't have been that important.

My eyes flickered open. I locked my gaze with Lev's, struggling to sit up higher to face him. "With all respect, Avtoritet, I want an explanation as to why you think it acceptable to make 'suggestions' to me." The sense of violation that had started in the bathroom and haunted me all the way to this apartment curdled and grew. "I've worked for you in good faith all these years. Or have I?"

"I've never risked this with you before, Alexi. The only reason I tried was to relieve your pain. Please." Lev pursed his lips, weighing his words. "Look... anything I say on this matter must never be repeated to anyone. Anyone. Not even if you suspect them of being a... spook. Not Vassily, not Nicolai. No one and nothing. Do you agree?"

This had to have been the first time he'd stuffed up like this, met someone who hadn't just let their mind be rolled. He was a spook, a different breed of mage to me. Lev had played his magical cards so close to his chest that he practically stuffed them in his mouth and chewed. "Fine. Agreed."

Lev sighed. He rose from his kneel, dragged a chair across, and set it by the sofa. When he sat, he perched on the edge and crossed an ankle over his other knee. "Sergei knows. He's always known. I discovered my ability after nearly dying in prison and honed it while serving with Sergei and your father in Kolyma."

Kolyma. Just the mention of the place made Lev's face gray and his fingers twitch while he moved, as if reflexively looking for the stub of a cigarette or the end rind of a piece of bread. That he had some magical ability explained how this soft, effeminate intellectual had survived the gold mines of northeastern Siberia. The name made my mouth turn dry and my palms itch. Perhaps it was an ancestral memory, inherited through the blood. "I understand why it is a secret, Avtoritet. No one else knows?"

"No. No one else knows. And they have no need to know. I'm only useful in some places and certain ways, Alexi. My ability has always been subtle... Suggestion, hypnosis, eavesdropping. A useful skill to have in prison."

A useful skill to have in the Organizatsiya. I could readily imagine him 'suggesting' that our old Avtoritet needed to be killed and replaced. Nic was right. Vassily was a fool to think of challenging Lev, and I'd been a fool to even entertain the thought that we'd find a way. "So Sergei knows Rodion is dead?"

"Of course. He ordered him killed." Lev leaned in a little. "Rod was only ever meant to be a temporary fix. He had no view of the big picture, and he was as corrupt as Semyon. Sergei has plans for this place, Alexi... but that is all I will say of this matter. You are not a captain, or Vor v Zakone. You are young and American. There are parts of the business you still have no right to know."

His words stung, and I looked down. When I thought back on my late teens—my grades, my horse-riding trophies, my accomplishments and first successful hits—I felt they were mine. My achievements. That is a very American way to think, but that was not how the old Soviet men thought. My achievements were theirs. They had put in the money, time, and energy, like I was a garden and they the gardeners. They'd sent me to the good school, bought the horse, taught me the skills that helped me succeed. He was right. Suddenly, my own early hardships and Vassily's hardships in prison, whatever they were, seemed vastly inconsequential. Compared to Kolyma, Fishkill was a palace resort. Neither of us could have survived the things our fathers endured. "Yes, Avtoritet."

"So, tell me how you ended up this way." Lev regarded me levelly, but he looked a little owlish, with bags under his eyes and lines around his mouth. "Nic said you were ambushed."

"At Vincent's," I replied. The details of the night were slippery, out of order. I struggled to prioritize them. "By a spook named Carmine. He works for Manelli and could even be the one who set up Semyon's security... but that isn't the most important thing. He doesn't know who Vincent Manelli is. He says Vincent is an imposter."

"That's not possible," Lev replied. The confidence in his tone was unsettling. "He's been vetted by George Laguetta and by me. He's been able to provide the contacts he claimed to have."

"The fact remains. They believe he's an imposter using the family name and are trying to find out his identity," I said. "And they've pinned Frank Nacari on us."

"They've... unless someone told them, they should have no idea that we are involved." Lev had the look of a man reaching his limit of stress. He wasn't the one who'd had a bomb set under his car and a pistol shoved in his mouth.

"Well, someone rigged my car. If it was the Manellis, then someone told them that I was on this job." I tried to keep the bitterness from my voice and failed. "Carmine mentioned that he had a 'little bird' who told him about Vincent. Someone is working against us."

"Already? I hoped this sort of thing would have died with Semyon." Lev frowned. "What a mess."

What an understatement. I pushed myself to the edge of the sofa, easing my feet to the ground. I couldn't bend my knee, but it was able to take my seated weight. "Do you have any idea who might be trying to take me out, Avtoritet?"

Lev regarded me in silence for a long moment, running his tongue over his teeth. I watched him carefully, but he showed none of the subtle signs of guilt. No contraction of the pupils, no nose or neck rubbing, no nervous hands, no flushed cheeks. "Not many people know that Vincent has gone missing. Did you tell Vassily, perhaps?"

"No." The word burst out before I could stop it. "Vassily had nothing to do with this."

"Well, Alexi, you have to understand something." Lev leaned in, hands folded between his knees. "Sergei still hopes to make Vassily Avtoritet of New York in the future... and you have been working for me. Loyally, I might add. Vassily has been gone for five years. He's an exceptionally good liar, and your acting out on your father has had quite a ripple effect, in terms of your place within the organization."

"I didn't 'act out.' He was a monster. A rabid dog." And a master at convincing people that he was never at fault. Everyone made excuses for him. "Vassily hardly knows anything about it."

"I heard that it was discussed with Vassily last night." Lev shrugged. "You probably should have told him before Petro did. He has been exposed to the worst possible version of the story already."

"He's only been out two days. I was planning to tell him when this happened." My head was throbbing, and it wasn't just from the headache. Every one of the words coming out of Lev's mouth nettled my ears. "Vassily is my sworn-brother. And Grisha deserved everything I gave him."

"It's arguable whether or not he deserved it." Lev grimaced. "And it doesn't change the fact that everyone is now frightened of what you're capable of. Including Vassily.

I can't think of any other people who would know you were on this job. I assume you told him?"

Arguable? When I remembered my father, I remembered a drunkard, a half-seen bestial shadow in the darkness of my bedroom. I remembered the rise and fall of a tire iron, but not the face of the man he'd beaten to death in front of me. I remembered... not all that much, in all honesty. The days before I had made the rainy midnight run to Vassily's family home and the period between my thirteenth birthday and my mid-teens was a black hole. There was nothing but nothing, the complete absence of memory. The few memories I had before then—that first witnessed murder behind a bakery in Red Hook, other odds and ends—had only returned after I'd killed him.

"Alexi?"

"I mentioned I was on a job, Avtoritet." I looked up at him, but it was an effort. "I did not share the details, and especially not the details of my appointments. You were the only one who could have known that."

The other man opened his mouth to speak, hesitated, and closed it again. His brows contracted together. "Well... I can't blame you for your suspicion, but I didn't hire you with the express intention of killing you. Someone may have you bugged, Alexi... someone may be wondering why I called you for a private conversation in my office. Given what happened to Grigori, and given that Sergei is returning to America, you can surely see why some of the men here might be concerned about what you're being sent out to do?"

"No." Everything he said sounded distant and dull in my own ears, as if he were speaking from far away. "No, I don't. No one talks about this to my face. The problem is that no one talks to me."

"Soon after you killed Grigori, there was talk of having you removed." Lev glanced at my face, not long enough. Why wouldn't he meet my eyes now? "The men in question are superstitious, and they fear. But I spoke for you."

How nice. Old Uncle Lev looking out for me. "And I guess you're not going to tell me who wanted me put down?"

Lev stopped trying to speak for a moment, exasperated. "No. I do not want another internal feud. The fact is that people wonder about someone capable of smashing his own father's head in with a hammer, and they think: 'Who's next?' That's how it was. Grigori was a friend to many."

So was Semyon. My ears were ringing. What a load of bullshit. Vassily had no cause to turn on me. Nic, Ovar, Vanya, even Petro... none of them had ever expressed concern in my presence. My memory flashed back to the Manelli spook. Carmine. The more I thought back—his contempt and arrogance, brashness, confidence—the angrier I felt. Someone was working with him, ratting out his own people to our enemy. "I hope you plan to have your office searched for bugs, Avtoritet. I'll resume my search tomorrow."

"Alexi, don't be ridiculous. You can't even walk." Lev glanced down at my legs, and his mouth drew across disapprovingly. "I will put Nic-"

"No." I counted to three and heaved myself to my feet. My head spun, the room looped, but I remained upright. While Lev watched me in silence, I limped to his living room door and caught hold of the jamb. "I resume tomorrow. I'll find Vincent. The Manellis are going to pay for my knee surgery."

CHAPTER 13

On the drive back, I lolled against the rear window of a hired car, brooding on nothing while I watched the city go by. The conversation with Lev left me feeling full and foggy and numb. My knee throbbed like a second heart, the discomfort echoing in my fingertips and the pulse under my tongue. The joint was slightly uneven, the patella smashed into several pieces and only just healed. It was better than nothing, but whatever Kutkha had done to help was not quite enough to put us all back together again.

The sensation of my Neshamah's presence was disquieting. I'd always known that the Higher Self was real, but he was always there now, humming like a cloud of ozone in the back of my mind. I had no idea what to make of this new, invasive consciousness. Once the euphoria of connection had worn off, it left me with the sense that I was constantly being coldly observed by a pair of alien eyes. Judged. I dared not seek or ask him questions until we were alone.

Vassily was waiting for us in the foyer. It was cool compared to the early morning heat outside, but Vassily looked like he'd been in a sauna with his clothes on. He was pale, sweaty, his eyes sunken, his t-shirt clinging to his wiry chest. He was awake, at least, but he took one look at me and scruffed his hair with both hands. "Mother of fuck. What did they *do* to you?"

"Take him, Vasya." Kir, my driver, was a spiky-haired Chechen with slow eyes and a very small mouth. He didn't really believe in saying hello.

"I can take myself." I checked the touch of impatience in my voice and hobble-hopped away from the back door, catching Vassily's offered arm. "Thank you for the help."

Kir flippantly saluted me before he turned and stomped out, his shoes ringing off the tiles. He hadn't said a word about my injury. That was the way of the Organization. Much of the time, no one would tell you what they thought. It was every man for himself.

"Alright, you. It's bedtime." Vassily ignored my protest and braced his arm under my armpit, grabbing my shirt when I tried to push him away by the ribs. "You and me, a one-way ticket to Sandmanland. I am sooo fucked up."

"No. No bed." I put a hand against his ribs and tried to move away, but Vassily was stronger. He half-led, half-dragged me towards the elevator. "Vassily, there's things I have to do."

"Dude. You look like you've been trying to bone a hornet's nest. You need to rest."

"I can't."

"Lexi..."

"Don't 'Lexi' me." My temper lunged through the cracks in my will with disgusting ease. "Vassily, there's business that can't wait."

"Okay, fine. Be an asshole about it, then." Vassily rolled his eyes. I noticed then that he was sweating more than the heat really warranted. His skin was waxen and clammy to touch, his face and hands twitchy. I read it through my fingers and through the dark, gritty smell of unwashed hair. "Go fuck yourself up some more. I don't fuckin' care."

"Are you... are you all right?" I asked.

The change in conversation made him pause. I could almost hear the gears grinding as he stared at me, catching up on the question. "Me? I'm fucking fantastic, but I want to know what the hell happened to you. Nic called before and said you got jumped. Who's gotta pay?"

Carmine would pay. How? I wasn't sure, yet. There wasn't any point trying to fight a guy who could clean your clock from across the room. "The Manellis. Someone tipped them off. Someone inside the Organization. But you didn't answer my question. Are *you* alright? You look ill."

"You'd get a fuckin' answer if you weren't being such a bitch." Vassily flushed an ugly shade of red across his face and throat. Something was not right. He smelled strange, a smell I didn't recognize. My synesthesia translated it to something pink, lurid pink, and greasy. "Stop being a bitch and go to bed when I say so, and I'll tell you."

"What on earth have you been drinking?" We got into the elevator. Vassily took a moment to deliberate over the scratched buttons. There were only four of them. "You smell dreadful."

"Antifreeze," he said, cheerfully.

I stared. "You had better be joking."

Vassily laughed. It had the edge of a bray to it, a high, manic pitch. "Just brandy, man. Just brandy. I'm fine, seriously."

When we got inside, I used my good foot to get the first shoe off but had to have Vassily remove the second. I lost all ability to concentrate as soon as we were in the house. My hands were itching and stinging in my gloves, and when I pulled them off, I recoiled. My hands were naturally smooth and pale from years of keeping them covered, and after cramming the gloves on over bloody, wet skin, they looked drowned. The backs and palms were puffy and torn, with old blood under my nails and in the creases of my fingers. The smell curdled in my nose, thick and putrid and violet.

Dead.

The stench morphed in my nostrils, and suddenly, I could smell it. The kitchen, from my parents' house. The old cabbage and stale sweat reek of angry, shouting people. Blood and urine on the old linoleum. Spilled *horilka*, the bottle half-empty on the floor. My vision clouded. I stumbled on Vassily's arm.

"Lexi? Hey, Lexi?"

My breathing sped. The sensory flood was merciless, the sensations as real as the day I'd last been home. I heard the cat howling inconsolably at the peeling window, saw the broken table and the long, cold shadow of the crooked ceiling fan. I was fourteen again, unable to move, unable to think... unable to do anything except look up at...

My vision cut. My eyes simply shut down as I barreled blindly past Vassily to the sink, struggling with the faucet. I plunged my hands underneath the cold water as the other parts of the flashback kept resolving, kept clarifying. The buzz of a single fly. The sound of my father throwing up in the bathroom down the hallway. The meowing hadn't stopped, but it wasn't the high-pitched mewing of mother's tabby calico. It was the deeper, resonant howl of a Siamese.

The flow of clean water shocked through my nerves, and my head jerked as colors and textures flooded my tongue and fingers, stabbing and hot. My vision beat back in, a kaleidoscope of unresolved colors throbbing in time with my heart.

"Hey." Vassily's head was a worried specter, light-rimmed, hovering in the mirror. "Alexi?"

The pour of water was an anesthetic, reinstating equilibrium, and it drew me back towards the present with its flow. I stared at the pair of faces in the mirror. Vassily was tall, lean, movie-star handsome. I was short and disappointing. I had my father's white eyes and burly build and my mother's height and pinched features.

"Hey uh... you want something to eat?" Vassily said. "I got some potato chips."

Potato chips. It was so inane that it hauled me back into the present moment. My mouth was so dry that chips would turn my tongue into jerky. "No. Can't."

Vassily's mouth drew to one side. I noticed his pupils were fully dilated under the bathroom light. He had bedroom eyes, junkie eyes. "Trust me, man. You might not be feeling shit-hot right now, but you gotta eat something. Not unless the Manellis were stuffing you with *foie gras* while they beat the shit out of you, you know? Getting bashed takes it out of a guy."

He was right. I knew he was right, but I wanted to resist. His blue fur voice made me twitch all over. It was so tactile that every word made my skin feel like it was being rubbed by sound. I flexed my nails against the porcelain sink and drew a deep breath.

"You okay?"

"Just..." The adrenaline had worn off, energy extinguished. Words blurred in my mouth, came out all wrong. Instead of trying to speak, I reached back, hand dripping wet, and awkwardly half-groped, half-clapped

Vassily on the arm. I felt like a clumsy assembly robot, unable to coordinate my limbs properly. "Over... stimulated. Dark. Need dark."

"All right. You get to bed, then." Vassily knew what "overstimulation" meant. Knew it meant I couldn't deal with too many words, too many sounds. He shortened his sentences automatically. "But food, soon."

"Soon," I echoed. I focused on my breathing, staring at my soggy hands under the water. They looked drowned, dead, too white. There was still blood under my nails. Goosebumps crawled over my arms, and I reached for the scrubbing brush. "Wash. Shower first."

Vassily sighed and moved aside, and I lost track of him while I scrubbed at my hands, back and forth, back and forth. It hurt, but it felt good.

"You got real close to the Reaper this time, didn't you?"

The sudden sound broke my momentary trance. I dropped the brush convulsively, and it clattered into the sink. It was several seconds more before I could speak. "Yes."

"Turn the water off. You're bleeding."

Numbly, I complied. The mirror showed me my own heavy-boned face, shadowed and pitted under the white light. I looked exhausted and dirty.

"I'm gonna talk to Lev. Get you off the hook." Vassily's voice was very low and unusually serious. "I can tell by looking at you, Lexi. You got the death-mark. You looked down the barrel of a gun."

My hands hurt. I gently shook my head and opened the mirror cabinet to look inside. The tumbler where I usually kept my spare pair was empty.

"Did you hear me? I'm gonna get you off this contract."

"No." Dry-mouthed, I gingerly patted my palms over with a clean towel. He was right: they were bleeding. They were clean, at least. "Don't you dare."

"No, you gotta understand me. I just got out of the fucking slammer, Lexi, and I didn't spend five years rotting in the boonies to get out just in time for your funeral. All right?"

The depth of anger in my friend's voice shocked me. I turned to face him, hands wrapped in terry cloth. Vassily was sweating like he had a fever, beads shining on his forehead. "Vassily, the men already disrespect me. Someone tried to bomb my car. I can't lose any more face. They'll kill me just for that."

"Right. So I'm gonna talk to Lev, and I'm gonna look at setting you up with something better. Something we can work on together. Fuck the three hundred G's. We'll make a million by the end of the year if we get back into credit cards. You remember the serial generator I was working on? That's the way of the future, man. Not this neighborhood racketeering shit."

"This is my duty," I said. "This is my responsibility."

"No!" Vassily threw his hands up. "You're two days into this gig, and look at you! Two days, Alexi! Look at you!"

"They weed out the weak. You want me to look weak in front of everyone?" I asked, incredulous.

"No one believes you're weak. They think you're a fucking psycho, but they don't think you're weak." Vassily's face was stormy.

"You do," I said. "You interrupted me when Petro was giving me shit. You think I'm weak."

"Petro was stomping all over you. What was I supposed to do? Stand by? Is that what you'd do if someone was doing that to me?"

"Of course not." The very idea was an affront. "I'd never abandon you. But I need to find Vincent."

"No, you don't. You need to survive. That's what we do." Vassily advanced on me, stabbing his finger against my chest. If I'd been stronger, I'd have caught his wrist. But I was tired, and this was too much already. "The graveyard is full of cowboys who tried to rush off into the sunset, Alexi. You think you're any better than them?"

My eyes narrowed. "I'll finish what I started. What kind of Vor v Zakone talks this way?"

"One who's had to bury his mother, his father, and the rest of his whole fucking family!" Vassily shoved back from me and stalked out the open door, slamming it behind him.

In the sudden silence, Binah jumped onto the sink and arched against my arm. I stroked her as I listened to Vassily curse his way down the hallway. The cat jumped when his bedroom door slammed, then resumed purring.

The outburst left me windless. Not angry. Anger made me stronger, not tired. I picked up Binah, draping her over my shoulder, and cast one sidelong look back at my haggard face and slumped shoulders before I limped away to the cold solace of my room.

The empty room seemed to hold the ghosts of every voice, every interaction I'd had in the past twenty-four hours. I set Binah on the bed while I found a spare set of gloves and looked down at her. She looked up at me with the same quiet wisdom I'd seen in Semyon's apartment. That was what her name meant. Wisdom.

I saw the same depth in her eyes that I'd seen in Kutkha's... and that reminded me of him. As my attention shifted back, I could see him in my mind's eye.

"So," I said aloud. "Kutkha. You have some explaining to do."

The faded awareness of my Neshamah sharpened in the moment before his voice returned to me in the stillness of the room. *"Do I, now? Do you think your own immortal soul is some fetch to be ordered about the place, Alexi?"*

I walked to my altar and eased down to the floor in front of it. I couldn't kneel, not with my knee the way it was, so I sort of leaned over until I could drop to my ass on the ground, legs in front. "Please, then."

"Well, never let it be said that I did not care for my Ruachim. I will do my best to explain your circumstances, on one condition."

"I didn't know one's own immortal soul set conditions for information." I reached across to beckon for the cat. "Before I make any more contracts with you, spirit, you need to prove you are what you say you are. 'Kutkha' is not even a real name. *Kutkh* was a Siberian culture hero and, I might add, a trickster."

"That he was: I am an admirer of his. You could just as readily call me Prometheus or Lucifer—it matters not. None of them are my true name, but you don't have a larynx capable of pronouncing the words which comprise it, Hu-Man."

A ruffling passed through the room, a small breeze. Binah hopped down to the floor and came to sit beside me. She was watching something, her eyes tracking motion I could not see.

"What you do not see, Alexi, is that you must prove yourself to <u>me</u>. You feel the truth of my being here. You accepted the bargain. I am not yours: you are mine."

"So, what is your condition, then?" I spoke cautiously. It was true that I had felt his arrival like a shattering, an epiphany, but spirits were often deceptive. I have never trusted feelings without evidence. I looked over at the collection of books around the altar table. Not a single one held the knowledge that could help me.

"You must eat eggs," Kutkha said, after a suitably dramatic pause. *"As many eggs as it takes to feel full. Then, you must shower and put yourself to bed."*

That was it? Before I could ask, the sudden desire for food overwhelmed all other thought. Fried eggs and sour cream. Ten minutes ago, I would have thrown up if I'd smelled food, but I found myself staggering up on my feet and limping to the kitchen before I really knew what I was doing, possessed of an impossibly strong desire to eat. Eggs, onions, sour cream. Greens, oh yes. Kale or spinach. How long had it been since I ate?

Aware that I'd been struck around the head, I started with two eggs. Five eggs later, I finally turned the stove off and leaned back from my plate at the kitchen table with a bulging stomach and surprisingly little nausea. I didn't feel Kutkha's presence again until we were back in the darkness of the bedroom and sprawled on top of the covers, stomach bulging. The rhythmic sound of the air conditioner washed over me in cool thrumming waves. I did feel better.

"So." Kutkha seemed to speak from the ceiling over my head. *"I suppose the first thing you want to know is how I come to be with you."*

"I want to know how to cast magic properly," I replied tersely. "And why God, or this G.O.D figures into this."

"Patience," Kutkha replied. *"GOD is a living organism which spans all known realities, of which every living thing is a single particle*

in its many billions of strands of genetic material. It does not have a HuMan face. It heeds no religion and knows nothing except itself."

Having it laid out so blandly, so efficiently, was oddly challenging. "I think we're talking about different gods."

"There are no gods as you understand," Kutkha said. *"No heaven or hell. No angels, though there are demons."*

Just as well I was an atheist. I'd never found meaning in Judaism, the religion of my mother, or entertained joining the rest of the Brighton Beach locals at their stuffy Ukrainian Eastern Orthodox church. I had a powerful sense of there being more "something" within myself, and possessed theoretical knowledge of a lot of different faiths, and that was the sum total of my spirituality.

"And is this... information that Carmine knows?" I was dubious. He hadn't really seemed like the philosophical type.

"That depends on his Neshamah and whether or not he listens to it," Kutkha said. *"Its age and experience. Its... motives... for empowering him. He seems like a powerful Phitometrist to you, but I suspect he has little Pressure behind his Art."*

"Pressure." And Flow, which my Neshamah had remarked on before. I frowned, thinking. "If Flow is the ability to... release or control Phi, which I assume is magical energy, then I can make an educated guess and say that Pressure has to do with how much is in reserve."

"Yes. A mage's power is dependent on their Pressure. Phi is a fluid, like water. It is the sap that flows through your being, which is a mirror of GOD's. Pressure is the amount of Phi you can keep in reserve. Flow is how that reserve is released. Though this feels like a revelation now, it has always been this way. Before Shevirah, Flow is... limited. The gate is closed. The key is pain of a very certain kind... the kind that exposes you to the concept of the Other. The kind which your shaman ancestors sought when they exiled themselves to the steppe."

"I had shaman ancestors?" Binah hopped up beside me on the bed, folded herself into my armpit, and began to knead my shoulder. I closed my eyes, drinking in the sky-blue image-texture of her purr.

"Your mother's blood is that of the People of the Reindeer in the far East, through her mother's line," Kutkha replied. *"Your father's line bears the Eyes of Tengri from the West. Have you never wondered at their strange color?"*

I hadn't. 'The Sokolsky Eyes', as my father had called them, were a very, very pale gray, almost white. At most, they were something people sometimes used to open a conversation with me. "And is that why I'm a mage?"

"No. Blood merely shapes the colors of your Art, and your blood is why I, of all possible creatures, am your Neshamah."

Kutkh was the Promethean spirit of the Chukchi, the indigenous people of Eastern Siberia. He was a trickster, a creative, a fire-bringer and innovator – and if memory served – a pervert with a voracious sexual appetite. In other words, he was the least suitable Neshamah for a boringly routine virgin in New York. "Does this mean I need to change the way I do magic?"

"The language you use and the symbols you make are irrelevant," Kutkha's voice was more strident now, though still sibilant and ethereal. *"You must merely free up the energy to fuel your will."*

I felt the corners of my eyes crinkle as I squinted up into the dark. "How? Carmine has magical tools, and those... summoned dogs of his. Can you do that?"

"No. And do not envy him, my Ruach." Kutkha was suddenly very serious and... uncomfortable. *"The hounds are his own Neshamah. He is like a deformed baby born with their organs exposed to the air. He fancies himself and his Neshamah to be powerful, but*

only because his exposed virgin flesh has not yet been touched by infection. His time might come... whether in this lifetime or the next."

"So tell me how to do what he does," I said. "Don't hide from me, Kutkha."

"I plan to." In my mind's eye, he tucked his head under his wing. *"But it is time for you to sleep."*

"God, not you too. Kutkha-"

"'Do you have the patience to wait until your mud settles and the water is clear?'" Kutkha recited the half-remembered verse in a softer voice. *"'Can you remain unmoving until the right action presents itself?'"*

"The *Tao Te Ching*." A pang shot through my chest. It reminded me of Vassily, alone in his room down the hall. "Verse Fifteen."

"Yes." Kutkha formed the word strangely, like an incantation.

"In other words, you're telling me to shut up."

There was no reply, save for a vague sense of amusement which might have been my own.

I had a feeling that my sleep was destined to be restless. The black sucked me under like thick mud, but I was lucid. I knew I was asleep when I could no longer hear the air conditioner or Binah's rumbling purr. The brief period of unconsciousness ended when I was ejected from nothing onto a dusty sandstone floor.

The dust in my nose felt very real as I snorted it out. The hallway was cool, and as I lifted my face, a perfumed wind danced across my skin and ruffled the downy hairs of my face.

Ahead of me was a doorway, hung with gauzy drapes that ballooned shallowly on the air. Beyond them was a darkness so deep it throbbed. A flight of stairs was behind me, and I knew without a doubt that they led up to the usual site of my lucid dreams, that childhood house with the haunted, empty rooms. I turned back to face the passage ahead. I could see nothing past the threshold, and for some reason, my throat clotted with fear.

I pushed myself to walk, pass the drapes, and enter into a blackness so thick it pressed into my nose and mouth like fingers. It sucked me into a bell-shaped chamber, a natural cavern with walls that ran with pure water. A plain silver ring was set into the polished black floor, thrumming like a dynamo core. A small woman with her wispy mousy hair up in a twist stood in the center, stripped to the waist, a proud cant to her jaw, neck, and shoulders. In one hand, she held a crescent sickle. In the other, she grasped my father's head.

"Nikla." My hands ached. I stepped to the edge of the circle in disbelief, my feet wooden and klutzy. "Mother... you're dead."

My mother was a tiny woman, tiny and thin. I looked more like her than I did my father, her prominent cheekbones and the same large, fine-bridged nose. My eyes were the same odd white-gray as my father's. Nikla's eyes were the blue of a summer sky, and they blazed with a radiant inner fire.

"*Oleksiy.*" She uttered my name thickly, stressing it in the way it was actually meant to be spelled, instead of the way I'd learned to write it at school. "It is time for you to choose."

"I already chose." My voice rang out, echoing. I tried to move towards her. When my toes touched the silver line, it rippled, halting my advance. "I told Kutkha that I agreed. What else is there?"

"Understanding." My mother's voice was as I'd always imagined it, light and dry and sweet. "The NO-thing X'd me. It wants to X you, too."

"Ex'd you?" I was rooted to the spot, staring at my father's head. "Who?"

Nikla threw the head on the floor in front of me, beyond the threshold of the circle. It landed with a dull crack on the stone.

Grigori Sokolsky was a bulldog of a man, even in death. His violet tongue lolled from behind his teeth. His eyes were missing, torn from his skull, and ichor gushed from the empty sockets. As I watched, Hebrew letters etched themselves across his brow, as if they were being drawn through the pallid flesh with the tip of a knife. אמת. *Truth*.

"DOG is GOD backwards," my mother said. "They're coming for you."

The black substance that leaked from Grigori's eyes gurgled, slopping out with sudden force. The Aleph turned to an X. The remaining letters formed a wholly different word. *Met*. Death.

My extremities were buzzing. I took a step backwards. "You need to stop speaking in riddles. I can't…"

The black stuff was creeping across the floor towards me in slow motion, crawling like a twist of worms. Grigori's mouth worked, fishlike, and then retched a great ball of the stuff, hacking it onto the marble. The stone was black, but in the presence of the creeping oil, the marble seemed colorful, nuanced and reflective. Wide-eyed, I backpedaled as it reached for me from the ground. The dead man's skull was beginning to dissolve and wheezed a tiny sigh as it crumpled. Metallic, insectoid things moved around inside the remains, stamping and needling one another as they strove to escape the brood.

"The Hunt." When I looked up, the woman who had been my mother no longer resembled her. This woman was tall and dark-skinned, the good red-brown of rich earth. Her hair was the brilliant white of burning magnesium, falling in a straight liquid pour down her body to her waist. I couldn't meet her eyes. They were a blue that had never existed in nature, impossible and terrifying. "The Hunt, Alexi, the endless question quest. They will X me. They X'd you!"

The black substance reared and lunged at me as I stumbled back and fled the room, back through the shrouded entrance and out into the sandstone hallway. It was strung in steely cobwebs, and in them hung chittering, shrieking insects. They had flat matte bodies and gaping pincer maws with needle-thin proboscises.

Let us X you, Alexi... X you X you X you X you X YOU X YOU X YOU X YOU!

I shouted at them wordlessly, covering my head. Things with too many legs fell on me, biting and sucking and feeding. I pulled one from my arm, and it came out with a thin plume of blood. The insect had my father's face. I crushed it with a snarl, barreling up the stairs. On my way past, I rubbed myself against the walls, the doorway, trying to scrape them off. "Fuck you both! You're dead! You're all dead!"

I nearly fell into the room at the apex of the stairs. It was no room I was familiar with in the house of my nightmares. It was long, like a chapel walkway, and candle-lit. At the other end was a crucifix. And I was nailed to it.

He was me, and not me. Bald, tattooed, incredibly powerful in the upper body, his legs withered, but I knew, somehow, that we were one and the same man. This other Alexi was eviscerated, shuddering around long iron spikes driven through his limbs. His mouth had been stuffed with his own intestines. He was chewing them. Slowly.

X you X you X you X you...

"You asked me to tell you everything." From behind me, a pair of feathered obsidian arms reached around my heaving chest in a surprisingly soft, sensual embrace. Kutkha hooked his obsidian talons painlessly through my chest, all the way to my heart. It didn't hurt. I felt it penetrate, and a thrill passed through me from nape to tailbone as I stared in fascinated disgust at the scene ahead. "This is the infection, Alexi. It X'd you before... will it X you again?"

I threw myself out of bed in the pitch darkness with a shout, skin still crawling with the sensation of biting insects. I promptly rediscovered my left knee as it buckled and sent me down hard to the floor.

Snarling in pain, I pulled myself up using the edge of the bed and stumbled to the light switch, knife in hand. I'd pulled it from the sheath without realizing what I'd done, clutching it as I recovered in the blurry light, fighting for breath. My forearms and neck were blotchy with hives. Binah was gone, hidden somewhere. "Binah? Vassily?"

There was no reply and no sound. I limped down to the second bedroom and cracked it open to look inside. "Vasya? Vassily?"

Vassily's room was empty. The air conditioner was off, the room warm and humid. I looked over the rumpled covers and the gathering pile of dirty laundry and felt a stirring of unease in the pit of my gut. A growing sense of wrongness haunted me through the length of the apartment on the way back to the kitchen.

A note had been left on the kitchen table. *"Gone to Mariya's. Don't fucking kill yourself."*

A tight, unpleasant feeling washed over me, another wave of anxiety-fueled déjà vu that had nothing to do with the note. I had about a second between the kick of intuition and the sound of someone banging heavily on my front door. One, two, three.

My eyes slid across, then down. I was still holding the knife. The silence hung heavily in the house for a thick heartbeat before the pounding resumed.

I knew better than to look through the peephole or open the door on the chain. Someone had already tried to kill me once this week, and I wasn't about to fall for one of my own tricks: knock on the door, put the muzzle to the wood, and fire two or three times. If the door was thin enough and the gun big enough, it was a cheap way to do a fast job.

I padded down the hall slowly on stocking feet and swung quietly into the doorway of the den. Ducked down. "Who is it?"

For a moment, there was no reply. Then, a thick, wet voice spoke from the other side of the wooden barrier.

"Yuri. Yuri Beretzniy

CHAPTER 14

My eyes widened. I knew the man's voice well enough, but hesitated before I went for the door.

"Hold on, Yuri. Give me... give me a moment," I called out and backed into the den. I folded the knife back into its grip. It didn't feel big enough. I needed shoes, a real weapon. A gun. There was a spare pistol in my desk drawer.

I went to my study. There, my gaze fell on the sledgehammer in its case. The iron gleamed dully in the light from outside, and briefly, I found myself torn between the hammer and the gun. The hammer had an intimidation factor the gun did not, but I wasn't as confident it would protect me if something went south. I lifted the lid, hand hovering over the haft before I changed my mind and went for the desk drawer and the .38 Special inside. I picked it up, checked the clip and the safety, and jammed it under the waistband of my pants.

Thump, thump, thump. Out in front of the apartment, Yuri's fist pounded on the wood.

"Coming!" I started back towards the front door, a tremor running through my arms. It was inexplicable. I wasn't scared, was I? Of Yuri? Unnerved, maybe, by his sudden reappearance after he'd been missing for three days. Despite my self-conviction, my palms were slippery against my gloves as I fumbled with the chain on the door and haltingly drew it across.

Outside, Yuri loomed down over me like a coffin on its heel. The old wolf was older than Nic, which meant he was cresting his early 60s. He was enormous, the kind of hoary man that could pound the shit out of thirty-year-old prizefighters in the ring without breaking a sweat. Now, his heavy shoulders were hunched in towards his chest, his hands buried in his pockets. His skin was clammy and pale.

"Yuri. You look... dreadful." I was, for a moment, bereft of words. "Where have you been?"

"Long time explaining." His voice caught and clicked weirdly, like he was talking through a mouthful of soggy bread and thumbtacks. There were awkward, painful pauses between his words. "Can I sit... down?"

Details filed into my awareness in seconds. The bruises under his eyes. The dried spittle at the corner of his lips. The coat he was wearing was too heavy for the summer heat. My nape prickled. "Perhaps. Tell me where you've been."

"Came back to talk about Vincent." He finally looked down at me then, and I recoiled slightly from the door. Yuri's eyes were normally dark, the whites a little yellow from hard years of prison hooch and nicotine. Now, they were black—a blackness that sucked in light and didn't return it. No reflection, no life, no anything. For a moment, they held me captive with the siren promise of knowledge. I knew somehow that Yuri, or the thing that had once been Yuri, now held more knowledge than my own curious mind could withstand.

Letting him in felt like a bad idea, but the mystery was irresistible. I licked my lips, throat suddenly dry, and opened the door to let him pass. "Shoes on the rack, please."

Yuri crossed the threshold. He didn't take off his shoes, and my brief captivation disappeared. Honestly. I really hated it when people didn't take their shoes off.

The huge man lumbered to the kitchen, turning his head one way, then the other. He stopped, neck craned, and stared at the icebox section of the refrigerator. The icebox. The seal was still in the tin chalice, in the icebox. My heart rate leapt.

"I've been underground." Yuri didn't look at me as he took his seat, shuffling heavily into a chair at the kitchen table. The table was a small, square thing, no bigger than a card table, and barely sat Vassily and me. Yuri, sitting side-on with his elbow braced down, dwarfed it. "Underground. I figured you might be interested in some new work."

"That depends on the nature of the work." I stayed standing. "I assume you don't want coffee?"

"No." Yuri swiveled his face towards me just as I was about to step in through the door. The look in the other man's eyes stopped me. "We have the kind of work you want. The kind you really want. None of this underpaid Girl Friday bullshit."

"Who's 'we'?" In the closeness of the kitchen, Yuri smelled like alcohol. Not liquor, like vodka or whiskey, but pure alcohol. The cold, nose-stinging smell of preservative. Surreptitiously, I rubbed my fingers together and pinched my own thigh. No, I wasn't still dreaming. "The Manellis?"

"Manelli." Yuri ground the word out like a woodchipper. It could have been agreement or just echolalia. "Hell no. I was sent t-to make you an offer. The kind that suits a true magus."

Now there was an expression you didn't hear every day. I stared at Yuri intently, trying to pick up anything I could. He wasn't right, but he wasn't... anything. I was beginning to mistrust things with a lack of aura, and I was beginning to think I'd made a mistake letting him into my house. "That seems reasonable. You have three minutes to make your pitch."

The big man looked up lazily with his void-black eyes and laid one of his hands on the table. "Power. Instruction. A position of leadership. And an out from the Organizatsiya, and the *geas* that Sergei has on the whole damn thing."

A creeping sensation ran up through my spine. I remembered the dream, though I could not recall the face of the pale-skinned, white-haired woman in the circle. I did remember the last stark image before rising: my mouth stuffed full of my own entrails. "You're not Yuri. Yuri knows nothing about these things."

"I do now," Yuri said. The words seemed to carry a weight to them, wielded like a fist through the thickness of his tongue. "And I'll tell you this, Lexi. You're so powerful that you could become a god."

I was rendered speechless. It was partly the awful cliché, but it was also because the thought had never genuinely occurred to me. I wanted to be better at my Art. Who wouldn't? Godhood was never on the agenda. "Why on earth would I want to be a god?"

"Men like you are either masters or slaves. Most of 'em are slaves. That's why the Vigiles take kids with the gift, Lexi. It's why operations have spooks, and don't let them out of their sight. You don't want to stay here." In that moment, Yuri sounded more like his old self, halting voice and all. "Living and d-dying... under someone like Sergei? Lev? They all think you belong to them."

The words hooked in my sense of pride. I tried reaching back inside, towards Kutkha, but I felt nothing there. It was as if I were walled off from him, left with nothing other than the distant sense of beating wings. "I have on good authority that gods don't exist."

"They do. Men become gods. Jehovah? He was a war leader and a spook. Alexander the Great? Jason and the fleece? Heroes and mages, the lot of 'em." Yuri's black eyes bored into me. "Just like Carmine."

My eyes narrowed. "How do you know Carmine?"

"Maybe he got the same offer. Maybe he said 'yes.' He was tired of being somebody's bitch. What about you?"

"I'm no one's 'bitch'," I replied, crisply.

"Psh. You're Sergei's bitch. I watched you grow up right into his design, kid. Grisha's skinny little weirdo, accidentally sorted out onto the conveyor belt for fighting cocks before he got thrown into the grinder with the rest of the chicks."

"Sergei is coming back to Brighton Beach," I said. "He will likely name Vassily Avtoritet, and I will be his second."

Yuri leaned in. The prickling was worsening, ringing cold bells through my nerves. There was something wrong about Yuri's skin. It was distended and tight, and when I looked down, I noticed his tattooed hands were bloated and puffy. "Kid, they haven't even made you a captain. They think you don't have the experience. Killing people doesn't put you in line for anything except a bullet between the eyes when the big cats vote you're too out of control. That's just cold hard reality. Did you ever wonder what Sergei sees in you?"

Of course I did. Numerous men had been born in or on the periphery of the Organization, and of all of them, Sergei had selected me and Vassily. I have one clear memory of him from my childhood: a memory of being hoisted up in tattooed hands the size of Christmas hams, looking down into his broad, beaming face and bushy beard. Sergei was as much a Slav as Vassily and I were, but he had red hair: red hair and violet eyes. I remember looking down into those twinkling purple-blue irises, understanding even then that they were full of cold humor and equally cold assessment. When he was here, he'd been a shadow over my shoulders, always watching. Every school report, every play, every equestrian competition. He watched everything with indulgent, predatory patience, rewarding the good and being outwardly disappointed by the bad. The same way you trained a dog.

"And how would you know?" I asked.

"Son, I was the first guy to bring heroin here from the 'Stans. Me and Nic. We took a convoy of poppy over the border all the way to a ship in Karachi." Yuri exhaled, and his throat buzzed with phlegm. "I knew Sergei before you were a gleam in your daddy's eye. Man is a Class-A shitbag. A real ringmaster. He'd fuck you with a razor blade for your jacket if he wanted it."

I glared at him in sullen, offended silence.

"I know what Sergei sees in you. Same thing he sees in all t-the rest of us poor motherfuckers." Yuri grinned. "Machine parts."

The undeniable truth of Yuri's words made me pause. I rubbed my hands on my thighs, leaning away. My fingers were stinging with salt, rubbed raw within the illusory security of their casings.

"Tiny, fragile, cheap... machine parts." Yuri's voice dropped to a brittle hiss. "Itty bitty. And there's lots of you. Lots of Alexis. Lots of Yuris. You're already a slave. Just like your mother."

"You don't know anything about my mother." That remark snapped the growing hypnotic fugue short. I reached back and pulled the gun free from my waistband.

"I know more than you do." Yuri's soulless eyes burned under the fluorescent lights of the kitchen. "You think your dad was her only man before she capped herself?"

"SHUT UP!" I barked.

A weird, choked sound bubbled up from Yuri's throat. It took me a moment to realize he was laughing. "She hated him. Hated you. She hated *us*. The Organization."

Shaking, I raised the pistol in a teacup grip. My arms, back, and stomach were taut with rage.

"Yeah. Get angry." Yuri sat back but didn't otherwise move. He didn't give two shits about the gun. "Think about it. You get t-to choose what Sergei did with you? Choose what you were born into? How you turned out?"

My nostrils trembled as I drew a deep, furious breath.

"Had your school paid up, car paid up, all sponsored... so you could do this. Pull a gun on the guy tellin' you how things work. You're a slave, kid. You joined the system, and they got you good."

It was true. It was all true. Sergei had put Vassily and me through The Knox School together, bought our cars. After my mother's funeral, Sergei had bought my first horse. They weren't gifts—they were investments. We'd both known it and worked hard out of gratitude and obligation and maybe more than a little fear. Our patron had checked us into college and assigned us our subjects. Finance. Business. He wanted white-collar leaders with a taste for comfortable living and big money. I had done everything he wanted—except one thing.

"So, you tell me, Alexi. Where'd it get you? Your loyalty?"

I lifted my chin. My instincts screamed at me to disengage, but pride wouldn't let me. I'd taken so much shit from the other *muzhiki* in this place. "I've got everything I need."

"You work like a dog, live in a shitty apartment, and half the Organization thinks you should be put down. There ain't no respect for spooks in this place, kid. I know the guys at work, what they say about you." Yuri didn't blink. "Rumor is you're a faggot."

"Say that again." Every muscle in my body trembled. It couldn't be true. My finger tightened on the trigger. In the ensuing silence, the small click seemed very, very loud.

"Faggot." He sounded it out long and slow, like I hadn't heard the first time. "You don't believe me? Ask Nic. Everyone thinks you make out like you're a big tough guy after killing your dad to hide it. But it doesn't have to be that way," Yuri replied. "You want your soul to walk beside you like it was real, like Carmine? You can do that. Want to learn how to walk on water? It's possible. Create gold? Skullfuck people from across the room? You can. I can sense it, Lexi. You woke up. You're one of the big boys now."

There was one thing that Yuri didn't know - and it was something that no one besides Sergei, Vassily and I ever discussed. I had opted out of my Economics degree and studied Psychology at college, without telling my *Pakhun*. He'd shot out my knee for disobeying him, but he let me graduate. That choice had been my one act of defiance against him, and against the system so eloquently laid out by the man in front of me. That training allowed me to keep an objective distance from Yuri's words. His speech tugged half-known feelings and old bitterness, but the rational, affectless part of my mind, the clinical observer I'd cultivated over so many years, ticked over each part of the advertisement. He had, indeed, spun me a sales pitch. The hook. The problem. The soothing empathy, and the inevitable solution. He was playing the Prisoner's Dilemma against me... that would be the next stage, if I listened to him. The only reward was paranoia, and eventual self-destruction.

"Fine. Then tell me where Vincent is." I lowered my face, as if sighting down along a horn.

"Preparing," Yuri wheezed. "To become a master of the knowledge of good and evil. We have a fruit from the T-Tree, Alexi. *The* Tree."

"As in... the Tree of Genesis? In Eden?" The God talk was definitely beginning to get to me. My trigger finger loosened again, but only slightly. "Yggdrasil? What tree? I'm not religious."

"I ain't talking about religion. I'm talking about reality." Yuri's face flushed. The slight increase in energy made his skin even more sallow, bringing out the purplish veins of his cheeks. His voice became clearer. "Vincent has joined us. He is the Hound, and he will harvest the fruit. It's here, in New York. You could be there. With us."

"And who, if I might ask, is 'us'?" I asked, cracking my neck.

Yuri's grin spread. "Wouldn't you like to know?"

"You know... Yuri, I never owned a television," I said, moving back slightly towards the door. "Partially because moving pictures make me queasy, and partially because I really, really hate advertisements."

Yuri's gaze fixed, and all the sick pleasure drained from his face. "I'm not lying, Lexi. You'd be the most powerful man in the Organization."

"Maybe I don't want to be the most powerful man in the Organization," I said. It felt like a weak retort.

Yuri dropped his face slightly, lips parted. Whatever was looking at me wasn't the terse ex-soldier I had known since my youth. Whatever was looking at me was not human. "Bullshit. If it didn't interest you, you'd have shot me half an hour ago. And besides... your soul's already injured. You think you can make it on your own with a gimpy Neshamah?"

Injured? My eyes narrowed, but his words caused an unmistakable, involuntary flush of fear. Injured? How could Kutkha be injured? My expression flattened. "I think you're wasting my time."

"You talk like you got time. You are... still weak." Yuri's mouth drooped open farther, and the thick buzzing sound in his voice began to intensify.

"And... to what 'Master' do you answer to, Yuri Juriovich?" My eyes tracked a trickle of pitch as it wound past his teeth, down his chin, slippery and slick. Shit.

Yuri's eyes flicked up slowly. "NO-thing. He sends his regards."

My nose and throat flooded with a scent like rotting sugar, like molasses-drowned bloated bodies left out in the sun. The stench was overwhelming; it filled my head with sudden buzzing hatred. Yuri's stare was relentless. Dizziness washed over me in a wave, and as my vision contracted, the other man's eyes deepened, distending inwards. The buzzing turned to gnashing and screeching, and the holes of Yuri's eyes spread into mouths of fanged black teeth.

Something hit me from behind: Hit hard enough to send me staggering, and then clung on with four sets of very sharp, very strong little claws. Binah. I shouted in surprise and pain and stumbled forward with the sensory shock, but it broke the trance.

"Banish it!" Kutkha struggled past whatever arcana had been spun around my mind from within and shrieked in a voice that filled my head with white noise. *"Now!"*

My finger convulsed on the trigger. One bullet went wide and spranged off the counter. The other two hit and took Yuri through the head, spraying black ichor behind him onto the sink and the row of potted plants on the windowsill. They hissed, shriveling, as I pumped another round into his chest. Binah detached herself from my back and scrambled away at the sound of gunfire while I stared ahead, breathing hard through my mouth. It was full of the scent of viscera, reflexively emptied bowels, and the old, half-remembered smell of another kitchen, another death.

"I said banish, not shoot!" Kutkha was panicking. Panicking?

"I don't exactly have time to go and get my chalk and Lotus Wand, asshole!" The corpse lolled in the chair, arms loose. Yuri's arms hadn't finished swinging when he slumped, spilling black fluid onto the tabletop. The goop turned into larval branches of living ooze. I backed away, steps punctuated by the anticlimactic blips of each silenced round. I hit two more times, and on the fourth impact, thin, whiplike tentacles burst forth from each bullet wound and every open orifice. They hauled Yuri to his feet like a marionette, kicking the chair back and the table towards me. I swung around the edge of the doorway. The table hit with a splintering crash, flinging slime across the floor. The worms. I couldn't let them get to my skin. "Fuck!"

"This is why we don't shoot the DOG, Alexi!"

I pressed back against the wall, scraping them from my clothes as I tried to aim with one hand. They were burning through my clothes. As I fumbled, half a dozen thick, prehensile tentacles whipped past the shattered doorjamb, and I fired blindly before remembering that the gun was useless. I threw it with a shout and lunged backwards down the hall, only to topple as something struck me around the ankle. The impact of the floor was more immediate than the grip of the lashing thing that wrenched me down. Struggling, twisting around to my back, I had just enough time to see myself being pulled towards a barbed starfish maw, larger than my torso, that blossomed from the ruin of Yuri's face.

CHAPTER 15

I caught the doorjamb as I flew past, kicking with my other foot as Yuri dragged me back into the kitchen. More fleshy limbs snapped around my chest, thighs, and calves, forcing my legs together as I fought and clawed and yelled into the darkened corridor ahead. I was hoisted nearly upside down off the ground. My knife tumbled from my pocket, clattering to the floor. The switchblade popped open, and just as the wooden doorjamb creaked and tore under my fingers, I lunged for the knife.

My feet hit something fleshy and wet. More barbed tendrils shot out from the screeching mouth, ripping fabric and flesh and wringing a harsh scream from my throat. I swung up and stabbed frantically at the biting tentacles that were feeding me feet-first into the gaping toothy void. The blade struck home, and the monstrosity shrieked once, then louder as I drove the point in through another tentacle, an eye, a small fanged mouth. The wounds oozed and discolored in the moment before I was flung into the hallway, where only years of horse-riding and training for falls saved me from breaking my neck. I tucked and rolled, skittered out across the floor, and stopped just shy of the front door. My knee went out from under me when I struggled to rise, pitching me down.

Framed by the doorway, Yuri's limbs ruptured: the black fleshy thing, half-formed, went to the ground like a malformed reptile and charged, umbrella maw agape. It was going to eat me, and if it got me, it would get Binah, and then Vassily when he returned. I rolled up with a snarl and pushed off from my good leg, blade first. Fear turned to rage, then to bloodlust as I leaped on its back. We rolled, tangled across the floor, and I stabbed and stabbed as it tried to twist and skewer me in turn. We crashed into a wall, into the rack of shoes, up against the front door. The knife wounds wracked the black flesh, causing it to shrivel and wrinkle. Teeth and drilling mouthparts flashed in my face in the gloom. Wherever its blood touched me, my skin burned.

The horror screamed and lashed, relenting as the mounting wounds caused it to weaken. I kicked it off with rage-fueled strength. The creature skidded back, the knife embedded in its back, and lurched against a wall as I scrambled up. It blocked the way to the bedroom. I backed into the den, throwing what I could at it as it stalked me into the room, towards the study. The radio. Books. Pillows. The case with my father's hammer was still open. It was all I had at this end of the house. Tendrils of sick flesh flopped and writhed through the entry, smashing it all to the sides of the room as it careened forward.

I pulled the hammer free and swung it down, straight into the distended snapping jaws that were lunging from the center of the fleshy-lobed flower of its face. The fifteen-pound head sunk straight into the creature's body; it made a gagging, sucking sound as the air around us throbbed. A wind that penetrated the remains of my clothing, my hair, and skin pulsed out from the haft, through my hands and teeth and spine, and then what had once been Yuri's head exploded in a wet welter of milk-like slime that drenched me, the shelves, the walls, and the desk. The corpse stumbled forward another step, convulsing, and crashed to the floor.

It began to break apart. The remains of Yuri's corpse split and divided, evaporating as it frantically tried to cling to unlife. I jabbed the hammer towards it, and the matter flinched back from it.

"How..." Heaving for breath, I answered my own question before I'd even really asked it. I knew how. I should have realized earlier. The hammer was forged in the 40s, taken from the Kolyma goldmines, and it had gone with my father across Siberia, slipped with him through the Iron Curtain in Germany, sailed across the Atlantic, then become his constant companion in America. He had killed many people with this hammer. He'd used it to terrorize his hits, his wife and his son, and the business end of this weapon was the last thing Grigori Sokolsky had ever seen. It was a sacrificial tool... it had built up some kind of charge that was anathema to this thing.

I hefted it over my shoulder and stared coldly at the floor as the last of Yuri's body disintegrated. Among the scraps of fabric and shriveling jelly lay a silver metal disk the size of a flattened bottle top, inscribed with another sigil I did not recognize. In terms of its workmanship, it was nearly identical to the one we'd found at Dock Number Four. I crouched and turned it over with the point of the slagged knife. On the other side were three familiar Hebrew letters. *Amet*.

My mouth drew into a one-sided, sloping grimace. A golem. Yuri had been turned into a golem. Someone was having their little joke.

I was in over my head. Vassily was right. There's a rule of boxing, which is that you never let the other guy push you around the ring in a match. You had to keep control, even if that meant faking out to lead the other guy into thinking he had the upper hand. I was the one being led around right now: my opponents were juiced up and experienced, and I was not keeping up with the blows. Yuri's words had struck me low. I'd always known the things he was talking about in some part of myself, but it was the first time I'd ever heard anyone say them aloud. I thought back to the discussion in Lev's living room. The way he had effortlessly induced shame.

No, not shame. Guilt. Even an unrepentant killer could be controlled by guilt, if he had been raised in it, steeped in it, like a foal trained to the bit and bridle on its way to adulthood. But maybe it wasn't just guilt that kept me here, working for Lev and Sergei, fighting for Vassily, striving in my own, small, dark way to serve the people I'd built my life around. My community. Maybe it was fear. They didn't respect me, thought I was... deviant. But they were all I had.

Wearily, I looked around at the mess of my study. Before whatever happened next, I had to destroy these sigils.

The kitchen smelled sweet and sick, and my plants were dead. The oily black liquid had dried up and vanished, like the rest of Yuri. I double-checked the room uneasily, and only when I was certain nothing was left did I set up the gas burner and get my tools. I found Binah under the bed, the preferred refuge of any cat. I was going to have to pick her up an extra can of salmon or something, given that she'd just saved my life.

I set up a crucible over the burner and drew a small circle around the stove with salt and chalk. The crucible was used to melt the seal I'd pulled from Yuri's remains, which I poured into a makeshift mold made from a jar lid. When I turned the small blackened metal ingot out, it was unremarkable, faceless. Nothing was left of its magic.

The tin chalice with Frank's seal was still in the freezer. I pursed my lips as I looked into the chalice and found the ice cracked and crumbly, the texture of a snow cone. It was brown, the water rimed with veins of corruption. I dried the unharmed sigil off before setting it on the crucible, where I watched it intently. It sat there and did not stir.

So much for that. I rubbed my jaw, turned the heat to full blast, and when that failed, picked the caster up in a pair of tongs and held it directly over the flame. It didn't even soften, in a wholly un-lead–like fashion.

"Well." I blinked, swallowing, and set it back in the cup. It entered the water with a hiss of spent heat. "That's not good."

"The energy attached to it must be absorbed or banished," Kutkha replied. "And either you must do it, or another Phitometrist."

I glared down at it, watching as air bubbles gathered around its surface. "I can assume a Phitometrist is someone capable of manipulating Phi. You've never explained to me what that is, Kutkha."

"You don't have the language for me to describe it to you."

How many languages did a man need? I already spoke three. I sighed and lifted my eyes to the ceiling. "Can you give me a rough approximation?"

An image flashed into my mind. I saw myself in a mirror that faced a long hallway of mirrors, each one reflecting my face back to infinity. I reached out to my reflection, and my hand entered the pane as if it were a fluid. Silver crept over my fingers, up my arm, then plunged painlessly through my chest. All of them. It connected every mirror in the illusion, linking my many selves into a chain which drew forward and back as far as the eye could see.

"Does that help?" Kutkha asked wryly.

I jerked on my feet as the vision passed, rubbed my eyes, and paused to regain my sense of place. Irritably, I reached out and turned off the burner. "Not really. And unfortunately, I don't know anyone who could do what you describe, except perhaps Lev, and Lev... Lev isn't powerful enough, is he?"

"No. His Mass is small and his Pressure is weak."

Mass, another familiar word in an unfamiliar context.

I took a box of salt and sprinkled the mineral into a new flask of water. "I can't just leave it like this. Whoever summoned this demon is using this artifact to spy on us. It must be Carmine. He summoned those dogs, or possessed them, or whatever it was he did. He could do this."

"I don't know. The Phitonic spoor has passed, and your foe already knows where we are," Kutkha said. My Neshamah's voice was as hazy as a silk shroud around my ears. *"One more day will not make a difference. Study and learn. Rest and recover, and we will try to track the summoner when they reveal themselves."*

He was right. I needed to find the symbol engraved on the caster and puzzle it out. Whatever it was, it would tell me something about the mage who enchanted it and how it could be used as an improvised tracking device.

First things first, though. A quick cold shower, then coffee. I poured the cold coffee from this morning's pot back through the machine, added more coffee in a new filter, and set it to brew jet fuel. Binah rediscovered her courage and came out to join me, purring as she threw herself at my shins.

"The feline enigma," I mused aloud. She had broken the trance Yuri had worked over me and, maybe, saved my life. Was she a familiar? Did she have kitty Stockholm syndrome? "What defines a familiar, Kutkha? Versus a normal but precocious pet?"

"As I told you, a soul has many branches, many Ruachim," my Neshamah replied. *"Not all of the branches are human."*

Binah made several complex murring and mewing sounds, the language of the Siamese, as she drew a figure eight of shed fur around my damp legs.

With coffee in hand, I gathered a few of my favorite old grimoires at my desk. I knew I'd seen the elements of the sigil design somewhere, but I couldn't remember where. This told me it was probably in one of the ones I'd read and paid attention to, but not studied in depth.

"So, let's say there were two of these enchanted lead casters. The other eye was ripped open and the caster removed," I said, sitting at my desk. "The question is, why the demonic seal AND the casters? Why not just the seal? And what do these things represent?"

Some mythologies had the dead sent along with false eyes made out of metals and precious stones, the better to guide them to their destination in the higher spheres. Greek and Egyptian funerary rites, to name two, but there was nothing holy about Frank Nacari's death. I thought back: the other empty eye socket had foamy spittle in it. Carmine's spirit hounds hadn't slavered, but what about the dog in the alley? Dogs were Carmine's creatures. If he used dogs as spies on the streets, he could have had one take the other caster: that would explain the gnawed face, and the car bomb. But why raid his own murder scene?

"All right. Assuming Carmine's torture didn't induce latent schizophrenia and I am not actually talking to a traumatic hallucination, I'm going to suggest, Kutkha, that you know a lot more about the operation of magic than I do," I said aloud. "So, start from the beginning. I need to understand why Carmine is so good at what he does, and why I am not. I need to learn how to get better. Preferably without selling my soul for the bargain."

"Fortunately for you, I don't come with a price tag." Kutkha sniffed, as much as a disembodied voice could sniff. *"There are many different kinds of Phitometrists, or mages, as you call them. Phitometry is just the ability to manipulate Phi under the pressure of your will. So the better question would be 'what kind of mage do I want to be?'"*

Wonderful. My conscious soul really was some kind of wiseass. "What kinds of mages are there? I was under the impression that you follow the rules, draw your figures correctly and speak the right words, and do whatever you please."

"You will always be limited by the rules that you follow," Kutkha said. *"The correct figures have power of their own, but even the most dynamic is still a static object. The only things you find in ceremony are comfort and pride in how clever and learned you are relative to the common man, my Ruach."*

I grimaced and pulled across the first book, *De Nigromancia*, a late Middle Ages tome dedicated to safety during demonic summoning. "So, tell me about these types of magi and how they work their magic, and I will summarily ignore five thousand years of Occult history to listen to a voice inside my head."

"An excellent idea," Kutkha said cheerfully. In my mind, I saw him: the ghostly raven from the warehouse dungeon,

perched on an arced span of gold in a darkened chamber. *"There are mages like Carmine, obviously. Inotropists."*

"Inotropy. That's a medical term," I said, turning to the table of contents. It was Middle English, and not terribly well organized. "An inotrope is an agent that alters the force or energy of muscular contractions."

"It is. And the Inotropist is an agent that increases or decreases the pressure of Phi in a local area, pumping it like a heart. They create fire, force and friction, manipulate gravity, and suchlike," Kutkha said. *"It causes inflammation and tends to harden the color of Phi in a given area to red."*

"Phi has different colors?" I asked, absently.

"All the colors of the prism, and then some. The basic spectrum is from violet to blue, then silver, white, glass. Red is a coarse energy, and common in this world. Violet is dirty Phi, used in Pravamancy. Demonic summoning, disease creation, corruption, leeching. Little better than pus from the skin of GOD, and just as likely to make me sick, if one was to imbibe too much of it."

I tapped my desktop with the end of a pen, bouncing it off the edge of the leather trim, while my eyes skimmed rows of neatly drawn circles, symbols, and spells in *De Nigromancia*. "I'll take that as a hint. And the others?"

"Orange is the color of deception and horror, the color of Illusionists and tricksters," Kutkha said. *"Yellow is the color of the mind and of time, which are both forms of mortal perception, and the mages who specialize in such things are called Mentalists and Temporalists."*

"Like Lev," I said.

"Like Lev. Green is the color of life, and mages who use this subtle form of energy are called Biomancers. This includes the raising of the dead, the revival and reanimation of corpses," Kutkha continued. *"Which I might add is a practice that is neither good nor*

evil in the greater scheme of things, though HuMans as a rule fixate on it as the height of diablerie."

"I see. And anything else?" The book was not looking particularly promising. *De Nigromancia* was a good tome for information on summoning, more advanced than the Goetia, but the symbol was not to be found. I set it aside.

"Blue is the color of Hierognosis, and the Hierognostic specialist is a Hierophant. Precognition, theurgy, the creation of wards and the rending of them. They guard the mystery. They create understanding."

"I see." That sounded a little like my own magic, but for some reason, the thought made me uncomfortable. Wardbreaking, déjà vu, dreams so real I woke with the sensation of sand in my nose. Maybe it was the ease with which Kutkha categorized it. "And how does one… pick up a specialization? Say I wanted to change mine and take up another."

"Each works according to their nature. The substance of a thing will dissolve into its own roots. HuMans are unique, in that they may have a dual or tripartite nature, and they may have talent in more than one area of magic. But each requires time to master."

"Huh." I picked up the next book on the stack, a thin volume with a pomegranate tree in bloom on the front cover. I opened it and flipped the pages until I finished the text, then skipped forward to flip through the pictures. "That seems simpler than I expected."

"Such matters are narrow, but very deep. Reality is often like that. Mortals feel the need to complicate things," Kutkha replied. *"Now look down."*

"What?" I glanced at the page I'd just opened. It was a column of planetary tables, the familiar symbols of each of the seven classical planets used in Astrology. They were set against horizontal rows of squiggly sigils, twelve in each row.

They seemed to move and shift on the page. For a moment, I wasn't certain what it was Kutkha was trying to point out to me—and then I saw it. The entire row of symbolic components for the Sun. They had been worked into one design.

"Wait... no. These are angelic binding symbols. These have nothing to do with demons." But there it was. Mesh them together, and you had the bell-and-spiral shape of the sigil I had found in Frank Nacari's eye. "The mage that murdered Nacari... he wasn't summoning Aamon at all."

"A red herring, as you might say," Kutkha added.

"So whoever did this made it look like an over-the-top Goetic rite to mislead... so they clearly expected to be dealing with another mage." Me? Were they expecting to have to contend with me? I wasn't nearly powerful enough to be worth that amount of effort. And if they'd been trying to summon some kind of angelic being, what about the smell? The unhallow, rotten strangeness? I mashed a hand through my hair and frowned down at the page. None of this made any sense.

I glanced at the clock and froze. Ten a.m.? When had it become ten a.m.? And it was Monday. Vassily wasn't home, and... he was supposed to meeting his parole officer at one.

"Goddammit, Vassily." I hesitated before marking the page and picking up the phone. Why did this sort of thing always fall on me to remember? He was an adult man, and I was almost exhausted beyond caring. Almost. Not enough to stop me from jamming the handset between shoulder and ear and dialing Mariya's number.

It rang several times before she picked up. "Maritka, it's Alexi. I was wondering if Vassily had left already? He has an appointment to go to, and hasn't arrived home yet."

"What?" Mariya sounded harried, like she had just rushed to speak to me. "Vassily isn't here, Alexi."

My heart turned cold. "He isn't? Did he leave already? He said he was visiting you."

"No, I haven't seen him today." In the background, I heard the laughter of children. Mariya's sometimes-boyfriend had two, a little girl and even younger boy. The sound carried through the handset, piercing the silence between Mariya and me. She sighed. "Alexi, you should know by now. Everything that comes out of that man's mouth is horseshit. He's probably at Vanya's."

The apologetic tone in her voice didn't soften the knowledge that Vassily had lied to me. He'd never lied to me before like this, not about his whereabouts. "Thank you. I'll check there."

"Brothers. Oy." She groaned before she hung up.

Vanya's phone rang out. With numb fingers, I tried a second time, stabbing the pen into a sticky note pad that was soon full of dark pinpoint holes. After five rings, a blurry voice I didn't immediately recognize picked up. "Whozat?"

"I want to speak with Vassily," I said, tonelessly.

There was a pause. "Who wants to know?"

When the speaker shifted from flippancy to suspicion, I was able to place the name to the voice. It was Mikhail, Lev's bodyguard. The one who had been at the scene with Nacari. "Mikhail, it's Alexi. You need to put Vassily on the phone."

"Oh, uh... hey, Molotchik. Fuck, man, he's, uh... he's still lying down," Mikhail slurred. "Yeah. In his room."

I could practically smell the alcohol on the other man's breath over the phone, and my lip curled in disgust. Drunk. Vassily would be drunk, too. "Throw some ice on him. I'll be there in twenty minutes to pick him up."

"Whoa, hang on, man. You might want to give him a whi—"

I slammed the receiver down and whirled up from the chair on my heel, storming off through the house to collect a bucket, and Vassily's best interview suit.

My dreams, invaded by the ghosts of the past. My home, invaded by a demon. And now, my best friend, lying to me. I wanted to kill something, but there was nothing to kill except Vassily... and I had a sneaking suspicion that he was already well on the road to killing himself.

CHAPTER 16

Vanya's house wasn't Vanya's actual residence, the split-level with his wife and children and Great Dane. When the *muzhiki* of the Organization said they were going to Vanya's, they meant the Coney Island penthouse with the wraparound windows, fully stocked bar, and generously proportioned callgirls.

I was so angry I was running a fever. A few seconds after I banged on the door, I heard a shuffling, lurching rustle from inside. An unfamiliar blonde woman answered, dressed in nothing but one of Vanya's enormous striped business shirts. Her eyes were red-rimmed. She had dried flakes of lipstick stuck to her lips. "Allo?"

"They're expecting me." The woman's shirt was open. I looked down sharply, staring at her vivid pink toenails. "Here to pick up Vassily."

She laughed a shrill laugh that was the same color as her nail polish and let me pass. "Vasyl? Vasyl is no good, my friend. He bombed it *out*."

I ground my teeth on the way past, scoping the room. Every single light in the house was on, the TV was on but tuned to a dead channel, the screen humming and blank. The fancy granite breakfast counter was cluttered with bottles, cigarette butts, and empty takeout containers. Mikhail lay face-down on the white leather sofa in his briefs. He still had the cordless phone in his hand, and peered up at me as I went by. "Sh'Lexi! You wan' Vvvasya? He's, he's..."

That was as far as he got before he had to lie back down and think about it some more. Fortunately, I already knew where Vassily would be.

The guest bedroom, like the rest of Vanya's house, was a study in Orientalist fetishism, with rice paper screens and fake silk and geisha dolls. Vanya was an Eric Lustbader fan, and despite being a racist slob, he had a thing for Japanese decor. His house was a temple to mafiya excess, wealth he gained through managing AEROMOR on Sergei's behalf. The guest bedroom was usually clean, in a sleazy, tasteless sort of way, but I was aghast to find it close and dank. Bags of trash were piled next to a dusty paper screen. The bed was unmade, empty whiskey bottles and beer cans scattered next to the dresser. The red silk sheets were dark with sweat.

The en suite door was open and occupied. I turned into the doorway and stopped, lips pressed together in a bloodless line as my gaze flicked from one point to the next. Vassily, naked and half-sprawled over the edge of the bathtub. A half-finished bottle of pepper horilka spilled beside him. A razor, powder residue, and an empty cellophane twist left on the lid of the toilet.

My stomach twisted in a very unpleasant way at the sour smell of vomit and alcohol. My hands ached, fingertips burning against the leather pads. I went over and nudged Vassily with a toe. A thin groan peeled from his lips, and the corners of my eyes began to tic.

"You *idiot*." I hauled Vassily's head back by the hair, pulled my glove off and jammed my fingers in against his pulse. He was alive, at least, but his heartbeat was thready and quick. "You goddamn *idiot*. Where the fuck did you get coke? Why the fuck are you doing coke?!"

"Lekshiii?" Vassily looked right through me. His nose was bloody, his eyes huge in a very pale, very sweaty face.

"Yes. Lexi, you insufferable, lying *moron*." My voice rose in anger. I should have been gentle, but I couldn't bring myself to baby him. I hauled Vassily back by his underarms and propped him against the side of the spa tub, fighting down the very real urge to kick him in the teeth. Instead, I pulled the glove back on and started the water to wash away the mess in the tub. "*Ka'kovo 'hooya?* What the *fuck* do you think you're doing?! What'll Mariya say to this? Don't think I won't tell her."

Vassily cringed away from my voice. He tried to reply, but as the words formed, so did the next round of spew. I clapped a hand on his skull and turned his head just in time, pointing his mouth at the porcelain so he puked violently into Vanya's fancy hot tub.

Between the noise and the smell and the fatigue from the night before, I was going to go off like an atom bomb. I left him to purge and stalked back out into the bedroom, looking for something to keep me busy besides homicide, anything to take the edge off the boiling, seething anger. I ended up stripping the bedsheets, taking the trash out into the kitchen, and putting the room in order, cleaning until the retching stopped. Only then did I go back inside the bathroom. Vassily was lying on his side on the floor, back turned towards me. I could see the fragile, serrated line of his spine, the play of muscles under the huge cross tattoo on his back.

In the doorway, I paused for a moment and sighed.

I mopped Vassily's face and hands before I eased him over my lap, cradling his cold weight in my arms. It was the first time I'd seen him undressed since he'd gotten out of prison, and now that there was time to look, I noticed things I hadn't had time to see before. He had a shank scar on his forearm: that was new. He was thinner, his ribs visible through his skin. His nails were cracked. The sight of his toenails, ridged from years of poor nutrition and high stress, brought me back to myself. I looked down the tattooed length of Vassily's body, back up to his face. He was rousing slowly, gaze wandering as he swam back to consciousness. Eventually, he fixed on my face. His eyes were as bright as black stars, and the expression of intoxicated longing in them made my mouth feel full and blue and bittersweet.

"Moron," I rumbled. "Can you sit up?"

"Sure. Maybe." Vassily rasped.

I eventually got him upright and, with some flailing arms and careful bracing, limped over with him to the bed. We had shared a double bed as young boys, but it was odd climbing in beside him as an adult. I was still furious and desperately needed sleep, and because I couldn't sleep, I wanted to beat the shit out of something. But I couldn't do that, either.

It was close to an hour before Vassily stirred again. I hadn't realized I was dozing until his arm groped over my chest, startling me out of a frustrated, dizzy reverie.

"Lekshi?"

My eyes didn't want to open. When they did, I glared at the rows of paper lamps overhead. They were gaudy and pointless. "What?"

"Sorry." Vassily patted me awkwardly. Chest, belly, arm. "You're... good friend. Good. Sorry."

"If you keep touching me like that, I will break your fingers."

"Sorry. Was real worried, you know. When you… gone. Sh' I knew… Lekshi's real good. Real tough. Sorry."

I wasn't certain what Vassily was apologizing for, but it didn't sound like he was apologizing for the right thing. I frowned. "You listen to me, because I'm only going to say it once. I spent nearly half my childhood dealing with this sort of shit, and I'm not going to put up with it with you."

"Put up? With what, Lekshi?"

"This bullshit. Your addiction." I sat up and turned so he couldn't see my face. "You're going to clean yourself up."

"Hey, hey. What? I'm not… not…"

"No. That's not how this works. I know it's not how it works. And if you don't get clean, that's it. You're moving out. I won't have this in my house."

My words hung in another protracted period of silence. When Vassily spoke again, his voice cracked. "That's fucked. You'd break off with me because… 'cause I went on a bender?"

I knew what cocaine did to people. I'd never used, never dreamed of using, but I'd seen enough people use it like this to know what happened afterward. The gibbering and gabbering, the violence, the superman complex, the burnout. "After your lecturing of me last night?" My voice felt cold in my own throat. "I watched my father destroy my mother and himself with this kind of behavior. Thanks to you, I just had to relive every day I spent cleaning up after them. If you want to kill yourself, fine. But I won't hold your hand while you jump."

Vassily lay on his pile of pillows, stunned. "You'd kill me?"

"I didn't say that," I replied. "You're putting words in my mouth."

"Yeah..." He looked up past his arm at the ceiling. "Yeah. I guess."

"And in unrelated news, you have a parole meeting in—" I checked my watch. "Fifty minutes."

"Parole?" Vassily's eyes narrowed, then widened like blue saucers. "Oh, fuck. FUCK! Shitfuckmothershit."

"Yes. And you're going. I brought your suit. So come on, get up."

As I pulled away from the bed, a wiry hand clapped around my wrist and stopped me in my tracks. Vassily's right hand, the one with the intricately inked skull. A snake's tail wove through it, part of a design that wound its way up his arm to his bare shoulder.

"Lexi... don't kick me out." His voice was higher than what I was used to hearing, fragile and desperate. "Please. I'm sorry. It won't happen again, all right?"

How many times had I heard it? The pleading, the 'it won't happen again'? Grigori always said the same thing. The last bender was always the last. Then came the storm clouds, the bad mood, the stressful day, and the bottles returned to the house.

"Sure thing." Heavily, I reached back and clasped Vassily's hand before peeling it from my arm. "Come on now, get up. It's time we got back to the real world."

*   *   *

We were nearly fifteen minutes late to the parole center. Every light on our route turned red before we reached the line, and by the time I'd dropped Vassily off at the office, surly but functionally sober, I wanted to kill something. My car smelled like vomit and pepper-flavored liquor. I wanted to take my fist to every jaywalking pedestrian, every yappy dog, and every shrieking toddler. I was stranded at the base of Maslow's hierarchy, unable to get a day—just one day—to rest.

The whole mess of circumstance contracted around me, a tight sheath of stress. Yuri, Carmine, my aching knee, the bruises and cuts from the night before—wholly unnoticed by my supposed best friend—the dreams and sense of impeding sickness. I parked on the side of the road and just fought to breathe, hands shaking. This was bullshit. Absolute bullshit. I wasn't supposed to feel like this. I was a hard man, a spook. And I was struggling with nothing. The oppressive stickiness of the air, the tackiness of my own skin. Nothing.

But a whole lot of nothing makes a something, a small voice said. *It makes a NO-thing.*

Vassily had done a lot of stupid shit in his life, but not drugs. He modeled his father religiously. Simon Lovenko had been everything my father was not, to hear Mariya tell it; a real Vor v Zakone, a handsome ringmaster steeped in thief's honor and gypsy romanticism. He'd sworn himself clean his whole life, and Vassily had followed in his footsteps... until now. It had been one of the things we'd kept to together as teens, as young adults. We sold drugs; we didn't take them. We were smarter than that.

What had happened to him in prison? What had they done to him?

Deliriously, I stepped out from the car onto the sweltering pavement. I was back on the Ave under the rail bridge. It was the end of the lunch hour rush, and Brighton Beach Avenue was a packed ambulating gallery of the soon-to-be-former USSR. The cacophony was almost too much to stand, but I had to eat. I had enough energy to either cook or start thinking and looking for Vincent. The former was the more optional option.

But where to even start? I knew how to find people, but missing persons leads weren't really my specialty. If I'd wanted to train as a detective, I'd have sold my soul to the *mussora*, the Vigiles Magicarum, for a badge. The only place I'd known to look for sure was Vincent's house, and I hadn't been able to find much there. It was a no-go zone now. The Laguettas probably knew his hangouts, but asking around too much about someone like Vincent was dangerous. The Mexican cartels wanted him. Manelli wanted him. Also, asking the wrong people—people who didn't know he was missing—would cost Lev face. It wasn't a good idea to cause your Avtoritet a loss of face. All I had after that was Jana, and maybe Yuri's friends. Of the two options, I preferred dealing with Jana.

That wasn't much, but it was something. I decided I'd deal with it at home: sleep, food, shower, not necessarily in that order, then a call in to Jana. It was almost a plan, but I still had the nagging sense that I was forgetting something. Something about Monday night, tonight.

I avoided Mariya's, even though I'd normally go there for lunch. I couldn't face her. Instead, I walked half a block to M & I, the neighborhood's old workhorse deli. I slunk in through the sliding doors and went for the self-serve window, where I numbly scooped chicken *katleti* and salad into a plastic dish. Kutkha was a distant presence, masked by a smokescreen of fatigue and self-pity. 'True Magus' my ass.

"Alexi!" A familiar smiling face with a braided corona of neat blonde hair loomed up in the corner of my bleary eye.

I nearly threw the dish and the ladle at the wall. I flinched and slammed the food down on the counter instead. "*Bozhe*, Jana. Oh. Good morning. Afternoon, I mean."

All faces briefly turned to look before they were once again downcast.

Jana's hand went to her mouth. She was made up and dressed for work, perfectly crisp in the muggy heat. There was not a single blemish on her spotless white blouse. "Sorry. I just saw you, and thought…"

"No. It's fine." It was in that moment I remembered that I hadn't shaved in two days. I probably reeked of vomit and certainly smelled of old fear, sweat, and violence. "In fact, I was about to go home and give you a call."

"You were?" she said. "That's funny. I was just getting lunch, and then I was going to call you and ask you how things were going."

If Kutkha was right and the universe was a living creature, then it was a merciless sadist with a bad sense of humor. I turned back to the double boiler and resumed dishing up, unable to stop the flush that crept across my cheeks and down my collar. "How serendipitous. I didn't know you came up this way for lunch."

"Mmhmm." Her mouth quirked ruefully, and she took a container herself. "My usual place closed for the day. The son of the manager died."

"No one escapes life alive," I replied. It felt dull and sour coming out of my mouth, and I fumbled with the lid as I boxed up the dish. "No… I apologize. For that. I shouldn't say such a thing."

"No, it's fine. I didn't know him–know him, you know?" Her whole body flooded with a smile that I caught when I glanced sidelong at her. "But yes… about that call. I have something I need to talk to you about in private. Do you have time to visit my house?"

Her house? My shoulders stiffened. "No, no. Not today, sorry. But we could go down to the boardwalk. No one will hear."

"Well, as in, I heard something around the office, and it needs to be somewhere really private." The smile fixed on her face like a mask. "What about your place?"

My place was a pigsty, post-Yuri. Under the best of circumstances, having a strange woman in my apartment was barely more comfortable than being in the apartment of a strange woman. I glanced furtively at the cashier. "There's another deli near here where I have access to the back. We can go there and talk."

"I don't know, Alexi." Jana ducked her head a little, and before I could stop her, she reached out and touched my bare forearm with light fingers. Her eyes widened, as surprised as I was by the brief contact, and her hand flew back like she'd been burned. Just as well. "It, um, it involves Lev. But I guess it can wait."

"Yes. In that case, it should wait." Feeling increasingly guarded and paranoid, I took a step back from her. If it involved Lev and my investigation, then it couldn't wait at all. "Look, the boardwalk will be busy, but no one will be listening. As long as we're moving in a crowd, it's the safest place for us to be. Even if someone I know sees us there, it's easily explained. You are clearly an attractive woman."

"All right, well, that works. Here, I'll pick that up for you." She blushed. This poised, confident attorney suddenly looked as shy and awkward as I felt, fumbling her purse a little as she bumped into me again. She slapped a ten down on the cash plate in front of the buxom cashier, who was watching the pair of us as judgmentally as only an old Russian woman could. I grimaced at her, bundled my cheap food, and snatched up the change before I followed Jana's swishing skirt out the door.

We stuck to the shadow of the bridge as we walked, shoulder to shoulder. Jana was vibrating with tension. I noticed she still had her jacket on, and she hadn't loosened the buttons. There was only ever one reason I did that when it was this hot: I was carrying. It was hard to say if she was, not without staring rudely at her chest.

As soon as we rounded the fruit stand and started up the quieter street towards the seashore, she sighed heavily and picked up the pace. It was quieter than I expected, which meant we could actually walk at a normal speed instead of being bogged down in beachgoing families and throngs of old people and fox terriers.

Jana waited until no one was nearby. "Alexi, I have to warn you. I think you need to get out of this mess. I don't know what you can do, but from what I overheard Lev say this morning, you're in real danger."

"That's not really anything I can control," I replied. "Things like this are inherently dangerous. What did you hear?"

"I don't think Vincent's even missing," she said. Her heels clicked quickly on the concrete beside my own silent shoes. "I overheard Lev talking to someone on the phone this morning. He was saying he had someone looking for Vincent, but from what I could make out, Lev's in on it with someone. I wanted to call you and warn you, but when I tried this morning…"

"I was out of the house." My intuition pinged me strangely as Jana spoke. It wouldn't surprise me if that was the case, that Lev was playing another level of subterfuge. The game of politics was one of direction and misdirection. But why?

"It's a sham, Alexi," Jana said. She looked around as we crossed the road and mounted the ramp leading up onto the boardwalk. It was busy, though not as much as I feared. There was space between the people. "The whole thing. I don't know as much about the business as you do, obviously, but I don't think it really has anything to do with Vincent at all."

Would Lev lie to my face like that? Probably. He and anyone else in the Organization would lie to their own grandmothers if it suited them, and Vassily's remark on the amount of money I was being offered to find Vincent Manelli was not out of turn. Maybe he'd hit it on the head. Maybe we were being herded down a cattle chute by our elders, and we needed to get them before they got us. "And what exactly was said?"

"There was some arguing, and that's what got me to stop by his door. It got quiet after that... but I heard him say Vincent was secure somewhere and he had 'someone' looking for him anyway." Jana's face flushed, whether from heat or embarrassment at having to report on her boss, I could not say. "I knew he was talking about you, and I also know Lev very well, Alexi. He's cunning, and he's ruthless."

It was true that the only other person who'd known I was searching for Vincent was my Avtoritet. I remembered Carmine's 'little bird' speech. Someone had tipped him off as to my whereabouts. Lev had known I was going to speak to Jana in the morning, and while I was waiting for and seeing her, my car was rigged. It seemed... elementary. One of those things that was so obvious you didn't want to see it. I looked out over the ocean, rubbing my tongue against the roof of my mouth. "That begs the question, though. Why would you be so eager to warn me of such a thing?"

"You seem like a polite and intelligent man, and, well…" Jana's mouth quirked, and she shrugged. "It's not very often I meet men in your line of work who can hold a conversation. I don't really have the moral high ground or anything, but I don't like hearing someone get set up by those in power without even the ability to defend themselves. That's why I became an attorney in the first place."

I felt an inexplicable chill pass through me, and with it came Yuri's words from the night before. *You're already a slave.* "Well, yes. And I think that's a very moral thing to do, actually. I appreciate it."

"Appreciate it enough you might want to go to Tatiana's with me on Wednesday night?" A sly gleam lit Jana's eyes, and suddenly, her confidence was back full-force. She could play the flirt from a distance, as long as we weren't actually touching, and maybe… maybe I could work with that.

That probably wasn't a bad idea. Crina wouldn't mind—or at least, I didn't think she'd mind—and Vassily would have no reason to continue to doubt my masculinity. As I considered my reply, I looked away and then behind us… and noticed the standout.

He had his hands in his jacket pockets: a heavy puffer jacket and jeans, like what a dockworker would wear. The coat was far, far too heavy for the weather, bulked out around the middle. But that wasn't the only thing I noticed. He was wearing a baseball cap that did nothing to disguise his likeness to Frank Nacari's license photo.

"We need to turn the corner and get back to the Ave," I said abruptly. I patted down my pockets. No knife, no mirror, no gun. I had left it all in the glove compartment. How professional.

"Hmm?" Jana's eyebrows quirked.

"We're being scoped," I replied. We had just passed the start of Brighton 3rd. As the mouth of the street loomed, the rest of my skin began to creep.

"Are you sure we're being followed? I mean—"

"Do you have a compact mirror?" I motioned to her purse.

Lips pressed together, Jana nodded. She fumbled around in her bag until she came up with her powder, which she opened and lifted up to reflect between us. I glanced back: sure enough, there he was. He was nearly the spitting image of Frank's license photo, but older. Different hairstyle, and not wholly identical, but closely related. His expression was one of blank determination.

"Listen. I want you to break away into the crowd and turn down this street. Get back to the main street," I said.

"I can't do that," Jana replied. She picked up her pace as I did. "I'm not leaving you here alone."

"Really. I insist." This was my world, not hers. Not really. She might've worked on the fringes, but she wasn't deep in its guts. "Go."

In the small reflection, I saw the other Nacari's eyes focus on me as he unzipped the front of his jacket. I had no weapons, but if I was able to concentrate, I could now hopefully work some kind of magic and get away. When we reached the stairs leading down to the street, I felt her hesitate and gave her a pointed little shove with my elbow. "Go!"

Jana stumbled briefly, her expression angry and brittle, but then tensely stalked off across the boardwalk, heels clacking on the wood. But she was not fast enough to get out of harm's way. No one was, as I turned just in time to see him pull a pistol, level it with the one-handed expertise of a talented marksman, and fire.

I threw up my hands and focused everything I had into averting the bullet. I expected a bang and a flash, maybe a zing. Instead, the pistol made a strange, mushy sound, like it were being fired underwater—and then the wind sucked in towards Nacari Senior with an invisible wave of weirdness that curdled the air and contorted the light around him. I saw Jana frozen out of the corner of my eye, her expression one of horror as the space around the pistol cracked into dark lines that then exploded, shattering into... insects.

For a moment, I was confused, unsure if I'd done something or not. But I knew that sound: it was the same as the human-faced insects in my dream.

"Run!" I barked aloud, not at anyone in particular, and staggered off at a limp towards Jana. "Run!"

She startled, her trance broken, her face a mask of fear, and I caught her arm as we fled down the boardwalk from the gathering cloud and the gathering screams. One male scream was louder than them all. As we ran, I turned to see the iron cloud wrapped around the hit man like a cyclone. He flailed at them, the gun fallen at his feet, as they ripped his clothes and began to strip the flesh off his face and hands. Other people were screaming and running or staring as he staggered back, flailing, and fell to his knees.

"Oh my god," Jana said. Her eyeliner was running a little. "Oh my god. What was that?"

"A very poor attempt at summoning," I said, breathlessly, and turned back for the stairs down to the street. "I think. Come on."

I turned at the railing. My would-be assassin was drowned in the crowd of panicking people, but the smell blew back to us: rotten meat and sugar. The elms that faced the ocean, growing in their stands near the end of the sidewalk, turned partly brown as the fetid wind passed over them and dissipated.

"You should get back," I said, keeping my voice low. "Back to the office."

"I—" she started.

"Please understand. This is between me and my people." I cut her off, shaking my head. "Your advice was invaluable. But it's all you need to give."

"And what about dinner?" The farther away we got from the chaos of the beach, the calmer she sounded. We were both used to working under stress, in our own ways, and her lips quirked in a predatory little smile.

"I don't date," I replied. "But I'll have dinner with you, assuming the Manellis continue to be this inept."

"Thursday," she said. "Seven, at Tatiana."

"I'll make a booking for two," I replied.

Her heart-shaped face flushed with something I wasn't wholly certain how to read. I didn't know her well enough, and strangers' faces take some getting used to.

I knew my body could not keep up without sleep by the time I got to my apartment. I stripped and showered with painful deliberation and ate my lukewarm food without appetite in the ringing silence of the kitchen. It was hot inside, the windows open to air out the rotten smell left by the demon. The place felt impure, unclean. Everything was broken and out of order. Vassily was not home, again. No one to quip with, no way to relieve stress. I was too tired for the gym.

"Well, Binah. It's not every day you see someone try and fail a mass shooting on the boardwalk," I said to the cat, watching her lick out the last bit of salad from the takeout dish. "Some days. But not every day."

She ignored me until she'd finished, then looked up at me with her eerie, pale eyes, licking her chops. With great studiousness, she began to groom her paw and face.

"Indeed," I said and sighed, to nothing in particular.

I had rarely been so grateful to see my bed, to climb in under the sheets with the cat. My mind should have been racing on what Jana had told me—but it was the opposite. It was black, empty, numb. I did not hear Kutkha's voice. No magical inspiration, déjà vu, good ideas. And I still couldn't remember what I was supposed to be doing tonight.

There were no nightmares this time: there was nothing, a balmy hum of sleep that was abruptly disturbed by an explosion of light and, then, a familiar, overly cheerful, still slightly raspy voice. "Yoo-hoo! Wakey wakey, rise from your gwavey."

"Uh? Vassily?" I slurred, covering my throbbing eyes. "Please just... let me sleep."

"Hey, don't give me that shit. You were the one that wanted to come along tonight." He threw something at me, and it landed heavily on my chest and sent the cat scattering. "What the fuck happened to the house today? Did we get robbed?"

"No. Long story." Groggily, I leaned up and peered down. He'd thrown me a shoulder holster. "What did I want to come... go to?"

"We're doing the laundry, remember? Nic's money?"

Oh, no. The casino. Atlantic City. The Laguettas. I was on bodyguard duty. GOD help me.

"So I cleaned the place up while you were getting your beauty sleep, and I got us a room at the Taj Mahal, just you and me." Vassily was half-dressed, throwing on a shirt to what looked like a new and fashionable suit. I caught a glimpse of the long, muscular line of his back before it was hidden from view and frowned, sitting up to rub my face.

"What time is it?"

"Nearly seven. What's up, Lexi? You don't look so great."

"I need… call," I blurted. "Crina. She should come."

"Oh." Vassily turned, but I saw him frown. "Well, I booked the room for two, but I guess you can get another if you want to shack up with your girl tonight."

"No, she can stay." I realized immediately that I hadn't thought that through. "I mean, yes, she can stay with me. Properly, in another room. Girlfriend."

He looked less pleased than I expected. "She better get her ass moving. We have to go in about forty-five minutes. Mikhail'll be here with a car."

"Forty-five. How late is this going to go?"

"Three or four or five a.m." Vassily laced his belt up around his shirt, smoothing it down over his belly. "I dunno if this is really the sort of gig for your girlfriend to come, Lexi. Crina might get a little familiar with the business, you know what I mean?"

"She's fine." I slid out of bed and tested my leg. It was still bruised, but I could walk. I didn't want to, but I could walk. "And you were right. Lev's trying to have me killed."

"Make sure you pack—what?" He turned, scowling, halfway through clipping on his tie. We could both tie real ties, but when you worked this business, you didn't wear them. You didn't want to wear anything that anyone could grab and choke you with, if a night turned to shit. "What?"

"You heard me. I think you're right. This job is bad news, and Lev is part of it."

"Holy shit," Vassily said. "Already? No way. You know for sure? How'd you find out?"

"One of the partners in his firm, Jana Volotsya, warned me after she overheard him from her office. It's not a hundred percent certain, given it's hearsay, but it's looking more and more likely."

Vassily blinked. "Yeah, it is. Well, fuck. Let me ask around a bit—I might be able to confirm or deny it. Ovar'd probably know. I'll ask him and Nic for you, all right?"

"You could, but it's getting harder to know who's on the chopping block, and why," I said. Now that I was awake, I could see Vassily was still haggard, pale, and jowly, but the fierceness was back in his voice and in his hands. "I don't trust them."

"We have to be able to trust somebody." Vassily tossed his hands in the air. "Oy. Go ring up your girl, man. We have to go."

The exclamation didn't have his usual ring of humor, and it didn't seem worth trying to explain what had happened with the other Nacari today. I hobbled away to my office as fast as my knee allowed. I got fresh clips for the Wardbreaker, fumbled with the phone and my wallet, and found Crina's card. It was plain red, matte, with her name and number embossed in black. It smelled of Charlie Gold perfume and clove cigarettes.

"'llo?"

"Crina, it's Alexi." I leaned on the ledger with my hand in my hair. "I apologize for calling you at this hour, but I was wondering if I could cancel your visit for tomorrow—"

"Oh, Alexi. That's fine, no problem." She cut me off, a little breathily. I wasn't certain, but she sounded disappointed.

"No, wait. I was wondering if you're free now." I exhaled thinly through my nose, massaging my scalp. "We're going to Atlantic City tonight."

"Atlantic City? I'd love to. I'm just eating breakfast… what time is 'tonight'?"

I winced. "In about forty minutes."

She laughed, a bright burst of yellow sound. "Forty? Alexi, my goodness. You really don't date, do you? Okay, I'll do it. But not for free."

"All expenses paid," I said. "And you can borrow as many books as you can carry."

"Deal."

Thank the Universe for small mercies. "I'll arrange to drive by and pick you up. Where should we meet you?"

"Outside Sirens. We all know where that is." I could hear her grin.

Forty minutes might be pushing it for her, but it was usually enough for me. I looked over at the hammer ruefully. I wanted to take it. After watching a gun eat a man alive, I was beginning to feel a bit superstitious about carrying one.

I reached out and pulled down my dictionary of Kabbalah, taking it with me on the way back to my closet. Nothing in there could stop car bombs, demonically possessed golems, or a hopped-up super-Guido and his pet hellhounds, but at least I'd look suitably wizardly while I figured out how, exactly, I was going to live out the week.

CHAPTER 17

Mob drivers are generally willing to do pretty much anything, provided you tip freely and well. Stopping by Sirens to collect Crina added an extra twenty minutes and twenty bucks to the three-hour trip to Atlantic City, but her presence was priceless. She was the only sane person in the car, as far as I was concerned. Kutkha was there in the back of my mind, which also helped. Even without a verbal reply from my Neshamah when I sought contact, his secret presence was reassuring.

I was seated to one side of the car. Vassily was in the middle, and his escort for the night to his left. Mikhail had the other door, chewing gum like a Jersey cow, while Crina was pressed in knee to knee with the blonde Russian girl from Vanya's place, the one who had answered the door naked. She was already drunk, braying with laughter at everything Mikhail said, while the other two women shot each other sympathetic glances. Crina had one of her PhD texts out, a first edition copy of *Kolyma Tales*. A fine pair we made, withdrawn from the conversation, books in our hands.

For my part, I focused on creating an impenetrable shell of concentrated brooding, trying to study words of power from the grimoire. Books are useful things for spooks. If someone looks over and glimpses a dense wall of text and unfamiliar symbols, they tend to lose the itch to make much chitchat. Maybe it was the added weight of my Neshamah's subliminal presence, but it seemed to work better than usual. Vassily's eyes shot across now and then, but he quickly looked away.

We skimmed two and a half hours of the finest scrubby pine barrens New Jersey had to offer on our trip down the parkway. The only good thing about Atlantic City was that it was neutral ground. Atlantic City gangs were small and localized, the Mob nearly nonexistent. No one faction controlled the powerful casino union, and the only guys running rackets were the Chinese. They were good hosts. A polite call ahead to one Mr. Leung and an expression of willingness to spend money at "his" casino was more than enough to grease those particular wheels.

I put the book away in my briefcase after we passed under the white-and-blue sign welcoming us to my least favorite city in the world. I had been here once before, back in the early 80s. Now, it was as if the whole place were addicted to crack and coke, skinned to the bone by addiction. While the others drank and chattered, I watched the streets go by, noting just how wasted and broken they looked. It had always been the most miserable playground in America, but now, the streets around the casino were some of the most desolate on the East Coast: a wasteland of broken lots, stripped cars, unconscious crackheads, and nervous streetwalkers. And it was our fault. We were one of the groups that had brought this drug to the USA. It was what Semyon had died over, maybe what I would die over, if Jana's intel was good. The truth of it—and the faint, clinging ammonia reek that seemed to hang around the cabin of the limo—settled into my guts and wouldn't let go. Yuri's spiel might have been a metaphor for all this... I'd heard Edenic terms used to describe Colombia before.

"Maybe he got the same offer. Maybe he said 'yes.' He was tired of being somebody's bitch. What about you?" Despite my best efforts, Yuri's words stuck with me. There was no way he'd literally been offering me an actual fruit from the tree of Genesis. It was a myth, at best. But when I searched back to solicit Kutkha's opinion, I encountered only a wall of silence. This was something he wanted me to work out myself.

If there was a Hell, I always suspected it would be a dark mirror of the Earth without beauty or life. In that hell, the Taj Mahal casino would replace the actual Taj Mahal. It was an insult to the beautiful Mughal mausoleum for which it was named, a tawdry mockery built for love of money instead for the love of a dead Sufi princess. The smell of the place hit me as soon as I stepped out into the muggy heat and flashing red and orange lights, a nauseating, sweet, fake cloud of perfume that bore into my sinuses. Underlying it was the scent of the city itself, metallic and unpleasant.

The other car was already waiting for us. Lev and Vanya waited inside the entry, smoking together with another pretty girl with no name. Vanya hadn't brought his wife, of course, that poor woman. Lev was alone, and he glanced archly at us as we approached in a gaggle.

"Vassily Simeovich, Alexi Grigoriovich." Lev greeted us by first name and patronymic with reassuring handshakes, the women with a kiss to the back of the hand. "And the lovely Katerina and Crina Pavloevna."

Crina was lovely, I thought. She had decided on a Chinese-style black-and-red silk dress which was both modest and deeply flattering. For all that I felt more like her brother than her boyfriend, I found myself assuming the postures of chivalry. When I caught Vanya staring at her chest, I stared back at him until he looked away.

"I'm pretty sure this wasn't here when I left," Vassily said to no one in particular. He arched his eyebrows at the overhead displays and fountains and alabaster onion domes. "Looks new."

"Yeah, it's somethin', ain't it? Thank Mr. Trump for that, haha." Vanya never seemed to talk without laughing. He was both fat and beaky, like some strange cross between Jabba the Hutt and a bald eagle. I'd said so once, while Vassily and I played chess at Mariya's. He laughed so hard then that he'd choked his milk tea over the chessboard.

I tuned out as Vanya began to extol the virtues of the place to Vassily on our way inside, breathing in a cloud of cold artificial perfume from the threshold. I surveyed the high ceilings and the narrowing entries to the main gaming floor, where the endless tinny ringing of the slot machines danced like Pop Rocks on my tongue. Vanya could coo all he wanted over the German crystal chandeliers, but all I saw was artifice. My eyes picked out the slightly uneven joins in the carpet, the chips and variances in the thin marble cladding. The whole thing was a confidence trick. Under the thin veneer of luxury was a well-greased, artfully constructed scam. The only authentic features were the hundreds of cameras that dotted the ceiling and walls. Every single one was able to zoom in on our faces, and the people behind them? They were a button away from dispatching the police, who would no doubt be delighted to find Vassily—a convicted felon put away for tax evasion and suspected money laundering—shaking hands with George Laguetta.

I also took some time to watch the bouncers. There were lots of them: patrolling, chatting, standing around, boredly loitering by banks of machines. I had a rough mental approximation of their procedures and personas. A minority of the guys who did security at places like this one were real hardcases, former club bouncers, ex-cops, and veteran soldiers who treated the gig like a retirement resort. The rest were mall cops at best, men and women who'd done two weeks of training and hoped they never got into anything the other guys couldn't handle. They did a whole lot of customer service, while the old soldiers trounced the troublemakers. Straggling behind Vassily, I idly played out various scenarios in my mind, from the most extreme ones where someone ended up shooting someone else, through to the mildest, where one or more of my party was asked to leave for being too drunk. In all scenarios, I concluded that resistance would lead to disaster. There were too many guards here. The cameras would be linked to a communications center, and every single bouncer could converge on the same location within a few minutes. I hoped the Laguettas were as steady as gossip made them out to be.

Lev fell back, and before I knew it, he was walking close to my other elbow, his mouth lifted in a secret smile. "How are things going, Alexi? We haven't had a chance to catch up since you fell down the stairs."

He had to know about the attempted hit today. I considered asking him about Vincent. My hand tightened on Crina's forearm. "Things are certainly going, Avtoritet. It's been an exciting few days, but I'm... confident things will settle down."

"Excellent," he replied. "Have you made any progress?"

My stress ratcheted up another notch. "Of course. I'll talk with you later."

Mikhail had fallen into line with him like a ghost, Katerina chattering to Vanya from his other arm. For a moment, I was reminded of Carmine's hounds.

"Chet," I said to Kutkha, mentally. *"That's the word I want to master. The barrier. Some kind of energy shield."*

"It isn't the word so much as the intent, my Ruach," Kutkha replied. His presence was a low rustling of feathers and dark, cold water. *"Master the intent. Use the word to gain mastery."*

Chet. I tried to focus on the meaning of the word as we walked, but there was too much distraction. The machines, the lights, the murmuring crowds, the heat of the gaming floor, the pistol tapping my ribs under my suit's jacket. Call me paranoid, but I couldn't help but think about Nacari's face being ripped off. Just like his brother's.

"Are you all right?" Crina said, keeping her voice low.

"Can't you smell it?" Her voice shook me out of my reverie. We were passing the slot machines with their scattered patrons. One here, one there—old men and women gambling their pensions, hookers on their breaks trying to win the next hit of crack. "The whole building smells like desperation."

"Mein Gott," she said and huffed. "Tell me about it."

That wasn't all that was troubling me. Vassily had barely said a word to anyone, though he was examining his surroundings with interest. I nudged Crina's elbow and pointed at a figure tiled into the ceiling. "You see that image of the woman and the five-pointed star? That's an embedded invocation to one of the faces of Venus, Lakshmi. This whole room is enchanted."

"Lakshmi? The Indian goddess of money?" She squinted up at it. "That seems quite blatant. What's it for?"

"Luck," I said. "But luck for the casino, not the patrons."

Lev was our ticket to the Chairman Club, where we'd be laundering Nic's money in irregular quantities, buying chips one, three, seven thousand at a time, then changing them back in. We had to take an elevator up to get there. The Club was screened off into semi-private smaller rooms for poker, blackjack, roulette, and baccarat. It had a restaurant and gaming table service, lounges, a bar, a nightclub. The reception to the gaming area was a seashell-shaped hall with a marble desk and a mirrored ceiling strung with sharp crystal decorations. If the flimsy-looking bolts ever gave way, the stylish receptionist would look like an elegantly dressed possum kebob. She flashed a magazine-perfect smile at our group, and if she was concerned about working under an armory's worth of dangling swords, it didn't show. "Good evening, Mr. Moskalysk. A pleasure to see you."

"And you, Yulia. You are as lovely as dream, as always," he replied in heavily accented English. It was the first time I'd heard Lev speak English in years. He already had his wallet in his hand and discreetly showed her the black card and his ID inside. "Do you happen to know if the Mr. Laguetta is waiting for us yet?"

"Yes, sir. He's already checked in to the Salon Privé," Julia said. She didn't even have to check her logbook.

"Ah, *kharosho*, excellent. Then please arrange for us one bottle of Coche-Dury Meursault, and one of eighty-four Dom Perignon Rosé?" Lev's English was thick, but his French was perfect.

"Of course." The woman replied as if the bottles of wine Lev had just ordered weren't worth more than her entire week's paycheck. "Anything else?"

"No, no, is all I could ask for from such a beautiful woman. Thank you." Lev smiled gracefully, polished polite as he split from the desk and led the way forward.

Mikhail tracked Julia wolfishly on the way past, and Vanya whispered something into Vassily's ear that made him laugh. I was the one who looked back to see the smile gone in an unguarded moment while Julia wrote her reminders on a well-used jotter. The brief exchange, in all of its formal artificiality, left me strangely cold on the trip upstairs.

"Someone walk over your grave, soldier?" Vassily's low voice disrupted my reverie.

I hadn't even noticed him, but he'd fallen in by my elbow just outside the elevator while the others walked ahead. Crina was talking about something at Sirens with Katerina, just ahead of us.

"It doesn't feel very real," I replied uncomfortably. I wasn't certain Vassily understood, but I wanted him to. "This place."

There was a thoughtful pause between us. I glanced over and found Vassily looking off into the distance.

He nodded. "Yeah... I know what you mean."

My mood lifted a little. "That, and there's too many cameras here. Approximately one every three feet, not counting each gaming table."

"Don't worry, man. We're just here to play." Vassily grinned, flashing teeth, and for a moment, the old sly light came back to his eyes. "It's Lev's chips, anyway."

It was technically Nic's, but who knew? The gracious concierge who offered to take our luggage, the gaming host who greeted us at the door, the cage cashiers—everyone there had a vested interest in us changing and spending their money. They didn't give a shit where it came from, as long as we kept playing and tipping.

We emerged into the orange-lit parlor at the end of the corridor and immediately beheld the well-dressed Laguetta entourage, who had taken the tables and sofas that commanded the best view of the door. Eight men, three of them already tipsily playing roulette with whoops and laughter. Only one man was under forty. When they saw our group enter, the seated men rose and turned to face us.

"Well, look who it is! Old Sly himself, and our young Mister Lovenko. Welcome back to the free world, Vassily." George Laguetta was an old grizzled lion of a man with a slow sloping grin, and he pronounced Vassily's name like "Vazli." He held out a ringed hand as we closed in: Lev shook first, then Vassily. Vanya hung slightly back, obviously keen for attention, but only getting it after the Avtoritet and the nominated heir of the leadership had their turn. I watched wryly from the back, hanging behind with Mikhail. We were the bulldog and the doberman, nameless unless introduced.

There was no house security was in here, just me, Mikhail, and George's bodyguards. The youngest man had a curly mullet and was cut and tanned like a competitive bodybuilder, and he was definitely on duty. The other soldier was a sallow, black-eyed wiseguy with a heavy five-o'clock shadow and a sagging Saturnine face. His smiles were dark and fleeting, placidly masking great attentiveness. I marked him as a good shot and a fast draw. He wore an open suit jacket that was a size too large, the lining weighed down with spare clips of ammo.

Besides us and Georgie's crew, the salon had other guests. A tired-looking Chinese man walked back and forth between tables eight and six, chain-smoking cigarettes from a red pack as he checked his bets on baccarat. A group of young women decked out in Gucci laughed and talked around one of the rear blackjack tables.

"...no, I'm telling you. Alexi back there kicks my ass at poker." I tuned back to the assembled when I heard my name, just in time to see Laguetta and his friends look over at me and Crina interestedly. "And he's totally playing baccarat tonight. I bet he'll be up ten thousand before the first hour's out."

I arched an eyebrow.

"Yeah, you got the eyes for poker. Shark eyes." George grinned broadly. "What d'ya think, Alexi? Reckon you can up Vassily here by ten grand?"

Everyone from the Organizatsiya laughed. Vassily was the best gambler out of the entire Yaroshenko crew, and they knew it. Beside me, Crina flashed an exaggerated cat's smile. I almost turned him down, demurred, and bought into the joke at my expense, but I spotted something bright and real in Vassily's eyes. His fingers moved by his thigh in a wave pattern. With a shock of pleasure, I recognized the old signal. Vassily wasn't making fun: he was giving me an in. It was as good as an apology, and I smiled as I was meant to. "Eleven thousand."

"Ohoh ohhh!" Laguetta clapped Vassily on the arm. "That sounds like a challenge to me. I'll wager on it."

"You're on." Vassily's face suffused with a wicked smile.

Mikhail and Vanya stirred restlessly at this sudden re-inclusion. They didn't look pleased as I left Crina and took my place at Vassily's right side, where I hardly came up to his jawline. He clapped me on the shoulder, and we got started on the game.

Four hours later, my sinuses were gummy with perfume and cigarette smoke, but I was up ten thousand and was playing at Laguetta's table, with Lev on my left and the hawkeyed Laguetta bodyguard on my right. His name had turned out to be Lazarus, and he was wholly relatable—quiet, serious, and cunning, if not book-smart. Everyone else but the two of us was heading towards being cheerfully drunk by the time I called my last bet. Nursing a cup of coffee and a stack of chips, I found that for once in my life, I didn't feel like a complete pariah as the dealer shuffled and laid out his own hand face-down on the table. "Place your bets, gentlemen."

Vassily came up behind me, and I caught the faint smell of whiskey and lime from over my shoulder. Lev was leading the bet, and regarded the others demurely as he pushed forward two five-thousand-dollar chips. My mouth twitched to one side, and I counted three of the heavy chips from my own stack, nudging them across. Vassily whistled.

"*Bozhe moy*. They don't call you Molotchik for nothing, do they?" Lev remarked.

"Haha, I'll match it." Vanya, sweating profusely, slapped down the same amount at the other end of the table. "Bring it on."

If I could appreciate any game in the world, it was the elegant simplicity and nearly-even odds of baccarat. If you had an eye for patterns and could card count, it was a little more than even odds. The dealer dealt us our cards while the others watched, then turned out his own onto the table. A two and a five.

"Oh, here we go." Vassily took a drink. "Did you just throw fifteen grand in the hole, Lexi?"

"Did we?" Crina leaned in over my shoulder as I thumbed back the very corners of my hand. When she saw the same thing I did, she waved her hand like she was fanning herself and had a draft of champagne from her flute as laughter bubbled up around her.

Lev won with his hand, to the cheers of the table. I was next and turned both cards over neatly, pushing them toward the dealer. "Three and seven. Perfect hand."

George thumped the table, and Vassily whooped behind me, cheering as I collected my new chips and sat back in my chair. It put me sixteen grand up from the starting bet. Lazarus laughed unhappily when he flipped his cards and turned up six, while Vanya pushed his losing hand—double twos—towards the dealer and left in disgust as he scraped the lost chips into the dealer's stack.

"With that streak, you should consider going all in." Lev looked at me sidelong, heavy-lidded and sly.

"Really, Avtoritet. We have all night to lose," I replied.

"You some kind of pussy, Jew boy?" Lazarus said on the other side.

Like smoke, my tentative regard for him vanished. I felt my face drain of all expression and saw the light fade in the other man's black eyes, an echo of my own deepening disregard. Neither of us were drunk. Both of us were proud, blooded predators.

"Now now," Lev chided. "No hard feelings, Mr. Valenti."

Something ghosted past me, creeping through my suit to the skin, but the wisp of energy bypassed me and engulfed Lazarus in a gentle, suggestive embrace. He blinked.

"Yeah, no hard feelings. I always was a shitty loser." He barked a laugh and extended a hand.

I uncomfortably accepted, and we shook, glove to glove. Lev had a sip of his Cognac like nothing had happened, and I remembered Jana's fear, her furtiveness. She had a right to be scared. Lev's magic terrified me in a way Carmine's could not. Carmine was fire and brimstone: Lev was poison gas crawling through cracks in the wall. A man with sufficient will and ambition could hold the world to ransom with that power. Maybe he was already planning for it. The back of my neck crawled.

"…this stuff's so pure you won't even know it topped you…" The snatch of conversation drifted through the room as the lull fell. I stiffened and broke off the handshake, turning while the dealer called for the next round. Mikhail was chopping lines of coke on the low drinks table in front of him.

"I believe you, seriously, but I'm done for the weekend," Vassily protested, but he was not moving away. "Not in front of the Mob guys, Misha."

I could hear the strain in Vassily's voice. He looked over at me with feverish blue eyes.

Across from him, Mikhail shrugged and snorted the first line with a thick sound of satisfaction.

Lazarus shook his head. "Crazy Russkies."

Beefbrick with the curly hair was far more interested. I watched him silently ask for clearance with arched eyebrows and a cock of his head towards toward the table. George Laguetta shook his head, a small grimace playing over his mouth and brow.

"You know, I need some fresh air." I lifted my voice enough to be heard and stood, knees cracking, and smoothed my hands over my hair. "Vassily?"

Mikhail shot me a dark look, glancing between the pair of us as Vassily wavered. Crina had frozen awkwardly, her glass held in both hands like a shield between her and the room.

"Give my lines to someone else," Vassily said. He moved towards me.

"That's awfully generous. Ain't like you, Zmechik." Vanya waved a fat ringed hand.

Vassily canted his chin as he turned on the other man, and for a moment, his face was a long, hard, lean thing of pointed lines and arrogant authority. "Sure it is. I'm cutting down," he said, in English. "So give them to someone else."

"Hey, lighten up. Take one and leave the rest." Vanya was nervous under Vassily's eye, but his grin was still wet and toothy. The expression made me look at him in a different way. Pinpoint pupils, shrunk from anxiety. Fingers, fidgeting nervously in his lap. He was worried about something—and suddenly, the pieces clicked.

Those sons of bitches.

"The balcony, Vassily?" I shoved my chips towards Lev, who took them without question. He was watching the exchange with a pleasant blank face.

"Sure." Vassily mimed a cigarette, but he was perspiring heavily.

I could see the sweat on his lip as I drew in against his side and linked an arm through his elbow. Up close, he smelled of barely suppressed desperation. As we withdrew, I looked back over my shoulder at Vanya and Mikhail, who were trying to pretend they hadn't noticed the intervention.

Vassily heaved a huge sigh outside, drawing deeply of the sweaty sea air and shuddering on the exhalation. I reached up, rubbing briefly between his shoulder blades with awkward sympathy.

"Fuck," Vassily said. He shook his head. "I feel like a french-fried asshole, Lexi."

"You did the right thing." I let my hand fall away. "They're setting you up to fall."

"Vanya? Nah, man... nah. It's not like they shoved this shit up my nose. It's my problem." Vassily looked up from the railing, facing the shimmering boardwalk and the sea beyond. "This...coke thing started about eight, nine months ago. That's how I got by in there. I dealt."

"And used." The realization weighed on me, and heavily. How had I not seen it? "And that is a setup, Vassily. They knew you'd use. They know what prison's like. You should have told me."

"How could I tell you?" Vassily threw a hand up, his speech harsh with frustration. "I knew what the fuck you'd say."

That stung. I frowned. "What I'd say? I'd have told you the truth, but I'd have been there for you during the recovery. I—"

"No. I knew you'd chew my ass out like you did this morning."

"You're putting words in my mouth again. Am I wrong?"

"No. Fuck. No. You're not, because you're never fucking wrong. That's the fucking problem, Alexi." Vassily turned on me. In the nighttime heat, he was sweating even more than he had been inside. Forehead, cheeks, throat. His hair was stuck flat to his scalp. "You always have to be right."

His words dried me out, making me brittle and sharp. His change in demeanor was disorienting, and my fists clenched by my thighs. "What do you expect me to do? Lie? Encourage you? Watch you destroy yourself without trying to help?"

"Listen. You never just listen to me." Vassily's brow furrowed. "I was wrong, man. You have changed. You don't fucking listen to a word I say anymore."

For a second, I honestly didn't know what to say to him in reply. He'd slammed the door in my face, cut off my ability to respond with anything believable. He knew as well as I did that it was impossible to deny a negative. "That's ridiculous. Vassily, you've hardly been home. You haven't told me anything. You didn't talk to me about any of this while you were in, and you've hardly spoken to me since you were released, and I…"

I had been fighting. Fighting and fighting to fulfill the contract our Avtoritet had assigned me. "You haven't been there. There hasn't been time to tell you, and you haven't asked, while I've been out on the streets getting injured, getting shot at. Working my ass off. I had another guy try to kill me today and I had one in my home yesterday. You didn't even bother to find out why."

Vassily turned back to glare at the ocean and fumbled at his pocket for his cigarettes. He said nothing.

"Vanya supplied you in prison, didn't he?"

"Yeah." Vassily grunted. He lit his smoke with a gold Zippo, breathing a cloud of green-smelling smoke into the dirty breeze. I adroitly sidestepped as it gusted towards me. "Him and Mikhail. They supplied for me and the boys inside."

"They want you to have this habit. It serves their interests to have you hooked." Beyond telling him the truth, I had no idea what to say to him. The truth was real, and he had a real problem.

"You don't understand," Vassily replied.

"So help me understand," I said, exasperated. "I don't even know what's wrong with you."

"No shit." He turned on me, eyes blazing. "All you're thinking about is the fucking coke."

"No. I'm not thinking about the coke, Vassily. I'm thinking about you." My face flushed hot. My temper has never been the best, and it was rising quickly. "You accused me of not listening. So I'm listening. Now talk."

He paused for several long seconds, lips twitching, then turned back towards the railing. "I can't. Not 'til I know if what the guys are saying about you is true. About your dad."

My gut chilled. "What part of it?"

"All of it." His eyes flicked across, then back. "I know you hated his guts, Lexi, but Misha says you took him down in front of everyone. Drilled his knees out and killed him with a hammer. Is that true?"

"Not in front of everyone." My eyes narrowed. What was he getting at? "In private. The others heard secondhand about it."

"What about the drill and hammer part?"

I couldn't lie to him. "That was true."

"That's a real shitty way to kill someone, Lexi." Vassily's tone turned accusatory. "There ain't nothing bad enough for someone to need to die like that. Even your dad."

"Yes. There is." I leaned in to him. Something savage and hot wound every muscle in my face until they sang. "There are things that are that bad. He made his choices, and they led him to that point."

"No." He chuffed, almost laughing, but it was bitter. "There ain't no justifying that kind of bullshit. You hated him, but he was still your dad."

"He was never my father," I replied, coldly. "And just because yours was a decent man and you lost him doesn't give you the right to judge how I dealt with mine."

"Choices, huh? Well, you fucking chose to get wrapped up in Lev's bullshit. You don't know what that's like, to not have a choice."

"You shut the hell up," I said. "Now. You're the one that said no one crammed that first hit up your nose."

"See? I told you that's all you were thinking about." His jaw set, and he sniffed, cocking his head. Just like he'd done to Vanya.

Before I could stop myself, my hands snapped out, and I shoved him along the balcony. He stumbled, mouth agape, and I rippled through with a twitch that turned into an explosive roundhouse punch and a sharp,ced wordless shout.

My fist hit the railing. The whole thing rattled under the impact.

"Jesus, Alexi—"

"You want to *lie?* You want to accuse me of *lying* about what I think?!" I roared, frustration and rage and insult curdling every word with a real force, anger red enough that it made Vassily take another step back from me. "You want to know what I'm like when I don't give a fuck? Fine! You can get the fuck out of my house!"

"Woah, hey-" Vassily's face turned the color of milk.

"Did I stutter?" I shouted back, lips peeled back from my teeth. "You think I'm gonna let you bring this shit into my life? You think I'm going to stand by and, and watch you lie to me? About me? I have dedicated my life to pursuing truth, Vassily, in all of its morbid, abject mortality, and if you are going to bring the lie back into my life, you can get the fuck away from me!"

Vassily took another step back. Whatever he saw in my face must have frightened him. "Lexi, I—"

"I nearly died three times this week, and do you give a fuck?" I advanced as he retreated and shoved him bonelessly into the railing. Vassily hit it without protest and bounced, too startled to do anything except gape.

His fingers twitched up, and for a moment, I thought he was going to draw on me. Instead, the nervous energy in his limbs drained out, and he turned back to the balcony door. "You get one good fuck, and this is what happens?" He sneered. "I don't need you."

I was horrified, and horrified by the feeling that welled up helplessly in my stomach and throat. Disgust. I wasn't supposed to be disgusted by Vassily. "Is that what this is about?"

He whirled, eyes blazing, and jerked his head at the doorway. "Is what about? It's not my business who you screw. I'm going inside."

My disgust intensified. Vassily was wrong: I hadn't changed, but he had. I looked at him, and I couldn't see anything other than the lie. A void, a shell that covered a sucking black thing of need and fear. "Crina's a beard, Vassily. She's in it for her own reasons."

"She's a hooker. And what does she do? Heroin?"

"Books," I replied stiffly. "She's a literature PhD."

"Her and every other crab-riddled bitch from the Balkans. They all say the same thing. They're here to study, get work.... whatever. It's all bullshit. She got brought over here to make money. You want to lay shit on me for a couple lines of coke—"

"Bags, Vassily. Bags of coke."

"Then you better fucking lay it on her junk-shooting cunt, too." Vassily glared at me with feverish eyes and stalked off back into the casino.

Lying. He would make up whatever stories made him feel better, and this time, it was me who backed away. I was certain the tight ringing in my gut was from panic, but I couldn't find a way to explain the subtle terror Vassily's denial of reality caused me. It felt sick, the way that Yuri and Nacari and the hit man that looked like him felt sick.

I turned to the Atlantic, to the curve of the seashore reaching back up along the coast to home. Miserable, polluted water.

"Alexi?" It was Crina, speaking from the entry to the balcony.

I grunted back wordlessly in reply.

"Is something the matter? Vassily just pushed on by. He looked pretty pissed off."

"He is." And so was I.

"He seems a bit prickly, doesn't he?" She tapped her way across to me and leaned beside my shoulder.

"Long story," I replied. "Let's... talk about something else for now. Like The Red Book. Have you seen it yet?"

Crina's face suffused, lips curling, eyes lighting up. "Yes. I saw it this morning, while I was in class. It's... it's more than anything I ever dreamed. You're going to love it."

That made me smile, however briefly. "Translated?"

"No, it's still in German. But I can read that just fine." She looked down. "Are we still on for tomorrow?"

"Absolutely," I said. "At my house. I insist."

Crina didn't really laugh so much as catch a single heated sound of pleasure behind her teeth as she grinned, her eyes half-closed. She pushed back. "Then it's a deal. But not a date. Come on… Mr. Mollusk was asking about you."

"My goodness. You didn't really just call him that, did you?" Amused and dismayed, I followed her back inside.

"I absolutely just did. But you won't tell him I said that, will you?" Crina glanced back over her shoulder. She was trying to cheer me up, and it was an earnest effort. Not misplaced, either. There was no place for showing weakness here.

We walked back into the hot parlor, and I caught Crina's arm, halting her in the doorway. I saw Vassily, Mikhail, Mikhail's girl, and Vanya bent over the coke table, while the Laguetta meathead cheered them on. George was deep in quiet, drunken conversation with Lev. The other goons were clustered around the poker table.

I paused there, watching them as a stranger might. Something in my heart sealed over, hard and bleak and lonely. Very lonely.

"Alexi?" Crina turned back to me. "Come on… we should go back inside."

I nodded, but I had to pause to take a deep breath before we did… and that moment of hesitation was the only reason I didn't catch a bullet as the parlor door burst in in a spray of machine gun fire and broken glass.

CHAPTER 18

Split seconds. It was Crina who dragged me to the ground as the room turned into a haze of blood mist and shattered furniture and glass. The guys at the roulette table weren't fast enough: three of George's men and the dealer went down like ragdolls. I heard Vassily drop with a scream of pain to my right, and my blood turned to ice.

I flung myself against the nearest baccarat table, dragging Crina behind the cover as the dealer, screaming and panicked, ran out into the room and bolted for the balcony entry. I didn't see what happened to her: I drew my non-enchanted pistol, and Crina motioned at me with a grabby hands gesture, wide-eyed. She wanted a gun. I gave her mine and drew the silenced Wardbreaker instead.

"Keep them busy!" A horribly familiar voice called out from the entry.

"Carmine," I grunted. "GOD dammit."

"Who?" Crina's hands were shaking, but she checked and took position like a soldier. East Germany. Of course.

"He's—" Shots rang out, deafening, then the machine guns. The guys at the door were taking turns: two guys firing, two guys reloading. "—a spook! Go to the bar, get Vassily. I'll cover you!"

Her eyes widened even more, but this table wasn't big enough for the pair of us. Bullets chewed up the sides, spraying wood past us in a stinging cloud. The bar was safer. I backed up in a crouch as Crina kicked her heels off and hitched the hem of her short silk dress up to her waist so she could move. She crawled around me and dashed low to the ground as I knelt up and fired over the table, drawing the next hail of bullets over my head. I wouldn't be far behind her: the firing squad was advancing, fanning out to start a search of the tables closest to the entry.

There was no time for fear. I pulled out my pocket mirror and looked around the edge of the table. Mikhail lay still on the ground, his swept-back hair a wet and bloody sprawl on the carpet. Worse was Carmine, bent in deep concentration around his pentacle ring. I felt something buckle and twist in the room, like my ribs were sucking in towards the inside of my chest. Carmine was the nexus of a small storm that rumbled, darkening the air around him as it began to coalesce into large, canine forms.

There was nothing we had that could stop those things once he got them started. But what did I have to head him off? I looked down at the Wardbreaker, its engraved glyphs of power. If I could defuse a ward, I could break a spell, but I needed the sacrifice. Death was everywhere, but not death spoken with the words of power I needed. Which left me.

Broken glass was scattered everywhere on the floor around me. With full intent to suffer, I seized a shard of it and stabbed it into my knee, the one that was still healing. The pain was raw and hot: I screamed, fighting to focus all my rage, all my pain, into the blood that burst out, and clapped the gun down against the fresh wound.

Blood whipped out into fine tendrils that wrapped into the grooves along the sides of the barrel, loading the charge with a ferocity and concreteness I had never felt before, a real push, like a hand behind the bullet as I reared up, took aim, and fired straight at Carmine's smarmy fucking face.

The bullet blew out with a sucking sound I'd never heard before, a *phwoomf* of backed-up force, and Carmine threw his hands up with a shout as the countermagic I'd spent so many patient years cultivating, sacrificing to, broke the spell he'd been weaving and sent him stumbling back. Whatever he'd cried out, it spun a kinetic web of force in a moment. The bullet zinged off his Phitonic shield and shattered it.

Crina, George, and Lazarus came up blazing from behind the bar, picking off two guys too slow to sense the shift in the battle. In between bursts, I heard shouts and screams from out in the hall behind the Manellis. The guards were here. The Manellis fell back as one: I got up to one leg to try to blast Carmine again but dropped when I saw him throw something into the room. It hit the wall and bounced with a tinny metallic sound. A grenade? I covered the head of the man next to me, burying my face against the floor with my arm wrapped around my ear.

The air sucked in as it detonated, spraying metal and wood over our heads. A sharp pain lanced through the left side of my face, but when I rolled up and felt for blood or a wound, there was nothing. My ear was ringing, and everything on that side sounded fuzzy. I could smell smoke, and it was getting hot…The building wouldn't burn down, but the inside of the room would, and that was enough to kill the lot of us.

Lev stumbled across to me from around the curve of the bar, milk white with shock. "Vas… Vassily's down. Go. Go get him and the women out of here, back to New York. I'll deal with this."

"Avtoritet, I can't leave you here." Even if Lev was trying to set me up, the old loyalty resurged in the heat of the moment.

"That's an order," he snapped. "Vassily, out. Get him to a hospital if you have to. Out!"

Couldn't argue with that. I hobbled up, stumbling when I put weight on my leg and it nearly crumpled. Oh right: the glass. I pulled it free without feeling anything other than a pinching pain, put it in my mouth, and sucked the blood off it. I put pressure over the wound as I went to join the others. It wasn't too deep, but it was bleeding.

The beefy bodyguard was dead behind the bar. Crina was there, putting pressure on Vassily's leg with a pile of blood-soaked linen napkins as he clutched at the floor in a silent rictus of agony. Vanya cowered with the blonde and Katerina, who was sobbing hysterically in his arms.

"We have to get him out. There's stairs down to the boardwalk!" I searched for something to use to tie more napkins to my leg. The blonde girl, wooden and doll-like with shock, silently held out her scarf. I bound my wound, stuffed my gun back under my jacket, and squatted on my heels as I slung Vassily up over my shoulders. "Up, up, up!"

Crina didn't say a word. Her face was a mask of determination as she took Vassily's other arm and helped to bear his weight. Vanya and the girls hauled up to their feet, and the six of us ran for the balcony, stepping over a dead dealer and racing for the outside door. The emergency gate that led to the shore was easy enough to open, but our doom lay on the other side of the boardwalk: a flashing wall of blue and red sirens.

"Anya, go get the car!" Crina said. "They won't look twice at you and Vanya if you don't run. Katya, you can spot for them. We'll meet you on the other side of the block."

Katerina didn't hesitate: she gave a nod and scrambled off. Anya was so stunned that she simply obeyed, stumbling down the stairs with Vanya's hand clutched in hers. He was wheezing like a pug, but he managed to shove his gun into my hands on the way past and half-run, half-wobble after her. Crina gave me a nod over Vassily's shoulder, and we dragged him swearing onto the sand, into the shadows, and waded our way up the mostly oblivious beachfront.

"Mother of FUCK!" Vassily spat aloud as soon as we were far enough away from people. He was hopping, almost exceeding us in speed. If I could give the coke credit for one thing, it was its anesthetic effect. "Fuck fuck *fuck*!"

"I haven't had a gunfight that good since I left Zagreb!" Crina said brightly, her voice high and shrill with stress.

We rounded the corner of the building to find Katerina hopping from foot to foot, stockings ripped, clutching her shoes by the straps. She waved us forward, and we made our way another half a block to the waiting car. Vassily swore angrily as we stuffed him into the backseat, head-first. We scrambled in after him, and the car roared off into the night as I slammed the door behind us. Vanya was in the front: it was Vassily, me, and the three women in the back.

"My leg," Vassily gasped. He reached down to paw at the enormous spreading bloodstain, pale and sweaty. "My motherfucking leg."

"Hands off." I rapped his knuckles and threw back my jacket, using it to put full-body pressure on the entry point. "You're lucky it didn't blow out the other side."

"Am I... is it..?" His voice was high with fear.

"You're not bleeding to death," I said, firmly. If only every spook had Lev's ability to magically calm people. "You'll be fine."

"Oh my god," Katerina whispered. "Oh my god. Misha's dead."

Anya said nothing. She curled into the corner of the leather seat and stared out the window.

Vassily grunted, writhing. The smell of blood was thick, turning the air heavy and humid. "Motherfucking shitcocking pieces of SHIT! That HURTS!"

I breathed in, out. *Calm*, I told myself. *You're calm.*

"We'll be back in New York soon, Vassily. Just hold on." Crina's voice was full of barely concealed panic. She'd kept it together while the adrenaline ran high, but now the rush was subsiding, she was feeling it. She might have seen some shit in her time, but she wasn't a hardened *muzhiki* off the street.

"In two and a half fucking hours, if we don't get pulled over." Vassily growled, face contorting. "How many did the guidos lose? There was five of them. What happened to George?"

"Eight of them. And I don't know," I said. "I didn't have time to count. But you know what? If he's alive, George will think we set this up."

"Oh god," Katerina said. "He will."

Vassily looked up at me in alarm. "Jesus Christ. You're right."

I was trying not to focus on how my jacket was soaking through with Vassily's blood. "Even if they realize that we did nothing, then they may use it to take the lion's share from the Organizatsiya."

"I'll kill 'em. We'll kill the fucking lot of them." Vassily lifted his voice to a near shout, calling through the tinted glass between the back of the car and the driver's side. "And for fuck's sake, Vanya, turn the radio on! I don't want die with nothing to fucking listen to except my own goddamned whining!"

After a moment, Vanya complied, switching on to a station seemingly picked at random. Johnny Cash burst from the speakers above and behind us, halfway through *Ring of Fire*. Crina shook her head in dismay, while our driver pulled out of Atlantic City, gunning for the parkway and the distant hope of home.

CHAPTER 19

By the time we reached Vanya's safe house, the sun had risen and the worst of Vassily's bleeding had stopped. Crina and I hauled him out—grim, stoic, and pale—and helped him into the building.

"I still say we should be taking you to the hospital," I said. "I can only do so much. You could get an infection, you could—"

"No. No fucking hospital," he growled through gritted teeth. "You might as well just take me straight back to jail."

"Can't you just, like, fix it?" Vanya said. He was trailing behind us, mopping his face with a handkerchief, seemingly unaware that he was wiping someone's blood onto himself.

Short of me sacrificing Vanya on the spot and hoping his saggy ass was enough to power the same kind of magic I'd used on Carmine's goons, there wasn't anything I knew that could help Vassily. "I left my magical leg-fixing wand in my other set of robes."

Crina made a choked sound in the back of her throat. Vanya glared at me before kneeling down beside Vassily. "How're you feeling, Zmechik?"

"Give me a shot of *horilka* and ask me after that."

Already halfway to the back room, I stopped and turned. "No. No alcohol. You cannot drink."

"Fucking hell." Vassily looked up at me hollowly. "Do you know how much this hurts?"

No, I'd only had my knee smashed in with a baseball bat not half a week ago. Exasperated, I left in frustrated silence for the kitchen, pawing around the freezer for icepacks. I collected a pile of clean towels and a folded sheet of plastic, the kind you used to line car trunks for transporting bodies. The plastic went down on the tiled floor. It was going to be a messy job. "Bring him over here."

Crina and Vanya carried Vassily from the sofa to the sheet. By the time they laid him out, Vanya, sweating and red-faced, was puffing, and he wore a look of strain nearly equal to Vassily's own. "Look uh... Alexi. You need any help? 'Cause blood and me don't—"

"Yes. Get me the two chairs from the kitchen, please." It was my turn to glare. No way in hell was he leaving now. The big man nodded, scruffing his hair, but he went off to get them anyway.

"*Dreksnest*," Crina said, with feeling. She puffed a lock of sweaty hair from her face. She was bloody with small cuts and scratches, her dress ripped, her stockings ripped beyond recognition. Her hair hung raggedly around her face.

"I can handle this," I said. "There's an en suite in the last room down the hall, if you want to clean up."

"Later. I'm fine." She waved a hand. "What else do you need?"

"Make sure he stays here." I snorted and stood.

"Fuck you. Asshole." Vassily rubbed his face, sniffing. "Can I at least have a smoke?"

"No."

Vassily, too exhausted to argue, nodded and slumped back down.

I got the largest medical kit we had from the back room and opened it up, extending the metal trays, and used the kitchen sink to strip my gloves and scrub up. I came back with them still damp, shaking them to dry. Crina went to do the same thing while I got my tools ready.

"Hey..." Vassily looked at me dully. The shadows around his deep-set eyes had spread, dark with stress and pain. "I don't even know what happened back there, Lexi. Us fighting."

I had a good notion what had happened and was about to tell him so when Vanya reentered. He grunted, setting the chairs near our place. "Fucking drama queen mobsters, haha. You handle this. I wanna try Lev's office, see if he's okay."

"Fine." Crina would be a better assistant anyway. I exhaled heavily and pulled out two pairs of latex gloves. I covered my hands and held the other pair out for Crina as she returned.

"Thank God they weren't throwing hollowpoints around, or I wouldn't have a leg." Vassily shifted on the tarp with a grunt of discomfort. "Can you get it out?"

I made a motion with my shoulders, agreement, then took up the short serrated scissors in the kit. First, I cut high around the tacky flat stain, the dry blood a palm-sized spread through the dark fabric of his slacks. I used one of the small saline bottles in the kit to dampen the stiff bloody fabric. "Crina, in the bathroom, you will find a spray bottle for the plants. I need it half-full of water from the kettle. Cold water, not boiling."

Crina heaved up with a sigh. "Sure thing, Doctor Sokolsky."

Under other circumstances, it might have brought a smile, but I was far too busy judging the wound. It had no streakiness, no signs of infection—yet. Vanya left in the midst of the exam, his actions audible from the bedroom.

"Like I was saying... look. We're both exhausted. This is all about being tired and fucked up." Vassily's eyes reddened as he stared fixedly at the studio lights above us. "You know it is. I don't want to fight with you. We can sort shit out. We've done it before."

I glared back down at him, unwrapping a needle and two syringes, a drip bag, tubing—the paraphernalia of the medic, almost as familiar as the tools of war. The gun and knife were not dissimilar to the syringe and scalpel. "Maybe."

Vassily frowned, pushing some of his hair over his face, back over his tacky forehead. When he spoke, his voice was low, soft enough that Crina wouldn't be able to hear. "Look, I'm sorry I put words in your mouth. I respect you, Lexi. You're my main man, my brother. I don't know why the fuck you weren't named standing Avtoritet."

"Because I put my father down." I set out a small surgical tray. Tweezers, forceps, gauze. I poured antiseptic over everything that needed sterilizing and left them to stew while I prepared two syringes of different antibiotics and a bag of fluids. "The rest of them thought I was out to steal their positions when I killed him."

"Well, yeah." Vassily turned his head so he could look at me, his blue eyes dull. "But like I said back home. You're the hardest man in this crew besides Nic. You came out like fucking Rambo tonight."

"If I don't finish the job I started, it won't matter. Not that you care about that." My voice was tense, and I barely stopped the next words that wanted to bubble out from my lips. That I wasn't sure I wanted any of this, anymore. The Organizatsiya. The fighting and the politics. I had always disdained the infighting, and because I'd tried not to get involved, I'd stayed alive. But now? It was wearing me out faster than my body and mind could keep up.

"Look, I do care. You didn't tell me any of this shit. You didn't tell me about the break-in, nothing. I'll speak for you." Vassily's eyes darkened for a moment. "We'll stop Lev from arranging whatever he's arranging, and I'll speak for you with Sergei."

"We don't even know what Lev and Jana and everyone else are—"

We fell silent again as Crina came back.

She set the spray bottle down with a thump. "Done. You need anything else?"

Levelly, I looked up at her face. "Yes. Sit beside him, on the other side. You will need to hold him down."

The operation couldn't be done with any strong painkillers: not with coke in his system. Vanya hid while the screams pierced the air of the apartment, but it wasn't long before I had the bullet out, the fluids and antibiotics in, and Vassily was sleeping off his blood loss. Crina was as exhausted as I was by the time we were done: we went to the bedroom, where she got the bed and I took the floor.

I got a couple hours of sleep before I roused at seven, restless and hypervigilant. With nothing else to do, I started cleaning the kitchen with compulsive fervor. Bagging, trashing garbage, sweeping, and spraying. I scrubbed obsessively at spots of dirt on the countertop, and it took several minutes of them refusing to budge for me to realize they were a part of the granite patterning.

An hour later, I called Mariya's house. My gut was tight and fluttering empty. How the hell was I going to tell her what had happened to her brother?

"Alexi, thank God," she said. Her voice was thick with relief. "Did you find him?"

"Yes, but Maritka, it's... I do not have good news," I said tensely. "He was shot last night."

There was a long pause. "Oh god. Alexi—"

"He's alive, just injured. It hit him in the thigh," I cut her off, before she could wind herself up. "All things considered, he was lucky. I've done everything I can for it, but he won't go to the hospital."

"How's he going to get to the parole center?" Her voice was high and frightened. "They'll know he was shot."

"I know. I know." I paused, debating briefly on what else to say. I decided, as I usually did, on the blunt and total truth. "This... it isn't all that's wrong with him. I found him passed out in Vanya's bathtub yesterday. He's been doing a lot of cocaine, and he's got a problem."

"Drugs? Vassily? No," his elder sister replied with disbelief.

My frustration grew horns and teeth, butting against the inside of my ribs. Not her too. I didn't need denial. We needed her help. "Yes, Mari. Drugs."

"Please, no. Cocaine's not the same as crack, is it?"

"Not exactly." I grimaced, trying to work out how to explain without downplaying. "But they are basically the same substance, and—"

"Well... was it a once-off?" She sounded nervous.

"No. He's an addict, Mariya. He's completely hooked. He... also drank nearly two bottles of liquor and almost killed himself the night before last." I paused for a moment, lips parted, unsure how to convey the cocktail of feelings the admission caused.

"It's all because of prison." The bitterness in her voice made my stomach tense. "I remember how Antoni was. It was just the same. Prison destroyed him, my poor brother. Just destroyed him."

"It's not just prison. The other men are all in on it. One person starts, then they drag their friends into this idiot addiction—you know how it is." I rubbed my forehead. Even through the gloves, it felt clammy and cold. "I hate to admit this, but I'm really not up to taking him home and caring for him. I haven't slept more than ten hours in the last three days."

"Don't you worry about a thing. I'll pick him up and take him. I want him to stay with me for the time being. He'll listen to me if I lay it on him, and I know him well enough. He'd never do anything like this around me."

It was the truth, and a good idea, but her words stimulated no hope: only a deep sense of failure. "I... look, yes. I would be very grateful. He's out of sorts. Highly erratic. You have to keep him away from Vanya and M—"

Oh, right. Mikhail was dead.

"Who?"

"Just Vanya and Nicolai," I said. "But yes. He's not very well right now, in more than one way. I'm sorry."

"No, Alexi. You don't get to apologize for this." Mariya's old scolding tone came back readily, and I almost expected her raised hand to come out of the phone. She'd never hit us as kids, but she'd been good at making us think she would. "I'll be around in twenty minutes or so. You just take care of yourself."

She hung up first, and I sat back with a sigh.

Self-care meant a cold bath, three aspirin, and a pitcher of bitter black coffee to reset my nerves and dull the synesthesia. I couldn't muster anything like enthusiasm when my adoptive sister showed up at the door. Even with the headache held at bay, Mariya's voice and smell nearly blinded me.

"You did a great job." Mariya kissed me on both cheeks and embraced me. Her arms felt strong and wiry, her chest very thin. "Thank you, Alexi."

"It's fine," I replied hollowly.

"It's not." She smiled, strain visible in the creases beside her eyes and the muscles of her jaw. "But it will be."

We had to get Vassily up and out, but his immune system was in full swing and he was so feverish he could barely walk. He was delirious as we loaded him into the back of her truck. I watched them leave, and Vassily, heavy-eyed, wiggled his fingers at me through the window with a blank opium grin.

It will be, my mind echoed. It sure as hell would be something.

Back upstairs, I found Crina awake and bleary. She had a cup of coffee and was sitting at the kitchen counter, her forehead resting on her linked hands. When I entered, she looked up me sourly. Without makeup, the bones of her face stood out in sharp relief.

"You get any sleep?" she said. "I saw that Vassily's gone."

"He's going to his sister's. It's the best place for him." I put on another carafe of java and sat at the other side of the breakfast counter. "What about you? Are you... all right?"

"Nothing I haven't seen before." She offered the ghost of a smile, brief and superficial. It didn't reach her eyes.

"You mentioned something about Zagreb."

She shrugged. "It's violent there. My family left when I was a little girl. We went to East Germany...but I didn't want to stay there, either. Too depressing, what with the wall running right through the middle of it."

I'd heard stories, and had to wonder how she'd left. You had to bribe or murder to part the Iron Curtain. My own parents had taken the subway route: my Jewish mother had family in West Germany. Her religious ticket out of the Soviet Union was the only reason Grigori Sokolsky, the psychopath, had married her.

"Naturally." My mouth drew to one side, and I leaned back. "I'm surprised you made it out."

"People had it worse than me." Crina's smile faded with some kind of half-hidden pain, and she leaned towards me. "But I wake up to the sound of mines and rifles going off, sometimes. The dogs. Some guy was always trying to make the run over the Wall and getting blown to bits. You know?"

"Well, New York isn't the place for peace and quiet. Not unless you have a lot of money and stay clean."

"It's good enough for you." Her expression turned sly.

I frowned slightly. "Yes. But I was born here."

"So that's why your English was so good." She cocked her head, like a curious bird. "Your parents must have gotten out... God. How old are you?"

"Twenty-nine."

Crina's eyebrows rose. "Is that all?"

I inclined my head. "I turn thirty in November."

"Wow, I thought you were older." She pressed her lips together, and leaned in towards me. "Here's a secret... I'm two years older than you."

My mouth quirked, and I ducked my face. It brought a laugh from her, filling my ears with a crisp, bright yellowness. Crina was good people. I decided I liked her, which put her in a category of person which only Vassily and Mariya really occupied.

"I have a question for you, Crina. Probably inappropriate." I frowned with thought as she watched. "But social interaction has never been a strong point of mine. Why have you been so interested to talk to me?"

"Oh. Well, lots of reasons. For one, you're really smart." Her moment of apprehension passed. "For another, you're not some meathead *muzhik*. Most guys play around. They smell like old school lockers. They drink."

"Aren't those supposed to be attractive qualities in men?"

Crina laughed again, more loudly than before. "Maybe if you're a masochist. And, well, I'll put it to you this way. If I were at Misha's or Petro's house, or pretty much any other guard's place, we wouldn't even be having this conversation."

I cocked my head. "What do you mean?"

"As in... none of them would know how to ask these questions, Alexi." Her smile became gentler. "It's all 'me me me' with those kinds of guys. Suck my cock, dance in my lap, but don't dare hang around: that'd be 'clingy.'"

It was true, and something which this whole mess had been making clearer and clearer as the days went by. I shrugged. "I did just ask you a very selfish question."

"Hey, you asked something about me first." She mirrored me, my head and hands. I noticed it because it was the sort of thing an interrogator would do. "What makes you think you're not good with people? You just seem like the quiet, confident type."

I looked at her clear brown eyes and held them for a moment before I concluded she wasn't trying to mine anything serious from me. She was safe. "To be honest, the only reason I'm still alive is Vassily. His family took me in at a young age when I left my home. It was… not a good place. I couldn't speak much, or communicate normally, and I was violent, angry. His grandmother and sister took me in… I protected Vassily from his elder brothers, and he taught me how to talk to other people."

"Taught you?" She looked confused but interested.

My expression turned distant, and I looked towards the bookshelves and the unused radio on the coffee table. "Yes. He would tell me when I needed to say certain things, or not. 'Hello,' 'thank you,' 'please.' I still forget, now and then—to say those things, that is. We worked out some hand signals, these little rituals to prompt me to do the right things at the right time. As I grew older, I got better at it. When he went to prison, I had to learn to do it myself."

"Have you met anyone else with the same problem?"

I shook my head. "No. Everything I've read suggests some kind of neurological disorder. Autism, maybe. But no… Vassily was a boon. He was very patient when he was younger. Now? Not so much. Our careers diverged at the end of college. He went into business and I… went into other business."

Crina sucked her lip under her teeth and let it go with a little pop. "Is the rage-thing better now you're older?"

"I don't really want to talk more about myself," I demurred, looking away.

"If you're worried that I'm bored, I'm really not."

The whole thing was making me increasingly uncomfortable. Vassily had taught me to take strangers at their word when they expressed curiosity, but to bring it back to the other person as soon as possible. "I don't know. The social element has been static. Fortunately, faces have patterns. If people stay the same, I look for the patterns and the colors."

"Colors?"

"In their voices." I'd never quite grasped how others missed them. The colors and textures and scents in sounds were so vivid as to be overwhelming. "And in sounds of all kinds, actually. They make... colors. Scents."

Crina seemed strangely impressed by that. She was silent for several seconds as she digested the concept, as Vassily had tried to do so long ago. "What color's my voice?"

"Yellow. Usually." I didn't hesitate, grateful she'd claimed her attention at last. "And effervescent. Sometimes it bleeds more towards green, and then it smooths out back towards yellow."

"Green's my favorite color." She grinned. "This is great, and I don't think you're really that awkward. Maybe you just need to hang around the right people. Get out of the ivory tower a bit more, let out your hair." She paused for a moment, then chuckled. "Not that I'm necessarily the 'right' people, but you know what I mean."

"Not really, I'm afraid. My dealings with living people are usually fairly short and to the point." I checked the clock on the other side of the room, noting the time, and slid from my seat. In defiance of what I'd just told her about being better with common cues, I nearly walked off on her and started packing up but remembered myself just as I jerked away from the breakfast bench. "I... really have to get going. There's things I must do at home."

"Okay." Crina rose and smoothed down her borrowed jeans. They fit her snugly but were rolled at the cuffs. I guessed they were Anya's. "I'll go with you. I really don't want to stay here with Vanya the Lounge Lizard."

"No doubt." I glanced aside for a moment. "Thank you."

"For what?" She'd been walking away herself, but stopped when I spoke.

"For last night. The beginning of the night, and the end."

Her mouth curled up in a cat's smile. "It sucked pretty hard... I can't lie. But that's okay. We aren't going to be able to make our date tonight, are we?"

"I don't think so." And I was genuinely regretful. "We both need sleep."

Crina's lips twitched as she looked down, then back at my face. Her eyes were very brown, a lambent amber that reminded me strongly of a bird of prey. "You owe me another one once all this is over. Don't forget it."

We got dressed and took the subway. It was only two stops to Brighton Beach. I got off there, and Crina carried on the Q line to wherever it was she lived. It was usually a seven-minute walk from the station to my apartment, but this time, it was more like twenty. The cut from the glass shard was inflamed and painful, though not infected. I considered the elevator but decided against it, hobbling up the stairs to my floor. A letter-sized, plain white envelope was stuffed half underneath my front door.

Curiously, I limped over and picked it up. I could be lucky, for once, and it was some vital clue from a helpful participant in the Manelli–Yaroshenko drama. Given how variable my luck was, it could also be that someone sent me a packet of anthrax. I cracked the seal carefully, holding my breath just in case, but it was nothing but an ordinary sheet of yellow steno notebook paper.

"Sergei arrived 0030 Tuesday," read Nic's blocky, heavy penciled hand. "Lev back in office. No arrests. Both S & L want to see you Wed 8pm at #2."

Sergei, back already? My heart froze in my chest. Back already, and he wanted to see me. And I had nothing to show for it, no success, and no excuse. No Vincent. I hadn't protected Vassily and Lev like I was supposed to. And Sergei was going to want to know how and why I'd killed my father.

Resigned, I tucked the letter into my sweaty jacket and let myself in. I went through the motions: fed the cat, showered, shaved, found a container of pelmeni and salad left over from that first lunch I'd had with Vassily. The dumplings were dry and the cabbage and mayonnaise a little too pink, but I ate mechanically, staring off into the too-quiet apartment.

Mariya had tried her best, but she was wrong. Things weren't going to be okay. I was cold as I thought back over the previous night. I was, quite frankly, fucked. I had no leads, no way to combat the array of half-seen forces against me. I was sure it all came back to Carmine, Carmine and Lev. If I didn't kill Carmine soon, he was going to kill me. He'd seen me at the casino, and even if by some miracle the Vigiles had caught him, he was probably going to get out sooner than later.

As if detecting my need for inspiration, Binah ran into the kitchen with a rolled-up sock in her mouth, meowing around it, and dropped it helpfully at my feet. I snorted, bent down, and threw it. She chased after it like a dog and brought it back again, making muffled sounds of triumph through the cotton. We played this until she dropped it near the fridge, batting and clawing at the toy as she scooted around on her side. I watched her indulgently—and then almost magnetically, my eyes were drawn to the freezer door. And suddenly, it clicked.

I stood quickly, shoving the table back from myself. "Carmine used that angelic seal to do... something. Yuri used it to find me." I spoke aloud, knowing Kutkha could hear me, even if I hadn't heard him. "It's still active, isn't it? The seal?"

My Neshamah stirred uncomfortably. My sense of his presence was as gradual as the dawn, but I felt his answer. Yes. There were no words, but it felt apprehensive.

"So, in theory, you could trace it back to the mage that is using it to spy." I paced agitatedly, an angular course around the small kitchen. "If I draw a summon circle and focus the ritual through something with a Phitonic charge—the Wardbreaker, my father's hammer or something—I could summon it. Summon it and find him and kill him."

"We could be deceived," Kutkha said, after a time. *"As I told you. There are no angels, only demons. The creatures and substance of GOD are physical. They cannot be summoned. Demons are formed of the cesspool to which all human minds contribute. They hold dark things—all dark things of which you could conceive. NO-things."*

"I know where they come from. I know it's a risk." I breathed in, out, and tried to relax on my feet. "But I am a ritualist, Kutkha. If there's any place I'm strong, it's ritual."

"All summoning is Pravamancy. You will tear a hole in yourself. That is how they are called. You tear a hole. You must hope that you can fill it in once it is done."

I went to the freezer and pulled out the chalice. It had been days without a water change, and the ice was brown and crumbly, like rust. "If I don't, we're dead anyway. If I have nothing to show, Sergei will shoot me like a dog on the street. Don't you know what he's like?"

Kutkha nearly said something. I felt him, the pressure of his intent—but he held back. Hiding something, from me?

"Very well. If you fail, you will go mad. You know not what you do."

It was the truth, but I was already on my way to the door. "No. Not really... but I'm about to find out."

CHAPTER 20

It took at least an hour to prepare a full circle. There was a particular setup illustrated in the grimoire where I'd found the sigil—the main circle was adjacent to another, smaller figure in which the demon would appear. The main circle featured a spiral it its center, a deceptively simple geometric figure that had to be rendered with great precision. With chalk and string and a two-foot measuring board, I laid down a ring containing a spiral, a perfect depiction of the Golden Ratio. The shape connected through positioned candles which led to the second, smaller circle. The summoning ring was made to take a beating: the shapes were simple, the lines tight, each border and sigil inscribed firmly and with care. I'd busted enough static enchantments to know how easy it was for imperfection to be exploited by a penetrating force. The fact was, other than a certain ability to sense and work with the currents of energy, I was working mostly from textbook knowledge. My fears had to be put aside, or I would fail from the expectation of failure.

Binah sat near the edge of the room, unnaturally attentive for an animal of her kind, watching me watching her as I wielded my onyx ritual knife through the chanting the incantation at each quarter of the circle. I felt a charge in it build as I went through each invocation, merging into the space through the stately choreography of ritual magic. Every hand gesture, each spoken word, the direction of our pacing—everything had its significance.

Kutkha hung between us like a shadow, and I felt his presence overlaying mine with every step in the rote, every vowel and dripping consonant—and when the last word hung, trembling on the air like a bell, I felt him merge like a wave in the ocean, a drop in the sea... just as we were overwhelmed by a sucking rush of power that dragged my weight into the floor, the same tactile hallucination that you could sometimes experience at the seashore as the rushing tide seemed to carry your feet into the spray.

The lines of the circle thrummed, gathering strength, then flared a deep vibrant orange. The engraved lead caster wobbled once, twice—and then the metal started to heave and boil, hissing as the entity bound to the seal began to struggle against the magic trying to control it.

"IAO!" I boomed over the sudden noise and movement, staring hard at the seal at the center of the spiral, the spiral that was gaining depth and power as we forced it to activate. I was conduit and controller, summoner and channel, and soon, something unseen began to test and challenge my will, seeking the cracks and holes it could leak in through.

"You, you, YOU... calling ME?!" Its voice crackled through the room like streaks of lightning, ringing off every surface. "You, of all magi?"

The room had gone very cold and smelled pungently of burning wax. I hadn't expected it to respond with the eloquence and force that it did. My surprise caused the chalk line to jitter on the floorboards, slowly charring it black. I mastered myself, as the extent of the danger I was in dawned in its full weight and breadth. I drew up to my full height, unimpressive as it was, my back stock straight. Whatever had come was certainly not an angel. Invisible, it gibbered frantically in the face of my stony silence. The initial burst of sound was followed by a hush as it pried and poked at my conviction and failed to move me.

"What is this? WHAT DO YOU WANT FROM ME?" The whispering built to a shriek, then dropped. Underlying its presence was the buzz of a hundred thousand hornets, a waveform pressure that peaked and ebbed under my growing control. I was gaining confidence. It was the next step up from the kind of magic I'd been doing my entire adult life, but as I began to verge into cockiness, I felt the entity picking at my mind like a hangnail.

"You! Creature, you will return to your last human summoner before me, and you will deal him agony." I spat each word with withering disdain, command bordering on but not quite falling into arrogance. "You will do it NOW."

It hissed at me before slithering into a pile of dancing motes, vaguely resembling the shape of a person, then a wheel, then a protoplasm. "Why not do it tomorrow, to catch the element of surprise? In the meantime, I could find you a lover... the man—"

"You will do it now." My lip curled as I hefted the hammer. "Or I will torture your seal for days before I lock it in a lead box of salt and holy resin and bury it. Do it NOW."

The threat caused the room to fill with wailing. The creature's form manifested in my mind's eye, a writhing bundle of lashing electric tendrils with no main body. The thing hissed, writhing in the air before being driven from the circle, inward, imploding to fly back towards its original summoner.

I bent my will to the rest of the task at hand—to destroy the seal itself. As I thought on it, the temptation to give into its desire only grew. It knew so much, and its tempting whispers lingered in my mind like cobwebs. The supreme math of the universe was at my fingertips, if only I could stand to listen to its voice. I burned with longing, and my mind was an engine on full throttle as I forced myself past desire, past covetousness—and with unerring speed, the spirit struck true.

It hit the other unseen magus like a Molotov, splashing fire and engulfing them in a roar that reverberated through the core of my being. I saw nothing—only a furious light that filled my eyes with infernal orange fire and sucked me inwards into physical blindness. But Kutkha could see.

Giddily, I realized I couldn't feel my body anymore. That I didn't have a body, but that I was moving, and I had no idea where I was.

"Now we've done it." Kutkha was the one speaking aloud here, slinking down a narrow corridor like an avian dinosaur shadow. He was neither bird or reptile, bipedal and sleek, his body made of clustering, freezing darkness. In this place, this space, I was the ghost in Kutkha's machine. "You call this Yesod, the plane of dreams and visions. And I do not know why you are here."

I could do nothing except go along for the ride. Water was rushing down the length of a progressively smaller and more constrictive corridor, flowing like blood from a wound where the demon had struck. Kutkha waded forward, and just before it narrowed into a doorway, we reached a sigil burnt into the wall, a single Hebrew letter. Chet. The letter was filled with mercury that swam and swirled as we approached. Beyond that point, the space was nebulous and indistinct, a cacophony of sound, shade, and color.

"I will not go beyond here." My Neshamah pulled back and turned, coalescing into his raven form. On wings of shadow, he glided back down the very tangible corridors of this other reality. "Our job is done, but… that is Ocean. We are in the Drink. This is already far too dange—"

The astral matter beyond the cliff's edge of my psyche began to resolve into points of light. I heard a dim buzz, like insects—the sound of their mandibles and legs rubbing together, and Kutkha swelled in size, his face sharpening to a bladed muzzle as he swiveled his head back to face the doorway. We watched a honeybee crawl onto the edge of the portal, then another: ten, a hundred, a million. Their wings whined with a building shrill, and behind them came a looming figure, blazing like a torch in a cave.

"This isn't an angel. You said they don't exist," I said, dragged back with Kutkha into the black stone passage. Fear hammered my intuition into overdrive. *"What the hell is it?"*

The bees could not get past the sigil, and they crawled out over the empty doorway as if it were a plate of glass. Each one shone like a tiny sun. The water stopped flowing along the floor as the bees covered the entire threshold, and there was a push, like a hot knife lancing through my insubstantial being.

"Fight it." Kutkha's body lifted up with a bristling layer of spines. "It's attacking you. Fight it!"

I struggled for focus as the penetration deepened, fought to ward back the heat, but it was slippery, and it felt its way in through the cracks of my psyche with inexorable, incredible force. To my horror, I realized that I could not stop the invasion. *"I can't!"*

"You must!"

Through the film of insects, a figure emerged: tall and thin, radiant, and remarkably, impossibly beautiful. It dragged along sheets of light as a garment, and as it emerged, a flush of heat as soft as sunlight spilled across us. My breath caught, and Kutkha stopped, eyes widening as light flooded the labyrinth hall. The pushing stopped. The angel-faced being was comforting, like a needy embrace that I had never been able to stand but somehow always craved. So close, so hot, that it might have been able to get into my skin, and I would never be alone again.

Alone. God help me, but I was sick of it.

Unwittingly, I yearned towards it, and Kutkha took a halting step forward. The tall figure reached out its hands. It sung a Solar song, pure and bittersweet, a silent bow that played the violin of my repressed emotions and coaxed me to run in, grasp it, hide my face—

"It's a DOG!" Kutkha snarled. "Do you want to die? Do you want Vassily to die?"

As Kutkha and I struggled to gain control over the other, the being opened its eyes, rolling them down from the back of its sockets to stare down at us. They were as bright and heartless as jewels: endlessly needy, greedy green eyes. The angelic thing smiled beatifically and spread its long arms open like an old friend. An old, false friend.

I knew the look of false friendship well, and as it fixed on us, I bared my teeth. Kutkha's hackles rippled, and he grew fangs of glass as he shrieked defiance, a thing of bright flashing claws, shadow, and ice.

The green-eyed being was fighting in its own way, wheedling its way under the skin into the channels of fatigue and pain, chipping at the hard shell that made me what I was.

With a jolt of terror, I felt it trying to replace my ego with itself. It was everything I could need or want, a sympathetic virus. The creature didn't judge me for my longings, for all the people I'd killed or the lies I'd told. It only wanted me. To possess me—to consume me.

United in desperation with Kutkha, we became a bestial thing. Lips peeled back from double rows of razor-sharp teeth, and we snarled, filling the corridor with a freezing, boiling presence. This time, the command to leave was wordless, a spear of pure will and intent. Like a caul, shadow encapsulated the penetrating radiance and pushed it back. For a moment, the pressure wavered, the siren call replaced by a quarterback rush of energies as the other magus rallied behind their countermagic, pushing against my fierce and sudden will.

And then I realized something. This thing, this viral, deceptive thing—it wasn't a demon. It was someone else's Neshamah.

With a roar of defiance, we charged in a surge of spines and shade and salt mist towards it. The other Neshamah's smile split its face in two to bear rows of long, needle-sharp fangs, and it screeched at us as the dark coldness shoved it away. Screaming, spitting, it was inexorably pushed back from where it had come, and when we battled it past the threshold, the gaping energetic wound it had left sealed up and threw us back into earthly reality.

I came to with the point of my onyx knife pressed up under my breastbone, the blade grasped in shaking hands. Gasping for air, bathed in crystallizing sweat, I was bent backwards over my own heels in grand mal, my hair brushing the ground. My knees ached viciously where they had hit the floor.

"Not... not Carmine." I gasped. I threw the knife aside and carefully, slowly extracted myself from the painful grand mal position. "That was not Carmine."

"No," Kutkha replied softly, a ruffled presence of shadowy plumage and bright, nervous eyes. *"It was not Carmine."*

I groaned and managed to slowly bend forward into a normal human shape. The muscles of my back were so tight they threatened to snap. Lying on my side and wracked with spasms, I felt like a honeybee after it had stung something, half-dead, its entrails embedded in its target as it slowly suffocated under the cold creep of death.

When I was able to pick myself up, I wearily surveyed the contents of the circle, wiping at a thin trail of blood oozing down from my sternum. The tin cup had splattered, liquefied, forming a spindly arc into the air where it had frozen solid. It had taken the dim shape of a tormented figure straining for release, clawing at itself in a contortion of agony.

It wasn't Carmine. I had looked into his eyes and known that his Neshamah was canine. The Hellhounds were his soul. When I thought back to Vincent's mansion, man and hounds had had the exact same colored eyes, just like me and Kutkha. At least it meant I knew who I had to kill, because I knew only one green-eyed mage. Lev Moskalysk.

As I recovered in the circle, exhausted, confused, and vaguely triumphant, I heard the tinny shrill of the phone from my office. My jaw worked, clenching tightly enough I felt the muscles of my face all the way up to my temples. After that bit of arcana, whoever was calling was not going to be anyone I wanted to talk to.

A sense of simmering dread deepened on the way from the bedroom to my office. When the phone stopped ringing, the answering machine clicked, but didn't record anything else. The phone hesitated only a second before the ringing started again. I switched on the light and watched the handset vibrate in its cradle before reaching out.

I heard no sound from the other end when I picked up the receiver, save for soft, raspy breathing.

"Lev," I said.

"I'm appalled, Alexi. All that effort, and you didn't even get my name." A polished mezzo-soprano, thick with dark, cruel amusement, spoke after several moments' pause.

For the second time that night, and the umpteenth time that week, I had been wrong. It wasn't Carmine. And it wasn't Lev.

"You just couldn't listen to me, take my advice to leave well alone, could you, sweetheart?" Jana was excited, but I could hear barely concealed strain in her voice. Whatever I had done, it had hurt her. She wasn't the only one hurt, though. The horrifying sensation of my mind leaking out from between my ears had ceased, but every one of my limbs trembled with exhaustion. "Alexi, you have half an hour to bring yourself to my house, or Vincent dies."

"I don't give a damn if he dies." My eyes narrowed. She thought she could ransom me, of all people? "He's a drug dealer. A leech."

"Don't be dumb. No one wants Vincent for the drugs." I heard her press and wet her lips, rubbing them against each other. Over the phone, the sound turned my stomach. "Maybe the mundanes in your two-bit protection racket, but there's more at stake than yuppie-dust. No, if he dies, you'll care a lot, Alexi, because that will leave you, and you alone, as the most precious resource in the city. You will never know peace again."

"And what's that supposed to mean?" My hand turned into a fist on the desk.

"Why would I tell you that?" Her voice lightened and smoothed. She was clearly enjoying the game. "You and Vincent share some… peculiar circumstances. But no one really knows, other than me. Yet. Carmine Mercurio, for example, doesn't know you're just what he's looking for... but I'm sure he'd like to."

I said nothing, nostrils flaring. "What are you talking about?"

"I told you. He said 'yes'."

My chest tightened.

"Carmine knows *of* you, *zolotka*, yes. When I told him that someone was using his uncle's family name for business, and was helping the Russian Mafia, he was keen to find out who that was. I gave him an address."

"Did you rig my car, too? Because that didn't work."

"Yuri set that up for me. He was a good host, better than Robert Nacari. Before we knew what you were, I was supposed to remove your piece from the board." Jana sighed. "So now, you have a choice. You come to me, or I dispatch Vincent, use his sacrifice to kill your butt-buddy while he's at your sister's place, then tell Carmine where he can find you."

"Go fuck yourself." My face flushed hot.

"16 Brown Street, Sheepshead Bay. Half an hour." She laughed and hung up on me.

I closed my eyes for several long moments, then looked down at the desk. If I only had thirty minutes, I needed to make them count.

CHAPTER 21

I spent fifteen minutes studying a single letter, the same one I had been studying and meditating on the way to Atlantic City. *Chet*, the barrier. I armed myself, pistol and knife, but doubted I'd get to keep them. Jana was right—I didn't really have much of a choice but to play her game. If I called for help, it was as good as telling Lev and Sergei I couldn't be relied on. One "aw-shit" was worth more than a hundred "attaboys." If I was going to do this, I'd have to do it myself.

The address she gave me looked like a perfectly normal Brooklyn row house, white clapboard with a chain-link fence, and unremarkable save for the exceptionally healthy red petunias she grew along her windowsill and over her stoop. They were a brilliant color, a red darker than blood. I didn't knock and didn't have to. As soon as I set a foot on the third step, the door opened of its own accord.

Jana's house was very well furnished, tasteful and decorated entirely in shades of white and cream with careful, small contrasts. Splashes of red in places, ambers and tawny browns. Her smell led me to her sitting room: it was all open-plan and white. Pure white. Everything was immaculately clean, white as polished bone. The woman herself was reclining on a white leather armchair in full view of the front door, seated with the stiff imperiousness of a nervous queen. She held a semiautomatic pistol in a loose, confident grip, the only black thing in the room.

"Come in." Her mouth curled at the corners. "But if I see you reach for anything, I'll blow your head off."

I edged inside, keeping my hands loose and my eyes slow. There was nothing at all to indicate that she was a magus. There had to be a room with tools and paraphernalia somewhere, an altar or a circle. My gaze fell on the sculptural lamp by her elbow. The base of the fitting was an inhumanly beautiful gazelle-like figure who arched like a gymnast, holding the spherical lamp on her shoulders. She was neither animal nor human and had long curving horns, like an antelope's.

The air ruffled strangely, warping from the power of an invisible, powerful will. Behind me, the door slammed shut.

"Coffee?" She arched a brow.

"No." I looked back at her. "Thank you."

"Don't feel like buying time?" She rose, neat in her prim dress and low heels, and moved around me in a slow circle.

"Would there be any point?"

She disappeared out of my peripheral vision, and I tensed. When she was behind me, she stopped. The cold muzzle of the pistol pressed in against my kidney.

"Not really," she said. "Walk ahead."

She pressed the gun in, and I moved off slowly, waiting for an opportunity. Waiting for inspiration. It was like my father always said: you could be the hardest sonovabitch in the neighborhood, but it didn't mean nothing at the business end of a piece.

Jana pressed me towards her bedroom. I looked over it with numb consternation as the door shut behind us. The bedroom, even more so than the living room, was white. Her bed, walls, carpets, everything. The blond wooden dressers had white sheets over them, with only the ankles showing. The only break in the monotony was dead things: Jana collected antlers, insects, bones, and pieces of amber mounted in wooden cases on her walls. White wooden cases.

"You like them?" she asked, girlishly. "I pictured you as a bit of a collector, you know."

"Oh, yes." What the hell was I supposed to say? Basically, the room had no cover, save for the bed. Nowhere to duck and shoot. "Just... lovely."

"Aren't they? Turn around."

Jana had a weird half-smile fixed on her lips, her eyes wide. Her cheeks were flushed with excitement, her lips moist. I regarded her sullenly, running over the word of power in my mind. *Chet, the Gate. The letter of the shield. Chet.*

"You know, I tried to ask nicely. I had Yuri visit and everything." She flashed a sympathetic, wholly insane grimace, wide-eyed and plaintive. "And that was before I knew what you are. But you didn't listen to me. They usually listen, you know, other mages. We love the magic for its own sake."

I thought back to the boardwalk. "So you killed Yuri and Frank. And what about the other guy?"

"Frank's brother? He was the one who found the Fruit." She said the word like it had a capital, like a title. "But he forgot where it was by the time I finally spoke to him. They do that, the norms—they forget. It's a defense, you see? If the unworthy behold the Fruit of the Tree of Knowledge, they forget where it is."

"I really have no idea what you're talking about."

"I was going to have him kill you," she said. "But then I finally got to touch you. Skin to skin. And I realized, Alexi—you're the real deal, better than Vincent. A true Wise Virgin. Do you have any idea how rare that is? A fully fledged mage with a clean cock?"

My face flushed with heat before I could stop it, and she laughed with delight.

"Strip." She dropped her chin slightly, her eyes locked with mine.

My mouth opened and then closed. I sputtered. "What!?"

She motioned slightly with the barrel of the gun, the black void at the tip never wavering below the neck. "I want to get a proper look at you. Strip. Make it slow."

The flush spread down my neck, and I bared my teeth, like a cornered animal. I was sick of being violated. "No."

I had no time to react before Jana fired. The bang caused my vision to white out and my mouth to sear with sensory overload. The air bowed with pressure. I was sure I'd been hit, but my heart continued to rush slickly in my chest while the bullet graze on my cheek began to bleed.

"I said strip." Jana's voice was cold.

"Where did... you learn to shoot like that?" I had to distract her while I searched for the out. I wasn't certain I could bring my hands up to start on my shirt collar buttons, but I was certain that I wanted to live. With shaking, fumbling fingers, I started on my clothes.

"I used to go hunting with my pa," Jana said languidly. "A real long time ago."

"You're... from the South?" I loosened one button, then the next, unable to stop my trembling. No one, nobody, had seen me like this. She was watching me hungrily, like food that hadn't died. Her nipples were hard. They stood out against the fabric of her dress.

"Tennessee."

I reached the last button on my shirt and let it drop behind me. My skin prickled with gooseflesh. "Why—"

"Shut up." She snapped, and her finger tensed. "No talking. Only time I want your mouth open is when there's something going in and out of it."

A tremor passed through my spine. I uncomfortably, unhappily stripped my undershirt up over my head. It brought an approving sound from Jana.

"That's it." Her voice had dropped, low and heated. "You're so shy. I never thought I'd see a shy Vor v Zakone."

I wasn't a Vor v Zakone, but she didn't look like she was receptive to being corrected. Haltingly, I forced my hands towards my belt, and when they reached it, they shook uncontrollably.

"You ain't ever shown anyone your little man before?" Jana's mouth spread in a crooked, lewd smile.

"No." I tried to pull the buckle out, but my hands were wooden. Jana twitched the gun warningly, and I somehow managed to undo it. My teeth chattered until I wired my jaws tight. "And I never want to."

"Oh, I know. I know, honey. And that's exactly why I need to see." She licked her lip and let her tongue linger, dark red on orange. "You're perfect. So pale."

I glared at her in hot defiance as I toed my shoes off. My cheek bled freely, and I licked at the corner of my mouth. The blood was a sweet iron tang. It felt effervescent on my tongue, crackling with some kind of subtle force.

Of course. Blood.

"I always wanted to see something like this." Jana gestured to my forgotten fly. "An honest Wise Virgin. You're the real deal. You can't imagine how I had to contort my magic to stop Rob from killing you on the boardwalk. That DOG wanted you so badly."

My legs felt like blocks as I stiffly stepped out of my trousers, moving slightly to the side and awkwardly bumping my knee into the corner of the bed.

Jana laughed, but I said nothing, jaw working. My skin crawled. The air felt wet and tacky.

"Socks first. If there's one thing I can't stand, it's a naked man in socks."

The only barrier between my body and her eyes after that were my trunks and my gloves. I had to face it: I had faced worse than this. As my focus grew, the mind-chatter went from turbulent terror to still apprehension, and I pulled off one sock, then the other, standing in her room on bare, soft white feet. My throat was tight, aching sharply. The bullet graze on my cheek burned cold, but Jana's intensity was daring me to try something. I knew through the pain in my gut and chest that I wouldn't be able to get the word of power out before she pulled the trigger in my face.

"And the gloves." Under other circumstances, her tone would have been teasing, flirtatious. It wasn't. She was soaking me up with her eyes, consuming my fear and loathing. But I couldn't do it.

"Please," I said. "No."

Jana lifted the gun and raised her eyebrows. "Gloves or your ear."

I would not fail this. My eyes and face burned red as I shakily pulled the gloves off, one at a time, and threw them angrily on the covers. It brought a soft sound from Jana. I growled back at her, mouth and nose full of the taste of blood. I felt like how I had in the bathtub, helpless and furious, and I stared at the tip of the pistol as I stripped the last off, ticcing, wincing as the waistband rasped over my soft fingertips. Without the protective second skin, my tongue rippled with the texture and the accompanying color.

"Uncircumcised? Look at you, all covered up," Jana exclaimed, chest expanding as she breathed deeply. Was she smelling me? She adjusted the gun, and it trembled slightly. Not enough.

I said nothing, clenching my trunks in one white-knuckled fist.

"Perfect," she said. With my gloves off, my body was a live antenna: I could hear every movement of fabric, every shift of her thighs, every small, wet sound made behind her teeth. My vision contracted. If she touched me, I was either going to break her arm or throw up on her before I died. Or both.

Jana didn't touch me. Instead, she reached into her collar and pulled free a long chain, like the one she'd worn in her office. This one wasn't silver: it was copper, with a drop pendant emblazoned with another Goetic seal, the seal of Ashtaroth. "Just perfect. And now comes the best part, Alexi—the part where you don't have to think anymore."

And now, now came whatever magic she had planned. I sighted down at her, pupils drawn to points, and lifted my chin as I sucked in a breath through narrowed nostrils. *Chet.*

"I'll brand you tonight, train you up. We'll find the Fruit, and then we'll go to Chicago together." She sucked her lip under her teeth and bit it until red welled up around her tooth. "I know people there that will take the time to break you in just right. Not like Frank—he couldn't even get it up."

In my mind's eye, I saw Yuri again, black tears streaming down his cheeks as he split from the inside. There was nothing worse than what Jana and her people, whoever they were, were going to do to me. My arm snapped out: I hurled the wad of cloth in my hand as I threw myself to the side. As I tumbled, I saw Jana track me with the experience of a hunter.

The certainty of death bore down like a mantle.

"CHET!" I roared as I hit the ground, drowned out by gunshot.

Hot pain seared through my knee: I shouted wordlessly as something cracked above my head. Jana screamed in agony.

Deafened, disoriented, I scrambled up to see Jana's eyes huge with shock. The front of her dress bloomed scarlet past her clutching hand, but she was already aiming again. I dove down beside the bed and ripped the sheets off, flinging them at her as she fired again and again. A bullet clipped my arm: I heard another tear through the material of her mattress as she spun around after me, tripped, and toppled over my naked chest with a harsh, bestial sound.

"Whore," Jana rasped, her gaze wandering over my face. "You're... just a... whore. Like all of them. Amma... Vmm Mmm... emet...gis..."

I fought out from under her dead weight in a panic and scrambled back in a crab crawl that landed me on my ass when I hit the dresser and bounced. I dragged up the sheets, covered myself, and scrubbed her blood from my chest. It clung stickily to my bare skin, and I ticced, spasming through face and fingers. Shaking, I staggered to my feet.

Jana's mouth was still working, her eyes hooded and dark. Whatever magic she was trying to work, she couldn't get the words past each wet, sucking breath. She was still looking at me when her head finally flopped lifelessly to the side. Blood welled across the carpet from under her weight, saturating the floor, her clothing, threatening to pool around my feet.

I barely made it into her en suite in time. I stumbled to my knees and threw up, retching until I garbled. That was it: the last straw. I couldn't do this. I punched the wall ahead of me. There was no strength in it. I could feel the clothes floating on my naked skin, my hands squirming in the gloves, and there was a second's pause before my heaving started again, every muscle in my body rebelling at the mingled, sickening smell of lilies and blood.

Through it all, I knew there was something I had to do, but I coughed and choked until nothing was left. Only once I stopped being sick did I remember, hazily, what'd I'd come here for in the first place. Vincent. And GOD help me, the police. The police would be here any minute.

Panic urged me to my feet. Vincent. My mouth was burning, a sensation barely relieved by cold water from the tap. Before I left the bathroom, I swilled and spat until I could no longer taste anything in my mouth.

"I did it," I rasped. "Kutkha. Magic."

The wraithlike weight of my Neshamah coiled around me in reply, a consoling and weighted presence. It didn't help much. I felt... dirty. Touched by filth. Jana hadn't gotten what she wanted, but I felt no triumph at having bested her. My stomach trembled again, but nothing was left to vomit up. I rubbed my hands on my thighs, composed what was left of me, and got back to my feet.

There was a stairwell down to a basement in the sparkling clean kitchen, a plain door with peeling magenta paint and a matte-black circle which contained the eye and cross symbol

I had seen in my dream. The air inside the next room was fetid, tropically humid, and smelled powerfully of living plants and rotten meat. I fumbled at the wall inside for a light switch, and flipped it up. Three blue lights flickered on overhead, then rows of grow lights illuminating a veritable jungle of plants. Marijuana, Angel's Trumpets, swamp lilies. The scent of decay was powerful, and there were cages about: heavy, roughly welded iron cages big enough for a man. A goat bleated in alarm as my footsteps scuffled on the concrete.

"Let me out of here, you crazy bitch! Hey!" a reedy man's voice cried out from somewhere deep inside.

I pushed on past the cage with the goat. The cage stacked on top of it had another one, dead, its tongue lolling from its rotting mouth. The pair of cages sat by a shoddily made door. I stopped in the entrance to assess the interior, my hair and clothing plastered to my body with sweat.

The small room beyond was lit by studio lamps, the floor almost wholly taken up with a Goetic summoning circle. The primary figure—the circle and triangle—were lovingly drawn on the whitewashed floor with thick permanent marker, half-filled in with chalk. A thin, unshaven, unkempt man was bound off to one side in a stress position, tied with ropes to a thick bamboo rods that held him like a rack. He was shorter than me, which is saying something – only around five feet tall.

"Who... The fuck are you?" Vincent was gray with shock, shaking, his hair a wet and bloodied mess. His skin had been carved with symbols from chest to beltline.

"Later." I went to him, dropped to my knees, and sawed at the ropes with my knife. "I'll get you out of here."

"Oh. Wonderful." Vincent grinned, before his eyes glazed over and he sagged like a doll against his bondage.

I freed him, laid him out, and looked over his injuries. Other than some deep bruises and the carvings, he looked to be sound: just dehydrated, shocked, and exhausted. I left him on his side and searched around the room. There were no tools in here. Some instinct drove me back out into the greenhouse area. Somewhere in here, I would find answers. Somewhere in here was the heart.

In the farthest reaches of the basement was a plain wooden trapdoor set unobtrusively into the floor. It opened up into a small square cellar that smelled powerfully of incense and formaldehyde. My nose wrinkled as I dropped down the ladder leading in, looking from one thing to the next. The first thing I saw was her altar—or at least, what I supposed was an altar. It was a square black cube table with nothing on it. An eye and cross symbol had been painted on the wall overhead, and I was fairly certain it was rendered in old blood.

Two of the four walls had bookshelves. One actually did hold books: the other carried a collection of skulls. I counted several humans, three cats, a dog, rabbit, and a deer. They had been glazed with amber, a hazed crust of sap over the bone that stained it red.

The fourth wall was home to Jana's desk. Unlike the altar, it was stacked with immaculately clean notebooks. Each one was bound in white leather. Aware that the cops were likely to turn up within minutes, I took an edgy seat and freed the oldest and newest books from the stack. Jana's older book, dated five years ago, was full of strikingly beautiful cursive. It was mostly an herbal, interspersed with a variety of notes on summoning, conjuration, and tool creation. Her latest grimoire, by contrast, was a chaotic mess. The writing was quick and scratchy, frenetically rendered in block paragraphs which barely linked together. A number of pages had been dedicated to sigil design. The rest, as I turned each page, was full of increasingly bizarre, fractured drawings. An entire page full of mouths with rows and rows of fanged teeth. Bizarre, hulking creatures formed by negative space in otherwise solid pages of ink. There was a short list of what looked like book titles: *Phitonis Harmonia*, *The Wayfarer's Rite* (Listen), and *Ars Phitomatrica*.

I re-read them, head swimming. As I had with the sigil used to summon... whatever had helped Jana do her dirty work, I felt I could, should know these things. Ars *Phitomatrica*. The title was powerfully familiar.

Towards the end of the notebook, I settled on the page which had the design of the solar sigil I'd entombed in my freezer. There was only one word of notation for the sigil itself: Puslicker. She had written below it: *"To find the champion of the Fruit, we need the Puslickers. They say Manellis have it. Where where WHERE?"*

The Fruit of Knowledge, the Fruit of the Tree? I frowned, skimming the rest of her notes. She hadn't written anything else about the Fruit, but I found the tipping point of her madness in an entry dated roughly eighteen months ago—December 23, 1989. The entry was full of photos that spilled out when I opened the page. Jana at her graduation, Jana with her friends. Everyone's faces had been cut out, except for her own. I turned back a page, and then another, through lines of grief-stricken, guilt-ridden writing. She'd experienced Shevirah when she and her best friend had been in a car accident and had awoken in a cold white hospital with Hyperion—her Neshamah, I could guess—whispering in her ears. It had convinced her that she'd murdered her friend.

"She went crazy after she underwent Shevirah?" I spoke aloud, voice high and tight.

"It would seem so." Kutkha was subdued.

"She lost her mind. This thing, Hyperion—that thing is insane. Are there things that can drive a Neshamah insane?"

For a moment, Kutkha did not reply. He rustled uncomfortably. *"There are. But I do not wish to speak of it."*

"Wait, no. You don't get to flake on me, you shit. Yuri said you were injured." I had figured he was lying and hadn't really given it much thought, but now? I opened another book which bulged slightly in the middle. A wave of crushed bees fell out of it onto the desktop, and I dropped it reflexively. "This could have happened to *me*."

"It is true..." Kutkha sighed. *"That I bear a scar."*

"So no wonder I was on the magical short bus. What caused this injury, wiseass?"

"You did," Kutkha said.

The answer caught me flat-footed. "Me? How?"

Kutkha did not reply. His withdrawal from me was as palpable as his contact.

Uncomfortably, I turned my attention instead to the notes Jana had left on the table. I knew I had to go: it was dangerous to be down here. Jana had gone from journaling properly in her books to keeping her thoughts on scraps, the newest left on the top.

"Frank Nacari no knowledge after retrieval. Brother, Robert Nacari, in charge of storage. Rob protected by ward: scry to find out WWHWW." Beneath it, she had noted in a far more rushed notation: *"Puslickers confirm. L says Fruit is local/nearby, secure V.M. to find. V.M. knows/knows who knows."*

L? Lev? I rifled through the stack of loose paper, my pulse trapped under my tongue. Other than vague references to L, an acronym turned up, over and over again. TVS. I could find no explanation.

Frowning, I turned my attention to Jana's desk drawers. I pushed aside bones and trinkets and dug out a small silver box emblazoned with a unicorn skull. Curiously, I opened it, and when I saw what lay inside, my lips parted in confusion.

Set into a velvet depression was the necklace Jana had worn on our first meeting, the silver teardrop pendant. Beside it was a small glass vial bound in copper wire. It was half-full of silver fluid that seethed and swirled. I touched it and jumped, startled, as it pulsed against my fingertip. Hesitantly, I picked it up.

"Oh..." Kutkha breathed in a hushed, reverent voice. *"Oh, my Ruach. This... is Phi."*

Kutkha's mirror analogy finally made more sense. I could see my reflection in the tiny vial, a miniature, undistorted rendering of my face that split and reformed like an unearthly mirror maze, reflecting many small Alexis under the light. It looked like mercury, but when I held the flask to the light, I saw the fluid crawling and evaporating, dripping upwards to the pool and reforming back into the mass. "It's stunning."

"Few men, few magi know the source of Phi. Fewer ever see it." My Neshamah was wary. Not of the Phi, I realized... but of me. *"We must go."*

"How do I use this?" I pocketed the bottle and the pendant and rose. My knee was throbbing and hot, my skin crawling with sweat. "I mean... can it be used?"

"Yes. You can consume it, if you wish to take the risk. But not here."

The impulse to uncap it and take the plunge then and there was strong, but common sense was telling me that I needed to collect my drug dealer and that we had to leave before we both ended up in the slammer. I pulled myself up, and collected Vincent, still unconscious, before I picked my way out of the basement, back up the stairs. I went to Jana's room, intending to look for anything that would help me learn more about this Fruit of hers, and froze in the doorway.

She was gone. The carpet was still dark with blood... but her body was gone. The room was thick with a sweet putrefaction smell... and as I searched for footprints, claw prints, anything, I noticed that the bloody carpet was moving, squirming with small purple-black larvae.

The skin of my neck and scalp prickled as I looked up, around, and backed away from the door. Fear drove me down the hall, out into the living room, then outside into the muggy heat. The air outside was fresh and sylvan in comparison to the smell in Jana's house. The smell of corruption... the smell I was coming to associate with Violet and Black, with demons, and the Gun.

CHAPTER 22

A storm had broken over the Atlantic by the time I got Vincent home, drenching the city in warm summer rain. Vincent was semiconscious, slurring in his sleep. I carried him inside the house, dressed him, tucked him up in a duvet on the sofa, and turned the air conditioner down to let the house warm up a little bit. Once he was seen to, I went to the bathroom and slammed the door hard enough that the hinges rattled.

In the ringing, whining silence, I stared at my reflection in the mirror. Trembling broke out through my body, spreading through my hands, my limbs, and my chest. My eyes were a mirror of my father's. I hardly recognized them as a part of my own reflection, trapped in the ringing silence of dissociation.

Jana had barely touched me, but she had some kind of power Carmine and his thugs did not. She'd cut me into pieces, objects for her scrutiny... and I had an awful feeling that she was out there somewhere, looking for me. I thought of Crina up on stage, in a booth, in a hotel room, performing under the gazes of men who did exactly the same thing. I had no idea how she endured it, night after night.

Shaking, I took the vial out of my pocket, and considered it for a moment.

"You don't like that I found this, Kutkha."

"I think it is too soon for you to become a Hound." My Neshamah's throaty voice held a bitter note.

Maybe if someone had explained what that was, I wouldn't have drunk it. With the naivety of the curious, I cracked the beeswax seal on the tiny bottle with jittery hands, and pulled the stopper.

The scent of Phi billowed out. It cleared the room. My bathroom turned into a fragrant temple, holy and sweet with the odor of night-blooming flowers, as if someone had taken the perfumes of honeysuckle, jasmine, and rose and dialed the saturation up until they transcended color and scent. It purified the air and cleared my head, even as it seared the inside of my nostrils with heat. It was the best thing I had ever smelled in my life, but it caused my chest to pang. Waves of wordless emotion gnawed at me... the sensation of loss and yearning was the strongest of all.

The mercurial fluid was pulling up in slender strands, disappearing into the air. It looked like *chordae tendineae*, heart strings. Before it vanished, I put the vial to my lips, and drank.

My body sucked up through my chest. Mind inverted.

I was a million miles above the ground and a million miles underneath as every vein, every organ, every cell filled with heat and sound. The sound penetrated everything, moved everything with its mass, moved between every atom and every moment in time.

...EverythingEverythingEverythingEverythingEverything...

I looked into sleepy eyes so blue they burned the heart out of me, and through them, a memory unfurled:

We were running, the White Woman moving ahead. Everything was frozen, the buildings cracking and crumbling, the ground itself churning to dust. The Earth, dipped in liquid nitrogen. The sky was orange, blazing orange, but there was no sun. I was myself, but not. My legs were missing from the knees down: I wore prostheses, recurved sprinter's legs, as something chased us like boiling, ghostly clouds of lightning.

...EverythingEverythingEverythingEverythingEverything...

The freeze was right behind us. Where it crept, color and light disappeared. I caught up to her, and as she turned to face me and offer her hand, I killed her. I watched my fist plunge a rainbow-hued knife right into her chest. She gaped, wide-eyed with shock as I pulled it free and pushed her, still alive, into the roiling gray sea.

...EverythingEverythingEverythingEverythingEverything...

I licked her silver blood from the knife, as sweet and floral as GOD's own perfume, then turned back into the frigid wind preceding the wave of ruin. Everything cracked dry and fell apart, a ripping cold so intense that it pulverized. It bathed me in fiery agony, a global necrosis that swept to the water's edge and took me as the sea froze and I opened my mouth and—

Oh GOD.

The pieces of me sucked back in and reformed, drawn by the inevitable pull of gravity. I came to on my bathroom floor, guts roiling with remembered pain. My mouth was open, throat wheezing as I screamed without sound. My body was bathed in sweet-smelling sweat that evaporated without a trace, just like the Phi.

"It's her." My voice cracked like a boy's. "*She's* the Fruit. The woman. That Phi was *blood*."

"*I told you that it was too soon. Yes... she is a Gift Horse.*" Kutkha loomed at the corner of my eye. He was projecting again, perched on the rim of my bathtub. Just like the first time.

"Which means what, exactly?" I rolled over, surprised to find that I wasn't in pain, that I wasn't bleeding or fucked up. My knee no longer hurt. My cheek no longer burned. My bruises were gone.

"Will you accept an explanation once you are centered and calm?"

I was fascinated by my knee. The crooked joint was straight again, almost as perfect as it had been when I'd first broken into Vincent's house. "I suppose."

"Then get a bathrobe. Get in the shower." Kutkha sounded as though he were standing right beside me.

I shivered my way through the shower, scrubbing Jana out of my skin. When I came out of the bathroom, I nearly ran headlong into Vincent in the hallway. The small man had his blanket clutched around his shoulders like a cape, framed by the doorway of the kitchen, eyes huge with surprise. They were sunken and bruised in his deer-like face.

He made a small, cracked sound. "Hi."

"Get back inside," I said. My voice came out like a whip. I hesitated, checking my tone before I spoke again. "Look... you can't even speak yet. I'll get you some water."

He turned and lurched back towards the den without a word. I double-knotted the belt of my robe and followed.

"Never seen a guy in bathrobe and gloves before." Vincent sounded like he'd been gargling glass. He collapsed back onto the sofa, pulling his blanket in around him. "Heard ya screamin'."

"You were hearing things. I'll get you some water." I didn't sit. "Stay here."

"Hey, before you run off... Who the fuck are you?"

I looked back from the doorway. "I was paid to find you."

"That kinda answers the question. I guess." He glared sulkily at the radio.

I left and got two glasses of warm water. When I brought them back, Vincent reached out urgently.

"Slowly, now, or you'll make yourself sick." I took my own chair, setting my glass aside on the reading table.

He had the look of a guzzler, but he had enough *compos mentis* to listen to the order and sip.

"You're one of the Russians." His voice was clearer after a drink, but vaguely accusative. Vincent was smiling, though, which confused me. His voice was higher than I was used to in men, a bright buzzing yellow. "Never thought I'd be glad to be in the clutches of the Russian Mafia."

'Clutches'. How dramatic. "I've been through a lot to find you, and seeing as you can speak, you're going to answer some questions." I rested my fingertips on the rim of my glass. "So let's start with Carmine."

"Oh, shit." Vincent grimaced as he sipped at his water. "Carmine's a total dick. I'm real sorry."

"Who is he?"

"You gonna at least tell me your name? Because I ain't answering nothing to someone whose name I don't know."

I sighed. I was too tired for the intimidation act. "Alexi."

"It was either gonna be Aleksey or Boris, wasn't it?" Vincent exaggerated the pronunciation of my name and offered me another hopeful, uncomfortable smile. "Do they make you great white shark motherfuckers in a factory out in Siberia or something?"

"I was born here."

"No shit? Okay, Alexi... you uh..." Vincent shuffled back against the sofa. "You deal in woo-woo, don't you? Big woo. Like Carmine."

Did I? I'd worked half-assed uncontrolled magic in desperation, botched one summoning, and managed to turn a bullet while I was naked and in fear of my life and virtue. Only the last one counted. "You could say that."

"I thought so. That blonde bitch had more woo on her than I've ever seen. I mean, that was some crazy, fucked-up shit she was doing in there. Torturing guys, cutting their fucking dicks off-."

"Wait." I lifted my hand. "No tangents. Start from the beginning. I want to know about Carmine, what happened to you, and whatever you know about the Fruit. In that order."

Vincent's face drew into set lines. He glanced at me, eyes flashing, before he curled back against the cushions. "Well... that's a real long story."

"We have all the time in the world."

"See, that's the problem. We don't, really. Not if the White Lady's got a thing to say about it."

I frowned. "The girl in your dream diary."

"You read my diary?" Vincent scowled, but he was too nervous to do anything about it. "Okay, look... I left my old man's place a few years back, for some real personal reasons. Things he couldn't deal with, you know what I mean? Meant I was out on the street. He's disowned me now. I lived pretty hard for a while, but I did what I had to do. I was having surgery for something when this voice in my head starts talking to me."

"Go on."

"Now, I remember Nonna, see. She was a Seer, full-blown Strega. My family's real superstitious. So I'm like, okay... I have this voice in my head now, and it's keepin' me from getting too down. Problem is, I start dreaming about weird shit. Probability. The future."

"Right." I sat back, steepling my fingers against my jaw. "You inherited her gift."

"Yeah. The Sight's a family thing. Goes right back to Roman times." Vincent sounded unaccountably tense. "So anyway, one of the things Spook-voice says to do is go see old man Laguetta. So I do that. It tells me: 'go to Cali.' Turned out two of my old street buddies were making it good in Colombia, so I hook Laguetta up with the two biggest coke suppliers in South America. Not just coke, either. Scopolamine, M.J.... So that's part of this, the drugs. But that's not the same as the Fruit."

"Where does that come into this?"

"Hang on. So there's two brothers in Dad's Family, right? Frank and Rob. Rob owns a fishing boat. Both of them love their coke, but my old man doesn't let his wiseguys ride the line. I could supply 'em, so they were my last link back to the Family, you know? I dealt to 'em after setting up with Laguetta, and they kept me in the gossip. So last time I sees Rob, he's all excited. Tells me that he and Frank were out dumping a body in the bay, and they found something weird. Super-weird."

I raised an eyebrow.

Vincent giggled. Not chuckled. Giggled. "Yeah. We're talking, like... a giant chestnut. James and the Giant Peach shit. Seven feet around. They find this thing out in the middle of the Atlantic, and they fish it out. No idea what it is, but they're opportunists, you know? Figger they can make money off it somehow."

"Naturally."

"After that, the weird shit starts happening. They put it somewhere, and nearly everyone that sees it forgets it exists. The few guys that do remember—because they keep seeing it in its hiding spot—they tried to crack it open, right? Some kinda goop shoots out of it and burns them alive. As soon as that happened, Dad calls in Carmine from my uncle's office in Vegas. He got real serious real fast, and Rob tells me that he put him under some kind of protection. We take magic pretty seriously. Rob shows me this pendant Carmine was making him wear, and he tells me that Carmine is looking for me."

"Because you're a Wise Virgin?" I glanced at the door to the den as Binah trotted in, her tail arched high.

Vincent's discomfort visibly increased. "Anyway, around about this time, I start having these dreams about the white land. Well, the Glass Land, is what she calls it. Eden. Every night after this thing is hauled ashore, I dream about her. First it was small stuff, then it got more and more intense. All these fucked-up, vivid scenes of this garden, and her in New York or Chicago getting killed, the world being wrecked and shit. She asks me to choose, but I can never answer her. I dunno what to say. Choose what?"

"I dreamed about her, too," I admitted, after a pause. "Soon after... being sent to find you by my superior."

"Lev, right? That guy is a total spook." Vincent's mouth quirked. "I got the Eye, man. I can see when someone's got woo."

I patted my thigh, and the cat jumped up onto my lap. "But no one can find the Fruit?"

"Nope. Frank, Rob, and Carmine knew where it is, but I saw Jana tear up Frank and Rob, and they both forgot long before she started torturing them." For a moment, the young man's face grew sober. "I don't even think you can use magic to find it. Jana tried a couple of different ways. The only one that knows now is probably Carmine, maybe my dad."

I thought on it, caressing Binah's ears and considering the puzzle pieces I'd been handed. "Jana was working for someone in Chicago, and she knew that the only person who can handle this Fruit is a Wise Virgin. That's a part of mythos related to unicorns. The only humans capable of gentling a unicorn were learned adult virgins, typically maidens. Nuns, priestesses. But not necessarily women."

For several long seconds, Vincent was silent. I watched him weigh up what to say and what not to say. "Yeah, I guess... But man...do you know how hard it is to find even normal virgins in the Mob? The Families ain't the place to be looking for virgins, I can tell you that much."

"Jana wanted to open the Fruit, and so does Carmine. I think he learned of Frank Nacari's death by accident, while Jana manipulated him for all this time." I frowned. "But if he's looking for you, he's learned something of this mythos."

"That's what I figure, too. Carmine will want that thing, man. He's like a nuclear reactor deep inside. He loves magic, he loves power. He's been obsessed with it his whole life. He was in a skiing accident way back. Got stuck in the mountains for a couple days with a broken leg. He survived, and he came out of it with this crazy woo he has now. He ain't normal. Most guys keep their spooky voices in their heads, but Carmine? There's something wrong with him. He has Fido and Goofy with him everywhere. Sometimes you see them, sometimes you don't, but they're real as shit."

His Neshamah could project a true physical form. Kutkha had said it, and I agreed: there was something wrong about it, but other than an odd feeling of unease, I didn't know exactly what. It was unnatural to expose your soul like that, I supposed. "You were close?"

"Me and Carmine? Hell no." Vincent shook his head. "Like I said, he's an asshole."

"Now, this is all fascinating," I said with a sigh. "But there is one problem. Carmine has no idea who you are."

Vincent drew in on himself in sudden agitation. His eyes went dark—dark and dangerous. "And it better stay that way. He'd fuckin' kill me."

"You need to give me the whole story. It's not only your life that's at stake." I matched his intensity, leaning forward on my knees. Vincent's eyes flicked from side to side. He was mapping his cover, his escape route.

When Vincent next spoke, his voice held bitterness far too concrete for his age. "You got no idea what's at stake. There's different ways of being killed."

"People tend to exaggerate and distort their personal issues," I replied. "And I have a reputation for discretion. Whatever it is, it won't leave this room."

Vincent glared at me suspiciously for several long moments, his blanket drawn up to his chin. "Mom and Pap had five boys. Two of us were in a car accident as kids. My bro died, and I got real fucked up. Jaws of Life, intensive care for six months, physical therapy. I lost half my colon, and my cock and balls."

I blinked rapidly. "Is that all?"

"What do you mean 'is that all'?" Vincent bristled.

"No, I don't mean it in a dismissive sense. I mean it is as in that was all that drove you from your family? Losing some parts of your body?"

"You don't understand, man." He wrapped his arms around his shin. "The Mob's just like a pack of wolves. They sense weakness, think you're not a 'real man'? I couldn't get a leg up after that. No promotion, no work, no respect. No one let me cover for them, or go on runs. They pretended to be all kinds of sympathy, but called me all sorts of shit behind my back. My dad told me that I was the most disappointing thing he'd ever made. So yeah, that's why I fell out with them. I faked my death, changed my name and everything. I wasn't called Vincent back then. No one else but you, Lev, and Georgie Laguetta knows I was part of the family. I've had guys put down for trying to speculate, you know what I mean?"

I nodded and clasped my hands together in thought. It was so completely irrational, but as Nic and I had pointed out to one another the week before, the Mafia were not known for their common sense. "It certainly explains why Carmine didn't know who you are, though I'd warn you now. He's found your house."

"He couldn't have."

"Jana knew I was going there and tipped him off. Do you know who or what the 'Temple' is? She might have called them the TVS."

"TVS? Nah. I heard her rant on about how she knew someone in Chicago, but she never said anything useful." Vincent twisted his fingers together. "I tell ya, this thing they caught out in the bay, it's nothing but bad news. So many guys are dead already, not counting whoever else is going to get fucked up. Dad'd have me done in the ass with a broomstick if they found me now."

"You're safe here, for the time being." It was a hollow assurance, but it was all I had.

"Sure." Vincent didn't sound particularly convinced. "So is that it? I need to catch more zees."

I thought for a space, looking at the spines of the books surrounding us in the den. "You said you saw the girl in your dream, on a dying world?"

Vincent sighed softly, tiredly. "Yeah?"

"Did you... see me with her?"

Vincent scratched his jaw, eyes narrowed in thought. "No. I saw someone, I dunno who it was. I called him the Bird Man, on account of the birds that always hung around him. Crows and shit."

With a shrug, I scooped Binah up over my shoulder and stood. "Well, time for sleep. Rest well. We're going to talk again."

"Yeah, man. I will. G'night."

With the cat wandering the floor, I stripped off in the hush and sudden privacy of my bedroom, head ringing. It wasn't until my head hit the pillow and the sheets were up around my ears that I realized the depth of my fatigue. The smallest edge of relaxation, and my bones began to throb in sympathy with the rest of my aching body. When had I last eaten? I reached up and ran a hand over my face. The stubble rasped against my leather palm, and I frowned in consternation. *When had I last shaved?* It was the last thing I remember thinking.

When the alarm went off, I stirred groggily and looked aside. It was going on six p.m.—only six p.m.? I couldn't remember the day of the week.

It took a great effort to sit up, and even more to turn on the bedside light and find my diary. Wednesday the 12th, a day ahead of what I'd thought.

Wednesday? I groaned and rubbed my face. The meeting at Sirens was supposed to start at eight.

It took a disproportionately long time to get out of bed, get dressed, and reach the phone. I dialed Nic's office number. Lev turned his handset off during meetings.

"Security," grunted the voice on the other end.

"Nicolai, it's Alexi. Can you put me through to Lev?" I had no energy for nicety. Fortunately, Nic never cared.

Nic hung up, and while the muzak played, I composed an address to my Avtoritet. I wasn't going to apologize for being late. I'd found what I'd been sent to look for, and I wanted my money and some reprieve while I considered what to do—if anything—about Jana's magical fruit.

"Alexi. Glad to see you're still with us." Lev's voice was slightly crisp.

"I have Vincent." I spoke in Ukrainian, snapping each word off cleanly so I didn't stammer from fatigue. "He's asleep in my living room. Beaten up, but otherwise sound."

There was a thick pause before Lev exhaled with relief. "That's... that's fantastic news. Thank you, Alexi, really. Where did you find him?"

"Jana's house." I listened carefully for his response.

"I..." he trailed off. "How did Jana have him?"

"You didn't know she was a spook?"

"No. No... but I suppose that... makes sense in retrospect." I could almost hear him frowning. "What did you do to her?"

"She's..." I nearly said 'dead', then I remembered the absent white hole on her bedroom floor. "She's around."

"Alright. Something to discuss in private, later in the night. Did we solve the mystery of Vincent's family story?"

"He was disowned by his dad when he was still a teen, apparently."

The pause this time was longer, broken only by Lev's tense breathing over the receiver. "I see. Look, Alexi. Are you still able to come into the office for that meeting with our Pakhun?"

"I can." I was immediately wary and glanced at the glass case, and the hammer. He wasn't telling me something, but there was no mistaking the surprise in Lev's voice. "But I'll be late."

"Good, and that's no problem. Come in at ten. Sergei won't be here until midnight, at least, and if you could bring Vincent and Vassily with you, that would be… advantageous."

"Vassily won't be able to make it. But I can bring Vincent." I rubbed my fingers on the edge of my bathrobe, over and over. Unaccountably, sweat beaded on my upper lip.

"Are you sure?"

"He's sweating off a fever."

"Not good. But bring Vincent. It will boost morale." Lev sighed. "I was able to talk us out of any arrests at the Taj Mahal, but there is bad talk over here, Alexi. Watch your back. There's wolves about, and they want our blood."

I hung up and moved away from the desk into the living room, unhappy and unsettled. Vincent was a white lump in the center of my sofa, and his breath filled the room with an ammonic reek. A dark head of hair protruded over the edge of the blanket bundle. It reminded me of Vassily, and with a pang of guilt, I realized I hadn't even thought about him before Lev brought him up. I needed to go and visit, but Lev would kill me if I left Vincent alone. I chewed a flake of skin from my lip as I pondered my decision and couldn't settle on any one thing. I was still exhausted. There was no time for sleep, though, no time for anything, except maybe food.

The smell of frying dumplings and butter was enough to rouse Vincent and pull him out of the living room. While he stared from the entry to the kitchen, I wordlessly dished out four eggs, two to a plate, alongside fried pelmeni and onions. The coffeemaker was on, and for the first time in a week, the kitchen smelled like normalcy. I heaped a large dollop of sour cream onto our eggs before taking the plates over and set one down in front of Vincent.

"Thanks." Vincent still sounded as tired as I felt. He poked curiously at the pelmeni. "Hey, I've heard of these. Russian pasta."

"Veal and cheese." I cut into my eggs and folded half of one over my fork. "So, you knew Lev was a Phi— a mage?"

"Nah. Figured it was likely, though."

I finished swallowing. "You know, for all that magi are supposedly rare, I seem to have encountered a lot of them in a very short period of time."

"Yeah, well. Like attracts like." Vincent pushed the onions aside and crammed an entire pelmeni into his mouth. "Who knows, man. I think there's some energy happening in the world or something. That's my opinion. But speaking of supernatural shit, what do you think Carmine wants with this thing? The Fruit?"

I wasn't sure I cared anymore. The more time passed since the vision of the White Woman, the less enthused I was about pursuing the lead. Whoever she was, she had ruined me in some past life, or fucked up my psyche to the point where I fully believed she had. The visions, the dreams... they felt like railroading. All I wanted was to return Vincent, get the meeting done and dusted, then head over to Mariya's.

She and Vassily were all I had left, and nothing else really mattered to me anymore. "I have no idea."

"Me either." Vincent's eyes narrowed as he looked down at his food. He was picking the egg white off from around the yolks. "I know that if I found a horkin' great big spiny thing bobbing around in the ocean, I wouldn't fuckin' pick it up. You know? Logic would kinda dictate something like that is bad news."

"Reason isn't the greatest strength of most men in our lines of work." I arched an eyebrow, fork partway to my lips.

"Yeah, but it ain't just the Families. People are dumb. It's how I'm making a mint off my business."

As I watched him devour the meal, his first in several days, it occurred to me that this man was, in part, responsible for Vassily's addiction. He was one link in a long chain stretching between the American continents. "Is it a messy business? The coke trade?"

"Jesus. You got no fucking idea. The stuff might as well just be made out of dead bodies." Vincent's appetite seemed to increase as he got into the spiel. "They gotta joke down there, translates to something like: God made Colombia the closest thing to Paradise. When other countries around the world started asking him: 'Hey God, wait a sec, what's the deal? Why do they get this fucking amazingly beautiful country and we get this shithole over here?' He tells them: 'Yeah sure, it's pretty, but wait until you see the motherfuckers I put there.'"

"Hmph." I snorted.

"I mean, Colombia is fucking gorgeous, but yeah. It's a bloody trade, and unless you're really tight with your suppliers, they'll fuck you over as soon as anyone else. Georgie's lucky he's got me and the Twins. If you don't know somebody down there, you'll get to see some of the prettiest forest in the world for maybe a couple days before you're dead in a firefight or having your ass robbed bare. A guy I knew, they put a bomb on his plane and blew him and three hundred other people out of the fucking sky. Just to nail one man."

I wanted to judge him, the ways in which his trade had ruined the lives of so many, but what ground did I have to stand on? I killed for money. Fact is, nearly everything we owned in this country—TVs, clothes, drugs, sex—came in at someone else's expense. It was as Jana, speaking through Yuri's corpse, had said: we were nothing but small cogs in a grand, capitalist machine. Between that and her deceptions—layers and layers of them—I wondered if that was how she'd gotten so deep under my skin. She'd spoken the truth. Even her lust had been sincere.

Suddenly, I didn't feel hungry anymore. I scraped the rest of my eggs onto Vincent's plate and took mine, now empty, to the sink. "Finish up. We have to head out. Sergei Yaroshenko has come back to America, and you and I have a meeting we must attend."

CHAPTER 23

The meet was being held in the Sirens VIP rooms. I dressed for business and gave Vincent one of my old college suits. It was too small for me nowadays, but it hung loose across Vincent's narrow shoulders.

By the time we drove in, it was close to ten p.m. Two dark-tinted town cars were in the guest lot, the engines still ticking. Petro was guarding the staff entry, lounging against the doorjamb with his radio piece loose and his arms crossed over his chest. He waggled his eyebrows at me as we came up on him, shoulder to shoulder. "That your new boyfriend? I was wondering why we were a man short tonight."

"I wasn't aware that any other men worked here." I walked past him without waiting for his reply.

"Ouch." Vincent chuckled when we were clear of the door. "That sounded like it felt good."

I led Vincent through the front of the club, up the stairs to the salon entrances. The suites were not usually manned by guards, but tonight, two unfamiliar men flanked the polished oak doors in identical Italian suits. They weren't even bothering to conceal: both of them packed machine guns on shoulder straps, resting their elbows on the stocks with the nonchalance of old soldiers.

Vincent and I followed Sergei's distinctive rolling laughter down to one of the salons, which also had a guard posted. He was a square-jawed man with the round head and swarthy cast of someone from the Balkans, and he opened the door to let us inside.

Lev looked up when we stepped in, and rose abruptly with an expression of plain relief when he saw Vincent, his glass of whiskey in hand—but it was Sergei who commanded Vincent's immediate attention. Sergei Vladimirovich Yaroshenko didn't look a day older than fifty. By all rights he was pushing seventy, but he was still a monster of a man, towering over the room from a black leather love seat like a red-haired, blue-eyed king. He was swathed in a Cossack-style fur wrap over a red suit, apparently immune to the lingering summer heat. His gaze bore down on me, and I lost track of everyone else as Sergei half-rose from his seat in greeting, his face a mask of carefully controlled delight.

"Well, look at you!" he boomed. "Alexi, you're not an inch taller than you were ten years ago, but I dare say you're looking well."

A man could choke to death on Sergei's charisma. Here was the man who had started me on my path: who had put me through school, through college, had supported me until I found my feet. My mouth stretched in an awkward smile as I went to shake his hand. "Pakhun. It is good to see you again."

Sergei engulfed my gloved fingers with his callused, tattooed paws, shaking with one hand clasped on my wrist. I let him pull me in to kiss cheeks, and when he let me go, he waved me to the seat beside him: the one on Lev's left. The empty chair on his right was usually reserved for Vassily. "Excellent, yes. You've done us good work tonight, Alexi

Grigoriovich. I think you deserve a drink. Go get this man a double shot of Kors, eh?"

"Of course." I didn't drink, but refusing a drink from Sergei was tantamount to throwing it in his face.

From the side of the room, one of the salon waitresses moved over to the bar as the tender poured, and Sergei turned his attention to Vincent... but while they sorted out their niceties, my attention was drawn past him to the drapes which framed the private pole and stage. Sergei's ever-present shadow was never far away from his side: Vera Akhatova, the only woman in the Organizatsiya who was neither call girl or family member. She was a lean silhouette from where I stood, half-hidden by the glare of the studio lights that framed the settee. Sergei was eccentric; Vera was eerie. Some said she and Nicolai were brother and sister, and that was how she had gotten into the business. I didn't believe it. While there was a certain similarity between their hard, thin faces and dry wiry builds, Vera was the dark to Nic's pale. She was sinewy and strong, with taut, freckled arms, a short bob of dry brown hair, and dead chocolate brown eyes. I'd heard a lot of gossip about her over the years. Most of the younger men wondered what she was about, if not a girlfriend, sister, or whore, but I never doubted. I had seen her shoot, only once, when one of the old-old crew from my father's day got up at a meeting and pulled a knife at the table. Sergei had motioned by his leg, and Vera had drawn her pistols and put two bullets in the guy's head, one in each eye.

The door opened again, and Nic stepped through, his hands deep in the pockets of his old BDUs. He grimaced lopsidedly when he saw Sergei and Vincent together and went over to shake his hand and kiss cheeks with our

Pakhun, a ritual repeated with Lev, and finally, with me. I wondered if his hand was a little tighter than normal, if the gesture was more perfunctory. I stopped wondering when Nic casually dropped down into the chair I knew was reserved for Vassily, absent but accounted for. It chilled something in me, deep inside.

"So, now we only await the illustrious presence of Vanya, seeing as our youngest Lovenko is incapacitated," Sergei said in Russian, resting his hands on his thighs. When he next spoke, it was in thickly accented, but perfectly fluent English. "And you, Vincent Manelli. Our million-dollar baby. I trust your time in enemy hands wasn't too hard?"

"It sucked enormous fat donkey balls." Vincent blinked rapidly as he accepted his drink and threw back half the glass. "Absolutely sucked. Your guy here got me out in one piece, though. I uh... I lost track of Yuri. Sorry."

It was my turn next. I took the glass of Kors and sniffed. At twenty-four grand a bottle, it should have smelled like something other than vodka, but no. It was still just vodka.

"It is the reality of war that soldiers are killed in the line of duty." Sergei fixed his gaze on him, and under it, Vincent seemed all the smaller. "His memorial is tomorrow. One of three. Two more men have died as of this evening. Our own Maximillian, and Mr. Laguetta's Captain, John Scappeli. They both met their ends at the hands of unknown hitmen."

I said nothing. Vincent made a spitting sound of frustration and a silent solo toast to their names.

"Of course, we have no intention of giving in to your estranged relatives. Joint monopoly on the world's most popular recreational substance—barring alcohol—is nothing to trifle with." Sergei grinned. It should have been friendly, but Sergei was never friendly: not really. His smile was the rictus of a predatory animal, broad and toothy as a shark's. "And history is built on a foundation of corpses, as they say."

"Yeah. They sure do say that." Vincent sipped his whiskey and tried to smile back.

The door opened again, and this time, it was Vanya. He looked unwell, pale and pasty and tired. The week's events had been hard on him, poor thing. I eased back, as much as I was able to, and as Lev lifted his glass, I joined him and had a mouthful of vodka. It was like drinking a ghost: a searing cold heat that burned down to my gut, nearly tasteless and vaguely sweet. A thousand U.S. dollars, down the hatch. If I managed the rest carefully, I could avoid having to accept another glass.

"Well, this is lovely," Sergei said. "Back together again, just the five of us. If only we could have Grisha and Syoma, Semyon and Rodion back again, eh? And Mikhail, bless his loyal soul."

That brought some uncomfortable glances to bear on me as the toast was made, and Vincent beamed innocently at one end of the table as he lifted his glass. He had no idea, and as far as I was concerned, no business knowing.

"It is good that you were able to make it here, Alexi," Sergei said. "But Vassily? Now there is a problem. How is his leg?"

"To my knowledge, it is fine. Painful, but fine." The muscles of my neck and shoulders wound taut. As one, the faces at the table had turned to look right at me.

"But the fact remains that he was shot, and he cannot be here tonight. And you were his bodyman at this event, at the casino?"

"Yes, Pakhun," I replied. I did not like where this was going. "I was."

"How was he shot, then?" Sergei spread his hands wide, like a magician unveiling his latest trick.

No matter what I said now, I failed. I could protest that I was outdoors, and the question would be "why were you outside?" I could say that we fought and Vassily stormed in a fit of pique to snort ten K worth of coke, and I'd be turning Sergei's ire on Vassily. I was angry with him, but not so angry that I'd rat him out. "I was not beside him, Pakhun."

"Just as well you weren't the one protecting Lev then, eh?" Sergei's eyes flashed angrily. The grin never left.

"So does my bringing Vincent back to you mean nothing?" I jerked my head at Vincent, whose eyes widened at the sound of his name. Even if he spoke Russian, he didn't speak this sort of Russian: the rough vulgar slang that grew out of the prisons and Communist industrial wastelands of the whole GRU. "Because I might have failed with one hand, but I succeeded with the other." It was their turn to be surprised. Lev's eyebrows rose, and even Nicolai looked up from his glass. Sergei's face drained of humor, but only for a moment before he slapped his leg and laughed uproariously, a sound which needed no chorus to fill the room.

"Yes, yes... you earned that one, Alexi Grigoriovich," he said. "You have grown these ten years, eh? Our resident *starets*. You can look me in the eye and say your piece. I respect that. Now, speaking of Vincent, let's figure out what to do with him."

I was all too happy to have his attention turned on something and someone else. The night had barely begun, and I was already feeling the trap tightening around me. While the captains fell to talking about Vincent, the coke trade, and how they were going to avoid incidents like this in the future, I sat back with my glass of vodka and pretended to drink it while watching their hands and faces. Nicolai seemed particularly animated, but he had the grayish complexion of someone masking illness.

"Hey, uh... Alexi, man. What are they saying?" Vincent whispered aside to me. "I keep hearing my name."

"You're being put up in a safe house, with a bodyguard." I dropped my voice. "That's all."

"That's it? I mean, I'm hearing a whole lot of 'Vincenti this, Vincenti that.'"

"It is decided, then." Sergei lifted a hand, breaking the bubble with his thickly accented English. "Vincent, my friend: I hate to interrupt your evening out, but we are going to send you to a safe house now, while the night is young and hunters are still sleeping. Do you agree?"

"Uh, sure." Vincent's voice was a little strangled. "That'd be great, actually. I could do with more sleep."

"Good, good. And couldn't we all." Sergei motioned to Vera. "Vera here will take you to the security office. You are getting two of our very best to keep you safe in your bed."

"Thanks. But this suit is—"

"Don't worry about the suit," I said. "I don't need it."

Vera broke from her static position, boots whispering on the plush carpet, and crooked her fingers to Vincent. Cheerful but shell-shocked, he followed her out like an eager puppy, stumbling a little over the points of his shoes. He was a childish, clownish man. It made me wonder, exactly, why the Santos Twins liked him so much.

Once they were gone, Sergei clapped his hands together. "Now we have time to relax before business. Lev has been telling me about his collection of beauties for years now, but I am yet to see a single one."

"You have only been here a few hours, Pakhun," Lev said. "They're merely a phone call away. What are you all looking for? Blonde, brunette...?"

Sergei waved a ringed hand. "I'll take your recommendation, Leva. Whatever one you like the best."

Something about their choice of words rubbed me the wrong way. It reminded me of Jana, and of the black nothing of the pistol in her hand. I spoke up before any of the other men could. "Call up Crina for me, Avtoritet."

"The small dark one?" Lev asked.

"I didn't know you indulged, Alexi." Sergei arched a brow. "You were always so virtuous."

I smiled thinly. "Men will always be men, Pakhun. And yes, Crina is small and dark, Avtoritet."

While they poured the second round and fell to small talk, I excused myself to the bathroom with my glass. The relief at finding Vincent and earning my crust was transient. Even if I paid out every cent of debt tomorrow, there was always going to be something I owed this man. He was already working the con: I could smell it. And I would not be able to fight back from my current place. Whatever Sergei spun tonight in front of Nicolai, Lev, Vanya... they would believe it. And nothing would change for me.

I wanted to be sick. Instead, I poured the rest of the vodka down the toilet and filled it with fresh water from the tap. It's not like they'd know the difference.

When I went back outside, the girls had arrived and were adding their yellow and green treble to the dull grayish grind of male conversation. Crina was sitting beside Lev, listening with one deep scarlet lip rolled under her teeth, and she glanced across when I emerged. Her eyes lit up, and she patted his thigh before breaking off to join me.

"Let's go to a booth." I jerked my head towards the curtains and watched Sergei watch me as I slid my hand around Crina's cinched waist.

Her eyes widened, but she made good on the giggling and teetering as I led her into relative privacy, the catcalls of the other men following us behind the hush of velvet and the lingering nausea of old cologne.

"What's gotten into you?" Crina kept her voice down as she gently pressed me back and straddled my lap. She did it slowly, but her hands stayed on my shoulder and upper arms, her knees on the cushions, and her crotch held off mine. "You don't-"

"Something is going down tonight," I replied. "Something bad. I don't know what's coming, but you need to get out of town as soon as you can."

She froze over me, her face deep in shadow. "What? Why?"

"I can't give you a concrete reason right now, but there is dangerous talk out there. It's a matter of time," I replied. "Sergei is back, and... the Organizatsiya is a monster, Crina, and it's hungry. Sergei has already criticized me over the casino incident. You were there. And they—"

She pressed a finger to my lips, looking back at the edge of the curtains. "All right, Alexi. I believe you. You're right. Maybe about tonight, maybe not... but I can tell you that I lost three clients this week. Gunned down, shot, strangled. And I nearly lost you."

I sighed. "I don't want you involved in any of this."

"I chose to be here." Her eyes were hard and fierce in the dim light, gleaming like jet. "But I always have an exit plan. Don't worry, okay? If you say things are going down, I believe you."

Relief swept through my chest. "Thank you."

"I'm a survivor," she whispered. Her fingers dug into my shoulders. "And so are you. So you make sure to take your own advice. You cut town, tonight. You're too good for these guys, Alexi. Don't let their world kill you."

Again. A wash of déjà vu passed over me, and for a moment, I remembered the flash of white hair, the smell of putrefaction and burning wax, the intense cold. My chest hurt with the remembered knowledge of everything dying, that *I* was dying, and that our only hope was to run for the sea and-

Crina must have felt my tension loosen because she leaned in closer, breaking off the ploy of lap dancing to hug me awkwardly, urgently, the same kind of one-armed hug I gave Vassily just before he went in to be sentenced for his bloodless crimes.

"I will. Thank you." It was all I could say.

When we emerged, there was a new bottle of vodka and the obligation to have another glass. I threw back my water and let them pour, nursing the new drink while conversation wound down, laughter became less frequent, and Sergei more contemplative and intense. When a natural silence fell, he nodded to Lev, who wrapped up with a quiet word. We waited until Nicolai and his escort came out of the bathroom, and then she left with the other women, Crina included. She didn't look back, and I couldn't help but wonder if I did love her, just a little bit. She would survive, no matter what.

Nicolai locked the door behind them as we settled back down expectantly. They were drunk, beaten off, relaxed. I was sober and not looking forward to whatever was about to be discussed.

"Well, gentlemen. I will get straight to the point." Sergei said, looking out over the rest of the table. "The USSR is dead. Now, we have to think about where this organization will be going in the future. How we will grow."

How could it grow? I thought of Rodion, the photo the press had gotten of his red-sprayed car window and slumped head. Semyon, cringing beside his bed, his cases full of dirty money. No growth was possible. Lev and Nic and Vanya looked to Sergei, rapt and attentive without any obvious sense of irony.

"It is time for a reorganization," Sergei said heavily, hand thudding on the tabletop in emphasis. "Because I know for a fact that everything is going to collapse. The announcement of the dissolution will be out any month now. It is said and done. This is the result of *perestroika*, which is - and I tell you now - brought about by the West in support of a union in Europe. America and Germany want this union, and they will do everything for it. They forgot what history has taught Russia about giving power to the West, and I tell you now… if the Slavic countries do not pull together in the decades to come, there will be a new kind of fascism in Europe. It will one day make Germany look like a play-date."

That did stun the room into silence, even me.

"Now. In the short term, chaos is good for us." Sergei's eyes glinted with anticipatory pleasure. "Very good. Business thrives on uncertainty, debt, speculation, risk. My friends are already looking at their pick for presidents in Ukraine, Russia, and Georgia. KGB men, the lot of them. But if we don't have a hand in this, we will miss out on a huge opportunity. So, I have decided that we will diversify. We are going to Ukraine to build a hub of trade that will link New York directly to Europe and Asia, my friends. Fuck South America. Goods will travel through the Middle East and up through Russia, then out to anywhere we want. The future is in China and Afghanistan, not Colombia."

Sergei's head swiveled towards Lev. "Lev, you are once again going to be my Advocate. I need you by my side. It falls to you to decide who will lead this community in your stead. My top choice has always been Vassily, who has grown up here and knows the U.S. better than anyone. But you, Nicolai, you always loved America. What do you have to say?"

All eyes turned to Nic. His mouth flickered in an approximation of a smile.

"Well. I'd say Vassily ain't fit to lead his head out of his own ass. He got hooked on product while he was in prison." While everyone else hung on his words, he looked me dead in the eye as icy, hard certainty settled in my chest. "And Alexi here... well, Pakhun. I told you about Grisha. And since then, it's just been one fuckup after another."

Lev glanced at me knowingly. He'd tried to warn me. But Nic? The man who had patiently mentored Vassily and me when we were green? He'd trained us to take these positions, to succeed him... and apparently, he'd decided that he didn't want to let go.

"I throw in behind Nicolai," Vanya added, a little too quickly. Politics had never really been his strong point, but he was apparently still better at pre-arrangement than I was.

Nic's eyes gleamed hungrily, victoriously. Damn his skinny, traitorous, ambitious ass.

"I see," Sergei said. He looked to me. "And you, Alexi?"

"What, exactly, did I do?" My voice was quiet, but for the moment, it carried. "What, exactly, did I fuck up?"

Nic shrugged. "How many times have I had to pull your ass out of the fire now? Three? First Semyon—"

"That went off without a hitch," I said. I couldn't keep the shock out of my voice.

"Then this Manelli spook, who wiped the floor with your ass, turns up and tries to hit us at the casino—"

I banged my hand on the table with enough force that he shut up. "I know exactly what you're driving at. He got nothing out of me. Not a single damn thing!"

Nic scoffed. He flicked a hand. "Then how'd they find out?"

"Jana Volotsya." Rage wound my voice tight, hard, and flat. Lev tensed.

"Who what now?" Vanya looked to me.

"Well... I can confirm that Jana was certainly involved in abducting Vincent," Lev said carefully. "We've started the cleanup at her house, but I'm still sorting through all her paperwork. Did you hear anything about what she was involved in?"

I wanted to say it. I wanted to tell them about the Fruit, to lay it out like a grand prize I'd been holding back so I could spit it in Nic's face. But I knew, even as I weighed up my answer, that none of these men would understand the Fruit's significance anyway. They'd laugh, at best, because what could it do for them? Would it make money? Add to the business? My dreams and visions, the struggles behind the scenes of the murders, the discovery of a fruit from the Tree of Knowledge meant nothing to them.

I'd never sought power in the Organizatsiya before, but I wanted it now. This was culmination of a long game played out with my life and the lives of people I cared about. Nic had spent years on this. He had us all lined up.

"She was working with the Manelli spook and Semyon." I grated the half-truth out flatly. "Working behind Lev's back. She organized Semyon's magical protection, maybe even facilitated him turning to the Feds. She played us off one another. And now, she's dead because of me. Vincent is safe, and the trade link with him. And you want to talk about my failures, Nicolai? What about your failure as lead enforcer to find the rats in our rank? You didn't know Jana was a threat."

"I don't have magic," Nic replied. "She was a freak, too. That's your job."

"No, it's not." I was pointing at him, and every time I moved my hand like a weapon, Vanya flinched. "And it was your job to protect Vassily's financial operation. He generated two million in stocks the year after graduation. He invented the credit card serial generator, and if we concentrated on that and oil instead of coke and guns? We'd have the richest operation in this country."

"So he's a nerd. Computers don't mean shit." Nicolai sneered.

"You set him up to go to prison, didn't you?" I knew I should have been subtler, but I blurted it out before I could stop myself. "You and Semyon."

"Alexi has a compelling point," Sergei said. He looked like he was enjoying the fight.

"Really? That's what you were trying to get at? Fuck off." Nicolai chuffed around his cigarette, cupping his hand to light up. "Semyon's dead. You can't prove shit."

He was as nonchalant as a tomcat, but I saw understanding dawn in Lev's eyes. He sat back and rubbed his brow. All of this had been happening under his nose, and his powers of persuasion, of subtle control, meant nothing. He was far too weak as a leader to wield it.

"You set him up the whole way." I wanted to do to Nic what I'd done to that guy in the bathroom: blow him apart. I tried to channel the energy, the power, but it was like squeezing clay from a tube. Something must have showed, because everyone froze warily.

"That is an interesting question. But I have one last question for you, Alexi, before I say my piece." Sergei sat back, hands clasped on his belly, just below his breastbone. "Why did you kill Grigori? With his own sledgehammer, no less?"

I wanted my chin. "He was a rabid dog. He killed my mother, and he wanted to kill me. I took him out before he could. This city wasn't big enough for us both."

Sergei nodded and rumbled low in his chest. Then he shook his head.

"My boy, you don't understand the most important thing about this mess," he said. "Because you forget one thing. Your mother killed herself."

"Because he beat her," I said. "He pushed and—"

"She broke. Because she was weak." Sergei's eyes flicked up to look at me then, full of disappointment... and warning. "And so are you."

There was a deeply uncomfortable pause around the table. In the silence, I set my glass down, still with half the shot of Kors, and stood.

"Sit down." Sergei motioned with his eyes to my seat.

Vanya and Nic tensed, and I remembered Lev's warning to me. They thought I was an atom bomb, primed to explode. I hadn't been: but I was now.

"With all respect, Pakhun, I'd rather go and study my Art." I turned a small, stiff smile on him. "Excuse me."

"You are not excused," came his brittle reply. "I haven't finished speaking."

"Then please, by all means, speak." I stayed in place, but I was not going to sit.

Nic folded his arms, watching me in silent triumph.

Sergei heaved a dramatic sigh. "Nicolai, I name you Avtoritet of New York, as Grigori Sokolsky—honestly, the man I wished could have managed Brighton Beach until his deathbed—is not here to claim that honor. Lev will be by my side as Advokat as we establish our Asian contacts. Vanya, your man Petro Yankovic has been voted by the others as suitable for the role of Cell Commander, and he will take Nic's place when he rises to his new station. As for you, Alexi, I have other work for you and Vassily befitting your age and skills."

Other than dog chum? I was genuinely surprised. With Nic as Avtoritet and Petro running the enforcement in the Beach, there would be no contracts for me. There would be nothing for me.

"Vassily is to go to Miami, to liaise with our younger, enterprising operation there and to assist with keeping the road to Colombia open and free. South America is still worth our time. He will have a chance to prove himself there." Sergei watched me with some amusement now. "And you will be coming with me and Lev for a tropical vacation. We are building a community in Thailand first of all, and we have business in Phuket which will require your particular skillset."

It took me a moment to process what he'd just told me. Leave the country? I knew what went on in Thailand. There would be no fuel racket there, no advancement into fake credit cards and careful money laundering. Southeast Asia provided three things to the black market: slaves, organs, and heroin. None of them were the sort of business I wanted to be involved with.

"I understand," I replied. "I will talk to you tomorrow, Pakhun. Avtoritet."

I directed the last to Lev with a slightly bowed head. Nicolai's eyes tracked me at a slow burn on the way out, but this time, no one tried to stop me from leaving.

CHAPTER 24

I reeled all the way back to my apartment and took the long way home, driving around and around the neighborhood in agitation. If I was pulled over tonight, I'd lose my shit. I'd kill a cop and end up in Wisconsin somewhere. At least it wouldn't be Thailand, but Vassily would still be stuck in Miami: addicted, alone, with Nic's forces arrayed against him, surrounded by strangers. He'd be dead within the month. It was one thing to tell him to get his crazy-making ass out of my house and clean himself up, quite another to be on the other side of the world, and probably never to see him again.

We had two choices. We got our asses out of New York, or I got really powerful, really fast. And then what? Kill everyone that hated me, and rule over a graveyard out of spite?

I was exhausted, wrung out from days of stress and strain. I went home to clean up before going to Mariya's to break the bad news, and found two letters in the letterbox and a package on my doorstep. The package had no address on either the back or front and no stamp. I sniffed the paper: it smelled like Crina's perfume. One letter looked like it had come from Lev's office, dropped off by a courier while I was still out. The other was the telephone bill, now well overdue.

The package was large and thick, but surprisingly light. I had not been expecting a package. I unwrapped it outside slowly and suspiciously, but relaxed as a red cover came into view. A post-it was tacked to the front.

"I promised I'd get this for you," the note read. "Sell it if you have to. And stay alive." Crina had signed her note with three suns, almost like a personal sigil.

It was *Das Rote Buch*. I smiled despite myself and tucked it under my arm while I looked at the other, unmarked letter. A slip of paper with an address written in Lev's deeply slanted hand: *14b Grove St*. It offered both satisfaction and confusion. The address was a safe house in Bushwick, which must have been where they were taking Vincent. But why was he confirming it for me? Out of respect? Consolation?

Jana's mysterious L, the name she hadn't written, was still in the back of my mind.

I took the book inside to the den, sat down, and savored the rest of the unveiling. Even though it was just a copy, it was beautiful, hand-bound, an authentic replica of the old German journal Jung had used to record his innermost revelations. I turned it, breathed in the scent of new ink and leather, and sighed as the muscles relaxed along my spine.

Tongue humming, I laid the book out on my knees and turned the first page. My eyes lit on some of the brightest, most stunning images I'd ever seen: beautiful illumination enmeshed with pages and pages of elegant German calligraphy. It looked like something from another time, and the illegibility of the text made the images stand out all the more. Mandalas wove into themselves with fearsome complexity; a many-footed snake ate itself as a naked man looked on in terror. What caught my attention and held it was a singular image of a tree that looked vaguely like a

Joshua tree, some kind of succulent plant with diamond-shaped leaves. The tree that Vincent had tried to draw so poorly in his diary was splendid in this painting, framed against a night sky with the moon—or was it the sun?—glowing trapped within the loose cage of its branches. It shone with a radiant corona that should have been impossible to depict in paint, framing a huge fruit-like rind that hung from a stout branch. A humanoid shadow was visible through the skin of the fruit, which was partly enfolded by the tree's branches just like the way a woman would embrace her own pregnant belly. The figure within was poised like a dancer in mid-air, hands lifted, hair flung up in an arc.

I pulled off a glove, blew on my hand until my fingers were dry, and reached out to stroke the image, tasting the crisp rasp of parchment under skin. I'd heard the book was beautiful, but beauty wasn't all I could appreciate. I felt like I was looking back on a photo of a time long past, of seeing something ancient and non-human rendered by human hands. It was as if Jung had painted something that was not actually from him, something that didn't belong to any of us... and with that, a new gravity settled over my shoulders. I didn't fully understand the implications of the Fruit being here in New York, but Jana had wanted it enough to torture men to death for it. She had been working for someone, someone who had given her tacit approval to move heaven and earth for this thing. What if they got it? And if the Manellis had it, what would *they* use it for? It was only a matter of time until they figured that out. Then what? Would there even *be* a New York to come back to, if Carmine was able to utilize the power of this primordial artifact?

And as I wondered, I had to ask myself: was I any better than he? A year ago—hell, a week ago—I probably wouldn't have wanted this sort of power for my own ends. But my first thought had been to attack the men who threatened and insulted me, to bring magic to bear on them. If there had been anything left in me - anything at all - I'd have set the VIP suite alight and burned myself with them out of spite. What would happen if someone like *me* harnessed the kind of magical power that Jana and Yuri had hinted at?

My eyes burned with fatigue. There was no way I was going to make it to Mariya's. I fed Binah and went to bed. I slept a deep, dreamless sleep, and when I rose in the evening, I drove straight to my adopted sister's place. Her car was in the lot next to Vassily's. I took the steel steps up the back of the building to her door, fist lifted to knock—except the door was already open and, where there had been a lock, there was only a blasted, gaping hole.

The world contracted into a small square of focus. My eyes throbbed. No. No one knew where Mariya lived... no one knew Vassily was there. Surely not. Acid rose in my throat. I reached back and drew my gun. "Mariya!? Vassily!"

No one answered me. I pressed the door in, the gun raised, and was greeted only by the smell of rotting meat.

I stepped inside, numb with disbelief, and looked around. The living room was trashed. A small cloud of flies had gathered in a lazy procession near the unmoving ceiling fan. Other than their hum, there was no sound. The kitchen was laid out for snacks: crackers, cream cheese, a pitcher of blended juice that had separated in the heat of the day. I sniffed it. Apples, carrots, and beets, with the fizzy tang of early fermentation. That meant it had been sitting here all day... while I was sleeping.

I turned from the living room. My face tingled as I half-ran, half-stumbled to Mariya's room. Neither she nor Vassily were there, but the place was torn up, littered with broken glass and bloodstained sheets. The next door I threw open was the bathroom.

She had been in the shower. The vase she kept on the windowsill was smashed across the floor, blue plastic poppies and daisies flung in a spray over the wet tiles. Mariya had fallen against the back wall. Someone had turned the water off: the tiles were painted with dried gore. Her eyes were wide, fixed and empty. Even in death, she looked surprised.

"Mariya." Fingers hovering, mouth dry, I was paralyzed in front of her. The tall, commonsense woman who'd raised us, the closest thing we'd had to a mother. Dead.

It took every ounce of restraint I had not to touch her. Instead, I clutched at myself, struggling with waves of agony that wracked my body and twisted my hands into painful claws. The color seemed to drain from the room, while denial beat at me, and then, grief. Horror. Rage. I didn't want to search the rest of the house, look into the other two bedrooms. I didn't want to find Vassily there.

Heaving, shuddering, I wrenched myself from the doorway into a forced march. Fear doesn't change reality, I silently chanted to myself. Fear doesn't change reality, and it never would. If Vassily was in there, he'd be dead whether I saw him or not.

My feet were heavy, but I was becoming numb to the smell of death. Rage was overwhelming despair. I didn't want a gun in my hands: I wanted a drill, a saw. Weapons of horror and torture. Revenge was something I could fixate on, and it was the certainty of cold, bloody revenge that drove me on to throw open the next door, and the next.

Every room was empty and clean. It was almost worse than just finding the body.

Vassily hadn't called. Hadn't raised an alarm, nothing, and the scene was cold. I went back to Mariya's bedroom and scanned it a second time, this time for the small details I might have missed. The bed was a mess: there was blood on the carpet, but not enough for a death. The dresser had been tipped over, a lamp thrown… and a white envelope had been set down, almost invisible against the tumbled pillows at the head of the bed.

I ripped the top off the envelope and unfolded the note inside. It was rough, a small slip torn off from a piece of plain copy paper. *"We know who this guy is. Bring Vincent. Crows Mill Rd Woodbridge T.Ship TransCorp parking lot 3am 8/16 or we kill him and send the tape."*

The hand was blocky, rough and practical, flat-bottomed, the handwriting of a killer. I stared at the paper, turned it over, then held it up to the light. No fingerprints, and I'd bet no hairs or trace evidence would be found. The gun that had been used to kill Mariya was long gone.

In the pictures, the world's gas men—whether they be Mafia or Organizatsiya or Cartel—are always sparing the women and kids. That was another Hollywood fantasy. As far as the average killer was concerned, women and children were just collateral. The guy who did this didn't know what kind of person my adopted sister had been. He didn't care. She was in the way.

Horror dawned as the involuntary memory of myself, staring down at Semyon, filtered back into my memory. "We always have choice," I said. What choice did Mariya have?

What decision had she made, that lead her to die like this? The decision to take care of me, all those years ago? To take her coke-addled baby brother, and nurse him back to health?

Good GOD. What the hell had I done?

What the hell had we done, all of us?

My hands were shaking as I folded the note and put it in my pocket. Then, I holstered my gun and straightened my shirt, making my way out of the house, down to my car. The gray humid sky beat down on the back of my neck. It was going to storm, and the whole parking lot smelled dead. I turned on the air conditioner and found myself unable to move.

I had no one I could call for help. Not a single one of those fuckers in the Organizatsiya. Even if Nic hadn't set this up—and I wasn't sure if he had or not—he'd still be happy to know that Vassily was gone. I didn't want to try Lev—he'd been there, listening to Sergei chew me out. He hadn't joined in, and had even tried to help in his own way, but he hadn't disagreed. Maybe it's just because Sergei was right. I *was* weak, at least compared to him and Carmine. But if there's one standout in all the things that piss me off... it's betrayal.

"I don't want to do this," I said aloud. "I don't want to be like them. I don't."

But Kutkha didn't have to descend from on high and tell me what I already knew. Vassily's mother and father died for the Organizatsiya. Syoma Lovenko had stolen a transport plane from Vladivostok and flown it to Japan to escape the Soviet Union and used the proceeds to buy his wife, eldest son, and widowed mother through the Iron Curtain, like some kind of fucking superhero. We lost them both to a plane crash, and Sergei didn't shed a damn tear at their funeral. Syoma Junior had died soon after arriving here, suicide by cop. Antoni, the second eldest and first born in America, died in prison after being arrested for his work in the protection racket. Lyosha died in a firefight. Then, there was my own family. My mother, the gentle pianist, a Jewish girl completely unprepared for life with my father, was a distant mystery even to me. When I tried to remember the circumstances of her death, there was nothing but the deep black. No one had ever told me her story. No one had ever bothered to find her out.

Just because Sergei and the Organizatsiya had furnished my cage didn't make it any less of a cage. Even if I let Vassily die, consigned him to his fate and the Fruit with him, what the hell was I going to do? Go to Thailand and train locals to deal drugs, protect gambling rackets, and raid villages for their children? The cold certainty of the action I needed to take fell across my mind like a shroud. Without a word spoken between my Neshamah and me, we were in instant agreement. I turned the engine, backed out of the lot, and drove the short distance home.

Binah was meowing at the door as I fumbled with my keys. She leaped into my arms from the floor as I went inside, scrabbling around my face until she hung over my shoulder. I let her stay there while I got the tools I needed. Rope, chloroform, a clean kitchen rag. When it was time to go, I set her down in the kitchen and rubbed her ears. She watched me with her big silver eyes while I filled up two bowls of chow and a big dish of water, and left the window ajar. It wouldn't be too easy for her to open it up, but if I didn't come home, she had enough time to figure her way outside. If she had a bit of me in her, she'd do alright out there in the city as long as she could stay ahead of the pound.

I emerged into a brooding summer wind. The change had come and turned the sky dark, and the storm wind whipped the collar of my shirt with gusts of salty, metallic-smelling air. I set my tools down on the passenger seat and made a token effort at concealment with the towel. The trunk of my car was always lined with fresh garden plastic for occasions like this. Kidnappings, body transport, scene cleanup… the hardware store carried all the things any gas man needed for his day-to-day business.

The safe house on 14b Grove Street was deliberately unassuming, indistinguishable from the many small row houses that crowded this part of Brooklyn. I parked outside in the No Standing zone, the closest place to the door. No one was outside. I carried my pistol down low, out of sight, and knocked with the other fist. My hands were sweating in my gloves, but my mind was ticking over like a slick engine while I ran through the many variables this snatch-and-run likely entailed. Vincent would have two guys guarding him here. They usually used a girl to answer the door, but this time, no one answered. I rapped the door again, twitchy, and looked up and down the cracked asphalt of the street. Crows called lustily out towards the rising moon, but there was no warning amongst them, no agitation. No one answered this time, either, so I holstered my gun and tried the door. Naturally, it was unlocked.

Cautiously, I slunk into the entry and down the narrow hall. Two guys I recognized from the AEROMOR Dockers Union were crumpled on the floor of the living room, handcuffed to the radiator. A golf club had been thrown carelessly from them, not far away. I crouched to look at them: they were both breathing, but one guy's hair was matted with blood. When I pushed it back, I found a lump the size of a tennis ball.

A notebook had been left in the middle of the rumpled sofa bed, a comp book just like the one I'd found at Vincent's house. I thumbed it open at a dog-eared page and read through it without expression.

"I know he's coming for me no matter what. I spent too long fighting to become who I am, and I'm not gonna lose it all on my family's altar. Count me out. I'd rather get fucked in the ass than stay on this sinking ship. Carmine doesn't have a reason to chase me anymore. Sorry."

I threw it before I realized I'd done it. The book hit the wall with a sharp bang and bounced to land on one of the *muzhiki*. He groaned, shifting on the floor as I stalked out, slamming the front door behind me on the way to the car.

There was only one option left to me.

If I added driving time, I had two and a half hours to spare before I needed to be at Woodbridge. At home, I shaved, changed clothes, and added weapons more easily concealed to my outfit. A garrote, knives. I kept the gun—they'd take it off me, and that was fine. I considered Kevlar but decided against it. I ate a bowl of *kasha*, the universal comfort food of Eastern Europe, and spent half an hour in meditation. Then I left my home again, maybe for the last time, driving towards the ocean with a cold heart and a hot stomach. My mind was buzzing and blank as I passed through the tollway and burst across the bridge towards New Jersey.

When I pulled into the lot where the exchange was meant to take place, I still had forty-five minutes to spare. A single pickup was waiting for me. He flashed his lights, and I flashed mine before I turned the engine off. The pickup door opened, and my chest knotted and braced, muscles armoring with tension. It wasn't a go-between that stepped out: it was Vassily, clambering down and shuffling out from the side of the car with a grimace of pain. From where I sat, I couldn't see the driver.

I wasn't incautious enough to open the door, so instead, I rolled the window halfway as Vassily approached. He looked exhausted, his eyes ringed by huge bruises, his skin clammy and pale. He had a new gunshot injury, a torn sleeve where a bullet had skimmed him. Otherwise, he looked remarkably normal for a man who had been kidnapped after the brutal murder of his sister.

"I knew you'd come." The relief was plain in his voice. "Where's Vincent? The driver says I can walk if you send him out across the lot."

"Vincent ran." My tongue felt heavy in my mouth. "He's not a Wise Virgin any more, but you need to tell them that I can do it. I'm what they need. I'll trade myself if they let you drive away."

Vassily nodded, as if in a daze. He straightened, swayed, then turned and limped his way back across the lot. I watched his slightly bowlegged swagger from behind, drew my gun under the shelter of the dash, and prayed to God, or GOD, that my aim was true.

Vassily leaned across the seat and spoke to the unseen driver in the cab. He couldn't be the only one there, watching the trade take place. I looked around through my windshield and windows but couldn't pick out anything in the gloom. As the conversation dragged on, I found myself wondering: was Vassily complying so readily because he had a backup plan or because deep down, he was as mercenary as every other gangster in New York?

In the distance, he turned and motioned with his hand. I exhaled heavily, undid my seat belt, and stepped out. I left the gun behind. In my mind, the word of power I'd been working to master and its sigil repeated itself over and over again. *Chet. Chet. The shield.* I could deflect gunfire for the precious seconds it took to throw Vassily down and get cover.

Vassily started towards me as I walked forward. On seeing his expression, my gut froze solid. He was... nonchalant. My intuition picked at me, but it gave no definite answer as we closed the distance and Vassily slowed.

"Vassily... do you know these guys killed Mari?" I said, quietly.

"What?" Up close, I saw his eyes. They were very red-rimmed and very dark, like he'd been snorting coke. "Don't do anything dumb, okay? Come here for a sec."

"Vassily?" I swallowed as instinct beat at the walls of my mind like an indigo velvet hammer. I flushed with adrenaline and stopped in place. "Vassily, I don't—"

He abruptly closed the distance between us, and before I could react, he ducked his face down and kissed me soundly on the mouth. I shoved him away and inhaled sharply with shock—and as I did, a mingled sweet, acrid smell flooded my nose, my sinuses, pushing tentacles up behind my eyes and deep into my brain. I lost control of my limbs, and I barely had a second to register the coldness of Vassily's lips before my vision darkened and I slumped bonelessly to the ground at his feet.

CHAPTER 25

I roused into a sleepwalk, the body shambling while the mind was trapped within a tight crystal cage. Disembodied, I watched from a distance behind my eyes as a mustachioed man walked up to the pair of us and ordered us forward.

This must be scopolamine, I thought. My body got into the car, and the roar of the engine blurred with the sound of a heartbeat in my ears. Motion had a texture: on the road, my vision was flooded by swirling orange light. At some point, I heard the driver speak, telling me to get out of the car. I felt my body comply with a sense of distant dismay. I was aware and conscious, but trapped. My legs complied with the directions we were given, an airplane on autopilot, steering through a woozy fog. *No, goddammit...*

Floodlights were shining down on a gravel yard that danced like glistening diamonds. We crunched and bobbed across it, headed towards a squat black cube with a gaping, fanged maw. As my vision rocked in the silence of his heartbeat, I saw the mouth open and close hungrily, large enough to engulf several trucks. *No.*

The air was a liquid, bubbling around me in a whispering river of sound. It was the strangest sensation, riding in the backseat of my body and walking shoulder to shoulder with

Vassily. He was breathing through his mouth, panting with pain, his eyes huge and black in his face.

We were drawn through the yawning warehouse maw. The interior was cold, and it smelled like meat, dust, and bird shit. We were led deep into the heart of the place, past a circle of leering men whose faces distorted into paint smears. Whatever the driver told my body to do, it did. I followed him up and down stairs, into an elevator, along a metal catwalk that chimed under our footfall like music as the three of us walked together in syncopated time. I tried to focus past the hallucinations from my remote position of observation. What was the Manellis' cover business? I tried to remember, but it was impossible to think backwards or forward in this drugged memetic cage. When I stopped trying, something rushed into my memory of its own accord. Elite Meats. Which meant we were out in Franklin Township.

We were led through stacks of boxes, wrapped and ready for transport, and into a section of factory cordoned off from the rest. And there it was, the Fruit. It roared high in my vision, looming like a gargantuan chestnut over the concrete floor, the assembled men, and a table laid out with tools. I thought I saw purple velvet, the clones of my father's sledge repeated, over and over again. I blinked, and my vision sliced apart, reformed, and focused. Tools, yes. Everything from axes to saws to a drill.

"Right. Well, idiot, you've definitely brought somebody." Carmine's sneering voice, grossly distorted, rumbled into my ears like bitumen being laid on a new road, and with the association came the smell of it, the burning, waxen tar. "Problem is, Manny, he's not the right motherfucking guy! Where's Vincent, you fuckup?!"

"Guy says he's got the same set of preconditions. Vincent cut and ran." From the way he used the word, it was clear he was repeating Vassily verbatim.

There was murmuring that might have been talking, but my inner eye was fixated on the Fruit. It pulsed in my vision, a blue dark enough that it seemed to suck in the light around it. I recognized a faint smell, even through the heightened state, that I could not help but breathe in. It was like the most fragrant peach I had ever smelled. In the back of my throat, it transmuted: the sweetness became aromatic and dizzying. Phi. It smelled like Phi.

"Scopolamine." One word leapt out from the babble. "Okay, get him on it."

A knife was thrust into my hand, and I was led forward. The driver, a swirling swarthy mass, his teeth made of light, turned me to face the Fruit squarely. "You heard him. Start chopping, and don't stop 'til you reach the middle."

As I advanced towards it, I had a vague memory of someone saying this thing had wiped out several guys. That it had sprayed them, something like that. But I couldn't stop going forward or stop my arm from lifting and the knife coming down. The blade made its first blow, sinking into the rind like butter, and the smell of Phi became overwhelming. My handler retreated hurriedly and left me alone in my labor as my arm rose and fell, rose and fell, like the piston in a machine.

Excitement turned the voices around me to a spiraling shrill that blended into the rest of the muted talk around the perimeter of the light.

"Fuck off, all of you!" Carmine barked. "I got this!"

His voice wasn't blurry. My head was clearing. With every passing moment, the drug was fading, and fast. My stabs slowed momentarily but then resumed as I struggled to keep the cover and not reveal the loosening lock on my mind. A door slammed behind me, and Carmine returned. In the sudden silence, Vassily's wheezing was all too audible.

At one point the knife began to thud and stick. I pulled it free, sunk it in again, and was struck square in the face by a jet of pure blue liquid that burst free under pressure from the pith. The stuff didn't burn me, and neither did it hit the floor; instead, it evaporated into fragrant steam before ever touching the ground.

The world swooped in a florid arc before it drew in to a point, sharp and clear. My body was mine once again. I chopped at the pith, and this time, the liquid slopped down the sides of the shell.

"Jesus and Mary..."

Out of the corner of my eye, I saw Carmine cross himself and kiss his ring, muttering in Latin. I changed the knife for my hands, pulling out chunks of soft sky-colored pith from inside the shell. I couldn't stop. I could have, if I'd wanted to, but I didn't want to stop. Elbow-deep in the mystery, I couldn't stop. What was inside? The woman in my dream, the one who had called me "father"? Nothing? Everything?

I broke through a thin inner skin and forced my arm in past it. It was hot inside the rind, as hot as a freshly cracked chest. I felt through a labyrinth of spongy, pulse-infused tissue up to my shoulder. It put me on my tiptoes, and I pressed my ear in against it as I groped around, searching for anything I could grasp and pull free. The shell reverberated with a low thrum up close, an impossibly huge heartbeat that surged as something unseen lunged forward and gripped my forearm.

I roared in mingled shock and pain, hauling back. Whatever had me held on as I pulled it through the final nacreous layers of the rind. Phi spilled everywhere as a woman - at least six feet tall and as athletic as a gymnast - slid out of the tunnel of the womb and fell on top of my chest in a spill of wet white hair. It was like living paint, a shade so pure it bent and flexed against light to hold its wholeness of color.

"Jesus Fucking... Shit!" Carmine screamed into the echoing hall of the warehouse, flinching away. "What the shit are you doing!?"

The nude woman, dripping blue, levered herself up on deceptively strong arms over my face. I couldn't breathe. She was the most graceful and powerful and fragile thing I'd ever laid eyes on, and she was powerfully, painfully familiar.

"Thank GOD," she whispered in Ukrainian. "You made it."

I knew her like my own face, and without thinking, I reached up to touch her cheek. My eyes blurred. Her name was on the tip of my tongue. "Z–Zar–ya?"

She was crying, laughing, and reached up to clap her hands over my cheeks, nodding when I said her name. Zarya. I had never seen her in my life. I scrabbled back from her, heaving for breath, too scared of her otherworldliness to do anything but react. I ran into Carmine's shins. Carmine was staring, and without looking down at me, he offered me a hand up. That wasn't how this was supposed to go, but in the face of Zarya's ability to exist? It made as much sense as anything else.

"*Bat'ko*, there's going to be a DOG here any minute." She spoke in accented English, educated, neither American or European. My accent. "Please, we have to go!"

"Dog? What dog?" Carmine blurted.

He took a step towards us, and Zarya shied back, as if warding him away. Without a second thought, I put myself in front of her and shoved him back. "Back it up, *pizdha*."

The bigger man's lips curled, and he snarled wordlessly as he took a step forward. "Back it... hey! You aren't calling the shots here, you little f-"

Before I could stop myself, I swung at Carmine's face. He wasn't expecting it, and my fist took him square in the jaw. He raised his ring hand, but before he got the word of power off, I kicked him in the jaw and he bit his own tongue with a bubbling squawk.

"No. You fucking shut your whore mouth," I said. "She's not 'yours.' Her *name* is Zarya."

"She knows!" Carmine spat, blood pouring down his chin, and pointed at her. I didn't dare turn to see what Zarya was doing. "She knows Everything!"

"*Blyat!*" Zarya said from behind me. "I can't use any of these guns! They're all... oh, GOD dammit..."

"So ask her from over there." I reached over to the tool bench and picked up another, larger knife. I was pretty sure I could land it in Carmine's face before he could get his hands up to work magic.

Carmine looked past me, shivering. His reddish eyes were full of the kind of desperation I'd ever only seen in junkies. "Fine, okay. Fine. Listen to me, lady. You listen. I need to know the answer to something."

"You g-g-got about a minute before we're all dead." She was chattering with cold or fear.

"I fuckin' died on that mountain." Carmine picked himself up and lurched a step forward. I tensed, but he stopped and turned away to pace sidelong to us both. "I know I did. I remember dying. Lady, you gotta tell me. What the fuck did I see? What the fuck was looking at me?"

"Ah." Zarya nearly made a sound but, instead, turned away to skim her hands over the array of tools on the table. "No, we don't have time. And you don't want to know."

"I have to know!" He had gone red in the face and whirled back to face us. "It's driven me nuts! Every night! Every dream! I see it staring at me. What the fuck is it!?"

"I..." She froze, trembling. "It's... it's the I. The I of GOD."

"God?" Carmine's expression fell. "And the voice?"

She made a small, needy sound, like a sound of hunger. "That's GOD, too. Look, we need to get—"

"It's freaking me the fuck out, is what it's doing!" Carmine was expressive in his agitation, waving his hands. "How do I stop it? Jana told me you could stop it."

"You... you can't." I felt her swallow.

"The only way you can stop GOD looking at you is by removing yourself from your enslavement to it," added a third voice from across the room. "Listen to the lady, Carmine Mercurio, and while you're at it, back it up."

Carmine whipped around on his feet, looking straight at what I also saw and couldn't believe I was seeing. The small, doughy face of Lev.

Lev held a slender silver pistol outstretched in one hand. He was flanked by three of Carmine's own enforcers. They had the stupefied, fixed expression of men under thrall. There was no visible turbulence around Lev: no light, no shadow, no flame. Lev's gaze was keen, and the skin was drawn tight across his jaw with effort. I felt the energy around him, the magic.

"Leave her, Alexi." Lev's voice carried through the warehouse. The four men stepped around Vassily. He was crumpled beside a stack of crates, his legs folded awkwardly under his weight. He was pale, a blue-white color that sent a chill through my chest. "Step aside, before I kill you both."

I looked back at him. "Lev! The hell's the matter with you?"

"Me? Why, nothing at all." The small man's smile was a tight-lipped mask. "I feel bad for you, Alexi. You've always been too earnest. Too hard-working. No one appreciates you in the Organizatsiya... but I have a lot to thank you for. Unlocking Jana's oratory, for one, and leaving it with all of its useful information intact, for another. I paid a visit, I broke her codes. Modified courtroom shorthand. I know everything she knew, about the Fruit, about this... retarded child consciousness that governs our reality. I had no idea she knew so much."

"I don't know what you're talking about." I couldn't quite mask the fear in my voice. Zarya broke away from my back, and my gut flashed uncomfortably.

"I always figured magic was just a useful skill, you know. Like being good at math or speed-reading. But it's so much more. I've really just begun to grasp the magnitude of what we are dealing with." Lev blinked rapidly. "Take the Gift Horse. Do you know what she is?"

"Please, Lev. Vassily—"

"I don't care about Vassily." Lev's eyes darkened. Foam was gathering at the corners of his mouth. "She is *magic*. Literally. Raw power. If I eat her, I'll be more powerful than both of you put together. Sergei can't strip me of my position. That scumbag, Nicolai, will be mine. I won't be playing second fiddle to anyone ever again. EVER."

"You and what fucking army?" Carmine said.

I wanted to kick him again.

"Anyone I please. I could rule the world with my kind of magic." Lev's gaze flicked to a point past his shoulder and stayed there. "If only I had a little more of it."

It was Carmine who pushed forward, hands raised. "You want magic? You want the girl? You can have her, motherfucker, over my dead body."

Lev's reply was to open fire. Carmine threw up a word of power and a gesture with a harsh shout that turned into a scream of pain as the bullets punched his magical shield with just enough delay that they didn't burst out of his body. He fell to the ground with an agonized shriek, rolling on the floor. The pain wasn't normal. I saw the wounds smoking, and his breath came shallower and more quickly as he looked back to Lev.

"You got that gun from Jana's, didn't you?" I began to back away. The knife might as well have been a toy. "Lev, you'll destroy her. She has to be handled by a virgin."

"No. The Gift Horse has to be *birthed* and fed by a virgin. It doesn't need to live for that long afterward." Lev's voice was still eerily calm. He was struggling to keep focused on me as Carmine screamed, eyes flicking down, then up again. "I mean... it's a fruit, isn't it? You eat it."

At first, I thought I was still hallucinating when the tip of Lev's gun began to ooze. The barrel was slowly leaking a familiar greasy oil that dripped from the muzzle and ran down along it, trembling before it broke off and hit the floor. It beaded like black mercury, wobbling—and then the drops began to move towards one another.

"Lev, your gun..." I took a big step back.

Zarya cried out. A knife flew past my face, flung with force from behind me. Lev's expression contorted: he fired and took the blade just under his collarbone at the same time. His finger convulsed with a wet click. I had seen that before.

"Run!" I backpedaled. A blast of violet-black emulsion spewed from the gun in a torrent: Lev turned ash-white and staggered, throwing the gun away with a yell. The weapon struck the coagulating mass of liquid, hissed on contact, and was absorbed into its mass.

The three Manelli soldiers broke their spell and started shouting, running into each other in their confusion. I started for Vassily as the fluid arched up into a gelatinous mass. It formed a roughly canine shape, but it had too many limbs and far too many teeth.

"DOG," Zarya gasped behind me. "DOG!"

Carmine sobbed in pain as he dragged himself up and staggered back, eyes darting between me and the DOG. "No, no way, fuck this. Fuck this fucking shit right back to hell."

Mouths unzipped across the entire length of the DOG's body as a terrier-like head formed at one end. It split and divided into sinewy tendrils that whipped and shot through the screaming, fleeing men. Its body split apart with a soggy sound into more mouths, which grinned and gnashed and squeaked as they dragged one, then another of the soldiers into its maws. One flew over my head as I dove for Vassily, grabbed him under the elbow, and hauled him up. A spined tentacle lunged for us: I slashed it with the knife, and it recoiled. Vassily was fighting to stay with me, but he was sagging in my grip.

"Chest," he wheezed. "Chest."

Carmine wasn't sticking it out: he was running away from us, towards the entryway. He and Lev were closest to the

DOG, which bounded after them, shrieking with laughter. They had nearly reached the door, and Lev had flung it open when a many-jointed extrusion flew from the demon's back like a harpoon. Carmine grabbed Lev's jacket and pulled him around, using him as a human shield, and Lev's piercing scream rang through the factory as it hooked him and dragged him back towards the gnashing mouths.

Zarya shook me out of it. She had knives in each hand. "Come on!"

"I've killed one of these before," I said. "Take Vassily and run. Something's wrong with him."

Her reply was to worm her way under Vassily's other arm, hissing through her teeth. On contact with his weight, her skin began to bubble like paint, bubbling and peeling with dark blue and silver blisters. "I don't have long. We're going."

Lev screamed a second time, a sound that blurred to garbling and wet mastication. The DOG was still chewing as it turned. It didn't whirl in place so much as reform to face us and began to lope and ooze across the ground. Lev's severed arm fell from between its teeth. I pushed Zarya and Vassily off towards the back of the factory and faced it down with the knife in my hand and my jaws clamped shut. *Kutkha, if you can do anything for me right now, make sure my aim's good.*

"HAHAHAHAhahahahHAhAHAAA!" The DOG was far, far larger than the last one and getting larger. Every dead thing in the room was being sucked into its body and incorporated. It was shrieking a hundred things at once as it slunk forward, crunching as bones splintered and the shards reset into its carapace. "WE LOVE YOU X YOU love ALEXI X YOU!"

I cocked my wrist and hurled the knife at the thing as it bore down. I felt gravity hitch, and the knife flew straight and true. It sunk to the hilt in the DOG's flesh, and it screamed: a hideous, many-throated, wailing shriek of rage. The demon fell back, tendrils whipping wildly as its substance sloughed from around the blade and evaporated in a foul-smelling cloud.

Now I could run. I caught up to Zarya and Vassily at the back of the factory, barreling under the man's other arm and catching her wrist, and the three of us ran while the DOG screamed on and on behind.

"How the hell do I know you?" I huffed the question out as we pelted across the floor, through a doorway and into the darkness of the factory proper.

"It's a long story, and we don't have much time." She ground the words out through gritted teeth. I could see Vassily's limp hand burning the skin of her back and arms. "I don't know you-you. But I knew other-you."

Other-me. Because that made sense. The DOG was shrieking, scraping itself along the floor to try to dislodge the blade still buried in its body. Between us, Vassily cried out weakly.

"His wound is infected." Zarya broke our stride to speak. She was bathed in sweat. "The DOG... everything near it putrefies."

"There's no time."

The DOG screamed pandemonium as it crossed at a limping run towards us. We hit a huge side-rolling door that was partly open. We squeezed through: I put my shoulders to it and tried to roll it across. Zarya staggered to my side, gripped it with her sinewy hands, and with strength far beyond her size, practically threw it shut.

Vassily was staring at Zarya in naked, semiconscious shock, his eyes dark and glassy. She was humanoid, but she was not human, not by the slender length of her throat, her long hands, or her eyes. They were the color of the Earth seen from space, too blue to be real. Zarya, on seeing Vassily's response to her, lowered her face as if sighting down along a horn. Her return look was one of reproach.

"Angel?" he croaked.

"Gift Horse," she replied. "Not the same thing."

He had no time to reply before the DOG hit the door with a heavy slapping sound, followed by the hiss and acrid odor of dissolving metal, and the three of us had to start running again.

"You are not... the first of you." She panted breathily as we headed away from the smoke and screams. "There's others. Other Ruachim. My Alexi... he died."

"Your Alexi?" I snapped back. We pressed through another metal door, slamming it closed behind us. It led into a room with coats and goggles hung on hooks and beyond that, a wide door hung with heavy plastic strips. No sound came from beyond. "The fuck is that supposed to mean?"

"It means there's many," she said. "The man I knew... the man who was my Hound. He wasn't the first, either. I don't know how to explain."

This was too weird. "If we head in and press through, there'll be an exit to the outside." I glanced behind as something screamed, high and loud. "I can guess that a DOG is opposite of GOD. What is a Gift Horse?"

Zarya's lips trembled for a moment, and briefly, her eyes unfocused. When she spoke, it was vague-sounding, growing stronger only as she went along. "The questing beast. The firebird. The daughter of the trees of knowledge. GOD's radio."

My breath sped in time with my pulse. "I... understand. Somehow. Come on."

"Lexi?" Vassily was sagging on his feet, head lolling. His voice was high and delirious. "Left arm."

"GOD dammit. He's having a heart attack," Zarya said.

"Don't you dare give up now," I snapped at him, blind with rising panic. It hit a dam of resolve and flowed back from him as I continued to drag Vassily's dead weight. "We can make it."

"Vassily, Vassily, please." The word from Zarya's lips sounded like an invocation. As she spoke, Vassily drew in a phlegmy breath.

He staggered forward, half his weight on my shoulder, his left arm hanging limp over Zarya's. "Don't feel... so good."

I knew why. "Scopolamine causes cardiac arrest. Breathe, Semych. Deep and steady. Come on."

The poultry processing plant was cavernous. We ran in near silence past cold processing machines, cutting belts, empty cages, and vats full of water that would be electrified if the equipment was active. Zarya was sobbing and shivering violently. She didn't touch anything, and when she accidentally bumped into a conveyor belt, she let out a stifled sound of pain. Her skin seared with a welt that looked like the lash of a bullwhip.

"You're not meant to be here," I spoke, puffing, as we pressed towards the back of the factory. "Where did you come from?"

"Eden," she said, "At first, but then I left. I lived... Elsewhere. Another Cell. A world, like this one, but it's dead.

You were there. But the whole Cell is dead. I'm not usually fragile like this—"

A triumphant chorus of howls rang out behind us, followed by the thump and crash of something very heavy hitting the floor. The steel door.

Zarya looked back, her hair swirling around her shoulders. "It's coming for me. It wants me."

"It's not going to get you." I was grim. "But I'm all out of knives."

"I'm not as strong as normal. I can't fight it." Zarya's voice was bubbly with mucous. She sounded asthmatic now, her breath wheezing on every intake. "If it gets you, it will eat your body and soul. DOGs are the violet hounds—they are the servants of the NO-thing."

"They drove Jana and Lev mad. I know they don't like knives. What else?"

"I don't know," she said, her voice high and desperate. In that moment, the newborn Gift Horse sounded terribly young. "I-I can't remember. I didn't even really remember it was you, until I saw you. Everything here is different."

The high-pitched giggling of the DOG began to resound through the factory, building to a manic chorus as it drew nearer. I pulled Zarya and Vassily into another doorway. We emerged into a loading room, filled with stacks of film-wrapped pallets waiting for transport. The smell in the room was alkaline and earthy. I looked around wildly for an exit that led out: the far wall had three truck loading doors.

"Go." I pushed Zarya towards it, looking over the stacks of crates. "Go, open it. Take Vassily. Save him, if you can."

"Alexi!"

"GO." I barely raised my voice, but the word carried emphatically.

She stared at me petulantly for a moment, but she obeyed, scooping Vassily up in her arms and carrying him away. I crossed to one of the stacks. Near one of them, I found a roll of plastic wrapping and a box cutter. A knife. My heart thumped. I took the box cutter and hacked at the plastic over one of the stacks, trying to see what was inside. It parted to reveal eggs, hundreds of them, resting in foam-lined open cartons.

I heard the screech of metal from the direction of the DOG.

I drew a deep breath, exhaled. I could do this. The deflection in Jana's room had worked. I'd stopped Carmine from blowing my head off. It was possible.

With a steady hand, I extended the blade of the cutter and pulled it across the flesh of my forearm. The world turned white, then red, as pain filled my mouth with pressure. I daubed my fingers in the blood that sprang forth and drew the symbol of Mars on the remaining plastic. The blood beaded on contact. The pallets weren't going to kill it, but they might incapacitate it long enough for me to stab it.

Through the archway slunk the DOG, oozing on each step. Its tendrils reached forward and almost delicately parted the plastic flaps ahead of it as it padded into the room. It was a mockery of living things—huge and hulking, chaotic, and foul.

"Deliciousdelicious smells delicious heeheeehee," it babbled deliriously with thirty maws, lurching on every step. Pseudopods burst into pincers at the end of each tendril, chomping black needle teeth as they loomed and darted over its back. Its flesh was melting and dripping, running down its bones and crawling back up. Human bones. They had been broken and reset to make a crude skeleton. "Deliciousoh it does... so brave bravebrave heeheehee..."

A sac of fluid erupted from the DOG's back and burst, and the air of the room seemed to sag around us. Vassily choked wetly, and as he collapsed, Zarya went down with him. I heard the scuffling, the thump, and Zarya's cry of alarm and terror but couldn't turn around to look. The DOG filled the room with the smell of rotten flesh, like dead whores preserved in sugar, the needles still in their veins. I licked my bloody arm as Kutkha gathered within and around me in a rising wave of pressure.

"I'll eat him and fuck the body," one mouth hissed in a syrupy baritone, lewd and slow. "Hear that? He's having a heart attack just thinking about it."

"Eateateateat!" shrilled another.

I could hear: the frothing, the thumping, Vassily's throat clicking as the foul miasma accelerated his condition and pitched him into cardiac arrest. Zarya was sobbing, but she was rotting away in the presence of the DOG, writhing where she had fallen. I was alone.

"Fuck you." I lowered my face, nostrils flaring. My voice was thick, the air around me building power and volume. "

The DOG laughed, sounding like Lev, Jana, and Yuri all at once, and as it built to a run and leaped, it converged into spiny, gaping rows of teeth—a huge bone-splintered orifice that came down to swallow me whole.

CHAPTER 26

I spat blood and roared wordlessly in the DOG's face. The pressure built to a maelstrom as magic caught and tore through the room, lifting my hair, my clothing. It was anger and grief: anger was the wind that snapped the sails taut, fueled by rage and grief so deep that it ripped something out of me. The pallets I'd marked lifted and flung forward, into the descending DOG. They struck it in the flanks, and it laughed as the pallets simply passed through and its body burst into ropes of tar that splattered across the floor, walls, and me.

The stuff burned through my clothes and gloves to my skin, and deeper. I screamed as pain worse than anything I'd ever known wracked my body, collapsing and convulsing as I futilely clawed at the wormlike stuff burrowing into my flesh. White needles of agony pushed through the roof of my mouth and up behind my eyes as the pallets smashed violently to the floor around me, building on the shrieking, yarping howls of the DOG. I heard the plastic hiss and rip. The eggs exploded, and I was covered in those, too. The acidic stuff eating into my arms writhed off to flop and squirm on the ground.

The pieces of the DOG jumped and hopped, baying in a clamor of alien sounds as it frantically contorted and squirmed to evade the wave of sticky albumen and yolk that now covered the floor. It grew legs and tried to skitter, which failed when they broke; then it tried to make wings, contortions of bone and slime that flapped uselessly against the floor. I tried to shake off enough of the pain to move and couldn't. I flinched when something sailed past my head. An egg. It hit the flapping, congealing form of the DOG and broke across it, pitching it back to the floor with a wail.

I heard Zarya's ragged, consumptive breathing intensify as she hefted again. Another egg flew by, and it hit. The DOG screeched, scrabbling and falling to the floor. It was a quarter of its previous size now, smoking and bubbling whenever it touched the mess of egg and shell. Whenever it slipped, it lost pieces of itself. NOthing was powerless when it was exposed to something that embodied potential life.

I heaved, choking back bile, and forced myself up to one knee. The wounds the DOG had left were burning cold, itching and running freely with watery blood. I touched the edge of one and gasped: the pain made my vision blur. The DOG had nearly taken my arms, chest, and shoulder down to the bone. I felt around until I found an unbroken egg and threw it at the parts of the struggling, snarling demon closest to me. It collapsed, dividing into fleshy gobbets that thrashed under their coating of egg, falling still as they shrank, then disappeared. Nothing was left, not even the bones of the fallen men it had consumed. Even the stench of it was clearing, while around me, the remaining albumen boiled and dried.

"Wh– wh–" I tried to speak, failed, and licked my chapped lips to moisten them before giving up on the attempt. I turned to find Zarya sprawling on the floor next to Vassily, who was gaping soundlessly. Agonal gasps.

The bottom fell out of me as I crawled across to them and tried to turn him on his side, pawing at his neck to turn his head and clear his airway. I tried to do chest compressions, but my arms buckled. I fell over his chest, struggled up, and knew that this was the end.

"No! NO!" I gathered him in my arms. Nothing. Fluid drained from his mouth, but he hung limp, convulsing in fits and starts. I've seen a lot of men die. I knew the signs: the fluttering eyes, the false breaths that never reached the lungs. Sure enough, his head lolled and he choked out foam and spittle onto the floor, but there was no response. His heart had already stopped. "You can't, Vassily, you can't..."

Zarya rasped beside me, her lungs full of phlegm. Bent over Vassily's body and heaving with dry, wracking sobs, I hardly heard her. No, dammit, no. I clutched him close and rocked. Back and forth, back and forth. No. Everything. Everyone. I'd lost everything.

"Ah–ah–lexi," Zarya whispered. "P-please..."

I couldn't look at her. Couldn't speak. I moaned, breathing in Vassily's smell through his shirt, then screamed, a harsh sound of pure agony and rage.

"Ah–lexi. Take... the knife," she gasped, louder. Her lips were flecked with bright silver. "Kill me. Try... feed him... heart's blood."

Her last words broke through my fugue. I hunched in a ball around Vassily's body, tear-streaked and shaking, unable to form any reply.

"Yes." She breathed the word as a fluted sigh. "Ah–lexi. Kill me. You must... fulfill the Pact. You must."

"I..." In all the times I'd killed, I'd never done that. I'd never eaten them or fed them to anyone else. "I don't—"

"Fruit." She looked up at me, shuddering with the effort. Her veins were visible, shot through with ugly violet streaks, which were spreading like poison as I watched. Her flesh was depressed and soft-looking, bruising under her own weight. Just like a rotting peach, she dimpled when pressed. "I'm... fruit. Made for it. Please."

I swallowed and lowered Vassily to the ground, touching his face, his unseeing eyes, his mouth. I turned to the Gift Horse, this strange familiar woman, and thumbed the box cutter blade to its full length. Her eyes were flickering, and as I watched, she heaved and brought up a gout of clotted silver streaked with black. The air was full of sweet perfume, but Zarya gagged, a horrible sound that wracked the air of the room. It was beginning to smell like Nacari on the docks... and I realized what the rotten sugar smell really was.

"Feed... him." She reached up, clawing weakly at my thigh. "My... heart's... blood. And eat. We will... see you again."

Beside her, I fell to my knees. "Zarya-"

"Trust... me." She smiled, and it was ghastly: her teeth were covered in tarnished chrome. "I'm... here, now. On this Cell. Trust... me."

I brought the knife up like a sacrificial priest. Zarya relaxed and fell back, lifting her chest up towards the blade, as if she'd done this a hundred million times. I brought it down without hesitation. Her flesh was so soft that I punched it through her ribcage without resistance, deep into her heart.

Zarya's eyes flew open, and she choked, staring up at my face with an expression of blissful relief. Unable to look away, I felt my Neshamah take my hand and draw the blade through her ribs and pulled it free. She cried out, and her pupils expanded completely until they filled her irises. They unfolded into a spiral that led my gaze down, down... drawing me into a vortex of energy that took my breath away.

"The Hunt will go on," her voice ruffled through my mind. "Until we meet again."

The blood that ran down her torso was mercurial, a thick spill of silver. I could see my reflection in it as it spilled over her chest and pooled on the floor, evaporating upwards in thin runnels that disappeared as they decayed. My face loomed larger and larger as I bent down over Zarya's body. She was gasping in agony now, chest rising towards me as I bowed towards her and, with a trembling tongue, lapped at the shivering pool that welled up from her heart.

Time slowed... then wound in to a single point in space.

I was gathered up in a rush of wings that carried me down a long tunnel, and they broke me into pieces, into dust that was carried, rushing, down a river of light; a water chute flung me out into a sea of endless GREEN.

A throbbing, booming sound rolled through my being, through every bone, every muscle, every cell as the scope of the ocean expanded exponentially. There was the seething Green cauldron, burning like the heart of an enormous star, and there were its innumerable, uncountable filaments— branches of GREEN bigger than my entire universe. At first, I thought they were veins, until I registered the minute twinkling flashes along their lengths and realized they were ropes of neural tissue. Each nerve strand was roped with pearls, and I knew without knowing that they were universes, entire universes, and there were BILLIONS of them. Billions and billions of flashing specks, in all directions, as far as my eyes could see. They expanded through a rippling aqueous structure that went from white to green to yellow to orange then red—but it was the core of this enormous thing which drew me to face it as the pounding, the booming, began to resolve into a chorus of genderless voice.

loveyouloveyouloveyouloveyouloveyouloveyouloveyouloveyou

It was looking back at me. The voice intensified and deepened. I was not even one cell within its mass. I was perforated, penetrated, a membrane full of holes that writhed and sobbed and screamed as my head was filled, full of it.

loveyouloveyouloveyouloveyouloveyouloveyouloveyouloveyou

Images flashed in a whirlpool of sensation. I saw myself split and brachiated along many of its nerves, living many lives on many worlds. I was a blond youth, laying my head down on a hexagonal stone in the seconds before a sacrificial hammer fell. I was on horseback, straight-backed and proud... I was riding in a car, I was sitting on a bench in the drop bay of a spacecraft. I saw Zarya and others like her. I saw Crina: female, male, arching back against a sofa, a stripper pole, braced with a gun in the door of a helicopter. And I saw Vassily, shadowed by the streetlights beyond a window as he came to me in bed...

loveyouloveyouloveyouloveyouloveyouloveyouloveyouloveyou

I woke over Zarya's body, sobbing. Seconds had passed, but I was no longer in pain. I scrambled upright, remembering her last words. *Feed him. Give him my heart's blood.*

The Gift Horse's flesh was turning translucent, trembling as it began to fade and peel away into the air. I cracked her chest and pulled her heart free. It was an enormous organ, half again as large as a human heart and with arteries like the spokes of a wagon wheel, blue and sweet smelling. Shaking, I shuffled on my knees to Vassily's cooling corpse and wrung it over his face and into his mouth. It felt stupid, and once more, the dry retching of grief began as I looked down into my sworn brother's wide black eyes and saw nothing there.

The silver fluid soaked into his skin, ran into his mouth, over his cheeks, disappearing into his pores as I watched with wide, frightened eyes, and set the organ down on the middle of his chest. The structure of it clarified, turning as clear as glass, then dissolved into his body.

I saw and felt some kind of energy ripple outwards from him, and his darkened eyes turned numinous, an incredible, fathomless blue shot through with stars. For a moment, I thought I saw him in there... but then the color left, and so did Vassily. Whatever I had seen in that moment – his Neshamah, my own desperation – left as quickly as it had come. I was too late.

He was gone.

EPILOGUE

Sunrise dawned hot over St. Vladimir's, raising fog from the hard pavement outside. The church was holding funerals early to avoid the worst of the heat because – even with the air conditioners on – the mortuary wax used to restore Mariya's body wouldn't hold its shape right come midday.

Ukrainian funerals were not private affairs. St. Vladimir's was packed with mourners for both brother and sister: Mariya's customers and friends, her tear-streaked ex-husband, his family, his friends, Vassily's friends, his released prison buddies, nearly every member of the *Organizatsiya* who cared to attend, and curious members of the local public streamed from the doors and down the aisle. The Orthodox church was not made for so many people, and they mingled and bickered and chattered out the door and onto the street, where Vanya's hand-picked bouncers guarded the gates.

Outside the church grounds, the street was full of gawkers. Police pretended to have a real reason to be there, while civilians clamored like crows at the fence, trying to get a glimpse of a rumored Mafia funeral.

I found my place by Vassily's side from the moment the doors opened. Both he and Mariya had open caskets, their bodies buried under piles of flowers. Mourners came to touch, kiss and lay more flowers and flags down over them.

Jewish flags, Ukrainian flags, white banners, even dollar bills. They came and left around us in a blur. Their words, their faces and scents bubbled formlessly around me. I only had eyes for my family.

Vassily was milk pale and sunken, his expression serene, eyes closed. His hands were folded over his chest, and I drank in every detail of his tattoos: the cat and dagger on the left, the snake and skull on the right. Each one commemorated his cunning and loyalty and determination, and for all his flaws, he'd earned them. The blue ink seemed to float just under the surface of his skin, as if it had turned to glass. He'd taken these images for his father, and Vassily had embodied them with the kind of passion that he'd be proud of, had he been alive to watch his youngest son grow to adulthood.

The Scopolamine fog made it impossible for me to tell which memories of that awful night were true and which were not. I was sure Zarya was real, and the DOG. I know I worked magic that took my breath away to think about. The rest? I couldn't say. All I do know is that this place, these people, and these sick men I grew up following are wrong. The Organizatsiya is a disease. Now, I realized why the smell of the DOG was so familiar: Because it smelled like home.

I only broke from my vigil once, to use the bathroom and check my arm. Two days had passed. My wounds were gone, but something had cut deeper than the DOG's talons. Zarya had healed me, and the flesh the DOG had chewed out of me was filled in, but the scars still ached. They wound up my forearm like twin serpents. Looking at them made me dizzy, and when I went back out, I lingered in the threshold of the bathroom, paralyzed until I caught a sweet draft of honeysuckle air from the open church door. It was as raw and pure as incense. The scent freed me of my freeze, but my hands remained heavy and hot.

Nervously, I put my gloves in my pocket and moved bare-handed back into the chapel hall. I wanted to go back to Vassily, but an impulse I could not name drew me outside. I stepped out onto the garden path, breathing deeply of the humid air, and scanned the crowd.

There was a line of men smoking near the door, killing themselves slowly while they paid their respects to the dead. Sergei's distinctive raucous laughter boomed from around the corner of the main building. I went around the corner of the chapel to see what he was laughing about, only to see him lift a screaming baby up high over his head, clasping it in huge meaty hands as he cooed and chuckled. Even at this distance, I could see the appraisal on the old man's face, the calculation.

He handed the baby back to his mother perfunctorily, praising her, and she blushed. Not thirty feet away, Vanya's three boys were playing around the only tree behind the church, a sickly looking maple that was shedding its leaves prematurely from the summer heat. The two older boys were bullying the youngest. I couldn't hear what they were saying, but I watched them push him to the ground with sticks and feet. The young boy didn't cry; he got angry, face burning, and picked up a stick of his own to charge them and continue the cycle of violence.

"Take them in as men and horses, and churn them out as numbered corpses." Kutkha said, whispering deep within my imagination. It was something I felt like I'd once read, but for the life of me, I couldn't remember the source.

Even as I tried to remember, something prickled at my skin. I refocused to my left. Sergei was watching me. He was overdressed, as always. The huge man wore a gaudy black velvet suit dressed with a heavy gold medallion that rested over his tie. He caught my eye and smiled knowingly with far too many teeth, then turned and went on to continue entertaining his guests, the couple breeding the next generation of cogs in his machine. Beside him, Vera stood with her hands folded behind her back, feet shoulder width apart, and stared at nothing with dead doll eyes.

A chill passed through my gut, a lance of unnatural cold that made my mouth itch. I bowed my head and peeled away from the wall, re-entering the church with a churning stomach.

Kutkha fluttered in my awareness with the pressure of protective wings. As I mounted the dais a second time, I felt the gentle indigo-black throb and pulse of his substance as he meshed quietly through my being, silent and supportive. I had my Neshamah. I had Binah, waiting for me at home. I had Zarya's final words. *"We will see you again."*

For the last time, I looked down at Vassily's face.

"Until we meet again." I leaned in to commit his smell to memory. Without really meaning to, I pressed my lips to the waxy skin of his forehead, lingering just long enough that I would always remember how it felt. Then I turned and walked away.

I didn't want to. A part of me wanted to join them. I didn't want to live, alone, in a world where people like Sergei and Nic survived and Mariya and Vassily did not. I didn't want the loneliness that would come with my decision. But I am a Magus, a Phitometrist, a catalyst. Whatever it is I must do, I would not find it here.

It was time to go.

Twenty shapeshifter children are kidnapped from a group home and their guardians murdered in a bizarre Occult ritual, and the werecreatures of New York City are baying for blood. Frustrated by weeks of botched Government investigation, they are taking the law into their own hands and need an Occult expert capable of doing the dirty work the police cannot. Someone like Alexi Sokolsky: mage, ex-Russian mafiya hitman, and reluctant finder of lost children.

Join Alexi in his bloody journey of revenge and redemption as he ventures out of the familiar world of the Russian Mafiya and into the unknown world of Stained Glass, the second installment in the occult horror Hound of Eden series.

STAINED GLASS: CHAPTER 1

Vengeance, like most fantasies, is better in the imagining than in the execution.

Snappy Joe Grassia – Manelli hitman, renowned sadist, and murdering piece of human waste – was hog-tied in my trunk. We were headed north along the Interstate, gunning for a place that a long-dead gangster had nicknamed Bozya Akra, God's Acre. The Yaroshenko Organizatsiya had been planting bodies there since my grandfather's day, and if the Feds ever found it, they'd have enough bones to keep the world in human ivory for the next decade.

It had been a long two weeks, and now that we were nearly there, I felt hollow, sour, even bored. This was the last kill I'd make in the USA, maybe for the rest of my life. I'd expected to feel satisfaction, some kind of relief. All I felt was nothing. When I glanced in the mirror at my face, it was stiff and cold, skin tight and grayish. I couldn't see anything through that shell of self-containment, the autistic armor I'd grown over the course of a short, violent life. There was only a mask: passionless, hard and proud.

The trip to Bozya Akra was nearly the reverse of the one Vassily and I had made earlier in August when we'd driven back from Fishkill Correctional. The wind blowing over us from the windows during that ride had been warm, the scents blue and bittersweet with the dog days of summer. He'd come out of prison thinned and brittle. He hadn't been strong enough to survive the odds arrayed against him when everything had gone to shit. The icing on the cake had been when he was kidnapped and his sister killed...and now, Snappy Joe and I were fated to share this moment.

The outer fence had rotted to stumps, and the frontage to Bozya Akra was so overgrown that it resembled the rest of the forest. We drove up along that long driveway very slowly, bumping and rumbling over the soft earth, and eventually came to a gentle stop in a clearing not too far from a deep, pre-dug pit. I collected the weapon I'd brought for the job, cut the engine and got out, the pulse in my tongue tap-tapping with the tick of cooling metal. The hissing trees filled the silence as I went around and popped the trunk.

Joe squealed when he saw me, eyes bugging over the top of his gag. He was a burly dog of a man, tough and bony as dry chicken. My hands itched in my gloves as I reached in and hauled him out like so much meat, rolling him to the ground with a wet thud. He was beaten to within an inch of his life, his body a coagulated mess of broken bones and livid bruises, and he swooned in a fresh faint as I – three inches shorter and a hand broader through the shoulders – grasped the top of his head by the hair and dragged him behind me through the mud.

In the dark of my mind, I felt something stir... the awareness of my Neshamah. Kutkha roused with dispassionate interest as I set Joe on his knees by the edge of the pit. There was just enough sun left in the day to us to see by. While he swayed and moaned, clawing his way back to consciousness, I cut his gag free, set a piece of razor-sharp broken window glass taken from Mariya's house against his twitching throat, and waited.

The sun was wavering red on the horizon by the time he gurked and lurched a little, catching himself before he toppled forward into the hole. The damp earth sighed under his weight. When he finally righted, he drew a sharp, frightened breath.

"Joseph Grassia," I spoke his name slowly, rolling out the 'ra' a little to taste the 's' that followed. "Do you know why we're here?"

Joe's throat worked a little under the blade as he swallowed, mouth working. We were in a clearing behind a thick stand of hemlock and trembling aspen, the trees shivering in the sweet evening breeze. Far from the New York city limit, fifteen miles from the nearest truck stop, we were utterly alone.

"R..Russian? The Russians?" He croaked. "No way. Come on, man... You-"

"Ukrainian." The blade was rocking, rocking, and beginning to draw a little red. "Three weeks ago, you raided an apartment to kidnap my sworn brother. You killed his sister and took him-"

"Please man, plEEE-!"

With a small shudder, I yanked the shiv in, and he cried out in a surprisingly high, wavering voice. "Be quiet while I am speaking, Joseph."

With the click of clenching teeth, he fell silent.

"You took him and you doped him up, and now he's dead, Joseph. Their names were Mariya and Vassily Lovenko." I smelled urine, and shuffled my feet apart so it wouldn't get on my shoes. "They took me in when I was a kid, when I had nowhere else to go. Do you know what that's like? The desolation of losing your only family?"

"Oh god. Oh god, stop." Joe rasped now, flesh quivering around the uneven edge of the knife. "Stop. Stop."

"Did you stop? Have you ever stopped to think about anything in your life? Do you think I had the choice to stop, when your Spook forced me to defile Zarya? The Gift Horse?"

"Oh god. You're the Spook. You're the f-fucking Spook." Joe's voice stayed high and girlish, squeaky. "Don't... please, I didn't fucking do it! I d-d- it was fucking Celso, man! He-"

My eyes narrowed. "Celso Manelli?"

"Yes... YES-S..." he stammered, unable to find his words for several seconds. "It was Celso, Celso called me in. It was you freakin' Russkies that started the war, I didn't have nothin' to do with it, they just wanted me to drive, all I was doin' was driving, I was just-!"

His voice slowly turned to a dim buzzing drone, and the filthiness of him, the un-reality of his being, suddenly became too much. I am not a telepath, but I didn't need any form of magic to see into Joe's mind. The thing in front of me was a man-shaped hole in place of a human being, a sucking void. A NO-thing, greedy and craven. The NO was an infection in the world that ran so deep and so virulent that there was no hope of a cure. This was what the Gift Horse had taught me. And in the bittering weeks since Vassily's death, I saw the influence of the NO in everything.

I pulled Joe up higher on his knees with the shard. He screamed, and kept screaming as I spoke against the nothingness I felt.

"*'I have done it again. One year in every ten, I manage it. A sort of walking miracle, my skin as bright as a Nazi lampshade, my face a featureless, fine Jew linen.'*"

"What the FUCK!?" Joe was nearly screaming now. He sounded like a frightened hen. "The fuck is this? The fuck-!"

Sylvia Plath's words continued to roll off my tongue in soft measured cadence, as natural as any wizard's spell. *"Peel off the napkin, O my enemy. Do I terrify?"*

"No, no no no, no NO NO-!"

I punched the shard, a remnant of Mariya's broken bathroom window, through the front of his throat just beside his Adam's Apple. Gristle bent and ground under the force of the improvised blade. Joe's lamb-like screams turned to garbles as his blood slopped over the back of my glove. I put the hard sole of my shoe against his thin back and pushed him into the pit, face-first, to suffocate his life out on the loose dirt. This was not a kind kill, a mercy stroke through the carotid artery. He would remain conscious until the end.

"*Dying, is an art.*" I looked down at him from overhead, pulling the latex gloves off one at a time and throwing them to the ground. "*And like everything else, I do it exceptionally well.*"

Joe had not known Mariya. The way she picked sour cherries out of the jar with us while we did homework after school, her patience with our grandmother as Lenina's mind dissolved in the grip of Alzheimer's Disease. He hadn't known Vassily: his broad shoulders, his long, tattooed hands, the wicked glint in his eyes or the flash of his smile across a room when he turned to face me. Joe would never know the dryness of my mouth when Vassily stripped off his shirt or laughed at my jokes; his effortless intensity when handling a new gadget, a deck of cards, a cigarette. Snappy Joe Grassia was sick, like everything and everyone in the underworld. And so was I.

A month to the day ago, I tasted the Gift Horse's blood and received a revelation. GOD, the Greater Optimistic Direction – was very real. Through Zarya, I'd felt its heartbeat, saw its capillary action, its respiration. I'd glimpsed the way that its body channeled highways of Phi, the stuff of magic, like lymphatic fluid. It was an organism, a flesh-and-blood living thing with tissues so massive that its cells spanned universes. The Every-Thing, an all-consuming, and all-encompassing entity of which I was one tiny, tiny organelle.

But I knew now that GOD was in pain. When I looked into that massive eye, I hadn't felt chosen. I'd felt dirty. Twisted up. In my visions, I knew instinctively that I was not part of the cure; I was still part of the disease.

The grave was filled and meticulously camouflaged, every shred of dirty evidence bagged and burned by the time I drove back down the bumpy winding road to the highway. I spent the trip back in a numb fugue: part dissociation, part adrenaline, part realization that no matter how many fingers I broke or how fast I did it, the job would be left unfinished. In perfect accord with Murphy's Law, Snappy Joe Grassia had named the one man who I could not possibly kill in the short window of time I had left. Celso GOD-damned Manelli.

The Manelli family was the biggest Mafia outfit in New York City and New Jersey. John Manelli, the Don of the family, was a ruthless cut-throat who spurned the traditions of the Cosa Nostra and dealt in drugs – lots of them. Celso was his father's Consigliere and renowned to be one of the most dangerous non-magical Made Men in the underworld. I didn't know much about him, and had never seen him in person. Rumor was that he'd killed more than a few Spooks – 'hitmages', as Vassily had once called us – and GOD knows how many norms. He was reputed to be smart, cool, and careful. All of the Murder Inc. guys could regularly be found at the club they owned and operated in Manhattan: The Gemini Lounge. It was quite likely that I could find Celso there… along with fifty other allied gangsters, street mages, and a partridge in a pear tree.

Joe could have been pulling my leg. Questioning someone who is about to die is a terrible way to get information, but something about his insistence that Celso had been there made sense. I had memorized the murder scene in a flash. The position of furniture, blood spatters, the signs of struggle and lack of it. Mariya's body, slumped like a worn doll over the edge of the bathtub. I'd been sucking on the details like a bad tooth, recalling them over and over. There had definitely been more than one person there. That person could indeed have been Celso.

If it was true, there was no way I could leave New York. Nicolai would pay. Sergei would pay. After their performance the month before, the Organizatsiya was dead to me. I'd wring every drop of blood from their bodies for Vassily and Mariya, for Zarya, and for me.

As plans to find Celso began to coagulate, the cold shadow that had cruised with me for the entire day, from Joe's capture to beating to execution, finally manifested himself. The cottony, dusty smell of feathers wafted through the cabin like smoke, filling the air with the subtle pressure of Phi, the substance of magic. It was Kutkha, my Neshamah: the conduit of my Art, and a sanctimonious pain in my behind.

From time immemorial, mages and mystics of all cultures have spoken of the Neshamah, the soul, as a real, conscious presence. It is the part of ourselves that all humans have, but few ever speak to. The Higher Self, the Holy Guardian Angel – call it what you will. Jung named his Thomas. Mine was Kutkha, named for the trickster deity of ancient Rus. Sort of.

"Alexi, we cannot do this." Kutkha spoke with no single voice. He sounded like the riffling wind, the air thrumming through feathers. *"We will not find him in time. Tonight, we must leave."*

I fixed ahead on the dark, wet road. "The Gemini Lounge isn't too far from our route home. There's time to cruise by before the flight. And if we miss this flight, I'll book another. We're not short of money."

"You will not find him. He is already gone. They know Joseph has disappeared."

My throat closed up with a sudden flash of heat so powerful that it flooded my eyes with white and gold. It caused my hands to tic, and I slowed to stop from losing control of the car. "No. You don't know that."

"Alexi..."

"I know you don't know shit about the future. You fucking listen to me, you -"

The shadows of the cabin quickened. Out of the corner of my eye I saw the ghostly impression of a raven, blue-black, its substance boiling into filaments of vapor. When he next spoke, it was stronger, something I heard with my ears as well as my mind. *"Your father used to say that to you, Alexi."*

"Don't." The urge to hit, to bite and grasp and tear at something, anything became overwhelming, but there was no one and nothing left to hurt. I was the only one in the car. "Don't ever bring Grisha up again, or I swear to GOD..."

"What?" Kutkha's tone twisted with dark amusement. *"Will you drill out my knees, too?"*

I exhaled thinly. It was starting to rain now, a light misty haze, and I fixated on the swirling particles to give my eyes something to chew on. "Stop being a smartass. Vassily-"

"Is still dead, my Ruach."

"Stop." I pulled over as the rain intensified, staring at the buildup on my screen as it began to blind me. The calm executioner's confidence drained out of me. The engine rumbled like a cat's purr while I clutched my head and willed Kutkha to shut up. But he wouldn't: his thoughts, his agenda were his own, but he was part of me. Or, more accurately, I was part of him. "Just stop."

Kutkha's eyes burned in the gloom. *"They are gone whether or not Celso Manelli lives or dies. They are gone when we are in Europe, or if we stay here. They are gone."*

Gone. *Gone gone gone.* "Please just let me-"

"No." The air was opaque now, blue-black and sucking. *"I will not 'just' let you live the Lie."*

I'll live a lie if I damn well want to, is what I wanted to say, but I couldn't voice my petulance with any seriousness. The unspoken words rattled around my otherwise blank, exhausted mind. What I really wanted was to turn around, dig up Joe, reanimate him and kill him again. Instead, I fumbled for the windshield wipers and turned them on, sweeping the rain off the glass.

"You vowed yourself to me, Alexi. You vowed that you would grow for our sake."

"I know." But the resistance remained.

"It is not safe to stay near Sergei." For a moment, Kutkha's voice was almost soft. *"We must go. You are done here."*

I didn't feel 'done', though not for lack of preparation. My luggage was packed with money, clothes, my most important books and magical tools, and I'd left a go-bag out in Sheepshead Bay in case anything went wrong. I'd spent the last two weeks securing a fake passport, a two-way ticket to Spain, and a one-way train ticket to Germany. I had my photos and papers, and a fake ancestral I.D. We were set. But I was going to have to leave knowing that another man had been at that apartment: the man who had blown Mariya's head back across her shower wall, and that he was alive and she was not.

"Do not make me regret empowering you, my Ruach." Kutkha swiveled his head, looking across with eyes like the core of a star, smoking white and churning with constant motion. Momentarily, I met his gaze... and their gravity caught and held me. *"By all rights, you should be dead... but you wanted to survive. And they would want that, too."*

Vassily and Mariya. My throat thickened. "I'm... I am abandoning them here, Kutkha."

"They are dead, Alexi. You cannot abandon what is no longer here."

The cold reminder did nothing to chase away the childish conviction that I was abandoning them to lie in their cold graves, while I fled the Organizatsiya and the life they had died to protect. Vassily had been a Vor v Zakone to his bones, the picture of a free-wheeling, quick-thinking thief-in-law. He'd been the kind of man who could spin a million dollars out of five hundred. Once, a long time ago, he debated better than most lawyers. Sergei had picked him for his brilliant mind... brilliance that proved so fragile that five years in prison and the machinations of his comrades had crushed him like a crane fly.

And now? He was dead. Even though I knew it wasn't my fault, it sure as hell felt like it.

I shifted gears, backed up, and pulled out onto the highway. Kutkha was right, as always. We had to follow the plan. It was a good plan, and if executed smoothly, it would work. Take the cat, leave the lights off, the car in the lot, the door locked and warded. We could get to the airport in the morning, be in England by the evening, and on our way to continental Europe the same day. We would change our money in Spain, convert the lot to Deutschmarks, and head to Bremen. In Germany, I could disappear into the Ukrainian Jewish diaspora without so much as a ripple, just as my parents had done when they'd fled Ukraine for America. But after that? No idea. I lived day to day as part of the New York Bratva, enjoying short periods of peace interspersed with episodes of hectic violence. There were days where I collapsed onto my bed in the mid-morning after working all night, sore and exhausted, patched up, amazed that I was still alive. This was the first time the future had ever existed as a concept.

Earlier in August, I'd faced down demons, DOGs, an insane sorceress, a sixteen-man shootout, and seen the I of GOD itself. My best friend had died in my arms; I'd had a gun shoved in my mouth, been tortured, kidnapped, and nearly car-bombed. I'd eaten from the Fruit of the Tree of Knowledge and faced death more times in that one week than I had in the last six years. But not a single one of those things were as intimidating as the prospect of freedom. I had most of a double degree in law and psychology that would get me approximately nowhere without grad school. Besides that, my only skills related to wet-work. Shoot a gun, throw a knife, sling a spell... sure thing. But hold a job? Finish grad school? Did they even have grad school in Germany?

The yawning expanse of that lifetime, all those years ahead, unseen... it felt like looking down the empty blackness of a gun barrel. A real gun would have been more comforting. At least the outcome was certain.

Something resolved in me: a deep, hot anger, the kind that burned a hole right through the gut. My jaws tensed until my teeth locked. I hauled the wheel and turned back out onto the road, wipers swiping the first rain of Fall off the windshield. "I'm checking out the club tonight."

"Alexi-"

"No. You'll get what you want. We'll be on that flight come hell or high water. But just remember that you helped me out once, you got me out of one bad situation, Kutkha. Every other time, it was just me. I killed the DOGs. I freed Zarya and shook off the dope. I coped just fine without you before, and I'll do it again if I have to."

"As you say, proud Ruach." Kutkha's molten white gaze bore into me from the arc of my peripheral vision, as bright and cold as the Morning Star at dawn. *"As you say."*

Get Stained Glass on Amazon.com:
http://hyperurl.co/stainedglassnovel

Get your Free Copy of Burn artist

GET YOUR FREE COPY OF BURN ARTIST AT:
WWW.JAMESOSIRIS.COM

More Books by James Osiris Baldwin

The Alexi Sokolsky Series

Prequel: Burn Artist

http://jamesosiris.com/alexi-sokolsky-starter-library/

Book 1: Blood Hound

http://hyperurl.co/bloodhoundnovel

Book 2: Stained Glass

http://hyperurl.co/stainedglassnovel

Book 3: Zero Sum

http://hyperurl.co/zerosumnovel

**Find all my books at
http://www.jamesosiris.com**

Other Titles

Fix Your Damn Book! – A Self-Editing Guide for Authors

Paperback, Kindle & Hardcover. Read on Kindle Unlimited!

STRUCTURE OF THE YAROSHENKO ORGANIZATSIYA

The Yaroschenko Organizatsiya is actually two gangs: the largely autonomous Brighton Beach/USA faction who identify with Sergei's surname, plus a larger Organizatsiya in Kiev, Ukraine who call themselves the Sviatoshyn Gang. As of August 1991, the hierarchy is as follows:

Pakhun (Overboss):
Sergei Yaroshenko
Avtoritet (Advisor)
Lev Moskalysk
Brighton Beach Advokat
Alexi Sokolsky (in training)
Volkhv/Spook
Alexi Sokolsky
Brighton Beach Kommandant
Nicolai Chiernenko
Brighton Beach Street Captain/Head of Security
Petro Kravets
Red Hook/East Village Kommandant
Vanya Kazupov
Red Hook Advokat
Yegor Gavrilyuk
Red Hook Street Captain
Ivan 'Ivanko' Andreichenko

AFTERWORD & ACKNOWLEDGMENTS

The first prototype for Alexi, Dante, started out as a character in an old IRC D&D group that I played with while I was in university. We were running a campaign in the Forgotten Realms setting - a protracted PVP murder-mystery style plot, where one of the characters was the murderer and had to pick off the other characters while they tried to figure out what was going on. The Dungeon Master asked me if I'd like to play the murderer. I made a Lawful Evil cleric with the ability to disguise his alignment, and deployed him as the healer for the party. He was so effective that they only worked out who it was when it was far too late. In a single session of absolute carnage, he strangled the paladin, poisoned the fortress well so that all our NPCs were sick, then let the forces of darkness in to overwhelm our weakened garrison. He then kidnapped the cute (male) rogue, who became his loyal brainwashed boy-toy, and took the artifact the garrison was supposed to be protecting. Everyone had a great time, but they were floored by this motherfucker: a fussy, thoughtful, outwardly compassionate but deeply bitter and merciless man capable of great foresight. Dante was compelling, confusing, and contradictory. I knew I'd found a winning archetype.

Alexi began to take more shape when I deployed his essential characteristics for a WOTC d20 Modern game, this time, as a mundane-but-talented crooked cop. As time went by, I gradually began to conceive of the character as being an organized criminal rather than a corrupt policeman, and the rest of his backstory followed. But it wasn't until I entered the Dermal Highway setting that I fully realized Alexi for what he was... a character who exists in multiple places and multiple times. Part James Bond, part Dr. Who, part Constantine. The first draft of the book was written in 2009.

While working as a bouncer in 2010, I got a telecommute job for a small magazine in Australia. Seeing the opportunity for what it was, I gave up all of my personal possessions and traveled the world for three years, moving from country to country and keeping up a long-distance relationship with my wife. But I knew, as soon as I left Australia, that all roads led to Brighton Beach. I got there at one in the morning on a very hot night in 2012. The train carriage had one sleeping, coked-out office worker, two Russian women, and me - a very nervous Australian backpacker. Expecting to be mugged at every turn, I eventually found Brighton 8th Street, where I walked in on a fight between a cat and a raccoon. The fight was being cheered on by a group of cheerful Slavic men in sleeveless undershirts and gold chains, bottles in their hands, cigarettes in the corners of their mouths. They welcomed me like I'd come home, as did everyone else I met there. In other words, the place was pretty much as I'd always imagined it.

This novel could not have been written without the help of many people: Canth?, Stacy, Joey, Joey, Amanda, #The_Highway and House Whitebird crews, and the many fleeting inspirations that were given to me by friends, family, strangers and enemies.

ABOUT THE AUTHOR

Dragon Award-nominated author James Osiris Baldwin writes gritty LGBT-inclusive, dark fantasy and science fiction. He was the former Contributing Editor for the Australian Journal of Dementia Care and has also worked for Alzheimer's Australia. He currently lives in Seattle with his lovely wife, a precocious cat, and far too many rats. His obsession with the Occult is matched only by his preoccupation with motorcycles.

Contact James by email: author@jamesosiris.com.
View more books at:
http://amazon.com/author/jamesosiris

If you'd like to review BLOOD HOUND and recommend it to other people, visit these shortened links and tell 'em what you think:
Amazon: http://hyperurl.co/bloodhoundnovel
Goodreads: http://bit.ly/BHGoodreads

You can get in touch with me (outside of the mailing list) at: author@jamesosiris.com. The hashtag on Twitter is #BloodHound. If you want to chat, add me with **@Jamesosirisb** in your Tweets.

Find me on Facebook
at: www.facebook.com/groups/houndofeden

Sign up to the New Releases Mailing List!
http://jamesosiris.com/alexi-sokolsky-starter-library/

Made in the USA
Lexington, KY
28 September 2017